SILVERHORSE

SILVERHORSE

Lene Kaaberbøl

MACMILLAN

First published 2007 by Macmillan Children's Books
a division of Macmillan Publishers Limited
20 New Wharf Road, London N1 9RR
Basingstoke and Oxford
www.panmacmillan.com

Associated companies throughout the world

ISBN: 978-1-4050-9047-6

Text copyright © Lene Kaaberbøl 2007

The right of Lene Kaaberbøl to be identified as the
author of this work has been asserted by her in accordance
with the Copyright, Designs and Patents Act 1988.

1 3 5 7 9 8 6 4 2

A CIP catalogue record for this book is available from
the British Library.

Typeset by Intype Libra Limited
Printed and bound in Great Britain by
Mackays of Chatham plc, Kent

CONTENTS

SILVERHORSE

It had been a gloomy, rainy day, and there was a wet and woolly smell in the inn's common room – a smell of damp clothes and cloaks spread out to dry. In the yard, thin mud oozed between the cobbles, and Kat had to kick off her clogs every time she stepped across the kitchen threshold. Even Tad, with his mild good nature, could be roused to a show of temper if you tracked mud all over his floor, and as for the tongue-lashing her mother would give her – well, better to not even think about it. But despite the care she took, Kat's stockinged feet left fuzzy damp footprints on the worn flagstones of the kitchen floor. And it seemed that whenever Tad had put her to work on something in the kitchens, her stepfather Cornelius would roar for her from the stables. When she went to help *him*, it was never long before Tad's milder voice called her back to the dirty dishes or the potato-peeling. To and fro, to and fro. Kat felt as if she had spent half a lifetime trudging back and forth across the muddy cobbles.

Kat did not particularly like her stepfather – especially not on a day like this, when the damp made his body sore and his temper foul. She would gladly have spent all day in the kitchens with Tad, even if it meant peeling potatoes from dawn to dusk. Actually, that would have been more fitting, too, for a girl, and an eldest daughter at that. But ever since Kat's two older brothers had left home, Cornelius had been short-handed in the stables, and whatever one might say about 'that redhead of Teresa's' – and Cornelius frequently said quite a lot – even he had to admit that she had a way with horses.

Kat picked yet another potato out of the bucket between her feet. It wasn't the work she minded – as a matter of fact she preferred stable chores to kitchen work. It was just that –

'Kat! Get out here, girl!'

– it was just that she hated the way he was always telling her what to do, yelling at her to 'do this and do that, girl'. Like she was his dog, or something. She bit her lip and carefully finished peeling the potato, slipped it into the pot on the table, and put the knife with great precision next to the sink. She took off her apron and hung it neatly on the hook by the door –

'*Now*, girl!'

Cornelius's roar could rouse a company of drunken mercenaries. He had had to often enough, once upon a time, and he was still proud of having made it to captain in Marker's Regiment before he retired. Ordinarily, his language would have been much fouler by now, so there must be customers present. Kat felt her face flush with the heat of her own temper. With fierce little jabs she tucked her shirt-tails into the waistline of her breeches.

'You had best be going.'

Tad rarely raised his voice, or ordered anyone to do anything. Somehow, though, Kat always ended up following his mild suggestions. Most people did.

'I'm on my way,' she muttered. From outside came a snort and a loud squeal. Somebody's ill-mannered hack, no doubt. Sighing, Kat pushed her feet into her sodden clogs and clattered back into the yard.

'About time,' snarled Cornelius, but for once Kat had no attention to spare for a smart comeback.

She would never forget it. It was like something out of a dream or a fairy tale. There, in the middle of the rainswept yard behind her mother's inn, was a horse like . . . a horse like . . . No. She could think of nothing that would do for comparison. Its slim-boned limbs were threads of silk compared to the sturdy mountain pony legs she was used to. Its head, too, was slender, like the point of a spear. And even in the pouring rain, even in the gloom of autumn dusk, the mare's body gleamed with a silver glow Kat had not imagined any animal could have. A fish, perhaps, leaping upstream in bright sunlight . . . but a horse?

For several long breaths, she could look at nothing else. Then she grew slowly aware of the rider. A woman, dressed in travel-worn grey leathers and an expensive cloak of Breda blue. A woman! Kat had her second shock of the day. A travelling woman, and on such a horse . . . it just wasn't

3

done. Decent women stayed faithful to the place they were born to, minding their houses and their businesses, and left the drifting about to the men.

'Stop gaping, girl.' Cornelius's voice jerked her from her reverie.

'I wasn't gaping!' she snapped back in defiance, although she knew she had been. 'It's just . . . she's so beautiful.'

The rider laughed. 'I take it you're talking about my horse,' she said. 'People don't usually pay me such heartfelt compliments.'

Kat felt her face flush once more, this time with embarrassment. She stole a look at the rider's face. True, not many people would call her beautiful – not with that wide scar flawing most of the left side of her face, puckering the skin and making her eye droop slightly on that side. It gave her a strange lopsided look, like Twoface in the puppet plays.

'I'm sorry, I didn't mean to . . . to . . .' she stuttered to a halt. She could feel Cornelius's fury even without looking at him.

'Take the horse,' he said. 'And mind you treat it right!'

As if I'd do anything else, she thought, reaching for the reins.

'No,' said the rider. 'I had better see to her myself.'

Kat straightened to her full height, which irritatingly still only brought her level with Cornelius's chest. 'I know my job,' she snapped, too angry to care that she was being rude to a guest. But apparently the guest did not mind. She looked at Kat for a careful moment. Then she nodded, slipping wearily from the saddle.

'All right,' she said, 'let's see how you manage. But if you need help, be sure to call me. Her kind . . . well, they're often a bit difficult.'

She handed the reins to Kat and let her lead the mare towards the stables.

The silver mare pranced a bit and swung her quarters sideways, refusing to walk in a straight line. Kat paid no attention. She put one hand on the sleek neck, just to feel it. It should be different, surely, from touching an ordinary horse's neck – she half expected it to be hard and cold, like metal – but it wasn't. Smoother, perhaps, that was all, with no trace of winter coat despite the autumn chill.

She put the mare in one of the few loose boxes they had. The rider hadn't ordered it, and Cornelius usually charged extra for such a privilege, but Kat simply couldn't make herself chain such a creature in a tie stall as if it were an ordinary everyday working horse. She pushed up the saddle flap, undid the buckles, and slipped the wet saddle off the mare's back. And at that moment, the horse turned its head and looked at her.

Horse? No. No horse had such eyes.

Cats, perhaps. Or something larger, and much fiercer.

Huge, they were, and golden, with black slits for pupils. The eyes of a predator that hunts at night.

Kat shuddered, despite herself. Old tales of ghosts and magic stirred inside her, and she felt herself drawn helplessly deeper and deeper into that fierce golden gaze.

'Are you . . . are you a Nightmare?' she breathed. Nightmares could talk; everybody knew that.

This one didn't, though. It merely turned its head once more and tugged a nibble of hay from the rack. Kat shivered slightly. She couldn't help herself. Crouching, she felt one fetlock carefully. No poison spurs. No cleft hooves, either. Gradually, her racing heart slowed its beat.

'What kind of horse are you?' Kat whispered to the mare. 'Not the ordinary kind, that's for sure.'

She talked to the horses at the inn all the time, but it felt particularly fitting to talk to this one. As if it was not inconceivable that it might suddenly decide to answer her.

Not this time, though. It merely shook its head, impatient to be rid of the bridle. Like any other horse at the end of a long day's ride.

She was busily rubbing down the mare – the *sheen* of that coat! – when Cornelius came into the stable. She could tell from the sound of his steps that he was in a temper, and inside her she felt something move: a familiar beast made from fear and anger, with claws and fangs that could slash and rend. She knew that beast so well that she could see it quite clearly in her mind's eye. It had a snout, and tusks like a wild boar, and harsh yellow bristles. It crouched in her belly like an unborn child, trapped and furious.

'You watch your mouth, girl,' said Cornelius. 'Getting fresh with me is one thing, but you better be polite to the guests, or you'll not like what's coming to you!'

'I was polite! You ask her if she thinks I was rude!'

Cornelius went on as if he hadn't heard her. 'And her a Silver, and all. A bredinari. What will she think of this place, after such a welcome? Ill-mannered whelp!'

Kat raised her head slowly. Anger boiled inside her. Who did he think he was, calling her ill-mannered? A foul-mouthed, broken-down old soldier like him?

'I've got better manners than you,' she said, although she knew where it would lead them.

'Dammit, girl! Do you *want* me to beat you?'

'I'm not scared of you!'

'Best say you're sorry,' he said in his lowest voice, the one that meant this was the last warning. 'Best say you're sorry, real quick.'

But she never learned. She couldn't learn. The yellow beast raised its spiny hackles and lashed out, and she started yelling at him.

'You don't get to tell me what to do! Why are you always picking on me? Just because you're not my father. You hate that, don't you? Mama loved somebody better than you, and you really hate that.'

Crash! Cornelius banged his great fist against the door-post. 'Shut *up*, girl! I'll teach you. I'll teach you to be rude to people!'

The silver mare flung back its head and pounded the floor with one hoof, hard enough to raise sparks.

'You're scaring the horse,' Kat said.

'Come here,' growled Cornelius, in the lowest voice of all.

Kat shook her head and clutched the wisp of straw she had been using on the mare.

'No,' she said. 'If you want me, you can come and get me!'

Because she knew, in one glorious moment of total superiority, that Cornelius did not want to come into the box, did not want to get too close to this strange not-horse with its predator's eyes. With a show of indifference that she knew would enrage him even more, she turned her back on him and began to rub the silver coat once more.

But that proved too much. Cornelius tore open the door to the box and seized her arm. He gave it such a yank that she tumbled across the aisle and hit the wall of the opposite stall with a thump. The silver mare squealed in anger and half reared, but he slammed the door shut on it and dropped the bar in place. Kat was already heading up the aisle towards freedom, but Cornelius caught her in three steps – he could still move when he wanted to. He dragged her along the row of stalls and into the hay barn at the end of it. Then he let go of her arm.

'Shirt off,' he told her.

She crossed her arms across her body and glared at him in defiance.

'Just because you're bigger doesn't mean you're right!' she hissed. It was something Tad often said, and she thought Cornelius needed to hear it more than she did.

He made no answer. He undid his belt, folded it double in one hand, and reached for her. She drew back from his grasp.

8

'Come here,' he said, but she couldn't, couldn't give in and come crawling just because he told her to. So he had to chase her round the barn, and every time he missed his catch he lashed at her, and the longer it went on the more furious he became, until he was puffing with both rage and exertion. Sooner or later he always caught her, though. This time he cornered her by the gate, seized her arm, and forced her down on her stomach across a bale of hay. Pinning her with his knee, he pulled up her shirt and bared her back. And there they were again, the way it always ended. The yellow beast was curled up now, spiny hackles jabbing in all directions. In the stalls, some horse kept squealing and kicking – probably the silver mare. And Cornelius raised his arm and belted her.

He was furious, even more than usual. He hit her so hard that she couldn't keep herself from yelling, and perhaps someone heard her. In any case, there was suddenly a cool voice behind them:

'What on earth is this?'

It was the woman traveller, the rider of the silver mare – what was it Cornelius had called her? A bredi- . . . bredi-something-or-other. She sounded angry. Cornelius let go of Kat and straightened slowly.

'No more'n she deserves,' he said, somewhat out of breath.

'Is that so?' the rider said, as if she didn't believe him. Kat pulled down her shirt and wanted to die on the spot, from shame and embarrassment. She wanted the rider to go away. She wanted her stepfather to go away. She wanted the whole world to go away and leave her in peace.

'Aye, that is so!' He always became more the mountain man when he was annoyed. 'What do you do to your fancy horse when it misbehaves? Tickle it with a feather, perhaps?'

'No good lessons are taught with the whip. To a horse *or* to a child,' said the rider. And then a truly odd thing happened. She put her hand on Cornelius's shoulder, as though she were praising him rather than upbraiding him. And the anger left him. Just like that.

'Aye, well, that's as may be,' he muttered.

The rider gave his shoulder a brief pat, and left them.

In the stable, the silver mare had finally grown calm. Kat got a curry-comb and began to brush travel dirt and bits of straw from its gleaming coat. Cornelius stood by the door of the box, watching her, but she knew from the way he was standing that the danger was past now. There was an odd lull between them, almost a kind of peace, the way there often was after an outbreak such as that.

'Kat,' he said.

She stopped working and turned to face him.

'Kat, I . . . Can you . . . ?' But he never quite apologized. Couldn't quite bring himself to. 'Once you're done with that one,' he said, 'tell Tad I said you could have a bowl of the good stew. You go and have a rest now.'

She nodded. He never said sorry. She never said thanks. That was the way it went.

'Did he hit you again?' Tad asked later, once the rush and flurry of the evening meal were over and they were alone in the kitchen.

'Why do you think so?' she asked.

'When he's being nice to you, it usually means he has a bad conscience.' Tad spoke quite sharply for a man who never raised his voice.

'It wasn't much.' And it hadn't been, not compared to other times, other days, when no rider had magically appeared to stop him. She didn't quite understand it. Why couldn't she just keep her mouth shut? Why did she have to cross that line every time, why did she have to poke and jab at him like that, until he lost his temper? And why did he get so furious, every single time?

'Tad,' she said, blowing gently on a spoonful of beef stew. 'That woman with the silver mare. Who is she? Cornelius called her a . . . a bredi-something-or-other.'

'Bredinari. Most people just call them Silvers. They serve the Bredani, in the City of Breda. Supposedly they bring her word and her justice to everyone in the country. We don't see them much around here though, not any more. I haven't seen a Silver in years.'

Kat shook her head without really knowing what she was shaking it at. Bredani, bredinari – it was like queens and princesses in the old days, something you heard about in fairy tales and puppet plays, not real life. She knew, of course, that the Bredani ruled the country of Breda from Breda City, just like her own mother Tess ruled Crowfoot Inn and everyone in it. But it seemed a hopelessly distant place, and she had no real picture of what went on there. Tad sometimes told the little ones the story of the Farmwife Who Wanted to be Bredani. Wait – wasn't there something about a silver horse in that one? 'She wanted to be Bredani and have horses of silver like the Bredani . . .' But of course, that was just a story. In real life, people were blacksmiths and farmers and weavers. Things like that. Soldiers, some-times. And some, she supposed, were robbers and thieves. But Crowfoot Inn saw few enough of those – Cornelius had a reputation as a fighter, a man it was unwise to cross, with or without a sword.

'What does a Bredani do?' she asked, nibbling at the hot stew.

'Rules the country, I suppose,' said Tad. 'How would I know? I'm not exactly royalty.' He grinned at her across one of the huge black cast-iron pots he was scrubbing.

'Your cooking is good enough for any kind of royalty,' Kat said fiercely. 'Why couldn't Mama have married *you*?'

As soon as the words had left her mouth, she knew it was a mistake. Tad's shoulders went tense and stiff, and he scrubbed the pots a lot harder than was necessary.

'She was too wise for that,' he said in a cutting tone, but his anger was all for himself.

'Tad . . .'

'No. It's true. She needed someone like Cornelius.

Someone who could keep the inn safe from drifter trash and other thieves. Cooks she can get by the score, without having to marry them.'

'We did just fine before he came,' asserted Kat, although the memory was somewhat dim in her mind.

'Those were different times,' Tad said, still scrubbing furiously. 'No, Teresa knows what she's doing, all right.'

Teresa. Kat had always thought that her mother's given name fitted her badly. It was much too soft and slow. Tess, the name most people called her by, was better: brief and sharp like the crack of a whip. But Tad always said 'Teresa', in that special gentle tone of voice, and this was how Kat had finally realized that Tad was in love with her mother.

Men in love with Tess was nothing new. Kat was just startled to see this disease infect kind and quiet Tad, whom she considered her own special friend. But Tess was dark and striking and vividly alive. Stronger men than Tad had fallen at her feet, and sometimes into her bed as well. Tess had nine living children, six of them born before Cornelius became a fixture at Crowfoot Inn. Who had fathered them only Tess knew, and she wasn't telling. Kat had not the least idea who her own father was. When she had grown old enough to realize that most people had fathers, she had asked. But Tess had merely shaken her head.

'You are *my* child,' she had said fiercely. 'That's enough, isn't it?'

And it had been. At least until Cornelius came.

She helped Tad wash and dry the last of the tankards and set them in their silent rows on the shelves in the common room. It was late. The rain had made the regulars stay longer, hoping for a break in the weather. None had come. The rain was still rattling against the roof when Kat climbed the last of the stairs to the attic where she and the rest of her siblings slept. Now, with Eskill and Dan gone, they were only seven, but as there were just three beds, everyone had to share. Kat, twelve years old and eldest now, might have ousted her younger sister Mattie and claimed a bed for herself, but they were used to each other, and she wasn't sure she would be able to sleep without feeling Mattie's gentle breath against the back of her neck.

Tonight, she was the last one up. The three littlest ones had of course been tucked in hours ago. She drew back the bed curtain to look in on them. Three-year-old Cor was on his stomach as usual, with his legs drawn up and his little bottom sticking up, a strange hump under the blankets. The twins, Tessa and Rose, were clutching each other in their sleep, such a tangle of arms and legs that it was hard to tell where one twin left off and the other began. From the bed Tim and Nicolas shared, there came a blurred murmur – Nicolas tended to talk in his sleep.

Mattie was still awake. Her eyes glittered in the dark.

'Is it bad?' she asked.

'No,' Kat said. 'He barely touched me.'

She had two tender stripes across her lower back and a red mark on one forearm where he had caught her with his belt as she ran. But no, it wasn't bad.

He never laid a finger on Mattie. Of course, Mattie was a shy and gentle girl who worked very hard at never

14

upsetting anyone. The little ones he noticed only to the extent of tickling a tummy now and then. But Nicolas and Tim got up to all kinds of trouble without unleashing anything like the beatings she got.

'It's not fair,' Mattie whispered, almost as if she had been following Kat's thoughts.

'Don't take it to heart,' said Kat. 'I don't like him, and he doesn't like me. We're even, that way. And anyway, who says I'm staying here forever?'

She said it without thinking. Mattie uttered a scared little sound.

'Don't leave me,' she said. 'You can't! I don't know what I'd do without you.'

'Hush.' Kat stroked her sister's hair. 'Don't be scared. If I ever do leave home, it'll be years and years from now. By then you'll be overjoyed to get rid of me!'

'No. Never!' Mattie clung fiercely to Kat. But even as she comforted her sister, Kat kept turning the thought over and over in her mind, like a new coin she had been given. It wasn't one she had ever had before. It was strange. Frightening. Girls did not *leave*, like boys did. Girls grew into women, and women ruled the houses and shops and farms they were born to. How could they do that if they went traipsing all over the countryside, travelling and drifting like men? Kat had heard of drifter women, but they were not the kind Tess would permit at the inn. Yet the silver rider had not looked like a harlot. And even Cornelius had treated her with respect.

Mattie had settled. She lay with her head tucked into

Kat's shoulder, and the feel of her breath against Kat's neck was warm and slow and easy. Perhaps she was already asleep. But Kat stayed awake for a while, thinking of the silver mare and its rider, who travelled round the country and was not bound to one place, one house, from her first day to her last.

When Kat woke the next morning, very early, she knew she would do something terrible. Something strictly forbidden.

She must have made her mind up in her dreams, because she certainly hadn't made the decision the night before. If she had, she would never have been able to sleep at all.

She wanted to ride the silver mare.

She *had* to. Just to sit on its back for a moment, in the stall. Just to know what it was like.

She slipped from the bed, careful not to wake Mattie. She had brought her clothes to bed with her last night and kept them under the covers, so that they would not be too cold and clammy in the morning. But instead of getting dressed, she clutched the bundle in her arms and sneaked down the stairs on cold, bare feet. The chill raised goose pimples on her skin, and the little hairs on her arms and legs stuck out in all directions. Halfway down she sat on the steps to put on her clothes. She could hear faint noises from the kitchen – Tad was already at work, making bread, but he wouldn't expect anyone else to be up and about yet. She eased open the back door as noiselessly as possible. It was still mostly dark outside. Above the roof of the stables there was a paleness in the sky, the merest promise of dawn.

In the stable, the horses were sleepy and slow. Only one was wakeful enough to neigh hopefully, begging to be fed, but she hurried past all of them, past the tie stalls to the row of boxes at the end.

The silver mare was waiting for her.

At least, that was what it looked like. As if it knew she would be coming. There was no sleepiness. It did not roll to its feet, like some of the others, shaking itself and stretching its long rear legs. It just stood there, waiting.

'Don't you sleep at all, Silverhorse?' she asked it. 'Do you just stand there, staring into the darkness with your night eyes?'

She didn't leap on to its back straight away. First she brushed it carefully, although it seemed the mare had not been lying down at all. After that she got a rag and rubbed the smooth coat, feeling as if she was burnishing a silver plate. She groomed the slender legs with another rag, soaked in cold water. And finally she knew that she was putting off the moment, shrinking from it, because she was as frightened as she was eager.

Don't do it, then, she told herself. But that thought was suddenly unbearable. So in the end, she pushed her toe into a crack between two boards, put her hand on the mare's neck, and swung herself on to its back.

It stood stock still at first. Then a long shiver ran through the slender body, a shiver of eagerness. In one smooth movement, the mare stepped up to the door of the box and leaned against it, as if trying to push it open.

'We can't!' Kat said, horrified. 'Cornelius will kill me!'

But even as she said the last words, a prickling wave of exhilaration mixed with fear rose inside her, and she knew that she would do it anyway. Leaning across the mare's neck, she could just reach the bar. She pushed it aside, and the door flew open. With eager steps the mare walked into the aisle.

'Not that way,' Kat said. 'We'll go out the back.'

She tried to guide the mare into a turn with her legs. It obeyed so promptly that she was almost unbalanced by it. This was a far cry from sullen, hard-mouthed livery horses that had to be jabbed and kicked into obedience!

They clattered along the aisle and into the little hay barn. Kat swivelled the crossbar that kept the gate shut. This was actually easier to do on horseback than from the ground, at least for someone no taller than Kat. Then they were out-side. The mare danced along the edge of the dungheap as though parading through the City of Breda itself.

'Wait,' said Kat. 'I have to close the gate . . .'

But the mare had had enough of waiting, and suddenly Kat cared not a whit for barn gates, or for Cornelius's fury. The mare sprang forward into a gallop, and they streaked across the hillside behind the stable, through the windbreak stand of pines and through to the other side, where the High Meadows waited, bright with dew and dawn.

This was like no ride Kat had ever had before. Everything was faster and fiercer, each leap longer and more forceful. The wind tore tears from her eyes. She could barely see, everything was a blur of gold sun-gleams and silver haze and yellow-green autumn fields. There was not a single thought in her head, only clear sharp air and body heat and thundering speed.

It took a long while for the mare to get to the end of that joyful rush. Kat lost her recklessness before the mare did. Thoughts of the barn down there, of the other horses, and of Cornelius, began to intrude.

And just exactly how do I stop a horse I didn't put a bridle on? she thought, furious at herself and her own care-lessness. But almost the moment she lost her taste for headlong gallop, the mare slowed to a walk. The silver body felt not just hot but incandescent, yet the neck was barely damp. It was as if the heat burned off the sweat and moisture before it had a chance to soak the silver coat. The mare was breathing deeply and regularly and looked as if it could have kept going all day. But tension clutched at Kat's stomach when she looked about and realized just how far up the mountain they had come, and how high the sun had risen into the sky.

She turned the mare around, heading down towards the stable. Her heart hammered in her chest at the enormity of the sin she had committed. To have taken a guest's horse (and it had to be *that* horse, of course, clearly the most expensive one) and ridden it into the ground . . . well, not into the ground exactly, the mare still seemed full of spirit, but ridden it much too fast and much too long with no thought for the day's journey ahead of it . . . And she had left the gates wide open too, letting the heat out and the cold in. Any horse that managed to pull free of its chain could wander straight out on to the mountainside.

Why had she done it? Sweet Our Lady. This time she really deserved the beating Cornelius would give her. Her only defence was a confused idea that the mare had wanted her to. But that was nonsense, horses did not *want* anything in that way. Or if they did, at most they wanted their feed, or to be let loose in the field.

As she came out of the windbreak she saw the rider and Cornelius both waiting for her by the barn. Kat wished she could somehow shrink. Small enough to disappear. Or small enough, at least, that everyone would agree she couldn't help it, it wasn't her fault, it would be no use scolding. The mare picked her way carefully down the slope, neat and sure-footed. They were close now, close enough that Kat could see the fury on Cornelius's face.

And suddenly things were turned upside down. She no longer wanted to be small. She wanted to be big, old enough and big enough to hit back, so that she would never have to shrink and crawl again. The yellow beast stirred inside her, and the mare snorted and leaped forward, almost as if it had felt the coarse prickly hackles of the beast. It began to dance beneath her, suddenly every bit as savage as Kat's feelings.

Cornelius's fury licked at her like flames.

'Down!' he ordered. And of course she stiffened and kept her place. He grabbed her ankle and jerked, unseating her, so that she ended up on her back in the mud. She rolled quickly, trying to escape him, but his hand closed on her arm like a vice. He yanked her to her feet, and she ducked to avoid the slap she knew was coming.

Only it didn't. A narrow silver muzzle shot between them, and with a startled yell Cornelius fell back, arms flailing. For a moment, his eyes were so wide that white was visible all around the brown. Kat's yellow beast reared up from its crouch, ready to lash out at anything and anybody, and at her back she could feel the mare like a glowing wave of heat and fury, refusing to let Cornelius near her. Odd behaviour for a horse, noted one small corner of her mind, but the rest of her was too angry to wonder at it.

'Child . . . what's your name?' asked the rider suddenly.

'I'm twelve,' Kat said angrily, not willing to be called a child right now. But then she remembered who she was talking to, and the fury dimmed and sang less loudly in her ears.

'Kat,' she muttered. 'That is . . . Katriona, if you want the whole thing.'

'I'm leaving after breakfast, Katriona. Will you see to it that Frost is ready? Fed, groomed, and saddled?'

Kat nodded dumbly. Frost! How could anyone pick such a name for a horse with so much heat in it?

'Thank you,' said the rider, turning to leave. 'Oh, and by the way . . .' she put her hand on Cornelius's shoulder, the way she had done the day before. 'You are not to punish Kat for this. Not now, nor after I have left. She has my permission. Is that clear?'

Cornelius gave a short, jerky nod. It was as if that hand

21

on his shoulder leached all the rage out of him. Kat wondered if there was something of witchcraft in this, although the rider did not look anything like the only witch Kat knew: dotty old Henbane who used to wander around in the Marshvale on moonlit nights, gathering berries and herbs. Sometimes he fell in, so that the goat girls had to rescue him.

Witchcraft or not, Cornelius did not hit her. And that was magical enough.

The rider came into the yard from the inn, saddlebags slung across her shoulder and an uneasy Nicolas at her heels. It was his job to carry the luggage, and he was worrying about what Tess would say. Kat stood, holding the silver mare, trying to tell herself that she didn't mind that it was leaving. She watched the rider carefully. Would she notice how the silver coat shone? Would she notice the glint of oil on the hooves? The scent of saddle soap and linseed oil from the tack? The rider fastened the saddlebags behind the saddle. Then she ran her hand across the smooth quarters.

'Beautifully done,' she said. 'My thanks.' She pulled out a small purse she carried around her neck and took something from it. 'This is for you, Katriona. Keep it carefully and let no one take it from you.'

Kat closed her hand around the rider's gift. It was a coin. Kat stared. Not just any coin. A silver coin. If a guest took it into his head to tip the stable girl, the most he would usually part with were a few iron pennies, or perhaps a copper. Kat had never before owned anything made of silver.

The rider swung on to the mare's back and set off. The clatter of hooves receded down the cobbled bit of street outside, then became a duller sound as mare and rider left the village behind and took the gravelly South Road, heading for the Kernland Pass. Kat was still staring at her silver coin and only later realized she hadn't even thanked Frost's rider.

It wasn't just that the coin was silver. One side of it bore the shape of a rearing horse. Silver coin, Silverhorse . . . She got a weird, dizzy feeling from looking at it, the way she sometimes did when Tad was trying to teach her how to spell a new word and she simply couldn't make sense of the letters he had scratched in the ashes of the hearth. There was a meaning hidden here as well, if only one knew how to read it, she thought. But the silver horse lay cool and silent in her palm.

ERMINE

Winter was tightening its grip on Three Valleys, and the Kernland Pass had been closed twice already. Cornelius and a score of men from South Vale had managed to open it again, but traffic was sparse, and few travellers stayed at Crowfoot Inn. Regulars from the Vale and the village still came for Tess's good ale, but the food these days was simple fare.

Most of the year, the Green Mountains around Three Valleys lived up to their name. Only a few peaks showed grey and bald above the treeline. But once the snows really arrived, not even the wide Kernland Pass could be kept open, and the mountains became a grey and white wall around the Valleys, letting nobody in and nobody out. Almost every year, some stranger would misjudge the speed and force of winter. If he was lucky, he ended up stranded in the Vale, waiting for spring. The less lucky were taken by the snows.

A few days after the Pass had been cleared for the

second time, a man came to the inn, riding a gaunt, exhausted horse. It was evening and already dark, and a fierce wind was whistling through the Vale. The lantern by the door of the inn was swinging wildly on its hook, causing yellow gleams of light to leap and dance on the wet cobbles. The sign, too, with Tess's family mark, the glacier crowfoot, was rocking in the wind, squeaking and rattling on its hinges. No one heard the hoofbeats through the din or realized that a guest had arrived until the door opened and a stranger stood on the threshold.

'Is this Cornelius Austerlin's inn?' asked the man. He looked huge and shapeless in his fur hat and sheepskin vest. His boots were so tall they reached all the way to the middle of his thighs.

'You must be a Southerner,' said Tess. 'This is Teresa's inn. But Cornelius lives here.'

The man gave a sort of grunt and plonked himself down at the table nearest the door.

'A bed for the night,' he said. 'And a meal on this table. My horse is outside.'

'Kat, see to it.' Tess nodded her head in the direction of the door, and Kat got off the bench where she and Mattie had been sitting, darning socks. Outside, the man had not even paused to tie his horse to the rail, but apparently it wasn't necessary. The horse looked as if it would drop dead if it had to take another step.

'Poor wretch,' muttered Kat. It was soaked from tail to forelock, and one eye drooped as if the horse lacked the strength to blink away the droplets caught in its lashes. Kat gently brushed her hand over that eye. Her fingers came away sticky. When she raised them into the light of the lantern, she saw that they were bloody.

'Did you cut yourself on something, horsey?'

But no, this was no scratch from a thorn or a branch. The gash was long and ugly, across the poll and down the forehead. The forelock was crusty with blood, and one ear drooped lopsidedly. This was a knife, or even a sword, Kat decided. Had the man been in a fight? Why hadn't he seen to the cut? No wonder the horse looked half dead, what with the bleeding and all.

Just then, the horse gave a hollow grunt and dropped to its knees, and then on to its side.

'Cornelius!' she yelled, at the top of her voice. 'Cornelius!'

He poked his head through the stable door, saw the horse on the cobbles, and crossed the yard at a run.

'What's wrong?' he asked. 'Did the idiot half kill it, trying to get here before nightfall?'

'It's wounded,' said Kat. 'Somebody cut it!'

Cornelius went down on one knee next to the horse. Kat pointed to the gash on its forehead. Cornelius grunted.

'Sword cut,' he said. 'To the poll. Clumsy bugger. Meant to get the rider.'

He got up and turned towards the inn. Kat knew what he was thinking. Swords meant trouble, and trouble was Cornelius's job.

'He is sitting quietly at a table waiting for his meal. And he knows your name,' Kat said. 'But this horse is dying!'

27

Cornelius stood indecisive for a moment, then he nodded.

'Have to get it to the stables,' he said. 'Let's see if we can get it on its feet. Fetch a bucket of oats.'

Kat ran across to the stables and filled a bucket. The other horses neighed when they heard the lid of the food bin rattle, but she paid them no attention. When she came back, Cornelius had managed to get the horse up on its belly, like a dog, instead of stretched flat on its side. Kat held out the bucket so that it could smell the oats. It flared its nostrils and craned its neck, trying to reach the food.

'It's strong enough to want to eat, at least,' she said.

'Let it have just a mouthful.'

She let the horse nibble at the oats. Then she held the bucket just out of reach.

'Come on, horse,' she said encouragingly. 'On your feet!'

Cornelius dug his shoulder into the horse's flank, shoving and lifting. The horse grunted with effort and managed to straighten its front legs. Its rear end wouldn't quite follow, and it would have collapsed again without the support Cornelius was providing. But finally one kicking leg got purchase on the wet cobbles, and the whole animal came shudderingly to its feet.

'The stables,' Cornelius snapped. 'Now.'

Step by wobbling step they proceeded, across the yard and through the door, into the nearest empty stall.

'Let it eat now,' said Cornelius. And Kat let the horse empty the bucket. Then it sighed and buckled down on to the straw. Cornelius put bales of hay on either side of it to keep it from collapsing completely. He got a heavy blanket from the tack room, and Kat covered the wet and shivering body with a thick layer of straw and then with the blanket.

'Get a bit of molasses and soak it in water. It needs the sugar and the water both. And then go see if Tad has some sheep-gut or something. That cut needs stitching.'

Kat nodded and did as she was told. She would be the one doing the stitching, she knew. Cornelius's broad and callused fists weren't as apt for the job as her girl's hands. She had stitched cuts before, on the horses or sometimes on a goat or a sheep.

Tad found some sheep-gut and scalded that and the needle for her. Kat washed her hands in water so hot they came out red and puckered like the skin on a newborn baby. With Cornelius holding the horse's head and Nicolas holding the lantern, she then closed the long gash, trying to pretend it was really no different than the darning she and Mattie had just been doing. The horse tried to toss its head a few times, but Cornelius's grip was firm, and the horse was very tired.

'Aye, then,' Cornelius finally said. 'We've done what we could. The rest is up to Our Lady. And now I want a word with the man who rode a horse in this state!'

The stranger was still sitting at the table by the door, now with the remains of a meal in front of him – breadcrumbs, soup bowl, cheese rinds and sausage skin. He had practically polished the bowl with his bread. Now he sat hunched over a tankard of beer – probably one more than he ought to have had, by the look of it. Tess was at the bar, laughing and talking with Anna Weaver and her journeyman Aren, but Kat could tell she was keeping an eye on the stranger all the same. Cornelius made for the table in a very straight line.

'Your horse was in a sorry state,' he said. 'We had to stitch the cut.'

It took a while for the stranger to raise his head. His tangled wet hair clung to his face, partly hiding his expression. The furrows by his nose and mouth were deep, the skin weather-tanned, and the eyes bloodshot.

'Cornelius Austerlin,' he muttered, slowly and thickly. 'Don't you recognize me?'

'Karel!' Cornelius's breath hissed through his teeth. 'What are you doing here? Aren't you with the Regiment any more?'

The man shook his head in the same slow, thick fashion.

'Ain't none. Not'ny more. Old Marker died, and Young Marker couldn't hold the pieces together. Been going downhill anyway, these past few years. Poor contracts. Bit of border patrol and such. No proper money in it. You were wise to get out when you did. Got yourself a fat berth, too, didn't you?' He nodded his head vaguely at the common room and leered at Tess.

Cornelius gave a grunt that could mean anything.

'About the horse,' he said.

'Cut its head on a sharp branch,' Karel said.

30

Cornelius snorted. 'Come off it, Karel. I just stitched that cut. More'n twenty stitches. That was a sword.'

Karel dropped his eyes. 'Didn't want to worry you unduly, is all. But you're right. Bunch of robbers. Attacked the merchants I was riding guard for. Had to make a run for it.'

'And the rest? The robbers? The merchants?'

'I was the only one who made it through the pass. Snow-slide. Road's closed, now.'

'We'll send someone to take a look,' Cornelius said, glancing with no enthusiasm at all towards the door. 'Some-one' was usually himself and Erold the blacksmith, who had also served with one of the mercenary regiments in his younger days.

'I told you, I was the only one!' Karel's voice rose, loud enough to bring Tess to her feet in disapproval. Then he continued more calmly: 'There's nothing you can do. There's nothing to take a look *at*.'

Cornelius stared at him for a long moment.

'If you say so, Karel . . .'

He drew up a chair and sat down across from the stranger. 'Is the beer to your liking? Damn, Karel, but it's good to see a face from the old days. Kat, bring me my tankard. And get Karel another.'

Kat took down Cornelius's special tankard from its hook above the bar. It was of white china, with a pewter lid, and his name painted in swirly blue and gold letters on the side. It had been a gift from his old commander, and he was intensely proud of it.

31

'See – I still have it,' he told Karel. 'Your health. And tell me what you've been up to . . .'

It fell to Kat to settle the stable for the night. Cornelius stayed in the common room, drinking beer and talking to Karel about the good old days in Marker's Regiment. Not a word was said, though, about what had happened to Karel's horse, or about what Karel had been doing since the Regiment was dissolved. Finally, it became harder and harder for Karel to speak intelligibly. Cornelius had to bend further and further across the table in order to hear him. Karel, too, bent further and further, until his head sank all the way down on to the table, and he started snoring. Cornelius gave an amused little snort.

'You take the luggage, Kat,' he said with a beery grin, 'and I'll take the guest!'

He seized Karel's wrist with one hand, hunched down level with Karel's belly, and rose to his feet with the limp body slung across his shoulder. It wasn't quite as easy for him as he would like to pretend – he grunted from the strain and grew red in the face – but he walked all the way up the stairs with his burden, never pausing, although Karel was by no means a small man.

The saddlebags, too, were large and heavy. Unusually heavy, Kat thought. What on earth had he put in them? Lumps of lead? His horseshoe collection? It was tempting to look, but Tess would be livid if she messed with the luggage of a guest, even such a one as Karel.

*

Karel never got that drunk again. But he spent a lot of time in the common room over the next few days.

'Sit down and talk a bit,' he would tell Cornelius. And Cornelius sat. Or Karel would say: 'Let's go and see if we can get a rabbit or two.' And then he and Cornelius disappeared up the mountain with snares and bows and the blacksmith's pointy-nosed setter, and no one would see them for the rest of the day.

Even though Cornelius and Erold, with Karel helping them, had managed to clear a passage through the Pass, there were hardly any travellers. Things in the stable were slow. Kat could handle the work on her own, and in the beginning she was only relieved to have Cornelius off her back. But it left little time to do chores for Tad. And Tad had to chop wood for the kitchen hearth and the big open fire in the common room by himself, a task that was normally Cornelius's.

After a week in this fashion, Kat heard Tess and Cornelius arguing in the scullery.

'I hope your good friend realizes that meals at this inn have to be paid for.'

Tess's voice was sharp enough to bring Kat up short. She had been on her way out to the stables, but now she stopped to eavesdrop.

'Of course he does,' grunted Cornelius in some irritation. 'He's already brought in quite a bit for the pot.'

'Two rabbits and a grouse,' Tess snorted, 'that Mattie had to skin and clean. It barely covers half the beer the two of you guzzle in one night. And just how long is he planning on staying?'

'Dammit, wife! Why are you so eager to see the back of him? I don't see a long line of paying customers waiting to get in. You ought to be pleased that *somebody* is willing to drink the mouse piss you call beer!'

'I've had about enough of this, Cornelius Austerlin!' snapped Tess.

'Really? Well, so have I. I've just about had it with you and your bossy manners, I've had it with slaving away all day to feed your brood of bastard brats! Don't be too certain of me, wife, or you might wake up one morning to find me gone. Gone to a place where a man can have a house and call it his own!'

'Where a man can have a house? Don't be daft. Nobody's that crazy, not even your precious Southerners. And as for the brats, they were made the good old-fashioned way, without this Southern marriage nonsense. I never should have agreed to that.'

'You think you know everything, Teresa.' Cornelius's voice had dropped to its lowest, most dangerous level, and Kat, listening by the door, held breathlessly still. 'But you don't. There *is* a place. And there are others like me. Why should a man not own a house, or a bit of land? Do we not work the land. Do we not defend it? Sweat for it and bleed for it, as much as you do? Why are we to be chased from place to place our whole life long, never to say, "This is *my* place, here I stay"?'

'Did Karel put this nonsense into your head?'

'*No, he did not*. Don't you think I'm capable of having a thought or two myself?'

'Oh, aye. That's why I'm so surprised to hear you spout a lot of gibberish another man came up with.'

Kat would never find out what answer Cornelius might have made to that. Suddenly, a rough hand seized her by the arm and shoved her into the scullery.

'Sorry to disturb you, Cornelius,' said Karel, delivering a flawless little bow, 'but it seems to me this girl could use a lesson on good manners. Or is eavesdropping customary in Three Valleys?'

Tess never hit any of her children. But there were times when Kat would have preferred Cornelius's kind of punishment. At least it was over and done with quickly.

Tess ran her forefinger along the sooty top of the fireplace. Then she drew a black line across Kat's forehead.

'The rest of the day.'

And those were the last words anybody at Crowfoot Inn spoke to Kat that day.

The black line meant Silence. No one talked to Kat. Nor did she try to talk to anyone. She wouldn't have been answered if she had. Not until Tess herself washed away the black line as a sign that she was now forgiven.

Kat hated the Silence. She vividly remembered the time when Cor had been born, and she hadn't wanted to have anything to do with him because he was Cornelius's son.

She refused to look after him, she wouldn't touch him, she wouldn't even look at him.

'He's your brother,' Tess had said, steel in her voice. 'And until you learn that this is so, you are not part of this family.'

And so the Silence had begun. It had been horrible. Not just for Kat, but for the others as well, particularly Mattie. But if anyone broke the Silence, they got the black line too. And Mattie could barely hold up for half a day without breaking down and sobbing for forgiveness.

Kat stood it for nearly two weeks. But she came to feel more and more transparent, as if she were no longer properly Kat. She had nightmares, thinking she had died and become a ghost that nobody could see. Sometimes she even dreamed of being buried, and woke up with the taste of dirt in her mouth and a heavy feeling in her chest. She would sit up in bed, gasping and listening to the sound of her own heart thudding away. She began to feel that she would have to start screaming and banging her head against a wall, if no one talked to her. But the only person in the house who did not know what the black line meant was Cor, who just lay there, cooing and gurgling, and sleeping most of the time. And one night, when the loneliness had become too much for her to bear, she had sneaked on to the porch where his cradle stood, pushed aside the netting, and taken the baby on to her lap, singing to him so softly that she didn't think anyone would hear.

'Congratulations,' came Tess's voice behind her. 'You have a brother.'

And then of course Kat had started to cry, harshly and loudly, as though her heart would break, and little Cor had come awake too, howling. Tess put her arms around the two of them and rocked them both at the same time.

'You are the stubbornest child I have,' she whispered, her cheek against Kat's bent neck. 'Sweet Our Lady, but I've missed you!'

'The rest of the day' was quite a long time, a harsher punishment than Tess would normally have dealt her for such an offence. Kat wondered whether she was being chastised not so much for eavesdropping, but because of what she had heard. The things Cornelius had said! Was it Karel that had made him think such thoughts? And was there really such a place, a place where men could own the houses and the land? And if there was, how did Karel know about it?

For days after that, they barely saw Cornelius. He and Karel left early in the morning and didn't come back until darkness had fallen. Tess was in a black mood from dawn to dusk and did everything with fierce movements and lots of noise, so that one could always tell where she was. Which was quite useful, as nobody wanted to get in her way.

In the stable, things were deliciously peaceful. Apart from Karel's poor wretch of a horse, she had Anna Weaver's pony team to look after, and Merchant Werle's fancy

Eastern mare which he dared not keep himself, as his stable was much colder than that of the inn. Then there were five 'autumn horses' – horses Cornelius had bought cheaply because their owners didn't want the cost of feeding them through the winter. In the spring prices would rise, and Cornelius would sell them at a good profit. He often bought, sold or swapped horses with the traders and travellers passing through South Vale. He had a good eye, and usually made a fair bit of money on his deals.

The easiest thing would have been to leave the autumn horses in the Low Field all winter. In the High Meadows it was too cold, even if one built them a lean-to. But last year, five horses had disappeared from the Low Field, without a trace. They never found out whether it was thieves or wolves. If wolves, why no gnawed remains? If thieves, how had they got in and out of the Vale at a time when the passes were closed with snow? Everyone in Three Valleys knew Cornelius's mark, and no one there would have dared keep such a horse without paying for it, that much was certain. And he had painted it large and clear on their quarters with everberry dye, so that it would stay there until their woolly winter coats dropped off in spring.

He had no time to guard a field of horses, so this year they were in the inn stables, even though that was more costly. That was why there were only five. Kat didn't mind though. It meant they had to be exercised, and so she got to ride.

This morning, it looked set to be a fine, clear day. She saddled Blackie, the gelding she liked best, and drove the other four up into the High Meadows to kick up their heels and graze as they wanted. They were used to the trip and made no trouble. She lazed about on Blackie's back and let him wander at will. She even let him graze with his bridle on, although it meant she would have to clean it when they got back. Globs of greeny-yellow foam dropped from his chomping jaws and on to his chest and forelegs.

Suddenly she heard somebody call her name – a scared, lonely voice. Nicolas. Nicolas in a state.

'Up here,' she called. 'Wait, Nico, I'm coming.'

Blackie's head shot up with a start as she squeezed him firmly with her legs and drove him into a sharp downhill canter. She came on Nicolas a bit further down, on the other side of the brook. To cross it on foot, one had to balance on some mossy, slippery rocks, and he didn't like doing that.

'Kat!' he said, and his voice was thin and frightened, so that one suddenly remembered that it was only last summer that he had been too young to be out on the mountain alone. 'I called and called, but you didn't answer . . .'

'I didn't hear you,' Kat said. 'Not till just now. What is it?'

'Mama . . .' He had to gulp a deep breath and start over. 'Mama says that you have to go and find Cornelius. Up near Saratown, she says. But hurry. There are six of them!'

'Six of *what*?' she asked, scared and irritated all at once. 'Dammit, Nicolas, why can you never get *anything* straight?'

'A gang. Or we think they might be. They came . . .' He waved his hands helplessly. Words had a way of deserting

Nicolas when things came to a head. 'They haven't done anything, not yet. Just smashed a pitcher. But Mama says . . .' He gulped again. 'Mama says Cornelius is to come. Now!'

'Why does she think he is at Saratown?'

'Erold says so. Hurry!'

'But the horses . . .' There was no time to drive them home. And if it really was a robber gang, they might be better off up here . . . but if she took off on Blackie, they might follow, and she couldn't go charging across the mountain with four loose horses at her heels!

'Nico, come here . . .' She let Blackie splash through the brook. 'Get up behind me.' She reached out and grasped his hand and made him put his foot in the stirrup so he could swing up on to Blackie's back. 'Hang on!'

Blackie splashed unhesitatingly back across the brook and trudged back up the hill. She didn't dare canter, not with Nicolas behind her.

'You will have to stay with the other horses,' she told him over her shoulder. 'We'll put the bridle on Brighella. If you can manage her, you'll manage the lot of them. They'll do what she does.'

'But if I get the bridle, what will you do?' Nicolas's voice was small and lonely still, and she felt sorry for him. This was a hard task for someone his age.

'I can manage Blackie with the halter,' she said, hoping it was true. 'I've a bit of rope that will do for reins.'

They caught Brighella and bridled her. Kat helped Nicolas on to her back.

'I'll be as quick as I can,' she promised. 'Take good care of them, and don't let Brighella follow Blackie.'

Nicolas nodded dumbly. Kat slipped the rope into Blackie's mouth and then through the halter rings, to form a kind of bit. It wasn't a bridle, and Blackie gummed the unfamiliar rope uneasily, but it was the best she could do. She wanted to take off at a gallop, but that would have been one sure way to stampede the others. She would have to keep to a walk, at least until they were out of sight. *Come on, Blackie, get on with it!* He didn't want to leave his herd, but she kicked him firmly, and he was used to doing what she told him to.

Once they had crossed the first ridge and left Nicolas and his charges behind, she urged Blackie into a canter. On the way to Saratown there weren't that many stretches of level ground, she had to make speed where she could. There was so little time. She hated to think what might be happening down at the inn, with Cornelius absent and only Erold Smith for protection. Six of them, Nicolas had said. *Sweet Our Lady, let them be all right.*

It wasn't until she was nearly there that she started to wonder what on earth Cornelius was doing at Saratown. It was not the obvious place to go rabbit hunting. Little grew there, and nobody lived there any more. The only reason anything had ever been built in that bleak place was an old pass, long since closed by a massive rockslide. Sometimes, when the flocks grazed the Upper Reaches in high summer, a shepherd might spend the night there, just to have a roof over his head, however dilapidated, but the rest of the time, owls and spiny rats had the place to themselves.

Or so she thought. But when she finally managed to boot a sweaty, sulky and increasingly contrary Blackie up the last ridge, she saw that there were horses in the paddock behind the old livery stables, and that smoke rose from several chimneys. Even at this distance, she could smell the wood-smoke. From pure surprise, she stopped urging Blackie forward, and he immediately halted. Then he caught the scent of fellow horses and took off at a trot down the path, whinnying shrilly. She tried to stop him, but a mere rope and halter proved a hopelessly inefficient brake once he had made his mind up. Whether she wanted to or not, she was going to arrive in Saratown at a loud, bouncy trot, and on a horse whinnying at the top of his lungs. He did not slow until he reached the paddock.

She scrambled off his back and managed to haul him away from the fence before a fight erupted between him and that big belligerent-looking bay with the stallion's neck. The fence looked none too solid. If either of the two horses broke it, she would hardly be popular with Saratown's new inhabitants. And who were they? Who would want to settle in such a bleak, desolate place?

She tied Blackie to a rail a fair distance from the paddock. The bay squealed menacingly and pounded the ground with one forefoot. Blackie snorted, and then pretended to be more interested in the spindly tufts of grass he could reach.

Almost all the windows in Saratown were boarded up,

and the place looked strange now, deserted and inhabited all at once. No one had come out to investigate the noise. She took a deep breath and knocked cautiously at the nearest door.

No answer. She lifted the latch and pushed tentatively. It opened.

With the windows boarded up, the place was gloomy even in daylight. Someone had slept in front of the fireplace recently, she could see. Pine boughs had been brought in for mattresses, and rolled-up woollen blankets and sleeping furs lay like lumpy dark sausage shapes in front of the fire. Mixed with the odours of damp and human sweat and wood-smoke was a full-bodied yeasty smell that Kat would recognize anywhere: Tess's very own beer. It seemed Cornelius really had been here!

There was almost no furniture in the room – only a huge oak table that had probably been too heavy for anyone to drag down off the mountain. On it were heaps and piles of clothes. Too many clothes, really. Kat rummaged curiously through one pile. Most of it was in the Southern style, with fancy stitching and embroidery, but there were a few heavier garments, cloaks and furry vests, that might have come from Three Valleys, or somewhere else where they knew a thing or two about sheepskin and how to keep warm in winter. Almost all of it was of good quality, and expensive. Two of the shirts had even been embroidered with gold thread.

Suddenly a chill went through her, and she felt an eerie prickling along her spine. One of the pretty shirts had been

43

mended. There was a jagged tear both in the front and the back, and although someone had done their best to launder and repair it, large brownish stains were still obvious. Whoever had bled on that shirt was unlikely to be still alive. Not after having a spear pushed right through him.

Kat dropped the shirt as if it had suddenly turned into a dead frog. Looking more closely at the clothes, she could see that many of them were similarly damaged. What *was* this?

'First I catch you eavesdropping, and now I find you pawing through other people's stuff? Someone needs to teach you some manners, girl.'

Now it was Kat's turn to become the dead frog – cold, clammy and stiff. Slowly, she turned round. Karel stood in the doorway, arms slightly extended, as if he meant to catch her if she tried to run. With the light at his back, he looked very large and dark. Dangerous. Kat felt a familiar taste in her mouth, all yellow and sour.

'At least I don't put holes in people,' she said, knowing full well she was being stupid. When the yellow beast was allowed its say, what came out was rarely pearls of wisdom. But Karel only laughed, loudly and ringingly.

'Neither do I. Or not since I retired. What gave you that idea? What have you found?'

As if you didn't know. She barely managed not to say it out loud.

'Clothes,' she muttered instead. 'With ugly holes in them.'

44

'Hmm,' he grunted, slowly approaching her and the table. 'Yes, that does look strange.'

'Where is Cornelius?' she asked, trying to keep her voice steady. 'I need to see him.'

'Who told you to come here?' He made a quick grab for her arm. 'Are you alone?'

His fingers dug into her elbow like claws. She didn't dare try to pull free.

'Erold,' she answered quickly. 'Erold told me. His horse cast a shoe, but he should be here any minute.'

Karel grabbed her other arm as well and pulled her close, so close she could feel his breath on her forehead.

'Come, now,' he said, in an eerily gentle voice. 'I think this little girl is lying. Now, why would you do a thing like that?'

'I'm not lying,' she shot back angrily.

'Really?' he said, clearly unmoved. Then it was suddenly his turn to snarl: 'Just how stupid do you think I am? You and your mother, all high and mighty, you could do with a lesson, the pair of you. Couple of bitches, thinking they can boss everyone around. Do this, dog. Do that. But I'm nobody's dog. And I'm nobody's fool either!'

He began to drag her towards the door, and she instinctively dug in her heels and struggled in his grasp.

'Oh? Well, you're asking for it then,' he said, changing his grip. 'Come along, Milady!'

His thumb was digging into a point by her elbow, and her arm was on fire. She had thought she knew about pain, what with the beltings Cornelius gave her. But he had never hurt her like this, never handled her in this frightening way, causing agony so easily.

She came. There was nothing else she could do. Obediently she hurried along at Karel's side, trying only to move in such a way that the pain would grow no worse.

Outside were four men, one of them holding Blackie.

'Was it just a girl?' one of them said, startled.

'The innkeeper's girl,' Karel said briefly, and Kat sensed that this changed things somehow.

'The innkeeper's . . . Does that mean we have to . . . ?'

'That's for Ermine to decide.' Karel dragged her along Saratown's short main street to the house that had once been the last Resting Place before the pass. The sign still hung above the door: a silvery grey horse in a circle of oak-leaves and the simple words even Kat could read: 'Shelter. Rest. Healing.' The sight of it made Kat think of the rider and the silver coin she had been given. She always wore it in a small bag around her neck. Suddenly she was aware of its light pressure against her breastbone, and somehow that made her arm hurt slightly less and she felt a bit braver. Then they had passed beneath the sign and into a darkened room, causing her to stumble with sudden blindness.

Karel stopped, and so perforce did she. The four men had followed them into the house, but they too stood quietly, waiting. The silence stretched.

'And what is this?'

The voice came from somewhere in the darkness, distinctive and yet somehow unplaceable. Man or woman? Kat couldn't tell.

'The innkeeper's girl,' said Karel once more. 'She claims Erold has sent her.'

'Erold . . . That would be the smith?'

'That's right,' said Karel. 'He's new.'

Another long, frightening silence. Then that voice again:

'Get Cornelius Austerlin. He will have to answer for this.'

Kat's eyes were growing used to the darkness now. She could just make out a human form, seated behind a table. Some kind of fur cloak blurred the shape. Then a door at the back of the room opened, and Cornelius came in – she would know his big square silhouette anywhere. Quickly she said:

'Cornelius, Tess sent me. Trouble at the inn. Some gang.'

Cornelius came to an abrupt halt.

'You promised . . .' he began. 'If they're yours—'

Ermine broke in. 'They're not. But – did you not say yourself, Austerlin, that a lesson might be needed? Yet here you are, rebelling at the very thought. You are too bound to that woman, Austerlin. Bound with the chains of desire. She holds you captive, and she will never let you go.'

A man, thought Kat. It must be a man. No woman would speak like that.

It was a while before Cornelius answered. 'Maestra – a man must have a woman. I cannot be like you.'

Maestra? Mistress of this place, like Tess was maestra of Crowfoot Inn? No man then. Who *was* this Ermine?

Cornelius suddenly straightened. 'The inn . . .' he said. 'I have to go!'

47

SILVERHORSE

'No, Austerlin,' said Ermine. 'Not yet. This girl. Is she obedient? Will she heed an order?'

'Obedient? Well, that . . . depends.'

'On who gives the order? Austerlin, she cannot be allowed to speak of what she has seen here. We must have her silence. One way or the other. Can you give an order she will heed? Will you answer for her, on your life?'

On your life . . . What was this? They couldn't mean that, could they? Not literally? But Kat remembered the gashed shirt and was suddenly certain of nothing except desperate danger. On your life. On pain of death.

Cornelius wouldn't. Never. Not to save the innkeeper's red-haired daughter who wasn't even his. And who had certainly never shown him much obedience before.

Skirting the table, Cornelius crossed the room to stand next to her. There was a tension in him, as if he might suddenly move very fast if he had to.

'She is my daughter,' he said. 'Of course she'll heed me.'

Kat peered at him, trying to make out his face in the darkness. His daughter. He had never called her that before. She stood, quiet as a mouse. For once she felt no desire to yell that he wasn't her father.

'Very well,' said Ermine, in that hard-to-place voice. 'She is your charge. You must see to her silence.'

'Yes,' said Cornelius quietly, and some of that tense, deadly stillness left his body. 'Thank you, maestra.'

'You may leave.'

Karel had let go of her arm. It felt numb and dead from

elbow to fingertips. She rubbed at it cautiously with her other hand.

'Come on,' said Cornelius through clenched teeth, and she followed him out of that dark room. The daylight seemed blazingly strong, the colours vivid, as if she had never truly noticed them before. The rocks, dark grey like a thunder-clouded sky shot with sparks of white and green, the mosses and the lichen, spreading in fine lacy patterns of rose and ochre and verdigris . . . The sandy-yellow tracks between the houses, and the houses themselves, silvery grey with age. The air burned her nose and the back of her throat, almost as if she had stopped breathing in there, and only now remembered what lungs were really for.

She caught sight of Blackie, now tied to the rail in front of the Resting Place.

'Blackie . . .' she began.

'I need him,' said Cornelius. 'You'll have to leg it. How many men?'

'Six. They smashed a pitcher.'

'And so Erold told you where I was?'

Kat nodded.

'And told Teresa too?'

She nodded again.

'Listen carefully, Kat. And even if you never do another thing I tell you to, this time you'll *listen*. Tell your mama that me and Karel were with a couple of drifter women. Nothing else.'

'Drifter women . . .' Kat felt her eyebrows shoot into her hair. 'She'll be *mad*.'

'That's my business,' snapped Cornelius. 'You just do as I say. Katriona, swear it!'

There was no yellow beast in her belly now. She looked him straight in the eyes and seriously declared:

'I, Katriona Teresa-Daughter, solemnly swear to do what my stepfather tells me to do.' And then, just to keep him on his toes, she added: 'This time.'

The last words brought him up short. Then a narrow smile tugged at his lips.

'Cheeky brat,' he said. 'Mind how you go.'

Turning, he loosened Blackie's rope reins and swung stiffly on to the gelding's back. He didn't much like riding, she knew. It made his leg ache, the one that had been wounded once. But he pushed Blackie forward into an even canter along the sandy-yellow track.

Karel came out of the Resting Place.

'So,' he said bitterly. 'There he goes. Mistress whistles, and the old dog hurries to do her bidding. Faithful old hound that he is.'

'Tell him that to his face, if you dare!' Kat snapped.

'Oh, so the puppy can bark too,' said Karel. 'But let me tell you something, puppy: Cornelius Austerlin is too good a man to be some woman's lapdog for the rest of his life. One day she'll be whistling in vain. And on that day, who will protect her little bastards?'

Kat could think of no answer harsh enough. He gave a brief, sneering laugh and went back into the house.

*

Kat hurried as much as she could, back to the place where she had left Nicolas and the horses, but the shadows had grown long and the day short and chill by the time she got there. Nicolas was still on Brighella's back. He had pulled his sleeves over his hands to warm them, and he was shivering with cold.

'We'll bring them down off the mountain now,' Kat decided. 'We can't stay here, not in this cold, not once it gets dark. We'll just have to hope for the best.'

She didn't even have a rope any more. In the end, she borrowed Nicolas's belt and attached it to the halter of one of the horses, a quiet brown gelding. Her legs felt rubbery from the day's tension and the long walk, and she had to use a rock for a mounting block. They headed for the inn, and with the scent of home in their nostrils, the horses soon became unstoppable. Keeping them to a safe speed was not easy. Kat had to yell at the gelding and pull back on the belt with all her might.

'Stupid horse! You'll break your silly legs! *Walk*.'

It didn't make much of an impression. The gelding went charging down the High Meadow, slipping and sliding and nearly colliding with Brighella. Brighella, none too pleased, laid back her ears and gave a warning kick. All in all, the last bit was a shambles, and by the time they reached the barn gate, the horses were pushing and shoving against each other relentlessly, trying to get through the gates first.

'Get off, Nico,' Kat said, leaping down herself. 'We'll just leave them to find their stalls themselves.'

She opened the gate and leaped to one side so as not to

51

be trampled. Squeals and clattering hooves echoed through the half-empty stable, but as she had expected, the loose horses were too hungry to do anything except head for their cribs. All she and Nicolas had to do, in the end, was tie them up. Someone had already put out the feed, a sign of normality that Kat found very encouraging.

'Stay here,' she told Nicolas. 'I'll come and get you once I've checked that everything is all right.'

'No,' said Nicolas, white-faced. 'I won't sit out here alone. I'm coming with you!'

Kat looked at him. He had held out for nearly four hours, out there on the mountain, without letting Brighella and the others head for home. No wonder he was tired of being told to stay behind.

'You did great with the horses, Nicolas,' she said. 'All right, come on then. We'll go and see what's happening.'

They stole across the yard and stood listening by the kitchen window. A thoroughly normal rattling of pots and pans sounded from within, and a little later she saw Tad by the oven. There seemed to be no one else in the room.

'Come on,' she said. 'Let's try and sneak in.'

They opened the back door as quietly as possible and stood there under the back stairs, in a darkness smelling of muddy boots and onions. No strangers lurked there, at least. Kat pushed open the door to the kitchen.

'Hello, Tad,' she said softly. 'What's going on?'

'They're still here,' he said, 'But it seems they're not robbers after all. You wouldn't know it to look at them, though, and they weren't too polite either. It was a good thing Cornelius came back, they've been a lot more civil since he walked in. They're Southerners, same as him, that probably helps. Nicolas, you look frozen blue. Come and sit by the fire.'

'Who are they, then? And where are their horses?'

'Out front. They're some kind of border guards.'

'What are they doing here, then?'

'Looking for robbers, as it happens. Some gang that's been harassing caravans on their side of the pass. They think the bandits must be from our side of the border. As if we'd shelter riff-raff like that! But that's what they think. Cornelius is trying to change their minds for them right now.'

Kat thought of the men at Saratown. Maybe that's the gang, she thought. Maybe they are robbers. But Cornelius had been respectful to Ermine, and he would never back some kind of robber chief. Would he?

She couldn't tell anyone about Ermine, or Saratown. She had sworn not to. So she kept her mouth shut, even when she heard the border guards' description of the robbers and realized that one robber bore a striking resemblance to Karel. And even when Karel's heavy saddlebags suddenly disappeared from his room all by themselves. Karel himself never came back, and after a few fruitless days of searching and questioning and generally pestering the people of the Vale, the Southerners went back to their own side of the border, and everybody just got on with surviving the winter.

THE SHRIKE

With Karel gone, Cornelius once more took over in the stables. He was hardly ever away, partly because unexplained absences made Tess hiss and spit at him for days, partly because of the ghostly threat of robbers who might or might not be in the Vale.

Strangely, Kat now found it even harder to obey him. He had stood in front of Ermine and said: 'She is my daughter.' The memory filled her with mixed emotions. He might have saved her life. And yet . . . she didn't want to be his. She didn't want his protection, she didn't want his care. Most of all, she didn't want him to tell her what to do. Only Tess had that right. Only Tess.

She knew something *had* happened, that day in the darkened room with Ermine. For one thing, Cornelius hadn't hit her once, since that day. Why did that make her want to fight him even more? She knew it made him furious whenever she argued with him. So she argued. She knew he hated untidiness, so she began to put things away messily or not at all. Or she took ages grooming a single horse, just so that he would shout at her. For some reason, it made the yellow beast feel better when he did. Stronger. More certain of things.

Sometimes, she had an odd, impatient feeling, as if waiting for something to happen. She didn't know precisely what. Perhaps she thought that Cornelius would complain to Tess? And that Tess would . . . would what? Kat wasn't quite sure. *Do* something, finally. But she never did. Never had. If she had ever told Cornelius not to hit her daughter, Kat had never heard it. And she never told Kat to behave either.

In any case, Tess, these days, seemed to have troubles of her own. One day she would sweep through the house like a bush fire, blazing at everything and everybody. The next, one might find her in the empty scullery, with idle hands and eyes turned inwards. That was how it went, in fits and starts, and you never knew where you were with her.

The entire inn suffered from it. Tad had gone all stiff and silent because she had lost her temper with him, yelling that he had no more manhood than a suckling pig. This made Kat lose *her* head and get into a loud and angry shouting match with Tess, making everything much, much worse. Kat even succeeded in getting into a fight with Mattie. Mattie! Who never argued with anybody.

'Why do you always have to fight people?' cried Mattie, pale with anger. 'Why all this screaming and yelling whenever you're around? Why can you never be at peace with *anybody*? You're such a shrike!'

Shrike. Butcherbird. Kat saw the picture in Mattie's head, as clearly as if it had been in her own. An ugly half-grown bird, shrieking and pecking at everybody. Impaling its prey on a thorn to prevent it from getting away, then pecking at it, pecking and pecking, until it was all bloody and dead. Her breath caught in her throat, and her eyes stung with tears. Crouched in his favourite spot under the kitchen table, Cor dropped the pine cone he had been playing with and looked up at them with frightened, stricken eyes.

'Mattie is mad,' he whispered. 'Mattie is really mad.'

Tad too had stopped what he was doing, ladle poised over the soup kettle. He wasn't looking at them, but he was listening. He had heard what Mattie said.

Shrike.

The kitchen blurred in front of Kat's eyes. If she had to stay here one moment longer she would burst. She spun on her heel and ran, across the yard to the stables. She snatched a bridle and put it on Blackie with such forceful movements that he trembled and looked at her white-eyed like a startled colt. She had no time for saddles. She flung herself on to the gelding's back and rode, pelting through the trees, upwards, across the High Meadow and further still. Shrike. Butcherbird. How could Mattie say such a thing? Did she really mean it?

Abruptly, Kat ceased her furious urgings and let Blackie drop to a walk. She clutched at her stomach as if she was the one being spitted on a thorn. Mattie always meant what she said. Always. Kat raised her head and glared at the mountain ridges as if they were a prison wall trapping her, holding her back. If she really were a shrike she could fly out of here. Cornelius could boss somebody else about for a change. Tess could scold whomever she wanted, and Mattie could . . . Mattie could . . . Mattie might cry her eyes out. See if Kat cared. She was a shrike. Shrikes had no feelings, did they?

It was starting to snow. Sharp little needles of ice, burning her skin. She had to get back. She didn't want to. She never wanted to go back.

Blackie's head drooped. He hated being out here on his own, but he had been too frightened of her anger to even try to baulk. She had to get him back, he needed a stable, he needed to be fed.

She halted the tired gelding. Halted him, and turned him around.

Nightfall soon. No way would she make it back before dark. It was snowing more heavily now, with larger, fluffier flakes. She cursed herself. Being out here, in the dark, during a blizzard . . . it could be lethal. And if the weather didn't kill you, there were other dangers. The hillfolk, for one. They lived underground, it was said, in the heart of the mountain. They only showed themselves at night, when they looked just like ordinary people. In sunlight, they were no more solid than mist. But if they got hold of you and brought you into the darkness under the mountain, you never got out again.

Or there were the Nightmares. Ghostly horse-shaped spirits with fangs and poison spurs. They had the gift of human speech, and if they managed to lure you on to their backs you were as good as dead. They would take off at a gallop, faster than any mortal horse could run, and toss you into a cleft or crevice, and trample you and tear you, and eat your flesh. They were said to be particularly fond of the heart.

She shuddered. Shrikes did have feelings after all, it seemed. They could feel frightened, and lonely, and small. She buried her hands in Blackie's mane, trying to warm them. The clatter of his hooves on the stony trail was a bleak and lonely sound, like someone beating a very small drum. The wind chilled her face, and she brushed away her tears before the cold could turn them into tracks of ice.

The night was utterly dark, and only Blackie's good sense got them home at all. *Stupid*, she cursed herself. Stupid, stupid, stupid. But finally lights popped out below her, and they were real human lights, not phantom lures. Blackie picked his way down the last slippery bit of the trail, calling out in his loneliness. Another horse, Brighella probably, answered him from within. But even without the ensuing chorus of neighs, she doubted she would have been able to sneak in unseen. By the gate stood Cornelius, lantern in hand. Waiting.

It was almost like that morning, that glorious morning when she had stolen her Silverhorse ride. But now it was cold, and dark, and no rider would come to stop him. Would he hit her? Would he finally hit her again?

'Where have you been?' he demanded.

'Nowhere,' she said, sullenly. A slow, sulky anger burned in her. The anger of the shrike.

'*Where*?' Cornelius grabbed her calf. 'At Saratown?'

'None of your business.' Why didn't she just say no? Why did she have to make him even more furious?

'Dammit, girl.' His voice shook with suppressed rage. 'Answer me!'

She sat silently on Blackie's back, looking down at him. The old litany started in her head. It's none of your business. You're not my father. Leave me alone. You're not my father. *You're not my father.*

Yellow. Acid. Spiny.

'Why don't you just leave me alone?' she said in a low voice. And then the words tumbled out, softly but clearly, one stinging jab after another:

'Why do you care? Who asked you to stay here? It's not your inn. I'm not your child. Why don't you just leave? Go on. Go join your fancy friends in Saratown. Do you think Tess would want you if she didn't need your sword? You're just a broken-down old mercenary, and that's all you'll ever be. Or do you have some notion that she really loves you? Look at yourself. Who would?'

Cornelius opened his mouth, but not a sound emerged. A shudder ran through him. And then he finally swung at her, a wild uncoordinated blow, with the lantern he happened to be holding.

The lantern. Glass and hot metal and scalding oil. Blackie leaped to one side and she ducked her head, but something hot and sharp hit her on the neck, just below the ear. She swayed dizzily, then fell clumsily on to the cobbles, down into a tumbling chaos of hooves and legs. Pain shot through her. Then Blackie was gone, and she heard the sound of his frantically skating hooves in the aisle inside. Then quiet.

'Kat?'

Cornelius was crouching next to her. She looked at him, but she could not seem to find the use of her voice or her body.

'Sweet Sacred Lady . . .' whispered Cornelius, and looked completely desperate. For one strange, calm moment, she nearly wanted to apologize. But *he* was the one who had hit *her*. And he wasn't her father.

She knew something was wrong. She was beginning to feel less dizzy now, but there was definitely something wrong with her arm, the one she had fallen on. And a burning sensation behind her ear told her that the lamp had scorched her where it hit.

'Kat,' said Cornelius, fear in his voice. 'Can you move? Can you move your feet?'

She nearly didn't. Let him think, for a moment, that she had broken her neck. Serve him right. But she was starting to feel frightened herself, and it was a relief to find that, yes, she could move her feet. In fact, she could move everything except her right arm. The numbness was leaving it. Pain thudded through it, and inside it, something moved that shouldn't.

'I think my arm is broken,' she said, hoarsely.

'You fell off,' said Cornelius.

She began to shake her head but gave it up. It hurt her neck.

'No,' she said. 'You hit me.'

'Not on the arm.'

'It was your fault I fell!'

Cornelius rose to his feet, looking down at her.

'I'll go get your mama,' he said. 'Say what you like to her.'

Tess put raw egg-whites on the burn and straightened the arm as best she could. Despite the snow and the darkness, Cornelius saddled Brighella, the most sensible horse in the stable, and rode off to fetch Keri Herbwife from her home in Junefield.

Kat was put to bed in one of the guest rooms on the first floor, but even though Tad made her drink an entire mug of strong, bitter valerian tea, she couldn't sleep. The arm was throbbing ceaselessly, and if she didn't stay completely still, the bones moved sickeningly inside it. It made nausea burn at the back of her throat. It felt so *wrong*.

Finally she began to dream, almost without falling properly asleep. She was alone on the mountain. She was trying to find her way home, but the trails did not go where they usually went, and the night was dark and foggy. Her feet became heavier and heavier, until finally she sat down on the ground, crying and calling for Mama. Suddenly something appeared in the mists. A shrouded shape in an ermine cloak. Her heart beat more loudly in her chest, but she was too tired to run.

'Please,' she whispered. 'Help me . . .'

The ermine shape came closer. It had no human face. Instead, a stoat was looking at her with beady red eyes, a stoat the size of a man. It had very white, needle-sharp teeth, and it opened its jaws and spoke to her.

'Come with me,' it said. 'You're mine now.'

'No, I'm not,' she said. 'I never saw you before in my life! How can I be yours?'

'You are mine,' said the stoat, raking her arm with its claws, 'because no one else wants you.' It pushed its white-toothed face quite close to hers. 'My little shrike!' it hissed tenderly, and bit her just below the ear, so that blood welled hot and scalding down her neck.

'She drives him to it,' Tess said. 'She keeps at him until he explodes. I've heard her. She never lets up.'

'She's a child of twelve. He's a grown man. Are you telling me you think she's only getting what she deserves?'

A voice so cutting and ironic she barely recognized it. Could Tad really talk like that? Even in her dreams?

'No. No, I'm not saying that. But Cornelius is not a vicious man. He gets on fine with the others. It's just Kat . . . She drives him crazy.'

No, she wasn't dreaming after all. It was Tess and Tad she was hearing, downstairs in the kitchen just below the room she was in.

'She's so fierce, Tad . . . so defiant. She can't seem to settle at all. Galloping all over the mountain, like some boy. If she had only *been* a boy, I think it would have been easier. But Cornelius keeps expecting her to behave like a girl, and be sensible and quiet and do as he tells her. And Kat just can't. Sometimes I think she was *meant* to be a boy.'

'But she isn't, is she? It can't go on. Teresa, you have to do something.'

The silence lasted for a long time, and Kat felt herself starting to drift away. But she resisted, she didn't want to go back to the fog and the ermine shape. And so she heard Tess answer, her voice so harsh and sad all at once that it cut Kat to the heart:

'No. You're right. We can't go on like this.'

Cornelius, thought Kat. She's sending Cornelius away. And everything will be the way it was before he came.

The fogs melted. The stoat had disappeared. Warm and content, she slept until dawn and fresh pain woke her.

Cornelius returned shortly before noon the next day with Keri Herbwife. She felt Kat's arm and said Tess had done a good job of setting it, but it needed better splints. The arm was wrapped in woolly bandages and a strange wicker-work contraption that could be folded into a tight tube, supporting and protecting the broken limb.

'Do you want your arm to become straight and strong again?' asked Keri.

What a strange question, thought Kat. Of course she did. She nodded.

'Then you will keep this on as long as I tell you to. No matter how much it itches. No matter how clumsy it feels. Even when it stops hurting, do you hear? And no falling, with or without a horse. You will stay on the ground, take it easy and do nothing sudden or rash. Are we clear on that?'

Kat nodded again. Having a broken arm sounded very boring. But at least Cornelius would not be able to boss her around until her arm was well again. And soon he wouldn't be able to boss her around at all. He would be gone. Thinking about it, she actually felt pity for him. She felt so sorry for him that she got into no fights with him at all for nearly three weeks. Until one night when she was coming down the stairs and saw Tess and Cornelius standing in the doorway to the bedroom they shared. Cornelius had one hand at the small of her mother's back, fingers spread wide. The other was buried somewhere in her dark hair, and they were kissing, slowly and thoroughly. Suddenly Kat knew without a doubt that Tess would not send Cornelius away. Not now, not ever. She spun and ran down the last steps, into the darkened kitchen where Tad was just putting out the last of the lamps.

'Kat – what is it?' he asked.

She didn't answer. She pushed open the door to the common room and took Cornelius's big tankard from its hook. For a moment she stood there, looking at it: the smooth white china, the swirly letters. 'Cornelius Austerlin', in blue and gold. Then she raised it high above her head and smashed it against the stone floor, shards flying in all directions.

Behind the scullery was a small room, not much larger than a cupboard. It was here that Tess kept her accounts, here she went to write her rare letters and to read the ones she received. The day after the tankard, Tess called Kat into this room.

Tad hadn't told on her. He hadn't said that she had smashed the tankard on purpose. But if she hadn't, what was she doing with it at all? Anyway, she wanted Cornelius to *know*. Otherwise the whole thing was pointless.

Kat waited. Dust motes danced in the air around them, and Tess just sat there quietly, looking unusually pale. Finally she broke the silence, but not to talk about the tankard, it seemed.

'I've written a letter,' she said. 'I want you to know what it says. Shall I read it to you, or can you manage it yourself?'

'I can read it,' Kat said, hoping that was true. She was better at numbers than letters.

Tess handed her the letter. She had taken pains with it, penning it clearly, in large, careful letters. All the same, Kat didn't get very far before the letters blurred and made no sense, and she understood only one single thing.

To Bria Dyer, Dyer's Yard, at Idabrook.
   Greetings from Teresa Katriona-Daughter, Crowfoot Inn, South Vale.

Hoping this letter finds you well and in good circumstances, I ask you to consider in all seriousness, for the sake of the friendship between our two families, if you will be willing to take into your household my eldest daughter Katriona . . .

Kat read no further. She placed the letter on her mother's desk, feeling her throat and her stomach and her eyes all tighten into almost nothing, so that she could neither move, nor see, nor speak.

Cornelius wasn't being sent away. She was. That was the single thing she understood.

'. . . not until spring . . .' she heard Tess say. '. . . when you are well again, and the roads are safe . . .'

She turned to leave, not waiting to hear the rest. But Tess's voice caught her on the threshold.

'Kat! Come back here. I haven't finished.'

Kat stopped, but did not turn around. Tess moved to stand behind her, putting her hand on her shoulder.

'Look at this,' she said. 'Do you know what this means?'

She held out the pendant she always wore at her throat, the glacier crowfoot pendant that had been passed from innkeeper to innkeeper for nobody knew how long.

Kat stared at it. Of course she knew what it meant. It was her mark too.

'Long, tough roots,' she said hoarsely. 'Almost impossible to uproot.'

'We hang on,' said Tess. 'That's what it means. We draw our strength and our lives from the land here, from the place where we live. And we do not move.' Gently, she stroked Kat's hair. 'But you move all the time. Never still. It's not just this thing with Cornelius. Sometimes I think you only fight him because you need to fight *somebody*.'

Shrike, thought Kat. That's what she means. Pecking at everything and everybody. Never content. Never at peace with anybody. Just like Mattie said.

'I don't want to leave,' she said. Her tongue felt thick and wooden, making it hard to talk. 'I want to stay. Please. I . . . I'll be good. I promise.'

Tess drew her into a hug.

'Oh, child,' she murmured into Kat's thick and crinkly red hair. 'It wouldn't work. You know it wouldn't.'

THE DYER'S YARD

On the day Kat was to leave, the morning dawned bright and sunny. She woke early. Sunlight fell through the gable window, and the attic was full of the familiar scent of sleeping children. Kat sat, hugging her knees and looking at Mattie, still asleep. Her sister had such fine, fair skin. She had begun to freckle, like she did every spring. Sun-freckles, Tess called them. In the winter they faded and disappeared.

Tentatively, Kat put out her hand to touch her sister's hair. Fair, like her skin, and smooth as water. Strong. It never frayed and frizzed and split, the way Kat's did. Kat was pretty certain that they had different fathers, she and Mattie. It saddened her to think of it, because it seemed a less solid bond, somehow. Half-sisters.

Tim's feet were poking through the curtains of the bed he shared with Nicolas. The soles were still soft and pink, but later in the summer they would grow yellow-brown and callused because he was always running about barefoot, even in the stables, although he wasn't supposed to. Who would tell him not to, now that she would not be here?

She had never been away from home before. She had never been outside the Vale. She had never slept in any place except this attic, unless one counted a few hot nights spent on the porch, and a guest room sometimes when she had been sick or hurt, like the time her arm was broken. Today she would join Anna Weaver's journeyman and a small caravan of traders, and they would travel for several days, through Three Valleys and further still, to Idabrook where the Dyer's Yard lay.

She had told the little ones that she was leaving. Tessa and Rose had nodded and eagerly repeated that Kat had to ride Blackie all the way to the Dyer's Yard together with Aren Journeyman and all the horses and mules and carts of the caravan, and that she would sleep in Aren's wagon six times before she arrived at Bria's house. But that she would be gone tomorrow, and would not be coming back – she was not at all sure they understood that. Would they be very sad? Or angry at her for leaving them? Would they miss her? Cor, a year older than the twins, understood a bit more, she thought. He had gone quiet and serious and had clung to her more than usual.

'Gone like Dan?' he had asked. He didn't remember Eskill.

'Yes,' she had said. 'Gone like Dan.'

Girls and women didn't travel. All the way to Bria's house she would be living among men and boys. And once she got there, there would be no visits home every now and then. If she did return, it would not be until her apprenticeship was over, three years from now. The little ones wouldn't remember her. Not even Cor.

It wasn't fair. It just wasn't fair.

Bitterness seethed in her. Why was she being sent away, and not Cornelius? *He* was the one who had hit *her*.

She washed, and began to put on her travel clothes. Tess had altered some of Dan's cast-offs to fit her – a decent pair of leather breeches, some linen shirts, a sheepskin coat for cold weather, and a woollen jacket for milder days. There was a cap, too, to hide her hair.

'Best you don't look too much like a girl,' Tess had said.

She put on breeches, shirt and jacket. Around her waist went a wide leather belt, a gift from Cornelius. It was a relic from his mercenary days that he had shortened to fit her, and it was full of loops and straps for tools, and small secret pockets. She pinned her hair, and put on the cap. From a distance, at least, she could pass for a boy.

She padded down the stairs on stockinged feet, and into the kitchen. Tad was making pancakes.

'At least I can give you a decent meal before you leave,' he said, not quite looking at her. In the frying pan the yellow batter was hissing and spitting and turning pale brown at the edges. He took a good grip on the pan handle and flipped the pancake in the air, the way he sometimes did to amuse Teresa's children, even though it was messier than turning it over with the spatula.

Kat had a lump in her throat and didn't feel hungry at

all, but she didn't have the heart to tell him that. And once the first pancake landed on the plate in front of her, steaming hot and smelling of butter and syrup, she found she could eat it after all.

'When they cool, I'll roll a couple with some of last night's stew, so you'll have a good lunch as well.'

She nodded. She didn't know what to say.

Tess was coming down the stairs. Kat recognized her steps easily – it sounded a bit like poking a willow stick into a cartwheel: clack-clack-clack – rapid and sharp, and full of sap.

'Good morning,' Tess said, entering the kitchen.

'Morning,' murmured Tad. Kat didn't say anything.

'Kat, I've written a letter for you to give to Bria when you arrive. Stow it in your belt so you don't lose it.'

She held out the letter. The paper was stiff and yellow, folded and sealed with red wax. Tess had put her mark on the wax, the glacier crowfoot. She always used the pendant. When you pressed it into the soft wax, it left a fine, clear impression, so that Bria would be able to tell who the letter was from, and that no one had opened it on the way. Kat wondered whether the pendant would now go to Mattie. She didn't think anyone would allow a travelled woman to become innkeeper at Crowfoot Inn.

Kat took the letter and slipped it into one of the secret pockets on the inside of the belt, still not saying anything.

Tess didn't move.

'Kat,' she said, in an unaccustomed gentle voice. 'Is there anything you'd like? Anything you'd like to take with you?'

Instantly Kat thought of the little rosewood box. It had a fine carved lid with birds and roses on it, and inside it were clever compartments for needles and spools of thread and buttons and so on. If she asked for it, she was sure Tess would give it to her. But she had made up her mind. She looked straight at Tess and was silent, silent with a will. If you did it right, the Silence worked even if it was only one person doing it.

Tess felt it. She went suddenly very still, and the fine lines around her grey eyes became much clearer. She waited for a while. Then she shook her head.

'Have it your way, then. Stubborn child.'

But her steps were less sappy as she walked away, and Kat knew she had managed to hurt her.

'Aren't you speaking to me either?' asked Tad quietly.

'Yes! Of course, Tad, it's not *you* . . .' Her voice became unsteady, and she had to stop.

Tad wiped his hands on his apron.

'Kitten,' he said, stroking her hair. 'It's no good with you and Cornelius, you know it isn't.'

'Then why isn't she sending *him* away?'

'I told you . . . Teresa needs Cornelius. The inn needs him.'

'And she doesn't need *me*?'

'Oh, yes,' said Tad, almost in a whisper. 'She needs you. Very much. We all do. But we'll just have to do without you for a while.'

'For years.' Kat sniffed, blinking furiously. She got to her feet. 'Bye, Tad. I'll go and see to Blackie.'

He reached, and brought her into a proper hug. Then he let her go.

'You're a lot like your mother,' he said. 'That's part of why she's doing this.'

She looked at him uncertainly. She didn't think she was much like Tess at all, and right now she wasn't sure she wanted to be either. But she knew he meant it as a compliment. After all, he was in love with her mother.

'Thanks for the pancakes,' she muttered, and left.

Aren was pulling his tall wagon out of its winter shed with the aid of Erold Smith. They had to put their backs into it – this was no light little market cart. The wagon was Aren's home for more than half the year, as he went travelling from place to place, selling Anna Weaver's goods and buying needles and specially dyed yarns for her, and metal buttons and other stuff that was hard to come by in Three Valleys.

It was almost like a very small house on wheels, with a real bed, and tables and lockers and a small stove you could cook on. Kat suddenly thought that this was the closest a man could come to owning a house. Aren loved it like a child. For weeks he had been oiling and polishing and sanding away, changing a board here and there, and freshening the paint. The wagon literally shone in the sunlight. The two faces of Our Lady were painted carefully above the door – one open-eyed, the other closed. Like most other wayfarers, Aren put his trust more in Our Lady than in the Locus Spirits.

'You can stow your things in the bench by the window,' said Aren.

She hadn't brought much. Clothes for summer and winter, a rolled-up sleeping mat and a blanket, a bit of food for the trip, and a bowl, plate, knife, spoon and cup. A pair of shoes. And the book Tad had given her.

'Promise that you'll read a bit every day,' he had said. 'A girl like you needs to know her letters.'

The book had its own wooden box. It had a leather cover, and the pages were a lot thinner than Kat was used to. They crackled crisply when you turned them. Worn gold letters spelled out the title: 'The Story of Sari Moon-Daughter and the Pedlar from Joss'. And on the first page was a picture of Sari Moon-Daughter and her ladies-in-waiting, looking at a fine length of cloth the Pedlar was showing them. Kat looked at it a bit before stowing away the book. She hoped she would be able to read it. Tad must have paid a lot of money for it – books were terribly expensive, she knew.

The square was getting crowded with horses and pack-mules and wagons. Cornelius brought out Blackie. Kat had brushed him herself, and oiled his hooves. She wanted him to look well turned-out and cared for, so that he could hold his head high in the herd of more experienced caravan horses.

'Take good care of him,' muttered Cornelius. 'And you keep your wits about you, girl, out there among the strangers. Stay out of trouble. And mind you stick by your word.'

Kat didn't look at him, but she nodded briefly. She had sworn to obey him just once, and she had to stick to that promise, even now. Besides, who would be interested in Saratown and Ermine where she was going? She would keep her promise, and her silence.

Tess came out. Kat stood by Blackie's head and watched her, seeing how she turned men's heads. She's so beautiful, thought Kat. It was like she gave off a special kind of warmth, so that you half expected the air around her to shimmer and blur, like it did over hot rocks on a scorching summer's day. She had braided her black hair and pinned it on top of her head, to keep it from getting in her way as she worked. It looked like a crown.

She took Kat's face between her hands. They were long and narrow and strong, and slightly damp and wrinkled now from washing the breakfast dishes. Kat could smell the soap.

'Be well, child. And behave.' Tess kissed her on the forehead with warm lips. Kat's own lips trembled, but still she said nothing. Tess gauged her with her eyes.

'Stubborn child,' she said. 'Watch out. Those who won't bend may end up breaking.' And those were the last words she said to her daughter before the caravan left.

Mattie wept. She tried not to, but she was no good at hardening her heart and steeling herself, the way Kat did. This made Cor cry, too, and Kat hurriedly hugged and kissed the whole brood. But the yellow beast put a sour, yellow thought in her head: they got to stay, and she didn't. She envied them.

'Time to leave, Kat,' said Aren quietly, already mounted on the box, reins in hand. 'Can't keep the wayfarers waiting.'

And so Kat had to swing on to Blackie's back, and ride away.

At first, Kat was a little frightened of the wayfarers. Aren had given her very careful orders: Don't get in the way, don't touch anything that isn't yours, and don't go into anyone's wagon, however warmly invited, unless I'm with you.

'They're not used to girls,' he said. 'Or at least, not girls like you. But most of them are good people when you get to know them.'

Kat wasn't sure she wanted to get to know them. A couple of them reminded her rather forcefully of Karel. But on the fourth day of her journey, they were invited very politely and formally to dinner by the driver of the wagon in front of theirs, a small square man with black hair and beard. Aren thanked him with equal politeness, and once they were halted for the night, he washed carefully, put on his good shirt, and told Kat to do the same.

'You bring your own plate and knife,' he said. 'And a cup too.' He opened a trapdoor and poked his head into the storage loft. When he re-emerged, he handed down a casket of Tess's best ale to her. 'When you are formally invited to dinner, the way Gelman Carter just invited us, you dress up nice and you bring a gift. If somebody asks you to share a meal, it's different. You come as you are and bring whatever you're having to the table, and everybody takes potluck.' He smiled at her. 'Wayfarer's Rules of Etiquette, Chapter One. You'll be an old hand by the time I get through with you.'

Gelman shared his wagon with two of his sons, one a young man, the other about Kat's age, or perhaps a bit younger. They eyed each other curiously across the fire, while Gelman carved the roast. It was a wild turkey, shot by Gelman's eldest. Kat couldn't help wondering if it was really as wild as Gelman claimed – there had been turkeys at the last village they passed through. She thought she had better not mention that.

Aren's gift was well received.

'Good ale,' said Gelman appreciatively after his first taste. Then he poured generous cupfuls for all of them. 'Your health, Aren. And your girlfriend's. Be welcome among the travellers, darling.'

'Kat is only travelling a short way with us,' said Aren carefully. 'She is to be apprenticed to Bria Dyer at Idabrook.'

Gelman looked appraisingly at Aren, as if he wasn't quite sure that Aren was telling the truth. Aren sat calmly, waiting for Gelman to look his fill.

Gelman nodded. 'So that's the way of it,' he said. 'Be welcome anyway, Katriona, even for a little while.'

They ate, and Gelman and Aren talked, and, by and by, Gelman's eldest, too. Neither Kat nor Gelman's youngest boy said much. But when they had finished their meal, Gelman went to his wagon to get out a small harp.

'Boy has a pretty voice,' he said. 'Sing to us, Allan.'

And so the boy sang, and Gelman played, quiet songs about the road that goes on forever, and the places men always have to leave.

'But I know Our Lady is waiting
In the Heartland, bright with sun
When the road has reached its turning
And my travelling is done
Call me home, Milady, call me home
Let me lie upon your breast
Let me dwell in your own country
And know my Place of Rest.'

Kat sat listening with tears in her eyes, both because she too had just had to leave a place, and because she was thinking of Aren and his house on wheels, and Cornelius, who had shouted at Tess about men and the land: 'Why are we to be chased from place to place our whole life long, never to say, "This is *my* place, here I stay"?'

When they had returned to Aren's wagon that night, she finally asked the question that had been on her mind since Gelman's toast.

'What did Gelman mean?' she said. 'Did he think I was your . . .' she nearly said 'harlot', because that was Tess's word for women like that, '. . . your girlfriend?'

Aren shrugged. 'What else was he to think? I told you, Kat – not many women follow the wagons. They're not used to girls, here.'

Kat turned her head to hide her blush. But I'm only twelve, she wanted to say. And Aren is . . . she didn't know how old Aren was. Old, that was all. How could they think that – that . . . ?

But apparently Gelman had.

Aren washed their plates and cups and put them away. There was never any untidiness in Aren's wagon. Everything was put away neatly in its place, and nothing went dirty or unmended for very long. He took good care of his gear.

'Go to bed,' he said. 'Don't worry about it. In a few days, we will be at Bria's, and you can forget all about me and Gelman and the other wayfarers.'

Kat didn't answer. In her memory, she could still hear Allan's voice, high and clear like a girl's, and tears came to her eyes all over again. *Call me home, Milady, call me home . . .* No, she did not think she would forget the wayfarers.

The Dyer's Yard was a great deal bigger than Kat had imagined – a village in itself, or perhaps even two villages: Old Quarters and New Quarters. In Old Quarters Bria had her house, and the original old dyer's shop, and lodgings for Bria's large family and personal staff. There were herb gardens, rose bushes and an orchard, an old stable and a small watermill. New Quarters was a much larger, barer place. All the buildings were bigger: Master's Hall and Prentice Hall, baths and kitchens, warehouses and workshops and caravan stables, and the tallest building of them all, the new Dyer's Hall.

The caravan halted in the empty yard in front of the caravan stables, and Kat helped Aren unhitch and care for his team. As she was sponging down the two sturdy ponies, a girl of fifteen or so came over and stood looking at her. Kat nodded politely, but the girl just kept standing there, staring, as if she had never seen a girl look after a horse before.

'Are you the new prentice?' she finally asked. 'You look like a boy.'

She herself certainly didn't – curved and attractive, dressed in a fine red woollen dress, and with long straight shiny brown hair. In comparison, Kat felt skinny-legged and grubby and out of place.

'She's a girl all right,' said Aren firmly, putting his hand on Kat's shoulder. 'Katriona Teresa-Daughter of South Vale. She needs to see Bria.'

'Not yet,' said the stranger. 'It's my duty to show all the new prentices around. The talk with Bria comes later.'

All the new prentices . . . How many were there? The girl made it sound as if greeting newcomers was a full-time job.

'I have a letter for Bria from my mother,' said Kat. 'I was to give it to her as soon as I got here.'

'I'm Bria's secretary,' said the girl. 'You can give it to me.'

Kat shook her head stubbornly. 'It's for Bria,' she said. 'It's sealed.' She showed the girl the red wax seal with Teresa's mark on it.

The girl narrowed her lips, and a pointed little 'Hm!' came from her throat. Without a word she turned and headed back through the orchard, towards one of the older houses.

'Best go with her, Kat,' said Aren. 'That's Bria's house she's headed for.'

'You're not leaving yet, are you, Aren?'

Kat could hear how small and scared her own voice sounded, almost like Nicolas's that day on the mountain.

Aren sighed. 'Better say goodbye now. I don't know how long I'll be here. Caravan's not staying overnight, Bria charges far too much for wagon space. When the rest head out of here, I got to follow.'

She hugged him, not caring that he smelled of sweat and dirt and horses. She was perilously close to tears.

'Kat, girl,' murmured Aren. 'Don't let them see you cry. You've got to be as hard as you can. I don't think they are particularly nice to newcomers around here.'

She sniffed a bit. Then she steeled herself as best she could.

'Bye, Aren. Bye, Blackie.' She patted the horse's round, black rump. Then she turned and followed the girl through the orchard to Bria's house.

Bria's house was painted a stately white and looked very trim and clean. There were three storeys, a balcony and a porch with a view of the garden. Kat crossed the porch and entered the house.

Bria had to be very rich. All along one wall in the parlour were cabinets with glass doors. And behind the doors were books. Whole *shelves* full of books. The other walls were covered in silky, pale blue tapestry, and on the floor were several large carpets that made Kat catch her breath in wonder. Unthinkingly, she crouched to run her hand through the rich, soft pile. The carpets had pictures on them, of strange trees and birds with long tails, and flowers unlike any she had ever seen in real life. There were skies, and water, and slim boats floating under willow trees. If I had such a rug, thought Kat, I'd spend the whole day looking at it!

'What are you doing here? Get out!'

Startled, Kat leaped to her feet. Had she done something wrong? A girl her own age was glaring at her, a black-haired girl dressed almost the same way the brown-haired one had been, in a fine red dress with a frilled white apron over it.

'My name is Kat. I have a letter for Bria.'

'You're not supposed to be in here! Go around to the back door.' Then the girl hesitated. 'Wait . . . Are you . . . you *are* a girl, aren't you?'

'Of course I am!' Kat was beginning to be annoyed. She didn't look *that* boyish, surely, now that she had taken off the cap.

'The new prentice?'

Kat nodded. 'Katriona Teresa-Daughter,' she said. Aren had taken pains to give her full name; perhaps it was wise to copy him.

The girl looked at her, as if trying to estimate something.

'New Quarters or Old Quarters?' she asked.

'How would I know? I haven't talked to anyone yet.'

'Didn't Asta show you around?'

'I have a letter. My mother said I was to give it to Bria right away.'

The girl seemed to make up her mind.

'All right,' she said. 'Come on, then. But in the future, you've got to use the back door. You're only a prentice, after all.'

'So? And what are you, then?' said Kat, somewhat belligerently.

'Bria's fosterling,' said the girl, in a tone that clearly meant 'So there!' Kat couldn't think of a suitable answer and contented herself with following the girl out of the parlour with the wonderful carpets, down a long hall, to a door at the end. The girl knocked.

'Who is it?' came a voice from inside.

'Celia with the new prentice. She has a letter.'

There was a rather long pause before permission arrived:

'Come in, then.'

Celia opened the door and let Kat pass her. For a moment, Kat was reminded of Saratown and the dark room where Ermine waited. But this room wasn't really dark, just a bit gloomy because heavy velvet drapes cut out most of the afternoon sunlight. By the tall window stood a shiny dark desk, and behind it a woman was seated, pen in hand, writing quickly and fluidly.

Kat watched in fascination. She had never seen anybody write that fast. It seemed almost lacking in respect to treat the art of writing so casually. Even Tad, who was the best penman Kat had ever known, penned his letters deliberately, with a certain solemnity.

The woman put down her pen, reached for a small silver tin with holes in the lid, and shook fine sand on to the lines she had just written. Only then did she look at Kat.

'Katriona,' she said. 'Are you named after your grandmother?'

Kat nodded. She had been Little-Kat to most people back when Gran had still been alive.

'Come over here and let me see you.'

Kat did as she was told, and took the chance to get a closer look at Bria. One could tell by all the wrinkles that she was old – almost as old as Gran had been when she died. But there was nothing slow or confused about her, not like Asa's old mother who lived on the farm across from the inn. Her hair was entirely white, and her eyes seemed pale, as if they too had lost their colour with age. They were grey, really, she supposed, but not the glittering storm-cloud grey of Tess's eyes.

'You have a letter for me?'

Kat nodded again. She had the feeling her voice would come out croaky and hoarse if she tried to talk. She brought the letter out of its secret pocket in the belt, and passed it to Bria. Bria looked at the seal for a moment.

'Ah yes, the glacier crowfoot.'

Then she broke it and started reading. Her eyes skipped down the paper with dizzying speed. Kat thought of the time it had taken Tess to write it, and again felt that Bria's rapid skim was somehow disrespectful. For no better reason than that, Kat began to grow angry at Bria, as if Bria had insulted Kat and her family.

'Do you know what it says?'

Kat shook her head. This one she had not been allowed to read before it was sealed.

'Your mother is asking me to adopt you. Did she tell you of this?'

Kat nodded.

'I can't do that,' Bria said. 'I have my own daughters, and daughters' daughters, to inherit my place as maestra here. I cannot bring you, a stranger, into my house and give you the rights of my own kin. But I am prepared to make you my foster-daughter.'

Suddenly Kat found there was nothing wrong with her voice after all.

'I don't want to be adopted, or fostered. Tess is my mother, and that's the way it will stay!'

Bria watched her carefully.

'Katriona, I'm not sure you understand this properly. By sending you away, your mother has disinherited you. By Law, someone who has left her place cannot be recognized as a true heir. You have become a stranger to the Locus Spirit. Didn't they teach you that?'

Kat nodded reluctantly. Yes, she had been given her proper lessons with the Locus priestesses of Three Valleys. Every place had its own spirit, its own small deity, and as land could not be owned in the way one might own a horse or a kettle or a cloak, land rights were won by pledging one's troth to the Locus Spirit. That was why the priestesses disapproved of the Southern custom of marriage. A woman, a maestra like Tess, ought not to marry a man, as she was already 'married' to the Locus Spirit. But in Border provinces like Three Valleys, customs were often bent to serve practicality. Kat would not inherit her mother's place as keeper of the Crowfoot Inn – but this was mostly because Tess thought that Mattie would make a better innkeeper.

'There's a restlessness in you, Kat, and I don't know how to cure it,' Tess had told her only a scant two weeks ago. 'You fight all restraints. I think you have to pit yourself against a wider world, like boys do, even if it is against the Law. But for now, go and offer the Locus Spirit your proper respects, so that we'll have less trouble with the priestesses when you return.'

And so Kat had walked to the Lower Vale, where the Motherhouse was. In the Hall of the Spirits, row upon row of clay figurines had looked at her, each in his little cubby-hole, from floor to ceiling and all around her. Kat went to the one painted with the crowfoot mark. A small manikin, white-skinned, black-haired, with eyes painted in red and green. Around his neck hung a locket almost twin to the pendant around Tess's neck. Inside the locket was a tiny scroll of parchment with Teresa's name and mark on it. This was the deed that made her Innkeeper and maestra.

Kat sang a song in honour of the Spirit, holding a small wooden tag in her hand. The tag had been carved in the shape of a crowfoot flower, and Tad had helped her pen her name on it.

'Forgive this parting,' chanted Kat, as she had been told

to do. 'It is neither scorn nor lack of love that drives me from you, but the call of other duties. Watch, as is your wont, over this place and its people, and recall me to your memory, though I am far from you. My body may be distant, but my soul still rests with you.'

As she did so, she thought silently: It's just a stupid clay figure. I don't believe in any of this. And then she grew frightened, for what if those silent thoughts had been heard, and the Spirit would never permit her return?

Bria broke into her thoughts.

'As my fosterling, at least you'll have a place in the world. Women who wander damage their souls. This is not an offer you should scorn so lightly. Your mother would tell you to accept it.'

Kat didn't understand how her mother could talk of adoption and fostering, and yet still pretend that Kat was one day coming back.

'Tess is my mother. I want no one else,' she repeated.

Bria regarded her coolly. 'As you wish. You will be apprenticed, then, like any other travelled girl. But if you have second thoughts, tell me. I owe your mother that much.'

She pulled on a rope half hidden by the drapes, and a bell sounded somewhere in the distance. Minutes later, the brown-haired girl appeared in the doorway.

'You may show Katriona around now, Asta.'

'Yes, maestra. Where is she to stay?' asked Asta quickly. 'Old Quarters or New?'

'New Quarters,' said Bria. 'Prentice Hall. For now.'

Asta made no comment until the door to Bria's room had closed behind them. Then she gave Kat a look full of contempt and triumph.

'Letter me this, and letter me that. Didn't help much, did it – drifter brat!'

'I'm no drifter's brat,' said Kat angrily. 'My mother is as good as yours!'

'Not around here, she isn't,' said Asta. 'Cos *my* mother is Bria!'

DRIFTER BRATS

Kat didn't see Aren again, or Blackie. Asta dragged her around from building to building, reeling off a million rules she was apparently supposed to remember. She was forced to take a bath – and a bath would have been nice after her journey, if only Asta hadn't been there, commenting on how dirty she was, and if the water hadn't been bitterly cold so that she was shaking all over by the time she was finished. The prentice baths were not much more than a shed with a pump in the middle and a huge kettle that could be fired up but apparently wasn't, or at least not just to heat water for one measly newcomer. And on top of that, Asta wanted to throw away her clothes!

'Filthy drifter rags,' she called them, but this was more than Kat would stand for.

'They may be filthy,' she said, because they were quite frankly dirty and smelled rather strongly of horse, 'but they're mine! And I'll wash them myself.'

'You won't be allowed to wear them,' Asta said. 'They're boy's clothes! Imagine what people would think . . .'

'I don't care,' said Kat, cheeks aflame. So what if they were boy's clothes? Who could work in a stable all day, wearing a skirt?

'Around here you'll have to dress according to the rules, or there'll be trouble,' Asta snapped. 'Black skirt and blouse, black stockings, black apron for workdays, white apron for holidays. You can use your own underwear.' Asta was pulling things off the drapery shelves as she spoke. 'Here you go. Put them on at once.'

And so she had to put on the skirt and blouse she was given. The black wool had a sour, acid smell, not sweat, but something else. Later she found out that this was the lye-and-sulphite smell of the dye vats. It got into one's clothes during the working day and couldn't be got rid of no matter how often they were washed.

'So why are *you* wearing a red dress?' Kat said acidly. 'Isn't that against the rules?'

'That's because *I'm* a fosterling,' said Asta. 'Black is for prentices.'

'Just how many girls is Bria fostering?'

'Just fourteen. So don't get up your hopes.'

'Fourteen! How on earth can she care properly for that many? And she has daughters of her own too!'

'None of your business,' said Asta curtly. 'You just do as you're told, and stop asking so many questions. We might have to teach you a lesson, else!' There was no mistaking the menace in her voice.

Kat shook her head slowly. What kind of a place *was* this?

Later, when dusk had begun to settle on the Dyer's Yard, Kat sat in a desolate slump on the cot she had been given in the prentice girl dormitory. She was so tired that she didn't even have the energy to take off her clothes and curl up under the black blankets. Almost everything the 'black-skirts' touched was black. That way, it showed less when stains and splashes from the dye vats left their mark.

There was such a whirl of noise and people here. More than a hundred and fifty, Asta had said. Bria and her proper family. Her many fosterlings. The Masters, the journeymen. The kitchen staff. The gardeners. The smith and his boys. And all the prentices. Kat had eaten her supper in the dining hall downstairs with nearly eighty other prentices, without taking in a word that was said to her, or tasting a single bite of the food she put in her mouth. When the other prentices had gone off noisily to their baths or their kitchen chores, she had come up here just to be alone for a moment. She had sat down. And now she didn't want to get up again. Finally she just kicked off her shoes and lay down on top of the blankets, still wearing all her scratchy new clothes.

She woke because something was moving on her cheek. She jerked upright, brushing at her face. Was it an insect? Bedbugs, or even a cockroach? She shuddered. The dorm was utterly dark and still. She listened, but could hear no sounds except somebody's quiet breathing. Finally she lay down again. Now it felt as if the darkness was full of scrabbling insect feet and waving antennae. Any moment another bug could drop on her . . .

There it was again! She whipped up a hand and for a moment touched something thin and furry. With a half-choked shriek she flung herself out of the cot. She stood in her stockinged feet, shaking from the cold and the shock of being torn from her sleep. No way would she share her bed with mysterious furry bugs. But how could she avoid it? She didn't even have a candle she could light, so that she would be able to see what she was dealing with.

Suddenly she realized the quiet breathing had changed to suppressed giggles. And then she understood. Oh, yes. That one. Dan and Eskill had played the trick on her, and she and Mattie in their turn had done it to Tim and Nicolas . . . It was so simple. All you needed was patience and a bit of fluffy yarn.

She moved quickly to the head of her cot where she knew the person dangling the yarn had to be. In the darkness, she misjudged slightly and banged her hip against the cot, but she managed to get hold of a fistful of shirt.

'Let me show you what I do to spiders,' she said, jerking the other girl on to the floor and pinning her there. 'I crush them flat!'

The girl wriggled and kicked and cried out, and suddenly the darkness was full of fists and arms and legs. Kat and the girl she was holding were buried under a crush of bodies, breathless and unable to move.

'Get a light,' said someone. 'Can't tell one from the other this way!'

There was the click and rasp of a tinderbox, and a candle was lit, making a fluttering yellow circle of light in the darkness. The girl pile dissolved into seven separate girls, slightly the worse for wear.

'So, New Girl likes to catch spiders,' said the biggest one, a big bony girl with a rough voice. Kat could tell that she was the one who had ordered the candle lit. 'What's your name, New Girl?'

'Kat.'

Of course, that brought on a flurry of giggles. 'Cat, Cat, Kitty-Cat . . .'

Kat felt her temper flare. 'What's so funny about that? I'd rather be a cat than a stupid spider!'

'Whoa, watch it, it's got claws!'

'Pet her and be nice, and she'll bring you mice . . . Kitty, kitty . . .'

Five or six hands began to stroke her hair with rough exaggeration. Furious, she struck at them.

'Stop that. Leave me alone!'

'Has it got whiskers?'

'Does it bite?'

'Where's the tail?' Hands flipped up the black skirt she was still wearing. She pushed them away.

'Stop it!'

'Meeeow . . .'

'Kitty, kitty, kitty . . .'

'Oooh, give Kitty a bit of milk . . .'

They wouldn't stop. They kept petting her roughly, tugging at her clothes, frizzing up her hair. Finally, she began to yell and scream, striking at them as best she could, but that only made them rougher and more heavy-handed. It wasn't a beating, though there was some hair-pulling and some scratches that were less than playful. It was more a sort of pawing over. And they didn't tire of their cat games until she lay curled into a ball on the floor and had long since stopped reacting.

'Kitty is tired . . . Let it sleep . . .'

Kat stayed on the floor until the dorm grew dark and silent once more. Then she got up, fumbled for her blankets in the darkness, and lay down on her cot. Her heart was hammering with fury and humiliation, and sleep was completely impossible now.

'Kat . . .'

It was the softest of whispers, from the cot next to hers. She didn't answer.

'Kat, don't mind them. They're always like that with the new girls. It'll stop.'

Kat propped herself on one elbow and peered into the darkness.

'Who are you?' she asked.

'Tia.'

There was a rustle as the other girl sat up. Kat could just make out a pale gleam of hair and eyes, and a quick flash of teeth. It was probably a smile, but somehow it made Kat think of something tough and skinny, a stray dog, perhaps, used to fighting for its share of the food.

'Are you a prentice too?' asked Kat warily. 'Or a foster-ling?'

Tia gave a short laugh. 'Me? A fosterling? No way. Just another low-down common drifter brat, like yourself.'

'I'm no drifter's brat,' said Kat stubbornly.

'Oh, come on,' said Tia. 'We all are.'

'Well, I'm not!' Kat said, temper flaring up again. '*My* mother's name is Teresa, and she is the innkeeper at Crowfoot Inn.'

'Oh, really? What are you doing here then?' Tia's voice was cold now, and she turned her back on Kat and lay down again, without waiting for an answer.

Kat wished she could have given her one. But what *was* she doing here? Why wasn't she at home in the attic, lying curled up with Mattie at her back, sweet Mattie who loved her and never teased her, or at least not for long. Kat felt tears coming on, and fought the urge to sniff. *Don't let them see you cry*, Aren had said. It seemed to be good advice.

In the Dyer's Hall, there were twelve great copper vats – one for each of the twelve basic colours the Yard produced: yellow, ochre, leaf green, dark green, cobalt, rose, indigo, purple, cinnabar red, lilac, aquamarine and black. The vats were so large that the prentices had to stand on scaffolding in order to stir the contents with long stakes and paddles. Each vat had two pumps, one that pumped water straight into the vat, and one which emptied it, sending the spent dye through long pipes into the river below the Dyer's

Yard. The rocks around the mouth of the pipes often had funny colours, and no plants grew there.

On her first day, Kat was put to work at the pumps. It took three prentices to work one pump, and it was grindingly heavy work. Long before nightfall, Kat had huge blisters on both palms and a backache that took her breath away. The second day was worse than the first. By the third day, she felt like screaming every time she had to raise her arms above shoulder height.

One of the Dyemasters finally noticed her winces and took both her and Tia off the pumps.

'You and you,' he said, not unkindly, 'go help the Storemaster for a while.'

The storeroom was huge and cavernous, and dust was thick in the air, but to Kat, anything that got her away from the pumps was pure bliss. She didn't even mind the fetching and the carrying and the pain it cost her back and shoulders and her blistered palms, because at least it was a *different* pain.

'Hey, you there – New Girl,' yelled the Storemaster. 'Go count how many sacks of red yarn we still need to load.'

Kat cast a quick look at the neat rows of sacks.

'Twenty-six,' she said.

The Storemaster furrowed his brow in irritation. 'Go count them properly, girl.'

'I did!' Kat stood her ground. 'Five rows of sacks with five sacks in each, that's twenty-five, and then one extra, that's twenty-six!'

'Who taught you arithmetic?' The Storemaster was visibly astonished.

Tad, thought Kat, but kept herself from saying it out loud. Here, of course, no one would know who Tad was.

'My mother's cook,' she finally said, although that was a pretty poor way of describing Tad. He was so much else. He was *Tad*. Her Tad.

'Your mother's cook . . . Sweet Lady, lass, who put you in with the drifter brats?'

Out of the corner of her eye Kat saw Tia pause, clutching a large unwieldy sack of yarn. She was obviously listening to the conversation, and she was scowling. Kat opened her mouth. Then closed it again. She shrugged.

'I don't know.'

Tia turned and walked away with her sack.

'Can you read, too?' asked the Storemaster.

'A little.' She was on the twenty-first page of Tad's book.

'And write?'

'Some. I'm better at numbers.'

'Listen, young lady. Tomorrow morning you go to my office instead of the Dyer's Hall. If you're good for something better than pumping dye and water, we had better find out.'

Kat saw Tia's scowl deepen, but didn't understand why.

'Eleven times twenty-six – no, in your head.'

Old Bookmaster Rikert asked the questions. Storemaster Alban and Dyemaster Tomas listened and watched.

Ten times twenty-six was two hundred and sixty, and then add twenty-six . . .

'Two hundred and eighty-six,' said Kat.

'Correct. And now – and you may use the slate . . . If, to dye twelve lengths of cloth we need eight cup-measures of purple, two ten-measures of sulphite and one and a half ten-measures of lye – how much, then, will we need for seven lengths of cloth?'

Kat wrote down numbers on her slate and did some hard thinking. For one length of cloth one would need . . . no, that wouldn't work. Wait, though. One cup-measure equalled six spoon-measures. So, for one length of cloth, four spoons of purple, ten spoons of sulphite, and . . . seven and a half spoons of lye. And for seven lengths . . .

'Twenty-eight spoon-measures of purple, seventy spoon-measures of sulphite, and fifty-two and a half spoon-measures of lye.'

'So – you don't know how to calculate decimals?'

Deci . . . deci-what? 'Mostly money,' Kat said uncertainly.

'I see,' said Rikert. 'So you calculate mostly in money . . . Well, you're hardly the only one in the Dyer's Yard to do so. At least you know how to multiply and divide. Now, show me how your spoon-measures may be written in a more practical form.'

In her mind's eye, Kat saw Dyemaster Tomas carefully counting spoon-measures: sixty-one, sixty-two, sixty-three . . . it would take all morning.

'Four cup-measures and four spoons, eleven cup – no,

one ten-measure, one cup-measure and four spoons, and then . . . eight cup-measures and four and a half spoon-measures.'

'Good. Will that be sufficient, Storemaster?'

Master Alban nodded.

'Excellent. Then let us move on to a test of the young lady's reading skills.'

The first one was easy. It was just a list from the stores. Kat hastened through bolts of linen, bales of cotton, wools and silks and skeins of yarn . . .

'Thank you, that will suffice. And this one?'

From the dye-shop. Somewhat harder. Cinnabar, Colmontian indigo . . . long, difficult words she barely knew and had never seen in writing before. She stumbled and stuttered, but Rikert didn't interrupt. He let her go on to the end of the list. When she was done, he silently gave her a new text.

'*In the country called Breda, in the city then called Silvers, there once lived a queen whose daughter was so beautiful that people called her . . .*'

Kat looked up in confusion. A few words into the text she recognized the story of Sari Moon-Daughter and the Pedlar from Joss. For a moment, she wondered if Master Rikert had looked through her things and found her book. Then she felt stupid, because of course her book was not the only Sari Moon-Daughter in the world. There had to be hundreds, or even thousands of copies of that story, and it seemed Master Rikert possessed one. She read on.

'. . . And at her birth it was said:
Widely to travel
Keenly to long
Harshly to suffer
Fiercely to fight
Savage in anger
Stronger in love
Little peace and many battles
Losing much and winning more
Such is the fate of the child.'

She broke off again. On this page in her book, Tad had left a note: 'Perhaps your fate too, Kitten. But remember, Sari Moon-Daughter thought herself happy in the end.' She had to close her eyes for a moment to hold back the tears. Oh, Tad . . .

'Katriona. We are waiting. It cannot be that hard for you.'

Rikert was watching her. She blinked a bit. Make yourself hard, Aren had said.

'No . . .' She managed to control her shaky breath. *'This prediction caused much unease among the people, and many voices said: "Must we be ruled by one with so fierce a destiny?" But the old queen upheld her choice and would take no other heir . . .'*

'So?' Tia slumped down on the bench next to her at dinner. 'Did they move you in with the other boot-lickers?'

'What do you mean?'

'You know. Going to rub shoulders with the snoots?'

'I have to work in the Bookmaster's office part of the time.'

Tia's scowl was back in place. And now the reason for it became apparent.

'Right,' she said, dipping her hunk of bread into her stew bowl. 'And I suppose you think that makes you better than the rest of us.'

Kat stopped chewing.

'No,' she said carefully. 'I don't think that.'

Tia threw her a furious look.

'Oh, come on. I heard you. Talking about your mother's cook, and all that.'

Kat felt her face redden.

'My mother happens to run an inn. Of course she has a cook. And it just so happens that he was the one who taught me to read. And do accounts and stuff. Tia, I can't help it if I can read and write. Did you want me to lie about it?'

Tia looked at her appraisingly.

'There are some among the drifter brats who can read,' she said. 'We're not all of us stupid or ignorant scum, the way *they* all think.'

'I never said you were.'

'No. But you don't think you are one of us.'

Kat looked into her stew.

'I don't think I'm better than you,' she repeated stubbornly. It was all she could think of to say.

'Well, this new move of yours is not going to make you

any more popular,' said Tia, and Kat couldn't quite tell whether Tia was sorry or not.

'I can't help that, can I? The masters make the decisions.'

'Hmm. Maybe. But I'd watch my back if I were you.'

It turned out Tia was right. Kat could feel the hostile stares, the cold silence, every time she entered the prentice dorm. She ignored it as best she could. But a few days later, Housemistress Tora came into the writing room next to the Bookmaster's office and stopped in front of the desk Kat was working at.

'Please follow me, Katriona.'

Puzzled, Kat put down her pen and trotted behind Mistress Tora across the yard and up the stairs to the prentice dormitory.

'I believe this is your bed?' said Tora, pointing.

Kat nodded. It was.

'Kindly take the sheets to the laundry room and clean them. In the future you will have to use a wet-rag.'

Kat looked at Mistress Tora in bafflement. 'But I haven't . . . I never . . .'

'No? What is this, then?' asked Tora and drew back the covers. On the sheet was a big wet stain. There was no doubt as to its nature. The sour smell of pee was quite penetrating.

'I realize being new here isn't easy. But this sort of mess is unacceptable. In the future you will use a wet-rag, and if you do have an accident during the night, you will clean it up first thing in the morning.'

'But I haven't . . .' Kat knew her face was burning with embarrassment. 'I never wet the bed.' She thought quickly. 'If I had, it would . . . it would show on my underwear, wouldn't it?' Even as she said it, she was thinking: If she wants me to pull up my skirt and show her, I'll die on the spot!

In reply, Tora merely lifted the edge of the blanket with one toe. On the floor beneath the bed was a crumpled pair of underpants. Naturally, they were soaked, and naturally, they were Kat's. One of her two spare pairs.

'I know you can't help this problem of yours,' said Tora sharply, 'but I'll not have you lying to me, nor will I tolerate filth and uncleanliness! Clean this up, and then go to your work.'

Kat ripped off the wet sheet and bundled it up with the treacherous underpants. The mattress, too, had been soaked.

'Put it in the sun,' said Tora. 'Scrub it with lye and leave it to dry in the open.'

She turned and left. Kat stood quite still for a long moment with the pee-soaked bundle in her arms and murder in her heart. She *knew* somebody had done this on purpose, and she knew it was because she had been 'put in with the snoots', as Tia called it. But they would be sorry. Sweet Lady, would they be sorry. If war was what they wanted, they would surely get one!

THE PEE WARS

All day Kat pondered her revenge. It would be easy to steal a chamber pot from somewhere and pay someone back in kind. Somebody like big, bony Tami, perhaps, who had led the 'spider' gang that first night. Kat felt pretty certain she was in on this too. But everyone would be able to guess who had done it, and there were more of them than of her. She would lose out in the end. No, she had to be cleverer than that. Make allies. Play one against the other, the way she sometimes had with Eskill and Dan.

Lunch was a torment. Giggles kept breaking out at the tables all around her, and some dimwit started a whispered song: 'Wee Kitty, Pee Kitty, Wee Wee Wee . . .' It was taken up by many of the other girls and spread around the room, a low, vicious chant. Kat felt herself flush. She banged her cup down and wanted to get up, to get *at* them, but to her surprise, Tia held her back.

'Don't. It's what they want. You'll get all the bruises, and the blame too, cos you'll be the one who started it.'

107

Kat nearly tore herself free of Tia's grasp, but she knew Tia was right, and that stopping her was actually an act of friendship on Tia's part. It still took all her self-control to stay seated, and she couldn't hold back an acid remark.

'Fat lot you care,' she snapped. 'I bet you were the one who told them about me and the snoots in the first place.'

It was Tia's turn to flush. 'I didn't mean anything by it . . . Honest, Kat. I'm not on Tami's side.'

'You're not on *my* side either, that's pretty clear.'

Tia's face hardened. 'You don't have a side, New Girl. You've got nobody. I'm risking my hide just talking to you.'

'Don't, then,' said Kat sourly and bit down savagely on her chunk of bread, pretending not to care. Then, all at once, an idea struck her. Slowly, she put down the bread. Yes. Oh, yes. She knew exactly what she was going to do.

'Tia,' she said, contritely, 'I'm sorry. I didn't mean that. I'm glad you talk to me. I'm glad you're not afraid of Tami.'

Tia bent her head, looking almost shy. 'Oh, well,' she mumbled. 'No reason Miss High-And-Mighty should have it all *her* way.'

Kat and Tia sat next to one another again at supper. Kat stuck close to Tia in the baths, too. She helped wash, rinse and comb Tia's long hair. It was not quite as fair as Mattie's, but just as smooth. Kat felt a twinge somewhere inside and almost regretted her plans. But then she hardened herself against the feeling. Aren was right. You had to be hard in a place like this. Hard as nails.

The next day, Kat's bed was wet once more. But so was Tia's. It wasn't discovered until lunchtime, and they both had to spend their midday break scrubbing mattresses. Tia was furious.

'They'll be sorry,' she sputtered. 'I'll get them for this. Who do they think they are?'

'Tia . . .' said Kat. 'I'm really sorry. This is all because you sit next to me in the dining hall. You'd better sit somewhere else.'

'Hell, no. No way are they getting away with this.'

Before nightfall Tami's bed was as wet as Kat's and Tia's. Retaliation the next morning struck not only Kat and Tia, but also two of Tia's friends among the drifter brats. After that, there was no stopping it. Of course, not even the most naive of grown-ups believed in such an epidemic of bed-wetting, but all Housemistress Tora's furious tongue-lashings were to no avail. The Great Pee Wars spread like wildfire. Nobody was safe. Even girls who thought they had been careful to make no enemies in either camp were attacked and forced to take sides. When a guard was set at the dorm, the Pee Fighters simply found new targets: a blouse hung out to dry, a kicked-off pair of shoes. And if pee was not available in sufficient quantities, other weapons could be found. Lye from the vats actually smelled worse, and more persistently. Eventually, the Pee Wars engulfed even the fosterlings. Somehow, a rumour began that the war had actually been started by them in order to make fools of the drifter brats. And on *their* red skirts, stains showed with such satisfying clarity.

'You do it,' Tia said to Kat. 'You're in there with Asta and her lot every day, in the writing room.'

'They'll know it's me.'

'So what? We'll watch out for you.'

'Every day in the writing room? Come on, Tia, they'll have me to themselves for hours when you lot are in the Dyer's Hall.'

'Rikert won't let them hurt you.'

'Rikert? Rikert doesn't see a thing unless you write it out for him on parchment. If they killed me, he'd only notice when the blood began to stain the paper.'

So it really wasn't Kat who poured cinnabar dye into Asta's button boots. But somebody did. And when Asta put her feet in them, the dye welled up round her ankles and spilled across the floor, and Asta's neat white stockings turned a glaring pink.

For a moment she just stood there. Then she looked directly at Kat.

'You did this!' she hissed. 'Don't try to deny it!'

Kat looked back at her with an empty feeling in the pit of her stomach. No, she wouldn't deny it. What good would that do? No matter what she said, they wouldn't believe her. She saved her breath and sprinted for the door, but Lora and Celia were both closer to it and barred the way. Asta made a grab for her collar. Kat dodged her and dived back into the writing room. It was deserted now, but in the next room Master Rikert would be at his desk, making his meticulous lists, and in spite of her contemptuous words to Tia, she didn't really believe he would let them hurt her. She got her hand on the latch too, before they all slammed into her. She ended up with three girls on top of her and the floorboards gritty and rough against her cheek.

'Check her pockets,' ordered Asta.

'Nothing there.' Or at least, nothing except lint and a button that had come off her blouse.

'Then look in her desk.'

Kat began to wriggle. In the desk she kept her Sari Moon-Daughter. She no longer dared leave it in the dorm. But it wasn't books they were looking for.

'Nothing,' said Lora. 'Just some old book.'

'Where did you steal that?' asked Asta, not really caring.

'Nowhere,' snarled Kat. 'It's mine!'

'Thief and drifter – one and the same. What about her jacket?'

In her jacket which had been hanging on its hook in the hallway all day, they found a small bottle of cinnabar dye. Lora held it up triumphantly.

'Still a bit left,' she said. 'Enough to give her a taste of her own medicine.'

'I didn't do it,' said Kat. 'You think I'm that stupid? Leaving the bottle here for anybody to find?'

But of course they didn't believe her. And she had to admit, Tami had been more cunning than usual. Two birds with one stone. Kat *and* Asta. Oh, well. At least the cinnabar wouldn't show on her black clothes.

Lora unstopped the bottle. She got down on one knee next to Kat, loosened her collar and began to pour the contents down Kat's neck. It stung a bit, and Kat squirmed in

Asta's grip, but actually she thought it was a fairly mild revenge. Perhaps Asta felt the same.

'Wait,' she said. 'That's too easy. It won't even show on her black drifter rags.' She thought about it for a bit. 'Get the book,' she finally said.

'No!' Kat screamed and tried to tear free of their grasp. Not the book! Not the book Tad had given her. She heaved with such violence that she nearly succeeded in freeing her arm, but Asta put one knee on her neck and leaned, until Kat nearly blacked out with the struggle to breathe.

'Lie still, Kitty-Cat,' she said quite softly.

'Wee Kitty, Pee Kitty,' said Lora with a giggle.

They put the book down on the floor next to her face, so that she would be able to see what they were doing. Then they opened it to a random page and emptied the bottle on to the fine, yellow-white paper. The red spot spread like a bloodstain, swallowing up the letters one by one. Asta took off one pink stocking and rubbed it across the paper, making the entire page illegible. For good measure, she then rubbed the stocking roughly across Kat's face.

'That's what you get for letting drifter rubbish into the writing room,' she said. 'Look. She can't even read a book without ruining it.'

The two other girls broke into a fresh fit of giggles.

When they had gone, Kat sat up wearily and tried to wipe the dye from the book with her sleeve. It did no good – the paper only crumbled and rolled itself into tiny pink sausage shapes. Too late she discovered that the dye had seeped down to destroy other pages as well, turning the crisp clean inky lines into fuzzy spider legs as it spread. Some letters were still legible, others were blurring in front of her eyes. If only she could read it before it disappeared, and remember it . . . but the blur spread much too quickly, and she was a slow reader at best. Sari Moon-Daughter's escape from the Castle of Breda disappeared into a chaos of inky whirls in a pool of cinnabar dye. In the end, Kat just sat there with the book in her lap and began to cry.

'Child . . .'

She got up hurriedly. Master Rikert was standing in the doorway. She blinked and tilted her head a bit, trying to keep the tears from brimming over.

'Master?' Her voice sounded nearly normal.

'What is that you have?'

'A book.' She closed it hastily. But he held out his hand. 'Let me see.'

For a moment she clutched it to her chest. He merely waited, hand outheld. Finally she surrendered the book. He took it, and a strange expression came over his face when he saw what it was.

'Sari Moon-Daughter and the Pedlar from Joss. Have you read it?'

'Only the first two chapters.'

'How do you come to have it?'

'It's mine!'

'Have I said otherwise? I am merely asking who gave it to you.'

'My mother's cook . . .'

'The one who taught you to read?'

Kat nodded.

Master Rikert smiled faintly. 'A man I should like to meet – your mother's cook. Have you any notion of the value of this book?'

He opened it gently to the title page, where roses, snakes and dragons twined about Sari's name so that the letters nearly disappeared in the maze of shapes and colours. With infinite caution, he stroked the illuminations with one finger.

Kat shook her head. 'I suppose it must have been expensive . . .' she said hesitantly.

Rikert raised his head.

'Expensive. Yes. You who calculate mostly in money . . . you will most likely never own a sum large enough to purchase another such. Take care of it. Take great care.'

Take care of it.

A sob rose all the way from her belly. Master Rikert looked at her in puzzlement. Then he must have noticed the red streaks of dye on her face and on the hand she had tried to wipe the pages with. His gaze fell once more on the book, and he leafed through it until he came to the stains. His own face turned scarlet with anger.

'Wretched girl!' he said through clenched teeth. 'This book . . . this book is a treasure, a priceless treasure, and you dare to treat it like some common ledger!'

The tears Kat had been trying to hold back spilled down

her cheeks. Rikert saw it, and put a rein on his anger. Deliberately, he softened his tone. 'How did this happen?'

Kat just stood there, at a loss for words. Telling tales . . . went against the grain, and besides, it would do no good. Who would believe the word of a drifter brat?

'I knocked over an inkwell,' she muttered.

'Child, I've been clerking for Bria for more than twenty years. I can tell ink from dye by now. This is dye. Cinnabar, in fact.' He looked at her in expectation. And kept looking, for what felt like hours. But she could think of nothing else to say. The silence grew between them, long and unpleasant.

'*And when she held her peace, no man could break her silence . . .*' Rikert finally said, and Kat just barely knew it for a line from Sari Moon-Daughter. Rikert sighed. 'Very well, then, Lady Silence. I suggest to you a trade. If I may read your book, I shall copy out for you the pages that were ruined. I possess a Sari Moon-Daughter myself.'

'But Master . . . If you already have a copy, why do you want to read mine?'

'Yours is older. There may be lines in it that have been lost in later copies.' He looked once more at the book in his hands, and there was a tender hunger in the way he held it. 'Well? Are we agreed?'

Kat slowly nodded. As long as her book was in Rikert's care, it was safe enough, she supposed. As long as he didn't think she would trade Tad's book for his.

'But I want *my* book back,' she said. 'Tad wrote

something in it.' She said that mostly so that he would know that she could recognize it.

Master Rikert looked at her sadly. 'You learn so much distrust in this place,' he murmured. 'So much distrust at such a young age. But perhaps that is true in other places too.'

That night Kat could barely make herself lie still in the overcrowded darkness of the dorm. They had ruined Tad's book. *Ruined* it.

Asta had been the one to pour the dye. But it seemed to her they had all been in on it somehow, all of them. The girls who had teased her the first night. The ones who had wet her bed for her, the first time and all the other times. Those who had whispered round the tables and chanted their mean little chant: 'Wee Kitty, Pee Kitty.' Tami. Lora. Asta. Even Tia. She hated them all.

She sat up, listening. The dorm was never totally still. There was always someone snoring, or a creaking as someone moved. Somewhere down the far end, two girls were whispering, almost soundlessly. Kat slid out of bed and crept to the head of the stairs on bare, silent feet. Down the smooth steps. Outside, into the clear, brilliant night.

There were stars. Not many, though, because the sky was so summer pale that only the brightest ones were visible. The courtyard gravel was damp with dew and clung to her feet, but once she moved into the orchard in Old Quarters, the tall grass brushed softly against her ankles. She sat down at the foot of an apple tree. Its blossoms shone palely in the darkness, filling it with scent. The moisture from the grass gradually soaked through the black skirt she was wearing, and her bottom grew damp with it, but she didn't care. She just wanted to be out here, alone.

But somebody had followed her.

'Kat?' It was Tia. Of course it was Tia. 'Kat, what is it?'

'Nothing.'

'Did they hit you? Does it hurt?' Tia sat down next to her and tried to put her arm around her.

'No.' Kat wriggled free of Tia's tentative embrace. 'They just poured dye down the back of my neck. It was nothing much.'

'What is it, then?'

'Nothing. I told you. Just leave me alone, can't you?'

'Why? Why is trying to get close to you such a crime, Kat? Aren't we friends?'

Kat didn't answer. Tia slowly dropped her arm.

'Aren't we?' she said, and this time she meant it for the kind of question that needed an answer.

'Tia, stop it.'

'I mean it. Cos if we aren't friends, I'd like to know.'

'What is it you want me to say? "Oh, Tia, I love you." "Tia, I'd do anything for you."' Kat jeered the words. 'Is that what you want?'

Tia got to her feet. 'You still think you're better than me,' she said bitterly.

'No, I don't.'

'Yes, you do. You look down on me. You think I won't be able to understand. You think you're so much more complicated, so much cleverer than me.'

'Tia, no . . .' But perhaps Tia wasn't totally wrong. She didn't want to tell Tia about the book because she was afraid Tia wouldn't understand why that had hurt. She was afraid Tia would think that a book was a dumb, useless thing to be lugging around. Or that she would even think Kat was trying to show off and be clever again, pretending to be all upset over a book. And although Kat knew it wasn't fair, although she knew it wasn't really Tia's fault, in some small bitter corner of her soul, she blamed Tia along with the rest of them. Just because Tia was part of this place, part of *them*.

Tia looked down at her. 'Yes,' she said stubbornly. 'You think you are smarter than me. But let me tell you one thing, snoot. Around here, you only make it if you have friends. And you are too dumb to see that. So really, *I'm* the clever one.'

Rage reared its spiny head in Kat's belly.

'Oh, is that what you think?' she said slowly. 'Is that how you think it is?' She got up and put herself in front of Tia, like a wall. 'If only you knew . . .' And there was a bitter yellow burning in her throat.

'Knew what?' said Tia scornfully.

'If only you knew who wet *your* bed the first time.'

'But I know that,' said Tia with a trace of uncertainty. 'Tami did.'

'No,' said Kat. 'I did.'

Tia froze. 'You . . .'

'Yes. Because I knew you'd come round to my side after that. I knew you'd want to revenge yourself on Tami. So don't tell me I'm too stupid to make *friends*.' She sneered the last word, as if it was the worst insult she could think to offer. 'I started the war . . . and the more people got wet, the louder I laughed. Nobody's going to treat *me* like that and get away with it.'

Tia was still standing quite still, and Kat could see that she was fighting back tears.

'You could do such a thing . . .' she whispered. 'Use me . . . pretend . . .'

Pretend you liked me. Pretend we were friends. Tia didn't have to say the words. Kat knew exactly what she was thinking.

I did like you, Tia, she thought. But I had to make myself hard. That was more important. I had to show them that nobody makes a fool of *me*.

But if that was so important, why did she feel like crying now? And why did it hurt so much to see the tears in Tia's eyes?

'You . . .' said Tia, and her voice broke a little before she got it under control again. 'You are the lowest . . . You are the worst kind of creep I've ever come across.'

She spun on her heel and ran, back towards Prentice Hall.

Kat stood, looking in that direction for a while. Then she tugged her sweater more closely around her, lay down in the tall grass and closed her eyes, as though she were asleep. She heard the night grow less quiet. She heard footsteps and low voices, and someone running on the path from New Quarters to Old Quarters. She heard more and more voices, more and more steps. But behind her closed eyelids she saw only one thing: a red stain spreading across white paper. And she made no attempt to run. She didn't even open her eyes.

Not until she heard Tami hiss: 'So. New Girl thinks she can fool *us*?' And knew that they had all come.

She got to her feet and looked around her. They were all there, red-skirts and black-skirts, fosterlings and drifter brats, crowded together. She gazed around the circle and took their measure, coldly and clearly, and then she began.

'You, Tia,' hissed the yellow beast, 'you want me to say I'm a drifter brat like the rest of you. But I have a mother. One who loves me. One who saw to it that I can read and write. Why should I pretend to be stupid? Why should I pretend that I was born in the back of some cart and never learned anything but begging and stealing? You can find *my* mother at Crowfoot Inn, South Vale. Where is yours, Tia? Do you even know? Living in some hole in the ground? Locked up in some jail for thieving? Well, Tia? Answer me this – where is *your* mother?'

Tia opened her mouth, lips trembling. But Kat knew she had no answer to give.

'And you . . .' She turned on Asta and the other red-skirts. 'You who are oh so proud of being Bria's fosterlings. What kind of fostering is that? Does she ever put her arms around you? Does she ever kiss you goodnight? Does she even notice if you're happy or sad? Not once, I bet. She cares only that you do your work and make no trouble. You aren't her daughters – you are her slaves. Foundlings and workhouse donkeys, one and all. Oh, I could have been one of you. Bria offered. But I turned her down. I laughed in her face. Because I have a *real* mother!'

Shut up, shut up! A small anxious voice was whispering frantically somewhere inside her, but she wasn't listening. The yellow beast was running things now. Gall was dripping from her every word, and she wanted to spit the venom at them, all of them, Tia, Tami, Asta – all.

She got to as many as she could, and for every one of them there was a particular grain of poison, some mean little truth she could tell. Perhaps she was spitting at Tess really, even though Tess wasn't there. If they hit me so hard I die, she thought, she'll be sorry. She'll be sorry for what she did. That was almost worth dying for. If only she could be there to see it, floating like a spirit over the stretcher when they brought her home to South Vale, see how her mother would fling herself at the poor dead body, calling over and over again, 'Kat, oh, Kat child, what have I done?' Even Cornelius might cry a bit, she thought. Well, maybe not cry. But be silent and heartbroken, perhaps. It would hurt him too.

She laughed when they caught hold of her. She kicked at them, hit them, scratched them. She bit them. But she knew that her words had already bitten them much deeper and more painfully than her blunt human teeth ever could. It made her feel warm inside, in the belly-cave where the yellow beast lived. She didn't care what they did to her now. She barely felt it.

Finally, the blows stopped coming. She could hear Tia shouting at them to stop, it was enough, they mustn't kill her. *Why not, Tia? I bit you harder than anyone.* But darkness curled in her head now, and she was very tired, and perhaps it was best if she didn't die. What if Tess didn't grieve after all? What if she simply didn't care, and only thought: Oh, so the shrike got her comeuppance in the end . . .

When her senses started to come back to her, she was lying on the floor in the Dyer's Hall. They had tied her hands with something woolly and scratchy, perhaps a stocking. She felt empty and heavy all at once. It made no sense. *If I'm empty, how come I'm not light?* Her brain worked very slowly. Why had they tied her up? What did they mean to do? She slowly realized they weren't done with her yet. There was a strong, sulphurous smell, as if someone had just added sulphite to one of the dye vats.

As if someone . . . but what did they mean to dye? All her clothes were black, and Master Rikert had her book – they wouldn't be able to get their hands on that this time.

'Tami . . . I think she's awake.' That was Asta's voice.

'Listen, Kitty-Cat . . .' Tami grabbed her by the collar and propped her against the vat. Her mouth was so close to Kat's ear that fine droplets of spit sprayed Kat's cheek when she talked. 'You shouldn't be so mean-tempered. It's not healthy.'

'We think it's all that red hair,' added Asta. 'It makes people all hot in the head, or so I've heard.'

'So we thought . . . blue. Blue is such a soothing colour.' Tami ruffled Kat's frizzy mane in a friendly manner. 'We think you'll like it.'

Blue . . . Kat finally realized what they meant to dye.

'Blue,' said Asta contentedly. 'Indigo blue. A very nice expensive colour. It *never* comes off, you know.' She smiled. 'It's even better than cinnabar that way.'

'It's probably best if you don't wriggle too much,' said Tami. 'You know what lye can do to the skin. Like acid. Wouldn't want to get it in your eyes now, would we?'

Kat was no longer empty. She was terrified. Her eyes stung, as if they could already feel the acid burn of the lye. No. No no no. *Not my eyes. I don't want to be blind, please, please* . . . She was still and pliant in their grasp and made no effort to resist them at all. The edge of the vat dug into the back of her neck, and the only defence she could think of was to screw her eyes up tight. The heat and the fumes from the vat made it hard to breathe and she had to fight back a cough, but she didn't dare cough, didn't dare *move*, while Tami called out the count in time with her pulse, the way Dyemaster Tomas had taught them.

'Ten times eighty beats for the full effect.' She could almost hear his voice. Ten times eighty made eight hundred. If she hadn't been able to work out numbers, would she be in this fix? If she hadn't learned to read. Or if she had ever learned to keep her mouth shut.

'Seventy-one, seventy-two . . .'

Asta, Tami, I didn't mean it, please. I'll be a good girl now . . . There was a whimper inside her, trying to get out.

'That's enough.'

Not Tami, not Asta. Tia, Tia again, telling them to stop.

'Why are you being such a busybody, Tia? Don't you think she's got it coming?' asked Tami.

'You stop now,' Tia said calmly. 'Or I'm getting Master Tomas to show him what you're using his most expensive dye for.'

Tami giggled. 'Yeah, that would set him off for sure . . . All right, Asta, I think that'll do, don't you?'

Asta reluctantly loosened her grip, and Kat rolled over on her side on the scaffolding. The dye had not got into her eyes. For a long time, that was the only thing that mattered. She was not going to be blind.

Tia tugged at the stocking knots and managed to free Kat's wrists. The hands felt completely numb.

'Come on,' Tia said, trying to get Kat to stand up. 'We need to rinse it. It can still burn you.'

'Tia – leave me alone.' She didn't know why she said it. It was probably just that she couldn't bear anyone tugging at her, prodding her, making her do things. She just wanted to be left alone for the rest of her life.

Tia let go. Kat looked up at her limply. Tia's fists were knotted at her sides, and her eyes were cold. Rubbing shoulders with the snoots – well, that might be forgiven. Even the deception might be forgiven, in time. She had paid for it, after all. But now Tia had once more held out her hand, and Kat had refused to take it. Again. So this was it. There would be no more chances.

'Have it your way,' said Tia in the hardest voice Kat had

ever heard her use. 'What do I care? Seems like you don't need me. Got your precious mother, after all. Who loves you so much she sent you *here*.'

It took a long time for Kat to get to her feet and limp her way to the baths to rinse her hair. She had to be careful – the dye was no longer full strength, but it still had a sting to it, and her new terror of damaging her eyes made her awkward and slow. Eyes. They suddenly seemed so fragile, so easily hurt. Her whole body felt battered and bruised, and every breath was painful, but there were no bits of bone moving, the way they had when her arm had been broken.

She knew she couldn't stay here. She simply could not wake up in that dorm tomorrow and face the rest of the girls. Perhaps if she hadn't become so scared . . . perhaps if she had fought them, kicking and screaming, when they dyed her hair. Or perhaps, if she had let Tia help her . . . But she had been limp and unresisting in their grasp, like some weak and newborn thing, and now they knew they could break her. And there would be no help from Tia next time.

She climbed the dorm stairs, silent as a shadow. If any-one heard her, at least they didn't say anything. From the box where she kept her things she took everything she had brought with her. The black prentice clothes she left behind.

It felt good to be free of the heavy skirts again. Dan's cast-off leather breeches were as comfortable as silk in com-parison. But this time there would be no need to hide her hair under the cap. She brought the long wet length of it forward over one shoulder. Then she took her knife, and started sawing. When she was done, she carefully collected the cut-off hair and put it in her bundle. She had heard that there were people who could do finder's magic with hair and nails. She didn't know if it was true, but she was taking no chances. Nothing and no one would call her back to *this* place, with or without magic.

The hardest thing was sneaking into Master Hall and finding Master Rikert's quarters, but there was no way she could leave without Tad's book. The old man was breathing heavily, and she felt certain that he was asleep. Fortunately, the book was on his desk, so that she didn't have to go rummaging through his chests and cabinets. She caressed the cover with one hand. Then she opened it. Where the damaged pages were, he had inserted some new sheets of paper – he had kept his word and copied out the missing bits. She would get to know what happened when Sari Moon-Daughter escaped from the Castle of Breda after all.

Quietly, she withdrew and began to close the door behind her. But just as she was about to turn away, she heard the old man's voice, quiet but alert:

'Farewell, Lady Silence. Take care of yourself – and of the book.'

For a moment she stood there, heart in her throat, clutching the book with one hand and the doorframe with the other. Then she got a grip on herself.

'Farewell, Master,' she whispered. 'And thank you.'

There was no answer.

THE RESTING PLACE

She didn't get very far the first night. She had been walking for less than an hour when she started to shake so violently that her legs would barely support her. Feeling sick, she crouched by the wayside and threw up in the ditch. She tried to walk on, but her legs felt as if they belonged to somebody else, and in the end she had to give up. She wrapped herself in her blanket and lay down in the shrubbery just off the caravan road. If anybody had come looking, they could have found her quite easily. But at the Dyer's Yard, no one cared for ungrateful prentices foolish enough to run away.

She lay there, still shaking and unable to sleep. If wasn't until the sun came up and brought a bit of warmth with it that she finally slept.

When she woke, it was past noon and the roiling in her stomach this time was hunger. Under the blanket, she was now sticky with sweat, and tiny black flies buzzed around her head, getting into her eyes and nostrils. She freed one arm from the blanket and brushed at them in irritation. Then she sat up slowly.

This was the first time she gave any thought at all to where she should run to. Yesterday, she had merely been running away. Now she realized that 'away' was not enough. What was she going to do? Her heart started to beat rapidly in panic. Tonight, when the sun went down, she would have nowhere to go. No wagon like Aren's, not even a drifter's cart. When the darkness came, and the cold, there would be no bed for her anywhere. Not tonight, or tomorrow night, or the night after. She wasn't just sleeping under the stars for the fun of it. She was homeless.

Suddenly, everything seemed dangerous. In her mind's eye she saw Nicolas's pale and anxious face the day she had left him alone on the mountain. Scared. Exposed. Scared of everything, because he was alone. Scared of every sound, of rain, of the dark, of wild animals and birds. Scared of falling, because there would be no one to pick him up. Scared of getting lost, because there would be no one to find him.

She had nobody now. And she was scared. Terrified. The sky no longer felt free and open above her head, it had become an enemy, a threat, something she needed to seek cover from. She was so full of fear she could barely move. In spite of the heat she drew the heavy blanket over her head like a tent. For a long time she sat there in her blanket cave with the sweat trickling down her face, hot and stinging in her eyes, and in the scratches from the night before.

Finally, something happened. Just when her fear had

grown so huge that it stopped all thought, an image slowly formed inside her. Silverhorse. Brilliant in the morning light, sparks flying from a flashing hoof, as it stood its ground to defend her from Cornelius. Glowing with life and strength and fierce defiance. She discovered that she was clutching something in her hand – the silver coin with the picture of the rearing horse on it. And then the image in her mind changed. No longer a living horse, but a painted one, on a sign, in a circle of oak leaves, and the words: SHELTER. REST. HEALING. A Resting Place. She and Aren had passed a Resting Place on their way to the Dyer's Yard. Deserted and dilapidated, like the one in Saratown, but still – it was a place to go. A roof over her head. And the sign with the silver-grey horse hanging over the door like a promise.

It took her four days. She was afraid to leave the caravan road completely, but also too scared to walk on the road itself most of the time. Every time she heard someone approaching, or thought she did, she took to the shrubbery or the woods that stretched on both sides.

It wasn't any one clear thing she feared. If someone had asked her, she would have said that she didn't want to be caught and brought back to Bria's. But in her heart of hearts, she knew that risk was small. Bria would never send anyone to bring back a single contrary and unwilling prentice. She could always get another, one who would be grateful for the bed and the food and the chance to stay in one place for more than a few nights. There were so many drifters –

fewer who could read and write, of course, but quite enough for Bria's purposes.

No, it wasn't that which made her cower in the bushes or drop to the damp ground among the trees, among the shadows, praying nobody would catch sight of her. She would lie there, face hidden against her arms, until the sounds of wheels and hooves, voices and footsteps had faded entirely. Because if anybody saw her now, she would not be the innkeeper's girl or Cornelius's stepdaughter. She would not even be Bria's prentice. She'd be nobody. And someone like that, who belonged to nobody, a lone drifter brat, and a girl at that – to many people, both travelled and settled, she would be fair game. Who would miss her? Who would make a fuss if she got hurt? If anyone was decent to her, it would be only out of the kindness of their heart. Kat remembered vividly how Tess treated the drifter women and drifter girls – some of them hardly older than Kat – who had dared to darken the doorway of her inn.

Most of the time, she was wet and scared. At night, she was cold. When she slept at all, it was mostly catnapping in the noonday sun. When the moon was out she would walk for as long as she could see the road in front of her.

She wished now that she had been wise and unscrupulous enough to steal some food from the kitchens before leaving. Her stomach ached with hunger and she got more and more dizzy. She found some wild rhubarb and picked as much as she could carry. There was not much nourishment in the red and green stalks, and they were sharp on the tongue and rough on the teeth, but at least they filled the belly a bit. There were also edible snails, but her stomach rebelled at the thought of eating them raw.

It was evening on the fourth day when she finally came to the place where she had seen the sign. For a while she simply stared at it. For the last couple of miles, she had begun to be afraid that it wouldn't be there, that her memory had betrayed her and it had never been there, except in some dream she had had. But there it was, like she remembered. Old and weathered, with barely legible lettering spelling out the words. Shelter. Rest. Healing. Well, shelter and rest she might get, but no one would be there to offer healing any more. Not like in the old days Tad had told her about, when every Resting Place had trained healers to care for the sick and the wounded.

She began to walk down the track branching off from the caravan road. There was a white, transparent feeling all through her body, as if she were slowly turning into a cloud. If I raise my feet off the ground, she thought, I'll float away. She didn't try. Pine needles cushioned her steps, and among the trees, an early twilight had fallen. Ahead of her, at the end of the track, light still blazed. There was a mossy stone wall and an old gate that swung open at her touch.

On the other side of the gate was a meadow, sunlit still, and buzzing with insects. The house itself sat waiting, grey and weathered, with its back to the woods and a porch in front, facing the grass and the evening sunlight, and on the far side of it a hazel-pole fence formed a paddock.

And there it was. Behind the fence.

Silverhorse.

It couldn't be. It had to be just an ordinary horse. If it looked silver, it must be because she was dizzy and had begun to turn into a cloud. She rubbed her eyes in tired annoyance. The horse was still silver. The evening sun bounced off its body like light on the blade of a knife. It was, it really *was* . . .

Kat dragged herself forward at a stumbling run. All caution, all thoughts of fear and clouds and hunger were forgotten. Like an arrow she flew across the meadow, not sure if she touched the ground or not. The silver mare's head came up, and a sound came from its throat, not really a neigh, more of a squeal. *Slow down, slow down, never run towards a horse* . . . but it was so hard, so nearly impossible to slow her steps and walk quietly, easily, the last few strides.

She didn't look the mare in the eyes, did not really want to meet that golden predator's gaze right now. She put her cheek against the smooth, shiny neck and breathed deeply and calmly, feeling welcome and protected at last.

She heard steps behind her. That would be Frost's rider, with the expensive blue cloak and the scar on one cheek. Kat didn't turn around. Explanations could wait, at least for a few more moments. She was sure the rider would understand. Hadn't she given Kat the silver coin herself?

'Who are you? What are you doing here?'

Kat whirled round. This was not her rider. He was dressed almost the same way – grey leathers, blue cloak – but this was a man, a tall dark man with the sun at his back making him even taller and darker. She couldn't see his face clearly, and words deserted her completely. This was not her rider, and perhaps the horse . . . that there might be other silver horses and other Silver riders in the world had not even entered her mind in that first rush of welcome.

'Who are you?' he repeated harshly. And she didn't know what to answer. She felt once more alone and uncertain. The silver mare snorted and threw up her head. Crash! A hoof slammed against the hazel poles of the fence. Kat started, and turned to soothe the horse. She looked straight into orange-golden hunter's eyes, and fear hit her like a fist to the belly, completely unexpected. A moment ago she had cuddled that slim silver neck. Now she was caught by the orange gaze, trapped and numbed. This is how a cat looks at a mouse, she thought, knowing perfectly well that this time she was not the cat.

'Back away from her,' the man said in a voice so flat it sounded as if he had deliberately squeezed all the emotions out of it. The mare snorted once more, reared restlessly, and kicked at the fence again. Two of the poles broke. And Kat backed up stiffly, on legs that did not quite behave the way she wanted them to.

'Keep going,' she was ordered. 'All the way up to the house. And stop looking at her!'

Kat did as she was told. Only when she reached the steps to the porch did she stop, folding up like a puppet with its strings cut. Fear would not let her go. She was so hollow from hunger that there was room for such a lot of fear. Huge, dizzying waves of it. She closed her eyes and tried not to retch. Faintly she heard the man murmuring to the mare, soft low words in the same kind of soothing tones she had used with the horses back home.

What was wrong with her? She wasn't afraid of horses. She could not remember the last time she had been scared of a horse. Perhaps once at the dawn of time, when she was just a little snotty-nosed kid, younger even than Tim. Back when she had been very small, and they had been very large . . . but it had never been like this. She had never felt so like a tiny, terrified animal, running for its life, running and running until the heart burst from panic alone . . .

'Think about something else,' the man said sharply, and again there was a dry crack of hooves against the hazel fence.

Think about something else? Easy for him to say. What else was there to think about? The sour smell of sulphite that still clung to her hair? The bumps, the bruises and the scratches? The starved hole in her belly? Mama? Tess, who had sent her away? How was all that supposed to make her feel less afraid?

Her hand had slipped to the silver coin again, clutching it, clutching it so hard, in fact, that her fingers hurt. And suddenly she did manage to think of something else. Of another silver mare she had not been afraid of, Frost, and that reckless, brilliant ride across the High Meadows, hooves hissing in the dew.

She opened her eyes. The fear had gone as abruptly as if it had been a candle she had finally managed to snuff. In the pasture the silver mare was squealing again, not with rage, this time, but playfully, whirling on its hind legs and trotting along the fence with airy dancer's steps, as if trying to impress another horse. The man laughed, saying something to the horse that she couldn't hear. Then he looked at her, and his face became flat and expressionless once more. With long, swift strides he came back to the porch, pausing only to pick up the bundle she had dropped in her rush to get to the mare.

'Inside,' he told her, with a jerk of his head. She rose, and went into the house.

Inside, it was dim and gloomy. He had opened two of the shutters, but the rest of the windows had been boarded up by travellers who were more concerned with cutting off the draught than with letting in air and sunlight. The room was quite large and reminded her a bit of the common room back home, except that here alcoves had been built along both gable walls. He had spread his bedroll on the floor, not in one of the alcoves. The straw there was probably mouldy and infested with all sorts of bugs. His gear was neatly set out – cooking pots, saddlebags, tinderbox, waterskin, cup, plate – there was a tidiness to his little indoor camp that reminded her of Aren Journeyman. He had lit a fire in the fireplace, and a kettle hung above the flames, hissing faintly.

'Sit,' he said, indicating the bench by the long table. She sat and so did he, on the bench opposite. For a while he simply looked at her, and she had no inkling as to his feelings. Anger? Annoyance? Or something else entirely? She couldn't tell. There was something unnatural about his lack of expression. Most people, thought Kat, tell you how they feel, one way or the other, with their faces or with their bodies. She could always tell Cornelius's moods just by listening to his steps.

'What did you want with my hellhorse?' he finally asked.

Hellhorse?

'Not to steal it, if that's what you think,' she said angrily. But he just kept looking at her, as if she hadn't answered him at all. She dropped her eyes. 'I just wanted to . . . to touch it,' she whispered.

'Why?'

Why? How was she supposed to answer a question like that? It was because of . . . because of everything. She shrugged. 'I just felt like it.'

'I saw you,' he said. 'I saw you run across the meadow. If you hadn't been running so quickly, I would have stopped you. People don't go running up to hellhorses just because they feel like it. Don't you know the first thing about them?'

'I rode one once,' she said defiantly. *Even if I didn't know what they were called. Hellhorses. What a name for something so beautiful!*

'Don't lie to me,' he said, with an edge of contempt showing through the flatness.

'I *did*,' she said, offended. 'I got paid for it too – a silver coin.' Not entirely true, of course. The coin was not for the ride, not for that glorious rush across the wet fields with the morning wind in her hair . . . but she held out the coin so that he could see that she had not been lying about the most important bit.

He snatched it from her fingers. 'Who gave you that?' he demanded, no longer expressionless.

'A rider. A . . . a Silver. A woman.' Unthinkingly, she put her hand to her face in the place where the woman had had her scar.

'Dorissa.' The man said it so softly it was hardly more than a breath. 'When? When did you meet her?'

'Last autumn.' Kat counted in her head. 'Eight months ago.'

'Where?'

Tears rose unbidden in her eyes. 'At an inn,' she said. 'The Crowfoot Inn in South Vale.'

'Where was she going? Kernland?'

'I expect so. She rode off in the direction of the Kernland Pass. And there really aren't all that many other places to go to from South Vale.'

The rider got to his feet and turned his back on her. Kat sat quietly, waiting.

'Can I have my coin back?' she asked eventually.

Still not saying a word, the rider put the coin on the table. Kat collected it and slipped it into the little bag she carried around her neck. She was so used to its light weight on her chest that she felt somehow bare without it.

The water had come to a boil. Carefully, he swung the kettle away from the fire and sprinkled some herbs into it. She could smell mint and lemon balm and something else she didn't recognize.

'I only have one cup,' he said in the same flat voice he had used before.

'I have my own,' Kat said, and rose to get it from her meagre bundle of belongings.

'So, Dorissa gave you her token,' he said slowly, 'eight months ago in South Vale. And here you are, still not knowing what that means.' He raised the kettle, poured the tea. 'Damn. I don't have *time* for you.'

Kat, who had had nothing either cold or hot since yesterday's rhubarb, folded her hands around her steaming tin cup and did not have the energy to wonder what he meant.

'Pardon my asking,' she said in a very small voice, because this was the first time in her life she had ever had to beg, 'but could you possibly spare a little food?'

'Yes,' he said drily, reaching for the saddlebags. 'I suppose I could.'

He fed her on mealy biscuits, some cheese, and a bit of cold rabbit. The biscuits were quite hard, and she had to force herself to chew them properly and not just bolt down the lot in six gulps. While she ate, he sat staring into the fire, saying nothing. After a while, the silence became rather awkward.

'You said that Dorissa gave me her token,' she finally said. 'What did you mean by that?'

'What you call a coin is really a medallion,' he said. 'A token, like I said. We use them for sealing letters and things like that. Dorissa gave you hers to show that she thought you could become one of us.'

'Why didn't she just tell me? And what do you mean, one of us?'

'I suppose she had the same problem I do. She had no time for you. And she probably didn't think you were going anywhere. She gave you her token to . . . to make sure that you had something, some proof, if she didn't make it back. What did she tell you to do with it?'

'Keep it carefully and let no one take it away from me, that's all.'

'She didn't say much, then. I wonder why.'

'One of us,' Kat persisted. 'What did she mean by that?'

'A bredinari. One of the Silvers, as I suppose you call us. She thought you might one day learn to manage a hell-horse.' He shrugged. 'You must have done better with Frost than you did with Grizel a while ago.'

Kat felt herself flush with shame. She didn't understand it. She was *not* afraid of horses. Not even horses with hunter's eyes. She hadn't been afraid of Frost, had she? Hardly at all, anyway. Perhaps a bit uneasy at first, that was all.

'Most people fear the hellhorses,' said the rider. 'And feeling fear can be dangerous. The hellhorses react to it, usually with savage attacks. Perhaps they can smell it, or maybe it is something else. But to control a hellhorse you must first control yourself.' He raised his cup and took a sip of his tea. 'In your case, I think there is quite a lot to control.

Aren't you the one who ran away from the Dyer's Yard four days ago?'

Kat jerked guiltily in her seat. 'Why do you think that?'

'Your hair has a rather unusual blue colour here and there, and Bria was still on about the ingratitude of youth when I passed her place yesterday. Was it you? Is your name Katriona?'

'I'm mostly called Kat,' she admitted.

'Kat. I'm Simon. Some call me Simon Jossa, because I'm from Joss. Master Rikert asked me to look for you on the road. But I didn't see you.'

'I didn't . . . stick to the road all the time.' She didn't want to tell him about hiding in the woods. What business was that of his?

'The inn you mentioned, where you met Dorissa. Was that your mother's inn?'

Kat nodded silently.

'Then how did you end up at Bria's?'

Her throat closed, but it had to be said.

'My mother . . . sent me away.'

He nodded without looking at her, and didn't ask her why. As if it was perfectly normal for mothers to send away their daughters like they were sons.

'I see,' he said. 'And are you on your way back to her, then?'

'I don't know.' Kat closed her eyes to hold back the tears. 'Probably not. She'd only send me away again.' The last bit came out acidly bitter, straight from the yellow beast. 'I don't care. I can manage just fine on my own.' She opened her eyes, struck by a sudden thought. 'Did you mean that? That bit about me becoming a Silver? A bredi . . . a bredi . . .'

'Bredinari. Yes. Dorissa is rarely wrong about things like that.'

That was almost enough to soothe the hackles of the yellow beast. A silver horse, a hellhorse of her own . . .

'Please. How do I . . . how do I do that?'

'Slow down,' said Simon. 'You don't really know what it means.'

'But if . . . if I wanted to be a Silver – how would I go about it?'

'First of all you'd have to know a lot more about what you're getting into. But if you are determined . . . your mother would have to give her permission and put her mark on a prenticeship letter. Then you would go to Breda City for your training. That takes a long time. Five or six years, usually.' He poured more tea for her. 'And at the end of that . . . it's not an easy life, Katriona. Particularly not for a girl. A lot of people have strong opinions about women who travel. And as a Silver, you would spend most of your life on the road. At least, some of us do.' Carefully he set the kettle down at the edge of the fireplace again. 'When someone asks me where I live, I usually tell them I live in Breda. And they think I mean the City. I don't. I'm in the capital perhaps one month of the year. The rest of the time the Breda I live in is the entire country, from Luna to Three Valleys, from Grana to Joss. Riding courier, or bringing the Law of the Bredani to people far from the capital. Or doing . . . other work, like now.'

141

'But at least you have a place to return to,' Kat whispered, with the ache of homelessness in her voice. 'I don't, now.'

'Bria would take you back, I think. Master Rikert certainly would.'

At first, Kat did not answer. Then she said, very loudly and clearly, 'If you force me to go back to the Dyer's Yard, I'll run away again. Doesn't matter where.'

He nodded slowly. 'Very well. I won't, then. We'll go to Three Valleys together first, so I can talk to your mother. And then we shall have to see.'

Simon went to check on Grizel and make sure she had water enough for the night. Kat unrolled her own bedding in front of the fire. She had a quick wash from the rainwater barrel, and then lay down under her blanket. She had food in her belly and a roof over her head, and she was no longer alone – although Simon, with his unnatural stillness, was hard to figure out, he was still *somebody*. She trusted him. She just wasn't sure why. And perhaps . . . perhaps she would one day be a Silver. A bredinari. She turned the word over in her mind. Whatever Simon said, it had to be a million times better than being a prentice at the Dyer's Yard.

She had already begun to drop off to sleep when Simon came back in. But there was one unanswered question still gnawing at her mind.

'Simon?'

'Yes?'

'You said you were doing "other work" now. What other work?'

He was crouching in front of the fireplace, carefully banking the fire, and the glow of embers lit his face from below. His still, unreadable face.

'I'm looking for Dorissa and Frost.'

'Are they . . . lost?'

He was closing the shutters, and didn't answer her right away. The room was very dark now, lit only by the weak glow of the banked fire, but Simon moved in the darkness with the confidence of a cat.

'They were supposed to return before winter closed the roads,' he said finally. 'Or in early spring at the latest. She should never have gone to Kernland on her own. It's a foreign place, too far from Breda's law.'

Kat nodded. 'People are different there,' she said, thinking of Karel and the border guards who had been so rude that Tess had thought they might be robbers, rather than men sent to *catch* the robbers.

She could hear the soft rustle of blankets as Simon lay down in his chosen spot. The room was silent for a while, and Kat floated off towards sleep. Then Simon said, so quietly that Kat wasn't sure she was meant to hear it:

'It's true we have a place to come back to. But there are some who never return.'

CROWFOOT

'If you start to feel afraid, like yesterday, then get off. Move away from her. And stay away until you're not afraid any more.'

Offended, Kat looked at Simon. 'I'm not scared—' she began.

'Everyone is scared,' Simon interrupted. 'Of one thing or another, sooner or later. There's no shame in it. I warn you, don't try to show off. If you get scared, get off. Immediately. Or I might not be able to hold her.' He gave her a twisted smile. 'When you feel something, Kat, you tend to feel it *strongly*. Grizel can sense you from quite a distance.'

He nodded in the direction of the hellhorse mare. 'When you're ready, go and say hello to her. It'll be easier once she is familiar with your scent.'

Kat looked at the mare, brilliant in the morning sun. Grizel. Not Frost, whom she had ridden, Frost who had defended her against Cornelius's fury. But yesterday when she had believed the hellhorse must be Frost, before Simon startled her – there had been nothing wrong then, no terrible fear, no numbing mouse-like terror.

She tried not to think. Tried to pretend this really was Frost. She walked up to the mare like she had the day before and put her hand on its shoulder and her cheek against its neck. If it wanted to, it would be able to bite her now. Or kick her down and trample her. It didn't. It merely lowered its head and blew softly against her back, exactly like Blackie would have done.

'Good,' said Simon. 'Excellent. You'll be all right.'

She helped him groom and saddle Grizel. Simon arranged the saddlebags and their bedrolls so that Kat would be able to fit behind the saddle. He swung up and extended a hand towards her. She took it, used the stirrup he had left empty for her, and managed to get up behind him in a not too inelegant fashion.

Once there, she suddenly felt shy about putting her arms around him, a stranger she had met only yesterday. But when he felt her hesitation, he resolutely brought her hand forward till she was clutching his waist.

'Hang on,' he said, and let Grizel move off at a walk, across the meadow and through the woods, on to the caravan road.

In spite of riding double, they moved much faster than when she had been travelling with Aren. Grizel hardly ever trotted. When a breather was needed, she walked. The rest of the time, she went at a slow, flat canter that she could keep up for hours. It seemed that Simon let the hellhorse set the pace. Kat never felt him urge her forward with his legs, and she herself was very careful not to bother the silver mare.

At noon, they stopped briefly in a village. There was no inn as such, but travellers could sit at a table in front of the smithy. Once Simon had shown his coin, properly minted with the Bredanis' mark on it, the mistress of the house filled their cups with thin, weak beer and brought them a hot meal. But a horse she would not sell them, no matter how good their money.

'Wrong time of the year,' said Kat. 'The ones they're willing to part with, they sell in the spring when the prices are good. Now they have only the breeding stock left. But next time you want to try, let me do it. One look at that cloak of yours, and their prices go up by at least a quarter.'

'Oh, really?' said Simon drily. 'And who do you expect will want to sell a horse to a raggedy drifter like you?'

What? She hadn't expected that kind of insult from Simon, and it took her a few moments to gather her outrage.

'Just who do you think—' she began, but Simon put a hand on her arm to halt her.

'Easy, Kat, easy. I'm just teasing you for the fun of it.'

Kat looked down at her plate, embarrassed and uncertain. She was not used to being teased for fun. Where she had just come from, such insults had been made in bloody earnest. But if nothing else, the wonderful taste and smell of roast chicken and summer cabbage was enough to convince her that she was very far indeed from the prentice tables in the Dyer's Yard.

They spent that night camped in the open, and the next as well. But Kat no longer felt scared and unsheltered. It was something, wasn't it, to be returning proudly astride a silver hellhorse? Even if she didn't hold the reins. A proper homecoming, this would be.

Or would it? Kat began to grow uneasy. What sort of a reception would she get? At this moment, Tess must think that she was busily learning the dyer's trade, might even think that Kat was Bria's fosterling now. And Cornelius . . . Kat's mind went completely blank when she tried to picture the welcome Cornelius would give her. She had absolutely no idea.

The closer they got to the Vale, the quieter she became. When they began to encounter people who knew her, she greeted them briefly, but said nothing more. Not everyone returned her greeting. Some went past with no sign of acknowledgement. It was perhaps just possible that they didn't recognize the innkeeper's red-haired daughter now that her hair was so much shorter and a bit less red in places. Certainly, they hadn't expected to see her again so soon. But it was a lot more likely that they didn't *want* to know her, that they no longer counted her among their own. Drifter girl. Traveller. The message was there in the faces that turned away so quickly.

If Simon noticed, he made no comment. But then, he was used to being treated like a stranger.

They went past Erold's smithy (Erold, at least, returned

her greeting) and past Anna Weaver's house. And then she could see the inn, and the Crowfoot sign, which had acquired a new coat of paint since she had seen it last. Barely three months ago. No more than that, although it felt like forever.

Hearing the hoofbeats, Cornelius came out to see to the guest's horse. And stopped, stock still. His broad shoulders rose and fell, and his face had become almost as expressionless as Simon's.

'Kat,' he said hoarsely, and opened his arms halfway, as if he wasn't sure whether she would let him or not. And Kat did something then that she had never dreamed she would do. She slid off Grizel, ran across the yard, and threw herself into her stepfather's embrace.

He closed his arms around her and hugged her tight, much too tight, of course: just like her, he did everything too much. But right now too much was a lot better than nothing. She heard Nicolas's voice from the back door:

'It's Kat! Mama! Tad! Mattie! It's Kat!'

And then the whole brood came swarming out to look at her and touch her and hug her, and she was home again.

Tess was the one she was unsure of now. She didn't know how to say hello, partly because she had refused to say goodbye. She had used the Silence on her mother. She had been so very angry, and she had wanted Tess to feel bad, as bad as possible. And the fact remained, still, that it was Tess who had sent her away.

'So. You've come back,' was all Tess said. 'Come in, then.'

As if she were a guest. A stranger.

At that moment, Kat made her decision.

'I'm not staying long,' she said. 'I want to go to Breda and learn how to be a Silver. A bredinari. If you'll let me.'

Simon went south, and was gone for nearly a fortnight. When he came back, he was wet, tired and silent, and had broken something in one hand. With him came a gaunt, silver ghost of a horse which started at the slightest sound and fought everyone who tried to go near it. Frost. It broke Kat's heart to look at her. And where was Dorissa?

'I have to go back to the City as quickly as possible,' said Simon. 'Are you still sure you want to come?'

'Yes,' said Kat without hesitation. 'But Dorissa . . . Do you know . . . ?'

'She is dead,' he said in his flattest, most expressionless voice. 'She must be. There is nothing left to hope for.'

He looked ill and desperately tired. Kat held her peace and left him alone, and Tess sent for Keri Herbwife, who took one look at Simon's hand and eyed him with displeasure.

'What have you done to it?' she asked.

'Just fix it,' he said wearily, and would answer none of her questions. She snorted in disapproval and made him a stiff glove-like bandage that left him hardly any movement in his fingers.

'Go easy on it,' she said. 'And come and see me in a week's time.'

Simon nodded and did not tell her that in a week's time, he reckoned on being halfway to Breda City.

It was another day before Kat gathered her courage to ask him if he had found out what had happened to Dorissa.

He shook his head. 'Not exactly. I have only a vague idea.'

She set down a bowl of stew in front of him. She had cut the meat herself, so that he would be able to eat it with only one hand.

'And Frost . . . ?' she asked.

'I found her with a farmwife who thought she had made a bargain. Such a fine horse at such a ridiculous price . . . It was only later that she found out that no one could get near the poor creature unless it had been drugged with poppy juice – the way the trader had done.'

'Did you find him, then – the horse trader?'

'Yes. But he wouldn't say much. And in Kernland I have no standing. By law, all I can do is ask. Politely.' He took a long swallow of his beer, soaked a bit of bread in the stew and raised his voice. 'Have any of you heard of a man or a woman called Ermine?'

Kat went very still. So did Cornelius. But Tess, who knew nothing, merely shook her head.

'No. Not from around these parts, I'd say. Not with a name like that.'

Cornelius was seated at a table to the rear, fixing Brighella's halter. His hands had stopped their movement the moment he had heard Ermine's name. Now he looked at Kat across the length of the common room, and she knew what he was thinking: *You promised me you would be silent.*

Kat bit her lip.

'Does this . . . Ermine . . . have anything to do with Dorissa's – I mean, if Dorissa is dead?'

Simon bit into the stew-soaked bread, chewed and swallowed, before answering her.

'I can't be sure,' he said finally. 'But Dorissa came here to look for him, or her.'

You promised. She didn't look at Cornelius again. But neither did she tell Simon about Karel, Saratown and Ermine. She couldn't go back on her word. It was the only time she had ever promised him anything. 'On your life,' had been Ermine's words. If she broke her silence, Ermine's people might try to kill Cornelius.

Her throat felt raw. She couldn't break her promise. But could she cover up a secret that might have cost Dorissa's life? Might have. *Might* have. Simon didn't know. He wasn't certain. And she had promised . . . She got up abruptly. Simon looked up at her.

'I have to see to the horses,' she said, and fled from the room.

Blackie was gone, sold by Aren somewhere up north. And at the moment she did not feel like seeing either of the two hellhorses, Grizel or Frost. She ended up in Brighella's stall, giving the old mare a grooming she didn't truly need. She hadn't been at it very long when she heard Cornelius's steps. He wasn't angry. There was no threat in the way he

152

walked. He went straight to Brighella's stall, as if he knew in advance where he would find her.

'If Ermine killed that Silver . . . if you find out that that's the way of it . . . then you must do what you think is right.' Calmly, he changed Brighella's makeshift halter for the one he had repaired.

'Thank you,' said Kat. But she was not sure that made things any easier. It all came down to her now. Her choice. Her responsibility.

Cornelius nodded briefly. In the twilight gloom of the stable she couldn't see his face properly, only his outline. He gave Brighella's neck a quick pat. Then he left.

'Thank you,' she muttered under her breath. 'I said thank you. Now all we need is for him to say he's sorry.'

And then she realized that perhaps that was what he had just done.

'Simon?'

He sat so still that Kat was wondering whether he had fallen asleep at the table, with the hood of his cloak shadowing his face and his head resting against the wall. But his eyes were open, and when she whispered his name, he straightened in his seat.

'Yes?'

'Simon . . . Why did you become a Silver?'

He rubbed his eyes with his good hand. 'Long story,' he said.

'I've got the time.'

He looked at her for a while. It was late now, and only a single lamp had been left burning in the common room. Beneath the hood, his face was all shadows. His eyes glinted faintly, but apart from that only his mouth and chin were clearly visible.

'Did your mother read the prenticeship letter?'

Kat nodded.

'What does she say?'

'That it's up to me.'

'And you still want to come with me to Breda?'

'Yes.' Her voice shook a tiny bit, but not because she was uncertain of her decision. It was because of Ermine. Because of Cornelius's secret that had now become hers. She could tell that it would be hard to carry around something that Simon wasn't supposed to know about. He had a way of looking at you, so calmly, just waiting . . . the words wanted to come trickling out, and she had to bite her lip to stop them.

Simon leaned forward so that his face disappeared completely into the shadows of the hood.

'I'm from Joss,' he said. 'We're used to drifting, men and women both. Most of us spend our entire lives wandering the plains, from winter grazing to summer pastures and back again. I was born in a tent. But my youngest brother was born in a Resting Place. And if there hadn't been bredinari in Joss back then, he wouldn't have been born at all.'

Simon raised his cup. It had only water in it now. When the pain from his hand grew bad, he would bring out a

154

small white pipe and smoke something which had a sweet
and spicy scent, and when he did that, he did not drink, not
even the weakest beer Tess had to offer.

'One summer there had been hardly any rain, and many
of our usual watering holes had dried out. When we finally
found one that still had some water in it, the animals drank
deeply. And a few hours later, they began to die.'

She couldn't see his face, but his voice had taken on
that dry, flat tone she had come to know quite well. She
was beginning to realize that the more he felt, the less he
showed it.

'A lot of people died too. My aunt and both her
husbands. Two of my cousins. But the animals suffered
most, because they had drunk more than we had. All our
horses died, and nearly all the sheep. The goats did a little
better, but even among them there were hardly any standing in the end – they just lay there in the dust, gasping and
trembling and refusing to get up.'

Simon took a long, slow swallow of the clear sweet
water from the inn's well.

'Some said it must be the Varanians who had poisoned
us. They had done so in the past, although that is a very
long time ago, now. My grandfather said that the water in
that hole had never been quite sweet, and that the heat had
probably turned it bad. It made little difference in the end.
All our animals were sick or dead, and we were stuck next
to a water hole we didn't dare drink from. It looked as if we
were all going to die, of sickness or of thirst. I was eight
years old. I still dream of it sometimes. I'm on fire, burning

everywhere, stomach, eyes, and throat, and the animals are lying in the dust, dying. Some of the horses went wild with pain, screaming almost like children. Finally we started killing them ourselves, to put an end to their agony. And in our tent, my mother lay with her legs apart under the sheet, groaning. She was in labour, but too weak for it. It was as if everything else about her had dried up, and all that was left was that belly, that enormous swollen belly. And inside it, my brother was fighting to be born.'

Simon's voice was as flat as ever, but the hand holding the cup had gone white around the knuckles.

'The sun burned so hotly that the plains were one big shimmering haze. And in that haze, in the middle of it, we could suddenly see something shining like silver.' Simon gave an odd little laugh. 'In the stories of the clans, Death is a rider who lifts you up behind him and takes you away. When I saw this silver horse come out of the shimmering, I thought I was dying, because I couldn't imagine that the rider of such a horse could be a real human being. But that was how I met my first bredinari. His name was Esa, and he had come all the way from Fulmark. In no time at all, it seemed, we were all at Esa's Resting Place, and Esa and his people were taking care of the sick, and of the surviving animals. My mother was given water and salt and sugar and strange herbs, and gave birth to my brother. It can't really have happened that quickly, but that was how it seemed, perhaps because I was ill with fever. One minute I saw Esa through the haze, the next we were at the Resting Place, and my mother was cradling this howling bluish-pink little monster in her arms. I had never even been inside a house before. I couldn't get over the *noise* it made when you walked on a floor. There was a tube in the kitchen that spilled water into a sink when you pulled on a lever. And a special little house just for peeing in! The whole thing seemed so magical to me that I sometimes wondered whether we had all been enchanted. And the hellhorses were the most magical thing of all. There were six of them, and I learned their names by heart and sang them to myself: Zephyr, Meretire and Rain, Silkie, Whisper and Grizel.'

He caught Kat's question even before she had time to speak it. 'No, not my Grizel. But what else should I call my hellhorse when I finally managed to bond one? Esa's Grizel has long since gone back to the breeding fields.'

He took another slow swallow from the cup.

'But there you are. That's why. I wanted to be such a Rider, someone who came out of the shimmery haze on a silver horse, and saved people from death.'

'So do I,' said Kat very softly.

But Simon laughed, his voice a little blurred and hoarse.

'Ah, but Katriona, my darling. It's not like that at all. In most of the border provinces there is hardly a Resting Place left. And I spend far too much of my time playing messenger boy for rich city families, who think that anything of importance in this country happens within the eight walls of Breda City.'

'You're nobody's messenger boy now,' said Kat fiercely. 'That's not what you are doing now!'

'No,' he murmured. 'What I'm doing now is bringing the hellhorse of a dead friend back to the City.'

'Don't you believe in it any more?' asked Kat. 'The shimmery haze and all that?'

At first he was silent.

'Yes,' he finally said, 'I suppose I still do, in spite of everything. Some of us do go out to places like Joss and Grana and Three Valleys. And there are still people at the Castle who care about what happens outside the heartlands.'

'That's good enough for me,' said Kat, taking his empty cup. 'Right now you're tired, and your hand hurts, and you're thinking about Dorissa. You'll feel better in the morning. Come on, I'll help you upstairs.'

'I don't need any help,' he said. But he did. He was tired and had had too much of pain, in both his mind and his body, and perhaps also too much of what was in the little white pipe. Kat draped his arm across her shoulder and supported him up the stairs to the room Tess had given him.

'Sleep,' she said, drawing off his boots. 'You need it.'

'Frost,' he muttered. 'She'll be climbing the walls. I had better . . .'

'I'll do it,' Kat said firmly, pushing him back on to the bed. She covered him with the blanket and blew out the candle. He made one brief sound, halfway between a cough and a snore. She knew he would be asleep in seconds.

She went down the stairs in the dark. The steps felt worn and familiar under her feet – she knew each crack and each creaking board by heart. From the hook under the scullery stairs she took the lantern they used in the barn, and lit it. Then she stepped into her old clogs that Mattie had probably inherited by now and trudged across the yard to the stable.

The horses turned their heads sleepily when she entered. They were not used to such late visits. Grizel put her head over the door of her stall, blowing softly down her nose. Frost made no move at all. She stood there, head drooping, and had not touched her oats.

'Hey, horsey . . .' murmured Kat. 'Why aren't you eating? Are you asleep?'

No, Frost was not asleep. The nostrils flared, and the orange eyes reflected the light like a cat's. Other than that, though, there was little left of the glorious creature Kat had stolen her morning's ride on nearly nine months ago. Kat thought back to that day, to sunlight and bright dews and a silvery body so hot it almost seared you. She thought of Dorissa and Ermine. Of Cornelius. Of Simon and everything he had said tonight.

'Did Ermine do this?' she whispered at Frost. 'I have to think about this. I have to think about it very carefully before I say anything.'

The mare lowered its head even more and closed its hunter's eyes. Kat checked that the water bucket was full and that there was nothing wrong with the oats. Then she took the lantern and stepped back out into the yard. It was a warm and quiet night, and the moon hung above the roof of the inn, huge and glowing orange, almost like Frost's and Grizel's eyes.

Tess was right. She couldn't stay here all her life. She had long tough Crowfoot roots, just like Tess and Mattie and the rest. But there was also something in her that yearned for more, for other sights and other places. She would not be satisfied living her life in the same pattern, year in, year out. There was so much she hadn't seen. So much she hardly knew existed. Simon's shimmering plains, the wayfarers and their caravans, the City, the hellhorses . . . It was time to leave. Time to become something more than Teresa Innkeeper's red-haired daughter.

She headed back to the inn. For a second, she was startled by the sight of someone standing in the open door. But it was only Tess, Tess with her big black shawl around her shoulders.

'You're up late,' she said softly.

'I was talking to Simon, and then I had to check on Frost.' Kat looked up at the orange moon. 'And then I just stood there for a while, thinking.'

Tess nodded, as if she knew perfectly well what kind of thoughts one thinks when looking at orange-golden moons.

'And have you made up your mind, then?'

'Yes. We leave as soon as Simon is up to it.'

'For Breda?'

'Yes,' said Kat. 'For the City.'

Tess took Kat's face between her hands. 'Do you know, child, that I have always wanted to see the City?' she said. 'Always.'

Her eyes were very dark and alive, and Kat could suddenly picture a much younger Tess, a Tess almost her own age. A Tess yearning for other places, other sights, like she did. But Tess had never left the Vale, nor ever would. Strange places came to her only with the men, the travelling men who spoke with a foreign ring to their voices, and bore strange scents and stories and tastes with them to the inn.

She kissed Kat's forehead. Her lips were very warm.

'Come back and tell me,' she said. 'Come back every once in a while, and tell me about everything you've seen.'

'I will,' said Kat. 'I promise.' And she rested her head against her mother's shoulder, knowing that this time she was not being sent away. This time she was leaving because she herself had chosen it so.

BREDA

The sun had risen, but a heavy mist clung to everything, as if a cloud had drifted down to settle around
them. Kat's blanket felt heavy and clammy with dew. The
smell of hay was so strong it tickled her nostrils as she lay,
floating somewhere between sleep and wakefulness. In her
dreams, her mother gave her a glacier crowfoot, saying:
'Will you look at the roots on this thing! But we managed to
pull them up, all the same.' Kat looked at the long, hairy
roots, brown and pale at the same time, and suddenly she
felt a stab of pain, and the taste of blood filled her mouth. It
took her a moment to realize what had happened: she had
clenched her teeth so hard that her last baby tooth, a canine,
had finally come loose and was hanging on by only a few
bloody threads.

She fingered the tooth, rocking it experimentally from
side to side. Ouch! It would probably be better just to get it
over with. Steeling herself, she tugged at it, once, twice . . .
and finally the last stubborn root gave up, and the tooth

came out. Holding it in her palm, she explored the new gap with her tongue. Damn. Why did it have to happen now? Now she would be riding into the City looking like some gap-toothed little kid. It wasn't fair. Mattie had lost all her milk teeth months ago, and she was a year younger than Kat!

There was a rustle in the hay. Beside her, Simon sat up. With the blanket over his head like a shawl, he looked like somebody's grandmother.

'You look like an old woman,' she said, unthinkingly. And of course he spotted the gap right away.

'Kat! You've lost a tooth!'

'I know,' she muttered darkly, clutching the offending canine. Why now?

'I would have thought you'd be finished with that stuff ages ago,' he said, making everything much worse.

'Well, I'm not,' she said sullenly, freeing herself from the clammy blanket. She got to her feet, shivering more at the wetness than at the cold.

'Seeing that you're up,' said Simon teasingly, 'you might go and get us the breakfast Elina promised us.'

Without another word, Kat turned her back on him and began trudging downhill towards the farm.

Elina Farmwife had greeted Simon with a hug and a kiss on the cheek the night before, and she had been bewildered and almost offended that they would not sleep in the farm-house. Simon had had to explain that one of the hellhorses could no longer bear to be near too many people at once.

'Sweet Our Lady,' said Elina. 'What has happened to it? And what have you done to your hand?'

But Simon would not tell her that. 'You know how it is with hellhorses,' he said to her vaguely. 'They get like that sometimes. And we'll be very comfortable in one of your haystacks.'

This morning Elina was flushed and busy, for the farm was a big one, and many rumbling morning bellies had to be satisfied. There was a great hissing of tea kettles and rattling of pans, and a smell of new bread that caused a stab of longing in Kat's chest, a longing for Tad and Mama and the familiar bustle of the Crowfoot Inn kitchens. She stood there patiently, waiting to be noticed, and Elina's eyes passed right over her several times before finally taking in her presence.

'Oh, it's the little bredinari,' said Elina suddenly, and Kat did not know whether to be flattered or offended. The 'little' stung, but being called a bredinari was quite a promotion for someone who had yet to set foot across the threshold of the Akademia Bredinari, where the Silvers were trained.

'Sit down, sit down, I'll get you your breakfast. Did you sleep well? I don't know what Simon Jossa is thinking of, dragging a young girl all over the country like that, and sleeping in haystacks! But he has a sound heart, so he has. I should know. Wasn't much older than you, was he, first time he sat at this table. Kosio, my eldest, used to bring him

SILVERHORSE

here on Memory Days, did he tell you that? And sometimes for the Midwinter Holiday too, when the weather was too rough for him to travel all the way to Joss. Kosio is a bredinari too, now, mostly up Luna way. But he does get back here for the holidays still, most years. Do you like goat's cheese?'

Kat nodded, a bit overwhelmed by the tide of words, and watched as Elina added a big brown round of cheese to the small mountain of food she was packing for them.

'Thank you, maestra,' she said politely. And was astonished to see Elina throw back her head and laugh.

'Me? Maestra? Whatever gave you that idea?'

'But . . . but aren't you the farmwife here?'

'Oh, I'm that right enough. Ever since my mother passed away, may Our Lady keep and guard her. But maestra? What made you think that? Do I look like a grand lady to you?'

No, Elina certainly did not match Kat's ideas of what grand ladies looked like. But what did that have to do with anything?

'But if you're the farmwife . . .' she said stubbornly.

Elina's busy hands grew still for a moment. She gazed at Kat for a while.

'Where're you from?' she asked.

'Three Valleys,' said Kat, and was annoyed to feel heat rising in her cheeks. There was nothing to blush about. Was there?

Elina nodded, as if in confirmation.

'Listen, girlie,' she said kindly. 'I think you know very

166

little about the City our Simon is dragging you into. It's not much like the borders. There are great families here, not just the Seven, but others too, others who have guarded their power over the land and the people on it for a long time. Too long, it may be, but that's another matter. Yes, I am the farmwife here. But my maestra is Sofia Esocine, head of the Esocine clan. This farm and the next, and the six beyond that, all lie on ancient Esocine lands, lands that have been in the family's keeping since the days of Sari Moon-Daughter.'

'But how can she . . . how can she be a proper maestra to that much land? That many people?'

'She just is,' said Elina. 'And I am her farmwife. And that is fine by me.'

Kat trudged across the stubble of the hayfield, her head churning with uncomfortable thoughts. How could one woman be a maestra to so much, to places she didn't even live in? It was like Bria, fostering so many girls, many more than she could ever be a proper foster-mother to. Kat wasn't sure she liked the idea. But on the other hand . . . the Bredani was a sort of maestra to the whole country, wasn't she? Not that you felt it much. At least not in Three Valleys. Perhaps her care and her ruling would be more noticeable here, so close to where she actually lived. Kat took a deep breath and tongued the gap where her canine used to be. Was Elina right? Did she know too little about the life she would be leading from now on? Simon had been telling her that all along. 'You don't know what you're getting into.'

But she had thought mostly of the hellhorses, of riding a beautiful silver mare of her own all over the country, seeing things and doing things, instead of spending her entire life hunched over a dye vat. Or a soup pot, for that matter.

To be a bredinari was to be in the service of the Bredani. Did that mean Kat would actually see her? The idea caused a flutter of unease in her stomach, and she unconsciously ran her free hand over her breeches, to rub away some of the grime. She couldn't, somehow, picture herself and the Bredani in one room. But serving someone you never even saw – that might be even stranger.

Despite his broken hand, Simon had managed to saddle both Grizel and Rane, Kat's brown gelding, by the time Kat returned with the food. He had long since cut away much of the rigid glove-like bandage Keri Herbwife had put on his hand, the better to be able to move his fingers, but on most of their journey he had left such chores to Kat's two healthy hands. Perhaps he was impatient because he reckoned they could reach Breda City today.

Frost stood next to Grizel, head and neck drooping, and Kat felt a quick stab of regret, thinking about the day last autumn when she had seen Frost for the first time. It had seemed to her that the hellhorse, the first she had ever seen, belonged not to the real world of the sodden, rain-swept yard behind the inn, but to some fairy-tale dream. Then Frost had been blazing not only with the incredible silver shimmer of her coat, but also with the fierceness of her spirit. Today, the sheen of the coat was almost unchanged, but the horse inside had turned into a different creature altogether, a hag-ridden wretch with no strength or courage to do anything more than stumble blindly from one day to the next. Some of it was due to the drug, the dulling herb essences Simon added to Frost's water bucket twice a day. Kat was sorry for the dullness it brought, but without it they would not have made it this far. Once, when they had been spending the night in the stable of an inn, Kat had woken to such a kicking, screaming chaos that she thought for a moment that the stable was on fire. A man had come tumbling out of the loose box Frost and Grizel shared, clutching his forehead with one hand and trying to hold up his trousers with the other. Blood was pouring down his face, and as Kat watched, his grip on his trousers slipped and he fell, flat on his stomach in the stable muck, his naked buttocks glistening palely in the darkness. It would have been comical, except that he was roaring in such agony that one could tell he was wild with pain and in terror for his life. And there was absolutely no comedy in the sight of Frost rearing in the doorway, screaming in fury and intent on plummeting hard hooves into a soft human body.

That man would probably have died, if not for Simon's habit of sleeping near the horses. It was Simon who had had the presence of mind to snatch up a water bucket and fling the icy contents into Frost's face, so that she dropped down and stood shivering and splay-footed, trying to shake the water from her ears. And it was Simon who got a rope around her neck and led her back into the stall before she could do more harm.

The man, it seemed, had been too drunk to find the

latrines and had chosen instead the worst possible stall for his errand. In the darkness, he had knocked into Frost, startling both the hellhorse and himself, and his stumbling and shouting and the smell of his fear had excited the madness in Frost's confused mind. Simon had to soothe the man with soft words and hard cash before he stopped demanding the immediate death of 'the mad monster'.

That had been the last time they had dared spend the night so close to other people. Of the other towns they had passed on the way, Kat had caught only hurried glimpses.

'That took you a while,' said Simon, catching sight of her.

'Elina . . .'

'I know.' Simon smiled. 'She does talk. But she has a kind heart. Her son was at the Academy with me, did she tell you? Kosio. He's a bredinari too.'

'Yes, she said.' Kat bit into one of the still-warm bread rolls Elina had given her. The other she tossed to Simon. 'Here. Catch.'

He caught it clumsily with his good hand.

'We can eat as we ride,' he said. 'I want to reach the City before sundown, and I'm not sure how quickly Frost will let us move.'

They reached Breda in the late afternoon. Sunlight slanted steeply between walls daubed mostly in ochre and red, and dust motes danced in the light. There were people everywhere. Pedlars' voices rose, hawking their wares, and the air was thick with charcoal smoke and grease, and with the stench and frightened roars and braying of cattle and sheep. There were so many houses and so many people that Kat couldn't see anything except city.

'Cattle market,' said Simon. 'Not the City's most pleasantly scented quarter.'

Kat barely heard him. She looked straight ahead between Rane's ears, and her hands, clutching the reins, were white-knuckled. There's nothing to be scared of, she told herself. Absolutely nothing. So why was her stomach roiling so? She was afraid to look anywhere but straight ahead, as if she might lose her balance if she did. She had never imagined that so many people, so many houses, could be in one place. It was like a forest, a forest of brick and beams, a landscape made from roofs and walls and muddy stony street canyons flooded with streaming crowds. Only the road she and Simon were on, the Castle Road, was free of crowding, because only those with Castle business were allowed to use it.

Suddenly there was a rapid clatter of hooves, and a rider came sweeping round the bend, almost at a full gallop. Simon put his hand on Frost's neck, but she still spooked, blocking the road with her quarters so that the oncoming rider had to haul back on the reins and brake his horse abruptly. It was a Silver, in grey leathers and a blue cloak just like Simon's, and he appeared to be in a hurry.

'Watch your step, you damn fool—' began the rider. Then he recognized Simon. 'Jossa! Is . . . Jossa, is that Frost?'

Simon nodded, and his face had gone stiff and

unreadable again, the way it always did when strong emotions moved him.

'And . . . Dorissa?'

'I found only Frost.'

The rider reached out as if to touch Simon's arm, but then let his hand drop on to his leather-clad thigh with a slap. 'I'm riding post-haste,' he said. 'To Castel Strigius, so I won't be back until tomorrow night. If they unbridle Frost tomorrow, will you pay my respects for me?'

Simon nodded briefly. The rider looked as if he meant to say more, but then he shook his head and edged his hell-horse around Frost. 'I have to go,' he called over his shoulder, already halfway round the next bend.

Simon and Kat rode on up the Castle Road, past the cattle market, past Tannery Row which smelled even worse, past carpenters' shops and smithies and barrel-makers, carters and tinkers, potters and coppersmiths . . . there seemed to be no end to it. Gradually, the artisans' quarters gave way to grander streets with shops selling cloth and spices, silverware and jewellery, and even books. Kat looked at the signs and thought of Tad as she spelled her way through their swirly letters. Could everyone read here? Surely not. But she was suddenly very glad of Tad's careful lessons, teaching her her letters by the kitchen fireplace with a charred stick for a pencil.

Tall walls rose on both sides of the road now, with gardens behind them, judging from the treetops and the sweet scent of blossoms and herbs. Once, Kat heard children's voices, laughter and running feet.

'Who lives here?' she asked Simon.

'The Old Families. The Seven. Around here mostly Esocine and Capra.'

And then they were there. The walls of Breda Castle rose like mountains above them, grey and craggy and striped with chalky runnels from green copper pipes. The sound of the horses' hooves echoed inside the gate, which was like a long dark tunnel under the walls. It was an eerie, underground sound, and Rane laid back his ears and bunched his quarters, wanting to spook but not quite daring to. But ahead of them sunlight beckoned, and then they were in a wide cobbled courtyard with a large stone trough in the centre. Grizel headed straight for the trough and buried her muzzle in the water. Simon gave her neck a quick pat, and slid to the ground.

A small, bow-legged man appeared from one of the buildings surrounding the courtyard.

'Jossa!' he said, a grin on his wrinkled face. 'About time!' And then he noticed Frost, and the grin faded. Slowly he approached the riderless hellhorse. He ran his hand across the still brilliant neck, but the mare moved not a muscle. Head hanging, it seemed not to notice its surroundings at all.

The man gave Simon a questioning look, but perhaps the stillness in Simon's face was answer enough. At any rate, he did not voice his question. He merely took Frost's reins and led her towards the open door to the stables.

'Come on, lass,' he muttered. 'At least you're home now.'

More people appeared. Some took Grizel, others Rane. Simon thrust his good hand into the water and rubbed it quickly over his face. Then he took Kat by the arm.

'Come on,' he said. 'I have to report, and they'll probably want your testimony too.'

Kat had to wait in a small whitewashed antechamber while Simon gave his report. It took a long time. The pale stripe of sunlight on the floor crept slowly towards her feet, up her legs, and over her head, and then disappeared entirely. From the other side of the heavy, dark door she could hear only the barest hint of voices, like rustling leaves. Finally the door opened, and a woman dressed in grey bredinari leathers asked her to enter.

She stood on a smooth stone floor, faced with eight people she had never seen before in her life. A man sat behind a large table, seven other men and women were seated in chairs along the walls. Simon was standing by the door. The stillness now went all through his body.

The man got up from behind the table and approached her. He was tall, with smooth black hair and eyes of an unusually bright blue, and there was something about him, something that made Kat feel she ought to go down on one knee, at least, if not both.

'My name is Alvar Alcedina,' he said, 'and I am the DomPrimus of the bredinari, the commander-in-chief. Rider Jossa may have told you that.'

No, Simon had not. Or he had perhaps mentioned the

name, but he had said nothing about what this Alcedina was *like*, nothing about ice-blue eyes that went right through you, and a voice that made you want to kneel.

'In important matters I am guided by my staff council, the ladies and gentlemen you see around you.' He raised a hand in their direction, but Kat had no attention to spare for more ordinary people. 'Tell us, Katriona, how you met Rider Granes.'

Granes? She knew nobody called Granes, did she?

'Dorissa,' prompted Simon, just as she herself realized who this Rider Granes had to be.

'She came to my mother's inn . . .' began Kat, trying not to open her mouth too widely and display the missing tooth. She told them about her meeting with Frost and Dorissa, about the stolen ride, about everything Dorissa had told her. About the silver coin – the medallion that Simon called a 'token'. She had to bring it out and hand it to Alcedina, who passed it on to a woman he called Signator Debra.

'Yes,' she said, after a brief examination. 'It does, indeed, bear Granes's code. There is no doubt of its provenance.'

'Thank you, Katriona,' said Alcedina. 'There is just one more test to pass now.' And he nodded at one of the councillors, an old man with a head as bald as an egg.

The old man rose and moved to stand just in front of Kat. She rubbed her hands nervously on her breeches. What sort of test? He was not dressed in grey leathers, but in a pale blue tunic that came all the way to his knees.

'Hold out your hand,' he said.

Kat did as he said. For a brief moment she thought of her brothers and the kind of pranks that would have followed such obedience – a lizard or a spider, or something gross and slimy from the pond. But what was put in her palm now was just an iron ball, cold and smooth, and heavy enough to be solid. She looked at it in confusion.

'Look at me, Katriona,' he said softly. 'Look into my eyes.'

A shudder went through her as she suddenly realized what he must be. A magus. A sorcerer capable of looking into people's heads and seeing the thoughts hiding there, if rumours were true. Unwillingly, she raised her eyes to his. His were blue, like Alcedina's, no, not quite like Alcedina's, more sort of green, or grey, or perhaps brown . . . red? Could they be red? Red like the eyes of the ermine . . . There was a brief sting of heat from the iron ball, just for a second, then it was cool once more. Very distantly, she heard her own voice talking, telling them once more of her meeting with Dorissa and the medallion she had been given.

'That will do, Ahlert,' said the wonderful Alcedina with the wonderful blue eyes, and a dry old hand loosened her grip on the iron sphere and relieved her of it. Her hand rose slowly in the air in front of her, as if suddenly adrift, now that the iron did not weigh it down.

'That is all, Katriona,' said the old man (Ahlert, was it?), and she came to her proper senses very suddenly and realized that they had been testing her to see if she was lying. Did they think she had stolen the medallion? Was that what they thought?

'I'm not lying,' she said angrily, forgetting all about her missing tooth. 'You had no reason to do this!'

'Calm yourself,' said Alcedina. 'We do not know you, so how else to test your honesty? Now we know you speak the truth. Now we *know* that you are honest.'

She said no more, but her urge to kneel to him had disappeared entirely. She glanced at Simon, and it seemed to her that she saw a faint smile hovering on his lips.

'Perhaps I may be permitted to point out that it has now been proven that Rider Granes considered Katriona a suitable candidate for the Academy,' he said. 'Having seen her conduct with Frost and my own Grizel, I wholly support Rider Granes's estimation. Katriona may become an excellent bredinari.'

DomPrimus Alcedina did not answer right away. Anger still sang in Kat's veins. They had doubted her word. They had put her through sorcery – sorcery! – to see if she was lying. Very straight and stiff with anger, she bore his inspection, and did not lower her eyes even though she had a feeling his ice-blue gaze was taking in every defiant line of her body, every unevenly sawn-off curl, every speck of dust on her worn jerkin.

'Very well,' he finally said. 'If the papers are in order, she may start tomorrow.'

He nodded briefly. Not until Simon touched her arm did she realize that it was a sign of dismissal.

*

'Did you know they were going to do that?' she asked Simon angrily, the minute the door had closed behind them. 'Did you know they were going to set that disgusting *sorcerer* on me?'

'Ahlert is not disgusting. He is actually quite a decent human being,' said Simon. 'But no, I didn't know they were going to subject you to that. Perhaps I should have guessed. People like Alcedina trust no one they're not related to, and even then they're cautious.'

'What would have happened if I had lied?'

'The iron ball would have become too hot for you to hold. And they probably wouldn't have let you into the Academy. Wait, we turn left here . . .'

Up a flight of stairs, across a hall and out of a door. They were outside again, in an open gallery overlooking a court-yard, but not the courtyard where they had left the horses. Kat had no idea where she was and would never have been able to find her way out. What happened to visitors who got lost here? Did they die from thirst and hunger somewhere in the upper galleries? Kat could practically see them, pale transparent ghosts still wandering the long corridors, whispering, 'Out. Let me out . . .' though death had long since stopped their hearts and withered their tongues . . .

'Simon – Simon, wait . . . Don't . . . don't leave me behind.'

He paused. 'I wasn't planning to. What's the matter with you? Usually you're the one charging ahead, leaving *me* to catch up.'

'It's just – all those corridors, all those stairs. Such a

crazy way to build a place. How can any normal person find their way around?'

'You'll get the hang of it.' His fingers brushed her cheek, tucking a rebellious strand of red hair behind her ear. 'Once a girl has lost her baby teeth she can do just about anything . . .'

She whacked him across the chest with the back of her hand, hard enough for the slap to echo under the gallery arches. But what she felt was not really anger. His face, normally so expressionless, had cracked into a wide, teasing grin, and there had been something very comforting about the gentle touch of his fingers against her cheek. Perhaps she was finally learning how to let herself be teased just for fun.

'Why do they all call you Jossa?' she asked.

'Because I'm from Joss.'

'Yes, I know that, but why not just Simon?'

'I'm not the only Simon in the corps. There is a Simon Capra and a Simon Ursinus as well. But in any case, there is a certain formality here. More than you're used to, probably. You might have to put up with being called Trivallia.'

'Trivallia?'

'Border brats like you and me don't have fine old family names, now, do we? So we're generally named after the place we come from. You're from Three Valleys, and so you are Trivallia. Simple as that. And now, Prentice Trivallia, we need to get your name down in the school records so that they will give you a bed.'

*

179

Simon was right. When Clerk Angia entered Kat's name in the records, she wrote: 'Katriona Trivallia, eldest daughter to maestra Teresa di Ranunculi, South Vale, Three Valleys.' It was furthermore carefully noted that at her arrival she had brought to the school a brown mountain gelding answering to the name of Rane. She had to put her mark on a separate form, to say that Rane, in return for his keep, would be used in the service of the corps as the Stable Master saw fit.

'Do you know how to write your own name?' asked the Clerk of Records.

Kat nodded, and the Clerk handed her a pen. Kat printed 'Katriona' in careful letters. And then, after a short hesitation, she added this new and unfamiliar name: 'Trivallia'. It looked strange. But perhaps there was a truth in it. Here she would not be Katriona Teresa-Daughter, the innkeeper's girl. She now was what Simon had jokingly called her: Prentice Trivallia.

The Clerk strewed sand across the page to make the ink dry more quickly.

'Are you a fairly quiet person?' she asked, giving Kat a sidelong look.

'Quiet?'

'Not noisy, are you?'

'Err . . . no, I don't think so.'

'Is she, Jossa?'

Grinning, Simon scratched his jaw. 'About as quiet as a thunderstorm, I'd say. But she doesn't snore, or talk in her sleep, if that's what you mean. And she's not the type to throw wild parties either.'

'Very well. There is a spare room above the hospital wing, a nice one with a view of the South Field. It's a bit of a walk to the girls' baths, but it's the best we can do now that the Lodge Brothers have taken over the old girls' wing.' Disapproval at this state of affairs came across very strongly. Kat wondered what the Lodge Brothers were.

'It'll be fine, I'm sure,' said Simon. 'Come on, Kat, I'll show you around.'

'No, you will *not*, Simon Jossa,' said the Clerk. 'You will go straight to Master Rodrian to have that hand taken care of – what on earth have you done to it? And then you will go to the baths, to the dining hall, and to bed. Hasn't anyone noticed that you are dead on your feet?'

The Clerk pushed back her chair and rose to her feet. She put a hand on Simon's shoulder, forestalling objections. 'So. Go now. I shall take care of young Trivallia.'

'Kat. She is used to being called Kat . . .' muttered Simon, and Kat could suddenly see that Clerk Angia was right. Simon looked grey with tiredness, and the fingers poking from the ill-treated bandage were swollen and bluish-black at the base.

'Go on, Simon,' she said quickly. 'I'll see you in the morning.'

He nodded vaguely, and Clerk Angia gave him a gentle push in the direction of the door.

'Off you go, then. And don't fall down the stairs.'

*

The most amazing thing about Breda was small enough to fit inside Kat's closed fist. It was a key. The key to Kat's own room. To a door she could lock, from the inside and outside.

She sat in front of her very own desk and looked out of her very own window across a field where more than thirty hellhorse mares were grazing in the evening twilight. Some of them had foals, black-coated and surprisingly normal-looking, except for being even more rangy and spindly-legged than ordinary foals. Kat looked at these with particular proprietory interest. Perhaps one of those gangly youngsters would grow up to be hers. Her very own hellhorse . . .

She yawned. Suddenly she felt completely unable to keep her eyes open. She rose from her chair and crossed the narrow space to the alcove where she was to sleep, tonight and perhaps for the next five or six years. A mattress stuffed with wool looked very inviting. Clerk Angia had ordered quilts and pillows to be brought from the stores and had provided her with a washbasin from the hospital ward downstairs, 'for the times when it is just too far to walk to the baths, dear.' Clerk Angia, on the whole, had been very kind and helpful and almost grandmotherly, in her own slightly distant way.

Gratefully, Kat snuggled under the quilts and let her head sink on to the pillows. She was so tired that her whole body was buzzing like a hornet's nest. Images flashed through her head: Elina Farmwife's laughter, the smell of new bread, Alcedina's kingfisher-blue eyes. Ahlert and his vile iron ball, mad Frost and the bare-buttocked man, Rane baulking in the dark gateway . . .

The door was ajar, and Clerk Angia's head was poking through it.

'Kat? Kat, are you awake?'

Kat heard, but her lips were thick with sleep, and it felt like too much effort to answer.

'The girl is asleep. There you are, Simon, she is perfectly fine. And you are going to bed too!'

'Yes, all right,' said Simon appeasingly.

The door closed softly, and the voices grew more muffled.

'I do hope she can stand up for herself,' said the Clerk. 'She seemed a bit quiet.'

Simon laughed softly. 'First appearances can be deceptive. If you want to worry, you had better worry about whether the school can stand up to Kat. There is enough sheer stubborn will packed into that little girl to equip three full-sized mules.'

'Little'? Kat gave a sleepy and offended snort. She'd give him 'little'. Tomorrow.

Later, she seemed to wake again. An owl and a polecat were crouched above her bed.

'Well? Is it her?' asked the owl harshly.

'Hush . . .' hissed the polecat. 'She wakes.'

The owl's face grew bigger. 'No,' it said. 'She sleeps. She dreams. She forgets. She has seen none of this.'

Kat slept on. She dreamt. But she did not entirely forget.

LEAVETAKING

She woke at dawn. The South Field was still hazy and untouched by the sun, but the treetops and the tall stone walls around it had their outlines traced in gold. In the grass beneath the trees dark horse-shaped shadows were dozing, heads low and hips cocked. She shivered a bit in the morning chill, her head still fuzzy with dreams. Ermine had been there, red eyes and sharp fangs, and other strange half-human beasts. An owl? Had there been an owl? She shook her head, and the dream memories scattered and melted like snowflakes when you tried to catch them in your hand.

She wasn't quite sure what to do with herself. The ward downstairs was quiet and probably empty. She was hungry and thirsty, and she desperately needed to pee. She had no idea where the kitchens were, or the latrines. No doubt Clerk Angia had told her yesterday, but Clerk Angia had told her about a thousand things, and at the moment she could hardly remember a single one.

185

She pushed aside the covers and got up. If she couldn't find the latrines, there was probably a bush somewhere that would take no harm from a bit of unauthorized watering. She really, *really* had to pee. She found her jerkin and put it on, but where were her boots? She seemed to remember leaving them at the foot of the alcove, but they weren't there now, and she really couldn't spend more time looking, or she'd have an accident. It was summer still, wasn't it? She could go barefoot – she used to do that all the time at home. She opened her door and peered into the corridor outside. Left or right? She had a feeling she should go left, and padded along to the stairway at the end. The stone steps spiralled downwards into deep gloom, and she had to feel her way, step by step. At the bottom there were three doors, and she chose the middle one, guided by a vague memory that this was the one that led out into the open air. It did, or nearly so. A short hallway – the Clerk's office was some-where to the right, she seemed to remember, and at the end of it a door with a fanlight above it. Pushing it open, she found herself in the hospital gardens, immediately below her own window. The South Field had to be beyond that tall garden wall, but here, at ground level, she couldn't see it.

The hospital gardens were very tidy and well ordered, with little brick paths and plants in neat beds. There was a heady smell of mint and sage and other herbs, and here and there water trickled in ceramic gutters and canals. Kat did not pause to admire this cleverness – at the moment the sound simply reminded her just how badly she had to pee.

Finding a spot for it was not as easy as she had

imagined. Everything looked so terribly tidy that it felt very improper . . . In the end she opted for a corner by the wall, shielded by a large laurel. She unlaced her underpants, pulled up her shirt, and squatted, with a feeling of exquisite relief.

She could neither wash nor wipe herself properly, but she did what she could with a handful of leaves from the laurel bush. When she straightened up, lacing her pants again, she felt like a new and better person.

This feeling was short-lived.

'Hold still,' came a voice. 'I have a crossbow aimed your way.'

Kat froze. *Robbers? This close to the castle?*

'Come on out. Quietly, no funny moves.'

The voice was harsh and flat, a bit like Cornelius's, used to giving orders. Kat rubbed her palms nervously on her thighs, casting a wild look around for a way out. There was none.

'Come on out,' repeated the voice. 'I'm giving you a count of three, and then I want to see you clearly. Or I fire.'

There was a short pause. Kat was in no doubt that he meant what he said.

'One,' he counted. 'Two . . .'

Kat stepped forward. In front of her, a few beds away, was a shape that in the faint light of dawn looked merely dark and square. But the crossbow she could see quite clearly. As a matter of fact, she had her eyes so firmly fixed on it that she did not at first notice that he was not alone.

Not, that is, until somebody yelled, 'I've got him!' and wrapped an arm about her throat from behind.

She moved without thinking. Cornelius had taught his stepdaughters a few tricks, just in case. Not all the inn's patrons were perfectly behaved. She slammed her elbow into his body and felt it connect. There was a hoarse gasp, and the grip on her throat slackened. She seized her attacker's arm with both hands, went down on one knee and threw her shoulders forwards. She didn't get it quite right. The arm's owner did not receive a flying flip and fall: more a sort of forward stumble. But he did go down, and she flung herself on top of him, digging for any sort of target, eyes, ears or throat, anything that would *hurt*.

'Hold!'

The man with the crossbow. He wouldn't dare, she thought, he might hit his mate . . . but he sounded as if that was a risk he was willing to take. She rolled sideways and tried to haul her unlucky assailant around to use for a shield, but he was too heavy, and he was starting to recover from the elbow, and in any case it would not get her anywhere. There was no way she could escape them. Giving up, she just lay there, watching the crossbow man as he stepped around a bed of mint and allheal.

'Get away from him, Claudi,' he said in annoyance. 'And stop that nonsense.'

His mate Claudi stopped trying to draw the knife at his belt. Instead he obediently crawled a few feet to one side of Kat. His breathing was still strained, and it was a few minutes before he was able to climb to his feet. Kat got to her knees.

'No,' said the crossbow. 'Lie down again. On your belly.'

Kat felt a familiar rage stir. So that was what he wanted – for her to crawl at his feet? To grovel in the dirt like a drunkard or a slave? Over her dead body!

'All I have to do is scream,' she said, 'and you'll be dead men. You and your buddy both. Have you any idea how many guards this Castle has?'

She hoped he did. She certainly didn't.

For a moment the crossbow man stood completely still. Then his shoulders started to shake, and a strange wheezing sound emerged. It took a moment for her to realize that it was laughter.

'Get up,' he said. 'And scream if you want. But I think there are quite enough guards here already.'

Kat pushed her hair out of her eyes and stared at the man. Once she gave herself time to look, it was really quite obvious that he was wearing a uniform, even though it was not Silver grey like Simon's. She got to her feet slowly, wishing with all her heart that she could have disappeared into the ground instead. The guard crossed yet another herb bed and approached more closely.

'Who the hell are you?' he said. 'And what are you doing here?' And then, as he came quite close, 'Hey! *You're* not a boy.'

'My name is Katriona Teresa-Daughter . . .' and then she thought of the Records and corrected herself, 'I mean Katriona Trivallia. I've just become a Silver Prentice.'

189

'Well, that's a lie for a start,' hissed the unlucky Claudi. 'The Academy doesn't *take* peasant scum like you!'

'They do so!' she snarled without thinking. 'I mean . . . I'm no peasant!' But she could hear that she didn't speak the way they did. In Three Valleys people sort of hung on to the words more, at the back of the mouth, they didn't push everything to the front, all pointed and dry, the way they did it here. Their way was probably more fancy. After all, that had to be the way the Bredani spoke, didn't it? And as she stood there, in a worn old jerkin that had obviously been cut down to size, with mud on her bare legs and no doubt a few laurel leaves in her hair . . . well, she did not exactly feel like the Queen of Breda.

'Ola, can't you see she's trying to fool us?' said Claudi, turning to appeal to the other guard. 'A scarecrow like that at the Academy? Where's her uniform? And what is she doing, sneaking around the hospital gardens and hiding in the bushes? There's something funny going on.'

The other guard looked at her appraisingly. 'You don't actually look like a greyling,' he said. 'And you still haven't said what you're doing here, in the garden.'

Kat's cheeks felt hot enough to burst into flame. She would rather die than tell them that she had come down to find a bush to pee behind.

'I woke early,' she said. 'I wanted a bit of fresh air.'

'Behind the laurel? What, is the air particularly fresh right there?'

'She was probably looking for belladonna. Or mandrake!' said Claudi, before Kat had had time to come up with an answer for that one.

'Belladonna?' she said in bewilderment. 'What would I want with belladonna?'

'Come off it,' said Claudi. 'Think I don't know what they pay for that down at the Market? Or maybe it's for yourself. Look at her eyes. They're very dark, aren't they?'

'No, they're not,' Kat yelled, losing her temper entirely. 'I haven't taken anything, I was just taking a walk, and if you don't believe me you can ask Simon. Simon Jossa, or Angia, ask them!'

'Jossa! He takes more than belladonna if—'

'That'll do, lad,' Ola cut in. 'That kind of gossip you can keep to yourself. As for you, Trivallia, or whatever your name is . . . I think we'll just take a turn around Joss's quarters, so he can vouch for you. And maybe you can get him to tell you how to find the latrines . . .'

His wheezy laughter shook his entire body this time. Kat stared at the ground. She knew how red her face was. Even her ears were burning. But perhaps it was better than being accused of stealing belladonna from the hospital gardens. Perhaps.

Simon was very pale and looked somewhat dazed, but he told the guard that yes, he knew Katriona Trivallia, and yes, she had indeed been accepted at the Academy. Claudi scowled. He had obviously hoped that Simon would deny knowing her. But Ola grabbed his partner by the elbow and raised his other hand in a sort of salute.

'Back to the beat, then. Or a real thief might come along and clean out every 'toxicating plant in the garden. Or every keg in the cellars, more like. Good morrow!'

He led Claudi along in a fashion that might be friendly but also looked distinctly firm.

'Come on in,' said Simon, holding the door open. 'Sit.'

'I'm sorry to bother—' Kat began, embarrassed. But Simon cut her off with a wave of his good hand.

'Wait,' he said. 'I'm still asleep. I can't think.'

He stood there, looking about him, as if he could barely remember where he was supposed to be. The room was large and fairly bare. There was a bench, a desk, a chest and a fireplace, with two wickerwork armchairs in front of it. In a recess in the wall were set several shelves, now mostly empty. Through a doorway she could just make out a smaller chamber with a brick-built alcove almost identical to her own. Simon's cloak and his saddlebags were slung on top of the chest, still not unpacked. There were no decorations on the walls, but on the floor was a rug in glowing gold, rose madder and viridian green. It made her think of the carpet she had seen in Bria's big house at the Dyer's Yard, but this was actually more beautiful, she thought. She had to fight an urge to crouch down and caress it.

Simon went to the chest and dug out a glass beaker, which he set on the desk. The glass was thick and cloudy, but the beaker had a neat lid of porcelain and pewter and reminded her a bit of Cornelius's old tankard, the one she had smashed after she had realized that her mother would never send Cornelius away. The pain of that still stung.

But not this time, she reminded herself. This time, she had chosen for herself. And she would show Claudi, and everyone else who thought as he did, that 'peasant scum' *could* become Silvers!

Simon got a leather flask from his pack and held it awkwardly between his thighs in order to pull the cork with his good hand. He poured some of the contents into the beaker. Whatever it was, it was a deep, dark red, darker than wine, and redolent with herbs. He tilted the beaker and drank until it was empty.

'See if there's any water in the kettle,' he said.

Kat lifted the kettle, which sat on the ledge in front of the fireplace. Water squelched when she rattled it.

'Almost full,' she said. 'Shall I put it on?' A fire had already been laid out, all she had to do was light it.

Simon nodded. 'You do that,' he said. 'It's a cold enough morning.'

Kat didn't think so, despite her bare legs. Simon was wearing a grey and brown striped robe, like those she knew were common among the shepherds of Joss. It went all the way to the floor and had a pointed hood which was thrown back on his shoulders now. But he really did look cold. Keri Herbwife's glove had gone, she noticed. Instead the whole hand was covered in a thick, white bandage.

'Did they treat your hand for you?' she asked.

Simon looked at it. 'Yes. Or so they said. It felt more like mistreatment.' He sat down heavily in one of the wicker armchairs. 'Please light the fire, will you?'

Kat hurriedly did as he asked. The wood was dry and well arranged, with shavings, twigs and birchbark at the bottom, so that the flames caught hold quickly. She hung the kettle on the big cast iron hook, and it soon began to hiss and steam.

'There's a jar of tea in the chest. And a pot on the shelf there. You can make us a cup,' said Simon, not taking his eyes off the flames. He sat there, hunched in his chair, making no attempt to help her. It felt strange, after so many mornings of sharing chores. She eyed him uneasily. Was he ill? What was the matter with him? And why had he not wanted to talk more about the things Ola and Claudi had said?

'Simon . . .' she said hesitantly.

'Tea,' he said. 'Then talk.'

All right, thought Kat, that was plain enough. Shut up and make the tea, and then we'll see.

She found the jar and the teapot, both of them decorated with leaping horses in pale yellow, rose madder and viridian. From Joss, she guessed, like the rug and the robe. And like Simon. Did he miss the plains? And his family? She pulled the big cork out of the jar and put some of the dried leaves into the pot. There were some she knew, rosehip and blackcurrant, but also some she had never seen before, narrow black ones with a heady scent.

Once the water boiled, she swung the kettle off the fire and tipped water into the teapot. She set it on the ledge above the fireplace to brew. All the while, Simon sat there, not saying a word. But gradually his face became less tense. And only then did she realize that he had, quite simply, been in pain. So much pain that he could barely move and talk normally.

'Mugs on the shelf,' he said, pointing with his good hand.

She got them, and poured the tea.

'And the flask,' he said. 'Would you hand me that as well?'

She did, uncorking it before she gave it to him. He poured a shot of dark red liquid into the tea.

'Sacrilege,' he muttered. 'But need is a harsh master.'

'Can I taste that?' said Kat curiously, when the scent of wine and herbs once more filled the room. Simon shook his head.

'Better not,' he said, with a faint smile. 'Bad enough that I receive young female prentices alone, in my robes. I don't want to be accused of drugging you as well.'

Kat blushed for the umpteenth time that morning.

Simon grew more relaxed. A touch of colour returned to his wan face, perhaps because of the wine.

'Did anybody bother to tell you what is going to happen today?' he asked.

'Angia . . . that is to say, Clerk Angia . . . She said something about unbridling Frost.'

'And you, of course, understood none of that?'

Kat looked at her feet. 'I suppose you think I'm ignorant peasant scum as well,' she said darkly.

'Whoa . . . don't bite until it's called for. Who was unintelligent enough to call you that?'

'The guards. Claudi. He said they don't take scum like me at the Academy.'

'That only goes to show that he is more ignorant than you are. Seeing that you *have* been accepted. But you had better get used to hearing that tune. There are plenty of people, inside the corps and out, who think that border riff-raff like you and I have no business wearing the greys. And there are things about City life that you cannot know, if you happen to have grown up in Three Valleys. Or in Joss, for that matter. So Kat . . . my red-haired friend . . .' He reached out three fingers and pushed a curl off her forehead, 'Would you do me *and* yourself a favour, and not flatten every thick-head who calls you peasant scum? Poor Claudi was still moving rather stiffly.'

'That wasn't . . . that was because . . .' Kat sputtered. And blushed. Again. 'I thought they were robbers . . . the peasant thing, that wasn't till after . . . and anyway, I didn't hit him *that* hard . . .' She looked at him and stopped trying to explain. She could tell by the crinkles around his eyes that he was laughing inside. But then that inner smile suddenly disappeared and he became completely serious.

'Kat. I mean it. You have to learn to rule your temper, or you will make enemies here. And you cannot afford that.' He took a deep breath. 'As for the unbridling of Frost . . . today, when the sun is at its highest, Frost will be released into the breeding fields. Her service with the bredinari is over. And at the same time we take our leave of Dorissa.'

She could tell from the flatness of his voice that there were feelings here he did not want to reveal.

'So now . . . you and I dress in our best and go and show our respects. What they call the final honour. She has deserved more than that, and better, but it is all that we can give her now.'

The hard, crisp roll of the drums started up so suddenly that Kat was startled by it. The seven drummers pounded the drumskins only with their bare hands, yet still the sound was sharp and dry like the snapping of twigs in a thunderstorm. It echoed between the mountain and the castle walls and took its time escaping. At first the rhythm was rapid and fevered like a dance beat. Gradually, very gradually, it slowed, until each blow hung solitary in the air and made Kat uncertain whether this was the final one, or this, or *this*. And then it really was the last, and the long silence following was broken only by the piper's tune, pure and sweet as a young boy's voice. Kat blinked away tears, because she recognized the melody. She had heard it among the Wayfarers, she had heard Gelman Carter's youngest son singing it, that night by the fire on her journey from Crowfoot Inn to the Dyer's Yard. The words floated through her mind, though no one was singing now:

> But I know Our Lady is waiting
> In the Heartland, bright with sun
> When the road has reached its turning

And my travelling is done
Call me home, Milady, call me home
Let me lie upon your breast
Let me dwell in your own country
And know my Place of Rest.

Was that where Dorissa was now? In the Heartland. Home. Home where she had come from before she was born, home where she belonged now that life was over. Kat had heard Erold Smith tell it often enough, back home in the Vale: the Heartland looked just like Breda, yet completely different. The Heartland was the real homeland where everything was the way it was meant to be from the beginning. A land that had never been laid waste by man or by the ice. 'The water is as pure,' said Erold, 'as purest spring water, even in lakes and streams. The air is so crisp and clear it tastes like grass, like juicy green meadow grass at midsummer. The stars are so clear it seems you can almost touch them. And nothing dies. Perhaps you are walking along a forest path, and then you see a light among the trees. Warm, golden light. You hear someone singing. There is the smell of bread baking. The light comes from a doorway, and behind that door She is waiting, just for you, and she is beautiful like rain and sunshine all at once. She breaks the bread and offers it to you, and it is soft and white and still warm from the oven. And once you accept it, you are home. Truly home.'

Even Kat's impatient mother Tess listened when Erold talked like that. He had once been at death's door from wound fever, so he knew more about those matters than most people. He said he had been close enough to actually hold the bread in his hand. But he had not eaten it. Instead he had returned to his sick body and had recovered. Sometimes he sounded as if he regretted it. In any case, there was a special longing in his voice when he spoke of Our Lady of the Bread, as he called her.

Was Dorissa walking along that forest path right now? Kat tried, but could not picture it. Out of long habit, she reached for the Silverhorse medallion, but her hand met an unfamiliar barrier: the new grey uniform had a tough leather front, almost a breastplate, and though she knew that the medallion rested in its usual place it bothered her that she could not reach it. She was leather all over. She *creaked* when she walked. How on earth did everyone else manage to move so naturally in all this gear? Thank Our Lady she was not expected to wear the full uniform all the time.

She cast a sideways look at Simon, but he stood utterly still, his face completely closed and deadened. Around her on the half-moon square between the Castle and Hellhorse Mountain was ranged every bredinari presently home. They stood as silently as Simon, and apart from the pipes not a single sound was heard.

Then the high pure notes stopped and faded. The gate to the Weapons Yard behind them was opened, and two bredinari led Frost on to the half-moon square. A tall man, dressed in grey leathers and a cloak of kingfisher blue, stepped up to the unmoving hellhorse. Kat recognized him at once – Alvar Alcedina, the DomPrimus of the corps.

'We are ignorant,' he said, his voice carrying easily even to the furthest rows of listening bredinari. It had almost the same flat ring as the drums, thought Kat. 'We know not how Rider Granes met her fate. And so we cannot mourn her the way we mourn other lost comrades. We know not if she met her end in fear or in acceptance, in pain or in relief. We even lack solid proof that she is no longer alive. But the hope that she will ever return to us has waned with the passing of the months. And so today we take leave of Granes's Frost. Her time in service is done. She returns now to the Mountain she came from, and our last and final hope must be that her Rider, too, will find her way home – if not with us, here in this world, then in the one beyond.'

He put his palm against Frost's forehead, squarely between the wideset eyes.

'The bond is severed,' he said. 'Go free!'

He stepped back, and turned to face the ranks. 'Studmaster Janek?'

A small thickset man stepped forward. He carried a very large, leatherbound book.

'Granes's Frost,' he intoned in a voice surprisingly loud and booming. 'Colour argent, of Blue Stock, formerly bound to Rider Dorissa Granes, now freed. Returns to the Mountain in Black Stock, this day in the sixteenth year of the rule of Cora Duodecima.'

He held out the huge Studbook so that Alcedina could witness the inscription.

200

Alcedina then raised his voice again. 'Though we have no proof of death, it has been decided that a memory page for Rider Granes should be added to the Records. Anyone who wishes to mark their respect may do so once the unbridling has been completed.

In the long curved wall facing the Mountain there were seven gates – yellow, white, green, black, blue, red and grey. Two bredinari unlocked and opened the black gate. Through its arched opening, Kat could see the first long grassy slope. There was neither path nor track, for this gate was only opened perhaps a dozen times a year. The grass moved in the morning breeze, fresh and untrodden.

The sight of it seemed finally to pierce the numbness of Frost's spirit. The mare's head came up, and a quiver went through the silverbright body. A man and a woman in grey bredinari uniforms removed first the saddle, then the bridle. Simon stirred uneasily.

'That should have been me,' he muttered, so softly that Kat only just caught the words. But the man on his other side heard them too.

'Don't be stupid, Jossa,' he snapped. 'With that hand you wouldn't even have been able to undo the buckles on your own. Besides, Granes was a Tertius. You, after all, are only a Quintus. It wouldn't have been fitting.'

Simon became still once more. 'Not fitting,' he said in a very flat voice. 'I see. No, of course it wouldn't.'

And after that he said not a word and moved not a muscle until the ceremony was over, and the pipe had sounded for the last time.

Kat was not quite sure of her own emotions as she watched Frost stand there, unsaddled and unbridled. Was this better? Was it best for her never to feel a hand on her muzzle again, a human being on her back? Or were they merely abandoning a sick animal that could no longer work for its keep?

Frost shook her head, as if to rid herself of the last sensation of straps and buckles, She snorted, and pounded the ground with her forefoot, just once. Her yellow gaze swept over the assembled humans, and Kat nearly took a step backwards. What she saw was no longer anybody's willing mount. This was a beast of the wild, a fierce and savage creature not wanting to be caged. The hellhorse fluttered its nostrils, and screamed. This was no neigh, no whinny. This was not a horse sound at all. It sounded more like the cry of a huge bird of prey. And somewhere, from the distant reaches of the Mountain, came an answering cry. Frost spun, then swept forward, hooves barely touching the ground. At the gateway, she hesitated only for a half-second before leaping across its shadow on the grass, and on to the green slope beyond.

Frost had returned to the Mountain. The gate was closed and locked. For a while they could hear the thud of galloping hooves, and Kat thought she caught a brief silver glimpse high up on the slope, among rocks and low shrubby pines. Then that sound, too, died away. Granes's Frost no longer served the bredinari.

Many came to put their mark on Dorissa's memory page. Some printed only their names, others wrote a sentence or two, a memory, a greeting, something Dorissa had done or said.

'Can I write something as well?' said Kat shyly, to Clerk Angia who had charge of the page.

'Of course. Why ever not?' said Angia, surprised. 'You knew her. You have her token.'

'Yes, but . . . I just thought . . . I'm just a prentice. And new here.' Claudi's contemptuous words still stung.

'This is for everybody,' said Angia firmly and handed her the pen.

And then, of course, she couldn't make up her mind what to write. She stood there for a moment, looking at all the other entries. She recognized Simon's name but could make neither head nor tail of what he had written.

'What does it say?' she asked Angia, pointing.

'You'll have to ask Jossa,' said Angia. 'He wrote this in the language of his clan.'

'But no one here will be able to read it!' said Kat, amazed.

'No,' said the Clerk. 'Perhaps that is the point.'

Kat blushed. She felt as if she had been caught eavesdropping, or something. But she suddenly knew what to write herself. Carefully, in her best handwriting, she printed the letters:

She showed me that the world was bigger than I thought. I want to be what she was. And she signed it *Prentice Katriona Teresa-Daughter Trivallia.* All right and proper.

Later, she asked Simon what he had written – much

later, because Simon had gone all distant and strange, and it took her days to work up the courage.

'It's just clan,' he said. 'Clan language.'

'Yes, Angia told me. But what does it mean?'

'It's just a greeting we use. A sort of farewell.'

And that was all he would say. It was years until she herself learned that greeting and guessed what he had written for Dorissa.

Tam'kora atavisa. Take care of my heart until we meet again.

GETTING LOST

'Excuse me. Could you tell me where to find Master Valentin's rooms?'

Kat was sick and tired of asking the way to this, that, or the other place. But how else would she ever get anywhere? Even places she had already been to more than once were difficult to find. There always seemed to be some unexpected wall in the way. Or stairs that ended in odd places. Or corridors that did not take her where she thought they would. Whenever there was a window or a gallery overlooking one of the courtyards, she used that to get her bearings. But even then she often found herself on the wrong floor or in the wrong wing, and getting up or down or around or across to the right one was no easy matter. So she asked. And asked. One total stranger after the other.

'Master Valentin's? That's up the stairs, to the right and through the blue door,' said the slender, dark-haired bredinari prentice. 'Go right in – he never hears you knocking anyway.'

He smiled at her – a nice smile, she thought. She thanked him and hurried up the stairs. She was afraid she might be late already. Fortunately she had no trouble finding the blue door, which was quite wide and handsomely carved with two kingfishers facing one another. And as instructed she went right in.

She realized her mistake almost at once. A room this large and splendid was hardly the domain of an ordinary study master. But before she had time to retreat, there were voices and footsteps, and a man and a woman emerged from the inner chambers.

'. . . an unnatural and scandalous situation,' the woman was saying. 'The matter must be settled immediately. I do hope we understand one another.'

'But of course, maestrina,' said the man, who had politely stood aside to let the woman pass through the door first. 'I shall do everything in my power to—'

And at that moment they both caught sight of Kat.

Kat felt as if her legs had turned to stone. The woman she had never seen before. But the man she knew. Alvar Alcedina, supreme commander of the bredinari. The man with the kingfisher-blue eyes. And he did not look happy to see her.

'What are you doing here?' he said sharply. His glare seemed to cut right through her, like a scythe.

'It . . . I . . . I didn't mean to . . .' stammered Kat. 'I lost my way. I need to find Master Valentin's rooms.'

'A somewhat peculiar mistake,' said Alcedina icily. 'The

good Master Valentin hardly ever teaches a class in my private quarters. And my door looks nothing like his.'

'But someone said—'

'Oh, I'm sure. No doubt the same someone told you to sneak in without knocking? It does not please me to be spied upon by my own prentices!'

'I wasn't spying,' Kat said angrily. All right, it had been a stupid mistake, but did he have to assume the worst the minute he saw her?

'Oh, I remember you now,' said Alcedina. 'The insubordinate little Vale girl that Jossa brought. What was your name?'

Something in the ice-blue glare made her anger falter and slink away.

'Trivallia,' she whispered.

'Trivallia,' he repeated. 'You are within an inch of being sent right back to your Three Valleys.'

'DomPrimus,' said the woman, putting her hand on Alcedina's arm. 'Leave the poor child be. It was an honest mistake, anyone can see that. How long have you been in this place, child? A week? Two weeks?'

'Four days,' muttered Kat, grateful for the woman's defence of her but also mortified that her inexperience showed so keenly.

'Four days. There you are, Alvar. How could it be anything other than a mistake? She probably has no idea who I am.'

Mutely, Kat shook her head. The woman was not young, Tess's age perhaps, or a bit older. She had a face full of sharpness: a narrow pointy nose, keen cheekbones, a small high jutting chin. Her hair was almost as red. as Kat's, but neatly and elaborately dressed in a pearl-studded net. She was wearing a silken overrobe embroidered with polecats on the chest and back. Kat vaguely remembered that the polecat was the emblem of one of Breda's old families, one of the Seven. No, Kat certainly hadn't seen her before; she would surely have remembered.

'My name is Felicia Capra-Mustela,' said the woman. 'And there is nothing covert or underhanded about my conversation with DomPrimus Alcedina. Yet I would still ask you not to speak of it to anyone, unless he or I ask it.' She caught Alcedina's gaze for a moment before returning her attention to Kat, and Kat had a very clear feeling that there was something teasing or triumphant in that quick glance. Felicia Capra-Mustela was nowhere near as displeased with being 'spied upon' as Alcedina was.

'Will you give me your word on that, Prentice Trivallia?' she asked.

Kat nodded. 'Yes. And I didn't do it on purpose. Honest.' She looked at Alcedina when she said that. He was the one she needed to convince. But it was the woman – Felicia Capra-Mustela – who answered.

'Of course not, child. Come on. Come with me now, so that your DomPrimus does not let anger cloud his judgement after all.'

Again that teasing tone. But this time Alcedina did not let himself be baited.

'Why should I be angry?' he said, with a cool smile. 'The

maestrina is right. So young and inexperienced a prentice has no part in power games and plots. She has one interest only: becoming a good and dutiful bredinari. Is that not so, Trivallia?'

'Yes,' said Kat. That was why she was here, after all. But Alcedina wasn't looking at her. So perhaps she was not the one he was really talking to.

The woman put an amiable hand on Kat's arm and led her to the blue door. Kat could not help casting a nervous look over her shoulder. Alvar Alcedina stood, arms crossed, and watched them leave. And he was no longer smiling.

The woman did not speak again until they had reached the end of the corridor.

'I cannot give you anything, little Trivallia,' she said. 'He would accuse me of trying to bribe his prentices. But I shall remember your name. And you will remember mine. And perhaps one day we can both be of service to one another.'

She put a cool hand on Kat's scarlet cheek – *why* did she always have to blush like that?

'You're a nice girl. Take care of yourself.'

Kat stood there, rattled and confused, and watched the intricate hair and the very straight polecat-embroidered back walk away down the stairs. What on earth had she got herself mixed up with? Then she remembered that she was late for Master Valentin's class. Where *were* his rooms? She practically ran down the corridor to the next stairwell. She would have to ask in the kitchens. Mistress Karolin, who ruled supreme in those regions, was a friendly woman, and almost everyone on the kitchen staff had received Kat kindly – apparently, they had never before met a prentice who actually volunteered to clear the tables and help with the dishes. They would not misdirect her. But the next time she saw the dark-haired joker who had led her astray, he would regret his little prank. To think that she had nearly lost her place at the Academy because of him!

She saw him sooner than she had anticipated. When she finally found Master Valentin's rooms, he was sitting at a large, round table along with seven other prentices, listening with innocent-looking attention to the Master's explanation of something called 'the Second Mark Conflict'.

'. . . and Darius writes that the Dykemasters of Fulmark did *not* raise any objection, but did indeed give over an area of land to the Eastern merchants. I have three questions for you. Why did the Dykemasters cede these areas to the Colmontians? Was their act lawful? And what, in your opinion, should Rider Morin have done?'

Master Valentin paused, and looked at his students expectantly. Either he had not heard her enter, or he was deliberately ignoring her. There was no free seat at the table. She stood uncertainly by the door, right behind the Master.

The dark-haired joker raised his hand. That, apparently, was a signal that he wanted to speak.

'Yes, DiCapra?'

'The Dykemasters were afraid to fight. They thought they could save their own hides by doing a deal with the enemy. That is clearly unlawful, and Rider Morin was right to take up arms. Only, he should have called in more troops so that he could have won a decisive victory right away.'

There was a disgusted snort from one of two girls at the table, a chubby, blonde freckleface of about Kat's age.

'That's all we ever hear from you, DiCapra,' she muttered, not raising her hand first. 'War, war, war . . .'

'Hand, Merian,' said the Master severely. 'Raise your hand before you speak! We are here to discuss in a civilized manner, not brawl like barbarians.'

Sighing, the girl raised a dutiful hand.

'Yes, Merian. Tell us how you would answer my three questions.'

'For one thing, Fulmark had plenty of legitimate reasons for allowing the Colmontians to settle,' said the girl. 'Sirimark had just put a tax on all goods brought in from Fulmark, which is a clear breach of the old Mark code. Strengthening trade with Colmonte was merely a sensible countermove.'

'But to give away Bredan soil to an alien power—' began one of the other boys.

'It was *not* Bredan soil. The Bredan Treaty had not yet been signed. And they did not give it away, they just allowed the Colmontians to build on it.'

'You're only saying that because you're from Ormark!' snapped DiCapra.

'I am not! If you'd bother to read the text . . .' shouted Merian.

'I know what the text says! It says that Mark peasants are cowardly traitors who sell out Breda lands!'

'Quiet!' snapped Master Valentin. 'Gentlemen! Ladies! If you are not capable of discussing in a sensible and courteous manner, you will have to give your arguments in writing. No less than two hundred words, please. Now! And legibly, please, Prentice Meiles.'

The class heaved a collective sigh. Valentin spun on his heel and nearly collided with Kat. Sighs turned into giggles.

'And who may you be?' asked the Master, eyeing Kat as if she were some lower form of insect life.

'Prentice Trivallia, Master,' said Kat. 'I'm sorry for being late, but—'

'But me no buts. I've had quite enough excuses for one day. Seeing that you're late, you will just have to read today's text on your own.'

He half-pushed her into the chair he had just vacated and slid a very large and heavy book under her nose.

'Here. Chapters Two and Three. And no skipping. You will stay here until you have finished, and tomorrow I shall test you on this myself.'

Chapters Two and Three . . . Kat looked at the text in disbelief. That had to be at least fifteen pages. Fifteen very large, very densely written pages.

'Well?' said Master Valentin severely.

'Yes, Master,' she said meekly, and bent over the text.

The study room was quiet except for the scratching of nibs across paper, as the other prentices wrote their essays. Master Valentin went into his private quarters, but left the door pointedly open, so that he would be able to hear any disturbance. Kat stared at the letters. They were squirly and strange-looking, and half of them added up to no sense at all. She understood perhaps one word in three. Even the words she could make out made no sense. What did 'mercantile' mean? What were 'in-loco powers'? And what in heaven's name did the Sixth Mark Code amount to? Desperately she raised her head from the text and caught DiCapra looking at her. He smiled. How had she ever thought that smile a nice one? It was not nice at all. It was superior. Condescending. Full of false pity. A 'poor-dim-peasant' kind of smile. She wanted to hit him with the book. Hard. But instead she let her eyes move across the words that made no sense, and when she thought a suitable time had gone by, she turned the page. At that moment she would rather have died than let on to DiCapra how slow a reader she really was.

One by one the other prentices finished, handed in their essays to Master Valentin, and left. Merian was one of the first, DiCapra second to last. Then a bell sounded, to signal that dinner was ready in the Refectory. Master Valentin came into the study room. His face was still disapproving and implacable.

'I am going down to dinner,' he said. 'I shall see to it that a meal is set by for you. You can eat when you are done. And remember, I will test you on this.'

And then he left.

Kat turned back the pages to the beginning of Chapter Two. She still understood hardly anything of what she was reading. Fifteen pages! And he was going to test her on it.

You are within an inch of being sent right back to your Three

Valleys. So Alcedina had told her. Would they send her home when they found out how badly she read? When they found out how little she knew about the Second Mark Conflict? Perhaps this really *was* too much for a mountain girl. Maybe she really was just peasant scum. Perhaps it would be better to give up now and go home while the roads were still good.

Her hand crept up to touch Dorissa's medallion, in its bag under her shirt. She remembered the day she had first ridden Frost. She remembered Dorissa and Simon. She knew that was what she wanted to do. Who she wanted to be. She wanted to ride a silver hellhorse to Resting Places all over the country, to help people who needed it. She wanted to travel from place to place and belong everywhere. And if she had to read fifteen pages about the Second Mark Conflict to get there, Our Lady help her, then she would damn well do so.

She began to read aloud. Some of the words she recognized when she heard them. Others remained alien. She guessed at what she didn't understand, and slowly worked her way down the page.

It took her all evening. Her stomach rumbled with hunger at first, but then it seemed to realize that dinner would not be forthcoming, and settled down to just a disgruntled pang now and then. When the light from the window became too dim for her to read by, she lit the lamp above the table, and the smell of hot stone oil enveloped the room.

At the bottom of the eleventh page, she started yawning.

By the middle of page thirteen, nothing made sense at all any more. She muttered the syllables one by one, slowly and brokenly, but her brain just wouldn't do it any more. She rubbed her eyes, and tried again.

'. . . and this un-pre-ce-den-ted breach of the ter-ri-to-ri-al treaty became the sub-stance of the ne-go-ti-a-tions of the Dykemasters with the Col-mon-ti-an de-le-ga-tion . . .' Unprece-what? And what was a delegation? Obviously something from Colmonte. Onwards.

'. . . at which junc-ture Rider Morin made a state-ment to the ef-fect that his in-loco-Bredani sta-tus fully em-powered him to take up arms . . .' She closed her eyes for a moment. Right. They got into a fight. Why couldn't the man just write *that*?

'Trivallia?'

'Mmmh . . .' She raised her head. Where was she? A middle-aged man with a nose like the blade of an axe . . . Valentin. Master Valentin. She straightened abruptly.

'Trivallia, how many years of schooling have you had?'

Here it came. They were going to send her away. She blinked, and stared down into the book.

'I . . . I've never really . . . gone to school. But I worked in the writing room at a Dyer's Yard, once.'

'For how long?'

Damn. 'Three weeks . . .' she whispered.

'And then what happened?'

'I ran away. But I *can* read. And write. And do sums.' At the Dyer's Yard, such skilfulness had been too much, causing the other girls to take against her. Here it appeared to be too little.

'Read to me,' he said, nodding at the book.

She hesitated. She knew what it would sound like. Stumbling. Broken-worded.

'Read,' he said.

She read. About four sentences.

'Thank you,' he said. 'That is sufficient.'

Her eyes seemed permanently locked on the book. It didn't matter. The last thing she wanted to do was look at Master Valentin.

He moved to the window and stood silent for a long while, drumming his fingers on the ledge.

'Tell me,' he finally said, 'what you made of the pages you managed to read.'

'The Mark-Lands had a trade deal. Sirimark broke it by putting a tax on goods from Fulmark. Then Fulmark began to trade with Colmonte instead, and let some Colmontian merchants settle in Fulmark. Some people from Sirimark got upset about that and complained to a bredinari called Morin, and then *he* got upset and thought it was a scandal and attacked one of the Colmontian merchant houses together with the people from Sirimark. Fulmark's Dykemasters got really angry about *that*, and I haven't found out how it ends yet.'

A sort of snuffle came from him, possibly laughter. 'Very concise,' he said. She did not know what 'concise' meant. She hoped it was nothing too bad.

216

'Trivallia, with your present level of skill you will not be able to keep up with this class.'

She swallowed. 'I'll try really hard . . .' she began, but he waved her to silence.

'Trying is not enough. You simply lack too many skills, and too much general knowledge.'

Stupid and ignorant. She blinked, so that tears would not drop on to the page and give her away.

'No,' he said, as if he was able to hear her thoughts. 'You are not stupid. You just lack the advantages that the others have had. Most of them are from families who have employed at least one tutor for them, and usually more. They learned to read when they were five or six. When did you start?'

She could not answer that. She wasn't sure how old she had been when Tad first began to draw letters in the ash. But she had probably been more than six.

'Why does there have to be so much reading?' she broke out. 'What does that have to do with the hellhorses?'

'Child. Being a bredinari is so much more than just riding a hellhorse. They should have told you that.'

They had. Simon had told her, countless times. But she hadn't wanted to hear it.

'I shall see to it that you get extra tuition,' said the Master. 'You may still attend my classes along with the rest, twice a week. But you must use the evenings and other spare time you may have to catch up on the skills you lack. It will be hard work for you, Trivallia. But necessary.'

It took a moment for her to realize that he was not

sending her away. That he did not want her thrown out of the Academy.

'Off with you,' he said, unhooking the lamp from above the table. 'You may not need such mundanities as food and sleep. But I do.'

'But . . . the book,' she said. 'I'm still two pages short.'

'They will keep until tomorrow,' he said, relieving her of the heavy volume. 'Go to bed, Trivallia.'

Sweat was pouring down her face, and her breath came in shortened gasps from strain and temper both. She aimed a stroke at her opponent's head, but he parried with ease, and turned the attack on her with such speed that she had to hop back ungracefully to avoid being hit. It was driving her crazy. Just once. Just *once*, to be able to land a blow on that oh-so-competent body . . . she leaped forward, totally concentrated on the blue helmet she meant to hit.

Once again he evaded with fluid ease, and before she had time to take in what was happening, her own helmet received a thwack that set her ears ringing. Her parry came up much too late and much too high, and Master Haryn had all the time in the world to put the tip of his wooden sword against her breastplate and shove her to the ground.

'Not good enough, Trivallia,' he said drily. 'You cannot beat me with temper. I offered you a low opening, but all you thought about was whacking me on the head. If this had been a real sword, and I a real enemy, you would now be dead.'

She lay in the dust of the Weapons Yard, looking up at him with a fury that verged on tears. He sighed.

'Trivallia, do you remember what I told you about *posa*?'

She nodded. 'Posa is the right poise, of body and of mind,' she said. 'Posa is not anger and is not fear. Posa is ease and serenity.' She knew the words by heart, and rattled them off with confidence. But Master Haryn did not look satisfied.

'It's not enough to learn the words, Trivallia. You have to take them to heart as well. And to mind!'

'Why can't I train with the others?' she asked sulkily, getting slowly to her feet. This made it the fourth time today that he had sent her sprawling.

'You can,' he said patiently. 'As soon as you learn to fight without losing your temper. Until then, I'm the only one you get to whack at. Come on. Once more.'

Kat did her best to push aside her temper. Of all the weapons masters, it was actually Master Haryn she got along with best, although he taught what she was undoubtedly the worst at: the old, classic Art of the Sword from Lunara. He never seemed to get impatient, he never taunted her for her clumsiness, and he did not appear to consider it beneath his dignity to tutor someone who was just a raw beginner, and a mountain girl to boot. It was nothing like Medes the Wrestling Master, who lost his temper daily at her 'total lack of style', and claimed that she fought like 'a drunken peasant in a bar-room brawl'.

Resignedly, she brought the wooden sword back into the guard position and took up the pose Master Haryn had

219

painstakingly taught her. She did quite well as long as they practised the set patterns and positions, but the ten minutes' worth of 'free fight' that usually ended the lesson practically killed her. Time and time again he took advantage of her openings to give her a small, sharp, humiliating tap, and every time he hit her, her temper rose another notch, until she completely lost her head and what poise she had, and started to 'whack away', as he called it. The punishment for *that* was never long in coming. He could, of course, take her down whenever he wanted to, and promptly did so, making her feel like a disobedient child who had once again strayed out of line.

'*Defend* yourself, Trivallia,' he said, again and again. 'Stay alive. You have very far to go before you can attempt an attack against a fencer of any experience at all.'

When she did attack, despite his advice, he let her do it, and even offered her an opening or two, she knew that perfectly well. But unfortunately he was right. Not even with a deliberate opening could she attack him competently.

He had taught her the first three patterns of defence: the Wall of Air, the Wall of Wood and the Wall of Steel. The Wall of Air she had mastered almost completely by now, and if she kept her head she would be able to stand her ground for a few minutes against a trained fencer. 'Long enough to scream for help,' Master Haryn had said. In moments of depression, Kat thought that that was all very well, but if her swordsmanship did not improve very soon, she would be hacked to pieces before even the nearest help could actually *get* there.

'Very well,' he finally said. 'That will do for today. Remember to put your gear away properly.'

She pulled off her helmet and trudged across the Yard to the Armoury, where all the practice equipment was kept. She had to tell herself not to drag her feet. She was completely exhausted. Probably black and blue all over. Her fingers felt like thick sausages, and she fumbled at the laces that tied the padded vest to her body. Carefully she put everything in its proper place – wooden sword, helmet, vest, arm guards, leg guards. It would be a while before she forgot the tongue-lashing Master Haryn had given her the day she had left the sword on the bench.

'But it's only wood . . .' she tried to defend herself, but that did no good.

'It's a weapon. A training weapon, yes, but a weapon all the same. If you are this sloppy with it, it will be a very long time before I allow you to touch a real sword.'

Don't rush it on my account, she thought. The practice swords were plenty hard enough, she was in no hurry to get beaten up with a real one.

She stepped on to the bench in front of the Armoury so that she could catch a glimpse of the clock tower on the Riders' Wing. Nearly lunchtime, but she would have time for a quick bath if she hurried.

She was still a bit embarrassed that she had had to ask her private tutor, Master Osual, to explain the clock to her. But in Three Valleys they didn't use things like that, or not much. Certainly the village had none. It was enough, back home, to know when it was morning, or noon, or night –

and anyone could tell that much by the sun. But here she had to present herself at Master Osual's at one o'clock sharp, and at Master Valentin's at three. And if she was late, she would be scolded. It was a different way to live.

She trotted across the Weapons Yard, past the kitchens, and into the baths. This was one of the really great things about the Castle. There were sunken tubs big enough for scores of people, big enough to swim in, even! The water in these pools was cold, but you could sit in one of the small, hot thermals first to scrub away the dirt, and right now a hot soak was just what Kat's tender muscles were crying out for.

She kicked off her boots in the antechamber and took a shortcut through the boys' bath. She had hoped it would be empty at this time of day, but apparently a couple of the Wrestling Master's students had fancied a noontime bath too. One of them was DiCapra.

'Why, hello, Trivallia,' he said, smiling. He always smiled that nice-looking smile when he saw her, but she knew better now than to trust it.

'Hello,' she said, not stopping. She went into the girls' side and sat down on the stone bench to take off her stockings. The door opened, and DiCapra and the two others came in. She gave them an irritated glare, but it rolled right off them, and they continued to stand there.

'Why don't you go to your own side?' she asked.

'Don't be so unfriendly,' said DiCapra. We just want to help you with your bath . . .'

And before she had time to react, two of them caught her

arms and DiCapra reached for her feet. She kicked at him, but hit him only in the chest, and not very hard at that. Then he got hold of her ankle, and despite her kicks and squirms she could not pull free. They swung her back and forth like a sack of meal.

'One . . . two . . . and three!' they called, and on 'Three!' they all let go, so that she sailed through the air and landed in the deep pool with a splash that rippled through the entire bathhouse.

Her nose and mouth filled with water, but the pool was shallow enough for her to touch bottom easily. Coughing and spluttering, she surfaced, to see the three boys standing at the pool's edge, laughing their heads off.

She was out of the water and up and at them faster than any of them seemed to expect. She brought one of them to his knees with one of the dirtiest kicks in Cornelius's bag of tricks before the other two had even begun to move. They backed away from her.

'Easy,' yelled DiCapra. 'Trivallia, it was just a bit of fun!'

Kat lost some of her fighting temper. For fun? Simon had told her, several times, that she had to learn to let herself be teased for fun.

'I didn't think it was very funny,' she said, still out of sorts.

'Well, Rubio isn't having much fun either,' said DiCapra. 'Trivallia, you *know* brawling is not allowed.'

'He asked for it,' said Kat, but somewhat less confident.

'She kicked me in the face!' wailed Rubio.

'I did not!' But his mouth did seem to be bleeding a

little. 'You must have bit your lip when you fell,' she said. 'I didn't kick anybody in the face!'

Or had she? No. She still didn't believe that.

'Come on, Rubio,' said DiCapra. 'Better get Master Rodrian to take a look at that.'

Kat watched helplessly as DiCapra picked up one of her abandoned socks and handed it to Rubio to dab his cut lip with.

'Come on,' said the third boy, 'Let's get out of here before she decides to attack us again.' He looked at Kat as if she were some kind of untrustworthy animal, and they all departed, Rubio complaining that he thought he might have a loose tooth.

Kat was confused. Here she was, dripping wet, and all her clothes, the shirt, the grey leather breeches, her under-wear – all of it was soaked, and all because those dimwits had attacked *her*. How come, then, that everything had somehow turned out to be her fault? How come she was suddenly the one who had behaved badly? *Had* it all been 'just a bit of fun', and she the one who didn't know the difference between a joke and a genuine attack?

There wasn't even time for a proper bath now. She would have to hurry if she wanted to get into some dry clothes before the noon bell rang.

'Simon?' She knocked hesitantly at his door. 'Simon, are you there?'

He opened. He was still in his greys even though it was evening and near bedtime.

'Can I come in for a bit?'

She was afraid he would refuse her. The first couple of days he had been there, somewhere in the background – just a quick word between classes or a faint smile from the other side of the Refectory, where the Riders ate. Prentices and Riders did not mingle much, it seemed, and she was soon so busy herself that she didn't have the time for long conversations. But at some point she realized she hadn't seen him in days. Somehow, his mealtimes never coincided with hers any more. He was never in the Weapons Yard when she looked for him, or in the hall outside her classrooms. It was as if he had withdrawn from her, and she had begun to wonder whether he *wanted* to see her at all. He had, after all, done his duty. He had seen to it that she was delivered safely to the Academy, and she was no longer his responsibility. She had thought she was more than a duty to him. She had thought they were friends. But perhaps she was the only one thinking that?

He certainly didn't look pleased to see her. He cast a quick glance up and down the hallway, but it was deserted. Then he nodded.

'Come on in.'

He closed the door behind her. He had a fire going in the fireplace, and the kettle was hissing quietly, but the heavy smell of wine and herbs from last time had gone.

'Would you like some tea?' he asked. 'Sit by the fire, if you want.'

She nodded, and sank into one of the wicker armchairs. He poured, into one of the thick glass beakers. The tea was strong and rich and golden, just like she remembered. The best tea she had ever had.

'It tastes so good,' she said, feeling shy all of a sudden.

'That's because it's real tea,' he said. 'Made with real tea leaves, from Vara. Much better than your usual herbal swill.' But he didn't smile, and he still did not look particularly happy that she was there.

'What did you want?' he asked.

She did have an excuse for coming. More than an excuse, actually. There was something she needed to talk to him about. But her errand stuck in her throat, and she couldn't help asking:

'Do I need a reason? Can't I just come round . . . to talk?'

He looked away. 'Better if you don't,' he said in his flat voice.

She grew cold all over. What was he saying? What did he mean by that?

'Don't you want me to?'

That sounded . . . a bit lost. But it had to be asked.

'It's not a question of what I want or don't want,' he said. 'You have to make friends here. I can't be here all the time. And maybe . . . you need better friends than me.'

Kat shook her head. She could feel tears prickling at the corners of her eyes. She *had* no one else here.

'I don't understand,' she said stubbornly.

'Friends your own age.'

'But they—'

226

'Kat,' he said, holding up a hand to cut her off. 'Katriona. You are strong, and you are stubborn. You can make it on your own. And you will have to. I have to leave soon. And there's something else. You have to know that not everyone in the corps is delighted at my existence. It's best if you don't come here too often.'

'But I—'

'Hush, Kat. Let's say no more about it. Drink your tea and talk to me. And after that, we say goodbye.'

She surged to her feet and banged her glass down on his desk, so violently that the teaspoon danced.

'Get up, sit down, drink your tea, don't do this and don't do that . . . Have you finished telling me what to do and not to do? If you're sick of me, say so. Then I'll leave.'

'I'm not sick of—'

'Well, then stop trying to decide who I'm allowed to like. I can make up my own mind about that, thank you very much!'

'You don't know what—'

'No, that's as may be. I'm just an ignorant mountain brat. "The insubordinate little Vale girl that Jossa brought." But I know who I like, and I don't stop liking them just cos some fancy City folk think that people from Joss are unreliable and . . . and use poisons and other stuff. If you think they say nicer things about people from Three Valleys, you're much mistaken.'

'Kat—'

'And if you think that nice, sweet prentices *my own age*

are lining up to be friends with me, you're dead wrong too. They wouldn't touch me with a poker.'

'If I could just—'

'They think I'm some kind of moron cos I don't read as fast as they do. And they think I'm mean and violent cos I hit back when someone throws me in the water. That dimwit Rubio has complained about me. I'll be lucky if they don't throw me out of the Academy. So before you toss me out too, you might give a thought to who *else* I have in this stinking place!'

'*If* I could just get a word in edgeways!' Simon's face was not expressionless now. As a matter of fact, he seemed to be quite red in the face. 'Sweet Lady, you do have a temper! No, I'm not sick of you. I like you. And I'm glad you're not ruled by gossip. But there are still good reasons why we shouldn't see each other too often. And you really must learn to cope on your own. I'm leaving in eight days.'

Kat looked at him, feeling lost. 'Eight days . . .' she said. He nodded.

'How long . . . how long will you be gone?'

'All winter. I'm reopening a Resting Place in Tora Vale.'

'Alone?'

'For the time being. Later Remus Varas will come to join me, and one of the prentice leeches, who has almost finished his prenticeship.'

Kat shook her head. She knew neither of them, and they didn't interest her right now.

'So you're going to Three Valleys.'

'Yes. If you want to write to your mother or anyone else in South Vale, I'll be your messenger.'

'Yes. Please. I'd like that.' She thought for a moment. The talk of letters had reminded her of her errand.

'Simon, I've had a letter too, of sorts.' She pulled up the grey leather vest that went with the uniform and poked her fingers into one of the compartments in the belt Cornelius had given her.

'Here – look at this,' she said, and showed Simon the tiny bit of parchment she had found hidden under her vest that morning after arms practice.

He read it quickly – there were only a few words – and a mask seemed to slip over his face.

'Who gave you that?' he asked.

'I don't know. It fell out of my vest when I went to put it on again after Master Haryn's class.'

'Did anyone see?'

'I don't think so.'

He looked at her for a long while. 'Sit down,' he finally said, 'and tell me about it.'

She didn't comply right away.

'It's a secret,' she said. 'The kind of thing you only tell a friend.'

'You never let up, do you? All right. You are right to be cautious. And you have my word, on my clan honour, that I am your friend, and that I promise not to tell your secret to anyone, unless you ask me to.'

'It's actually not *my* secret,' said Kat. 'Or not just mine.' And then she told him what had happened the day DiCapra sent her up the wrong stairs. Simon listened to her without interruptions.

'And you think this is from her?' he finally asked.

'Who else would it be from?'

The rolled-up bit of parchment bore only four words: *Remember what you heard*. And then the imprint of a polecat, done in red wax. Such a message could only be from Felicia Capra-Mustela, Kat felt.

'I don't know,' said Simon. 'But it would be easy enough to steal or fake the seal of Mustela. And in matters concerning the Seven, you should never trust appearances.' He rose and crossed to the window. It was completely dark outside now, and he would not be able to see anything except his own mirror image in the glass. Yet he still stayed there for a while.

'Burn it,' he said. 'And stay away from her. She is dangerous.'

'She seemed quite nice . . .' began Kat.

'For all I know, she may be. But what she is involved in is dangerous. You don't belong in that world, Kat. You don't know the rules they play by, and in their power games, the life of a twelve-year-old Vale girl counts for very little.'

'Thirteen,' she corrected him.

'Thirteen? You haven't had your birthday yet, have you?'

She ducked her head a bit. 'Well, nearly thirteen,' she said. 'In twenty-one days.'

It seemed he was quick at sums. 'The first day of the Storm Season,' he said with a smile. 'I might have guessed . . .' Then he was completely serious once more. 'No, I mean it, Kat. You have no idea what's at stake here.'

'You keep saying that. But how am I ever *supposed* to know, when nobody will tell me?'

He sighed. 'All right. I'll tell you. Enough so that you will understand why you have to stay clear of it.'

He poured fresh tea for both of them, put another log on the fire, and sat down in one of the wicker chairs.

'You may have heard,' he said carefully, 'that for nigh on a year, Mustela has had no maestra.'

Kat felt her eyes widen, but tried not to let her amazement show too much. Maybe it was completely normal for a City family to have no maestra. Who knew? Better not to let on.

'No,' she answered casually. 'Why don't they?'

Simon smiled, a somewhat harsh smile. 'It turned out their maestra was a man.'

Kat could keep her casual pretence no longer.

'A . . . a *man*?' she sputtered.

'Mustela's old maestra, Ivana Mustela, was very nearly barren. When she finally succeded in producing a child, it was a boy – and she told no one. She pretended to everyone that the child was a girl, and raised it to become her heir.'

'She must have been mad!'

'Probably.'

'But surely people . . . surely *someone* would find out . . .'

'If anyone did, Ivana ensured their silence. One way or another.'

'But . . . but, when he got older . . .' Kat could not quite find the words. A small boy might be taken for a girl, yes, but when he became older, and his voice changed . . . she still remembered how peculiar Dan had sounded, one moment hoarse and deep, the next, crack, up his voice went, like a startled bird.

'She had a leech cut him when he was still small.'

Cut?

'What do you mean . . . cut?'

He threw her a gauging look.

'You're a country girl. A border brat like me. You must have seen them cut a colt.'

Kat nodded, somewhat pale. She had never liked to watch that, and the mere thought that someone would do that to a person, to a *child* . . .

'It did, of course, come out in the end. But not until Ivana was dead, and Tedora – the boygirl – had been Mustela's maestra for some years.'

'Then what happened?'

'They're still looking for him.'

'He ran, then?'

'Yes. But the Motherhouse Keepers won't give up so easily. They'll look until they find him, I think.'

'And then . . . do what?'

'They got the Bredani to cast him out. You know, like in the story of the Soulless Man: "You, Creature, my land will not suffer you. The earth you walk on shall burn beneath your feet. The food you eat shall turn to poison in your mouth. All gifts of the land shall be denied you – food, sleep and comfort – from this time till you die."'

232

'Does that work?'

'She did it once before. A long time ago, but no one has forgotten. The man sickened and paled away to nothing, and they say some sort of madness came over him. Within ten days he died.'

'But that's sorcery,' said Kat, eyes wide, 'cursing someone so they die!'

Simon smiled, a crooked, somewhat sour smile. 'Perhaps he had a bit of help. Something slipped into his food, who knows? In any case, he died. And you can be sure Tedora will die too – if they can catch him.'

'Poor man.'

'Don't voice such sentiments too loudly. And in any case, I'm not sure he is worth your pity. He and his mother, by all accounts, stopped at nothing to keep his secret. There is enough blood on his hands to warrant even such a punishment. And so, Mustela has no maestra. But there are two women who would like to become rulers of that Family. And one of them is Felicia Capra-Mustela.'

'Alcedina called her maestrina,' Kat said.

'Yes. That might be a sign that our DomPrimus supports her claim. And as he is our Bredani's very own brother, his support is far from insignificant. Possibly that is what Felicia wants you to remember. She may want to use you as a witness, to pressure him.'

'And that is dangerous?'

'Oh, yes. He is not a man who likes being goaded. Arin Medes-Mustela – the other claimant – has her following too. Many of them in this corps. She happens to be a bredinari.'

'First he called me insubordinate – Alcedina, that is,' said Kat thoughtfully, 'and then he turned around and said I was just an inexperienced prentice who only wanted to become a good and dutiful bredinari.'

'And aren't you?'

'Yes. Yes, of course I am.'

'Good. Then burn that message.'

Reluctantly, she got up and tossed the bit of parchment on to the fire. It caught immediately, and the wax sizzled and melted, so that the polecat seal became oddly distorted, and finally disappeared altogether.

Simon had risen too.

'Stay away from those people,' he said. 'Be polite when you have to, but stay away. Or you will be trapped, and possibly hurt. And I would like to keep the friends I have . . .'

'I never wanted to get mixed up in anything like that,' she said. 'But Simon, it's so hard not to get lost in this place.'

She was not just talking about all the stairs and galleries and corridors, and when she looked at him, she could see that he understood that.

'Maybe it was wrong,' he said. 'Maybe I was wrong to take you from Three Valleys. Would you like to come back with me? We can probably get an annulment of the prentice letter, if you want.'

'No,' she said. 'This is what I want. And I'll learn. I want to be a Silver. Just like you.'

'Hopefully not just like me,' he said. 'Hopefully better and stronger and wiser than me.'

He looked tired now, almost as tired as the morning Ola and Claudi had dragged her to his door.

'Does your hand hurt?' she asked.

'No,' he said. 'It's much better. And you really do have to go now. It's very late.'

LU

'Ceuta, you can practise with Trivallia. First Wave, Second Wave, Wall of Air, Wall of Wood.'

Kat cast a wary glance at nut-brown, long-limbed Lusiana Ceuta. She was Master Haryn's star pupil, the only one of the prentices who could float effortlessly through all the forms and patterns, as if that was the *only* way to move. Kat thought she looked as slim and elegant as a deer, and neat with it – the coal-black hair was braided tightly to her skull so that no opponent could easily get a grip on it; not that that kind of thing was allowed in Master Haryn's classes, of course, but rumour had it that Lusiana Ceuta could look after herself in less stylish contests, too. What would Lusiana say to being paired with the rawest, most hopeless beginner in Master Haryn's entire class? And it wasn't just the difference in skill. Ceuta was a fine, old Breda family – not one of the Seven, of course, but almost as highly placed. Lusiana might be one of the people who thought that border brats like Kat had no business wearing the greys. Every so often, an elbow would accidentally hit Kat's midriff in the lunchtime crush, or a leg might just as accidentally trip her as she went past. Kat had acquired quite an array of bruises in that way, and made more enemies by pushing back. If bruises were what Lusiana had in mind, sparring with her would be no fun at all. Wooden the practice swords might be, but the wood was tough white ash, and they could do a lot of damage in the hands of someone who knew what she was doing. As Lusiana undoubtedly did.

But if Lusiana had any hostile feelings, or felt that her new opponent was beneath her, she didn't deign to show it. She merely nodded, and fell into the stance required for the pattern Master Haryn called the First Wave. Not even the ghost of a sneer curled her lip.

'Go on then, Trivallia,' said Master Haryn, 'but remember –' and he tapped her breastplate with a finger, 'don't lose your temper!'

That's easy for him to say, thought Kat. But if that leggy fighting machine over there whacks me on the head, I whack back!

The 'fighting machine' showed no signs of wanting to whack anybody on the head. She was merely waiting patiently for Kat to join her in the pattern. Kat took a deep breath, adjusted a helmet that didn't need adjusting, and set to.

The First Wave was a carefully calculated set pattern of movements – this thrust to meet that parry, this sweeping stroke to be answered by that whirling evasion. One fencer

– Kat, this time – was always the attacker, the other always the defender. All the time, Lusiana's parries came exactly when and where they should, with a lazy ease that was somehow infuriating. Despite Master Haryn's warning, Kat felt her temper stir, and upped the pace a bit. Lu followed with no sign of strain. Was there even a slight smile on her face? I'll teach her to laugh at me, thought Kat, and spun a shade more quickly. And then more so. And more. Until she was whirling like a water demon – they both were, faster and faster, while the dust rose around them and the swords thwacked one against the other, never a moment too early, never a moment too late, and Lusiana's face, the dark eyes aloof and unchanged, was the only thing she truly saw. And suddenly Kat's temper left her. Why hurry? They were already there. Always, both of them, no matter how quickly they moved. No hurry. No strain. She felt as if she was completely still, completely unmoving. And yet she knew that in the last few moments of this calculated dance of arms she did move, in a blur of speed she had never thought possible before.

They stopped. For a few moments, Kat could still feel that strange unearthly calm. I think my eyes look like Lusiana's right now, she thought. And then she discovered that her heart was pounding so hard that it felt painful, and her arms and legs were completely leaden. After one pattern! She grimaced. If they kept this up, she might actually drop dead of exhaustion before the lesson was over.

Lusiana was watching her, almost as if they were still

engaged in the pattern. The same poise, the same complete attention. And suddenly Kat felt a hand on her shoulder, and her nostrils picked up the unique mixture of metal and leather and linseed oil that was Master Haryn's scent.

'Well, Kat,' he said slowly. 'It seems there is hope for you after all.'

She turned and stared. He had never before called her by her first name. He hardly ever called anyone by their first name. Only every once in a while when Lusiana had been particularly brilliant, or when Tobin Brest, his journeyman-at-arms, had surpassed himself. Then he might award them a 'Well done, Lu!' or a 'Well, finally, Tobin!'

And now, here he was, calling her by her first name – she hadn't even been aware he knew it – and giving her the same sparse praise he normally saved for his best.

She couldn't help herself.

'Why do you say that?' she burst out, and then inwardly cursed herself for behaving like a clumsy country brat with straw in her hair and one big question mark underneath it.

'Because you have finally seen the light,' he said. 'I wouldn't have thought anybody could reach posa through sheer bloody-minded temper, but it seems you can.'

Posa? Was *that* what he meant with his talk of serenity, balance and poise?

That was what I felt, she whispered to herself, wonderingly. That was where I was, those few moments when everything went still even though we were spinning like weathervanes in a whirlwind. And she realized now that this was what Lu had. This was what put her miles beyond any of the other prentices.

'Shall we get on with it?' said Lusiana suddenly, and Kat was almost startled to hear her voice. Those were the first words Lu had ever spoken to her. 'We haven't done the Second Wave yet. And this time, *you* get to parry.' She grinned widely and ruthlessly at Kat's involuntary moan. 'There are a few things I could show you, if you like. About the moves, I mean. You keep flapping your arms like a bird trying to get off the ground.'

Kat smiled cautiously back at Lusiana.

'All right,' she said. 'Better get on with it, then.'

And that was how it started. Kat and Lu. Later, they became friends.

It was Memory Day – the one completely school-free day of the week. Those prentices who could went home to their family house to 'show their respect for the Locus Spirit', as it was officially called. For most of them, it was mainly a chance to spend time with the family they were born or fostered to.

Kat had nowhere to go. Three Valleys, of course, was hopelessly far away. She might not even be able to make it home for the Midwinter Holidays, because winter often closed the passes, and thus the roads into the Vales. She could have gone to a Motherhouse here to show her respect for the Locus of all Breda, but it wasn't really the same. This was why she sat on the hospital garden wall, dangling her legs and looking out across the South Field where the broodmares were grazing. The foals were not really foals any more. They were nearly as long-limbed as the grown hellhorses now, and they were beginning to shed the woolly coats of nurslings. Bright silver showed in the spots most easily rubbed or scratched at.

She missed Simon. He had only been gone for a week, and she missed him already. And as if that was not enough, a terrible thought had occurred to her almost the moment she had watched him ride through the Castle Gate.

He said he was going to Tora Vale to reopen a Resting Place. But she knew better. Oh, no doubt he would do that. But he would also continue to look high and low for any trace of Dorissa.

Damn him. His hand was barely healed. What if he did find a lead? What would he do then? Follow it until he got himself killed too? So that the only thing they ever found would be a crazed Grizel that they could then release on to the mountain to join mad Frost?

And even that was not the end of it. What if he found Ermine? Ermine was just as dangerous as whoever killed Dorissa. Ermine might even *be* Dorissa's killer. What would happen, then, to Cornelius and to Crowfoot Inn?

She had given him letters. One for Tess. One for Tad. One for Mattie. And one that was more for all of them. They weren't all that long, the letters. She still was no dab hand at writing. But she had taken pains with them, especially with Tad's. She wanted so badly to show him that she was getting better. Perhaps he would be proud of her. He would be pleased, she thought, because it was Tad who had patiently drawn one letter after the other in the ash, until she could copy them, and it was Tad who had given her her most precious possession next to Dorissa's medallion, the book about Sari Moon-Daughter and the Pedlar from Joss. She still read at least a few pages every night, and she had nearly finished now.

She hadn't written a letter to Cornelius. She wouldn't have known what to write. She was not at all sure what she felt any more. She didn't think she was angry with him. Only sometimes, when she was tired or upset and longed to be back at the inn where at least she knew everybody, and nobody called her a brat – then she would sometimes get mad at him again, because it was his fault that she was here, and not there. But if Simon found Ermine . . . and if Ermine thought that *she* had betrayed the secret . . . and if Ermine blamed Cornelius for that betrayal . . . then Cornelius would die. Ermine had said so. *Will you answer for her, on your life?* And Cornelius had agreed. Cornelius had saved her life by risking his. How would she ever be able to face Tess if anything happened to him? How would she be able to face *herself*?

Damn Simon for stirring up that hornet's nest. Why did he have to go haring off, with a hand that could hardly hold the reins yet, and leave her stuck here, alone and friendless? Kat was scared. And furious with him. And jealous, though she knew it was crazy, of Dorissa. He had abandoned Kat for Dorissa, hadn't he? Even though she knew that that was not the way of it at all. She had not been abandoned. She was safe here. While nobody knew exactly what had become of Dorissa, or whether there was any hope that she might still be alive. And as for Kat's awkward pact with Cornelius, Simon knew nothing about that.

But damn him all the same.

A window in the hospital wing was opened, and Clerk Angia's narrow face poked through it.

'Kat? Where are you, girl?'

'Here,' said Kat, hastily hopping down off the wall. The hellhorse field was out of bounds to the prentices, and sitting on the wall came a little too close to disobedience for comfort.

'Ceuta is asking for you,' Angia called. 'I've shown her to your room.'

'I'm coming.'

Trotting along the brick paths of the gardens, Kat wondered what Lu wanted. Why hadn't she gone home to her family last night? Most people did.

Lusiana stood rather awkwardly in the middle of the room, as if afraid she might knock into something if she moved. Perhaps it was because she was wearing a dress today, with very full skirts and a froth of lace at the wrists and neck. It all took up much more space than her everyday uniform of breeches, shirt and vest.

'Hello,' she said, smiling in relief when she saw Kat. 'I hope you don't mind . . .' her gesture indicated her presence in Kat's room. 'Clerk Angia let me in. What a lovely view you have.'

'Yes. That's the best thing about the room,' said Kat, who

had a shrewd suspicion that Lu was used to somewhat more spacious surroundings. 'Would you like a cup of tea?'

Angia let her use the small stove in the Archives, and Simon had left her a small precious supply of real tea as a parting gift.

'No thanks,' said Lu. 'I'm on my way home. Which is why I'm wearing this carnival outfit.' She waved a disgusted hand, causing the lace to rustle. 'No, I only came to ask you . . . would you like to come with me?'

She looked suddenly uncertain, as if she was afraid of a refusal. And it was that uncertainty that made Kat agree right away, without thinking, without considering what sort of a reception a no-account Vale girl might get at the residence of one of Breda's more prominent families.

'I'd love to. But . . .' she took in more details of Lu's appearance. Her black hair was gathered in a jewelled net, almost like Felicia Capra-Mustela's. The overrobe of her dress was of dark green velvet, draped to show off the pale green silken underskirt, and the bodice was embroidered with pearls and little sparkly green crystals, matching the ones in her hair. Kat stared. If those weren't glass, Lu was wearing a fortune. And even if they *were* glass . . . Kat had never seen such colour, such clarity, such perfect shape. They *looked* like emeralds. 'I haven't got a dress that's anything like *that* . . .' she finished. Actually, she didn't have a dress of any kind, but she didn't like to say that.

'Put on your dress uniform,' said Lu. 'That's perfectly acceptable.'

Kat put on her dress greys. She hadn't worn them since

245

the day Frost was unbridled, and they were still rather stiff and creaky. She felt as if she was wearing one of the armoured suits hanging in Master Haryn's storerooms. But she looked presentable, and that was all that mattered right now.

'Would you like me to braid your hair for you?' asked Lu.

Kat pushed a hand through her mass of frizzy red curls.

'You can try,' she said. 'I used to be able to braid it back when it was properly long, but now . . .'

'If you'd ever seen mine when I let it down, you wouldn't worry,' said Lusiana. 'Believe me, I know *everything* there is to know about making frizzy hair behave.'

She braided Kat's hair so that it was swept neatly back from her forehead, and secured it in a short ponytail at the back.

'So,' she said. 'I think we're ready.'

It was the first time Kat had been outside the Castle since the day of her arrival. She had been so busy trying to find her way around the Castle grounds that she had had no urge to go further afield, and besides, prentices needed a permit. They weren't usually very difficult to get, it had just never occurred to her to try. But in Lu's company, it was easy. You simply swept by the gate guard who greeted 'Domnessa Ceuta' politely and apparently would not dream of stopping anyone accompanying her.

'The stupid skirts are no good for long walks,' said Lu in

irritation, 'but it's just too silly to drag two horses from the stables for such a short ride.'

Kat didn't answer. She was busy taking in her surroundings. They were on a terraced path in the middle of a wide strip of turf. On both sides of the grass, drifts of roses clung to green metal frames, so that it was a bit like walking through a gallery with pillars and arches of living flowers. Kat had never seen grass trimmed so artfully short, nor such a wealth of flowers. It was still warm, though summer was coming to an end. Petals fell in a steady drift from the arches and scattered like snowflakes on the grass.

'Where are we?' asked Kat.

'Oh, this is Millerosa. The Rose Path. Beautiful, isn't it? And quite a useful short cut, if you're on foot.'

Lu dived through one of the rose arches and followed a much narrower path between tall yellow brick walls. Then she turned down a wide gravelled avenue flanked by tall linden trees. The traffic here was much heavier, and there were both riders and carriages. People on foot had to stay on the grassy verge under the trees, and leave the gravelly centre to the horses. Several of the people they passed greeted Lusiana politely. She returned their greetings just as politely, nodding or bowing according to some system Kat could not quite make out.

They crossed a bridge. The water under it tumbled rapidly along, confined between stone walls.

'Castle Falls,' Lu told her. 'You're actually looking at our bath water.'

'Looks cold,' said Kat, shuddering a bit at the thought. 'I think I like the thermals better.'

They walked along the Falls for a bit, on a narrow path between the gorge and a tall whitewashed wall. Suddenly, there was a gate, which Lu proceeded to unlock with a key she had carried in a small purse hidden among all the skirts.

'Here we are then,' she said. 'Home, sweet home. This is the rear entrance.'

Though the lock looked rusty, the key turned smoothly and soundlessly, so it seemed the rear entrance was used quite frequently.

'Come on,' said Lu.

Kat cast a last look across the bridge and the Falls. And suddenly a shiver ran through her. On the bridge was a man. A man with the head of a polecat. And he was looking at them.

'Lu . . .' She grabbed Lu by the elbow. 'Look!'

Lu followed her gaze. But the man was already turning away, melting into the crowd. They caught a few glimpses of the red fur hood among the other strollers under the tall lime trees. Then he was gone.

'It was just a Lodge Brother,' said Lu. 'Why did you want me to see him?'

'He was looking at us,' muttered Kat.

'So? Under that mask of his he has eyes like any other man. He was looking at two pretty girls, that's all.'

'Maybe,' said Kat. But there was something about that mask – the flattened predatory skull, the gaping jaws. The

248

flat beady glass eyes on top of the man's own. Suddenly she was shaking with terror, and she didn't even know why.

'Kat . . .' said Lu. 'You look like you've seen a ghost. You *can't* be that frightened of the stupid Lodge masks. Can you?'

'Why do they have to wear them?' said Kat. 'I don't like not being able to see people's faces.' But it wasn't all the masks that frightened her. The goatheads of the Chamois Lodge, or the weird reptilian salamander masks didn't bother her at all. Nor did the raven, the pike or the king-fisher. It was just the polecats – and the owls. Just those two.

'It's just kids' stuff, really,' said Lu. 'Grown men dressing up and holding "secret" meetings. Secret! Everyone knows it's going on. The Motherhouse Keepers rant at it occasion-ally because they use the Sacred Beasts. But the Seven support them, so of course nothing is ever done about it.'

'Is the Polecat Lodge part of Mustela?'

'That's a matter of opinion. Mustela supports them. And there are probably many Mustela-born men among the Polecat Brothers. But others too. You don't have to be born to the Seven to be accepted by the Lodges.' Lu pushed open the gate. 'Come on. Forget about them. I want you to meet my family.'

Kat followed Lu through the narrow gate. But she couldn't quite forget about the polecat man.

There was a guard on the other side.

'Hi, Jona,' said Lu. 'It's just me.'

'Yes, I could hear that,' he said, 'or I would have stopped you.'

'I didn't know Mama was posting guards by the Falls Gate too. Has anything happened?'

'Not that I know of,' said the guard. 'But you can ask your mother. She does the postings, after all. Who's your friend?'

'Kat Trivallia,' said Lu, 'may I introduce my cousin Jona?'

Cousin Jona bowed elegantly. Kat attempted to copy him. Her dress greys creaked.

'Welcome to Castel Ceuta,' he said. 'If you get bored up there at the Big House with all the dignified Maters, come and keep me company.'

'You just keep your mind on your duties,' said Lu. 'Kat's too good for you, anyway.'

Cousin Jona struck at Lu with the staff he was armed with. But even dressed in velvet skirts, Lu was still Master Haryn's star pupil, and he hit nothing but air. Which seemed to be exactly what he expected.

'Still fit, I see,' he said. 'Good for you, Lu.'

'Fitter than you,' his cousin snorted. 'Let's go, Kat.' She gathered her skirts and swept up the garden path with an air that made it clear that *this* was a lady, born and bred. Kat followed somewhat less elegantly in her wake. Behind her, she heard Jona giggling like mad.

As soon as they were out of sight, Lu dropped the I'm-a-lady pose.

'He's all right really,' she said. 'He and Mama taught me, before I joined the Academy. He even told Mama that she had to let me become a bredinari.' She giggled. 'As a matter of fact, he told Mama that if she *wouldn't* let me join, he would find work with Maria Esocine instead. And Mama can't stand Maria Esocine.'

Kat wasn't listening properly. Castel Ceuta might not be quite the size of the Castle, but at first sight it certainly looked that way. The white walls of what Jona had called the Big House rose fortress-like above a small village of stables, workshops and smaller dwellings. Once it had been a defensible stronghold, one could see. But now most of the moat had been filled in, and the battlements were hidden under a fuzzy blur of wisterias. Porches and balconies had sprouted on what had once been unscalable walls, and narrow archery slits had been widened and glassed over to become handsome bay windows.

A bell began to toll – clear, deep peals that seemed to stay in the air, still trembling, much longer than they should.

'Seven bells,' cursed Lu. 'We'll be late. Run!'

They reached Ceuta's Memory Grove just as the bell stopped pealing. Lu's Aunt Toria sang the Memory Chorus, and Ceuta's maestra, Nina Ceuta, held up a handful of Ceuta soil and repeated her maestra vows for all to hear: never to abuse the land, never to make herself master of it and trade with it as if it were a dead possession anyone might own. One by one, Ceuta's people went to touch her hand, the one that held the soil, and whisper their own vows. Only Kat hung back. She could not swear on Ceuta's soil, because this was not where she belonged. She felt a sharp stab of longing for the Vale, for hazy mornings in the valley and sparkling nights in the High Meadows, waiting for some mare to foal. The leaves would be turning just now, starting high on the ridge with a crisp dotting of yellow, gold and scarlet among the dusty summer green. For a moment, she was almost able to smell them.

When the remembrance was over, people scattered to eat the Memory Day meal with their most immediate family. Kat was introduced to Lusiana's mother and her three sisters, and bowed self-consciously in her creaking leathers. Then dinner was served.

The table was full of things Kat had no idea how to eat. Those scarlet crayfish, for instance, glaring at you with dead black pinhead eyes. She managed by watching Lu carefully and eating only what Lu ate, in the way Lu ate it. Probably it tasted wonderful, but she was too tense to notice.

'How long have you been at the Academy, Katriona?' asked Lu's mother.

'Nearly three months,' said Kat, eyeing Lu's plate. Were you really supposed to dig that stuff out of its *claws*?

'Do you like it?'

Like it? That was a difficult question. Sometimes it was awful. Sometimes . . . exciting.

'It's what I want,' she answered hesitantly, hoping that that would be enough. It seemed so, for Lu's mother merely nodded.

'That's what Lu says too. We must only hope that it proves the right decision in the long run.'

'Oh, Mama,' said Lu in an exasperated voice. 'Of course it does. When are you going to stop worrying so?'

Marietta Ceuta did not answer. She clamped the pliers around her crayfish with so much force that there was a loud crunch, and a spurt of pale juice squirted out on to the tablecloth.

'How clumsy of me,' she murmured, dabbing at the wet spot with her napkin.

'Mama,' said Lu. 'You trained me. Why can't you be glad I'm good at it?'

'Perhaps we should try to get through just one Memory Day meal without having an argument?' said Lu's mother. 'Particularly now that you have brought us a guest.'

Lu glared at her crayfish as if she needed to murder something and was sorry that the creature was already dead.

'Yes, Mama,' she said.

After which, silence reigned for a very long time.

Kat sat quite still, not saying a word. She couldn't even put food in her mouth, for as long as Lu wasn't eating, Kat didn't dare to either.

It was a very long meal.

'Why does she keep *doing* that?' snarled Lu between clenched teeth. 'She has three well-bred, civilized daughters who are perfectly able and willing to take over the household duties when their turn comes. Why can't she just let me get on with what *I* want to do, and wish me good luck?'

253

Kat just shook her head. How was she supposed to answer that?

'*She* was the one who made me train. Now she's suddenly saying that self-defence is all very well, but she did not raise her children to become "silvered mercenaries". She thinks I'm only doing this because I want to ride around on a hellhorse all day.'

'Mothers can be difficult,' Kat offered cautiously. That much she did feel able to say with some authority.

'Is *your* mother like that?'

'No, not like that . . . or maybe, sort of, but in a different way.' Tess was not the least bit like Marietta Ceuta. But there was, all the same, something very familiar about Lu's complaints.

None of Lu's sisters looked like her at all, and it was also difficult to see anything of Marietta Ceuta in Lu. Perhaps there was a likeness about the nose and eyes, but the small similarities were overshadowed by the big difference: that Marietta was pale-skinned and fair-haired, while Lu was as brown as a hazelnut and had hair the colour of a moonless night.

'Do you know who your father is?' asked Kat.

'No,' said Lu. 'She won't talk about him.'

'I don't either.' Kat paused. 'The others are saying that you must have Esocine blood.' Esocine was one of the Seven, so such a bloodline was considered very noble, even if it was only through the father.

'They say that of everyone who has dark skin,' said Lu. 'But actually I think my father may have been of Esocine. At any rate, I know Mama had a grandmother of a row with Esocine about the time I was born.'

'What about?'

'She won't say, but I think they wanted to adopt me. That's Esocine's way of hanging on to the father-born. They probably thought she would be honoured to have a daughter adopted into the Seven.' Lu grinned. 'I can just imagine what Mama had to say to *that*.'

Lu showed Kat around the whole of Castel Ceuta. It was really a small village, with its own smithy, lots of other workshops, and even a small hospital. Ceuta had more foster-daughters than Bria, even. Some lived at the Big House, others had their own cottages and lived there with their families. Ceuta's riches were founded on two things: trade, and a special kind of glass that only they knew how to make – the 'jewels' on Lu's dress really were glass. Kat was staggered to learn that Ceuta sent caravans all the way through the Norlands to the ocean and the great trade cities there. And Lu said they had three ships sailing the Greater Circle Sea, bringing in tea and spices from Vara and indigo and silver from Colmonte.

'Yes, but how . . .' Kat tried to settle the confusion in her head. 'How can you do that when you live – here?' How was it possible to own and run three ships on the Greater Circle Sea, way beyond the Marklands, impossibly distant from Breda City – ships that Ceuta's maestra could never have seen with her own eyes?

'Oh, that's because we know how to hang on to our men,' said Lu with a crooked grin. 'Ceuta's sons have no call to go begging other families for shelter or work. There is quite enough for them to do here. And they know we won't throw them out once they are too old to work. Loyalty works both ways. That's why they stay, and that's why so many of them swear fidelity to Ceuta when they come of age. I think we have more oathsmen than any other family except maybe Capra.'

Kat sighed. Lu would probably think her stupid, but . . .

'Lu? What is an oathsman?'

Lu glanced at her. 'I keep forgetting that you're from the country,' she said. 'I don't suppose you have oathsmen in Three Valleys?'

Kat shook her head. If they did, she wouldn't be asking, would she?

'Oathsmen have sworn lifelong fidelity to a certain maestra. It's a bit like becoming a foster-daughter, only for men, of course. So we have oathsmen in Sira and Colmonte and Varena, who belong to this family almost as if they were daughters. You should meet my Uncle Felipe. He is the one in charge of the Circle Sea shipping. What he does not know about trading and sailing and dirty tricks is definitely not worth knowing. Capra would pay through the nose to get him, but he is just as much Ceuta's as I am.'

It was dark by the time they returned to the Big House to say goodbye. The whole place was brilliantly lit. One of the specialities of the Ceuta Glassworks were the crystal chandeliers that scattered the light from the oil lamps in bright reflections all over the walls and floors.

'Where is Mama?' Lu asked her youngest sister, Carlotta, who was crouched in one of the window seats with a book.

'Guardhouse,' said Carlotta briefly, without raising her eyes from the page.

'I'm leaving now. See you next week.'

'Mmh. Bye, then.'

Lu reached out and tousled her younger sister's hair. Carlotta pushed her hand away, like someone brushing off a fly. When they left she still hadn't looked at them.

'That must be a really good book,' ventured Kat.

Lu grinned. 'Not necessarily. She's always like that.'

In the Guardhouse, Marietta Ceuta stood over a chart table, still wearing her rich golden-green Memory Day robes. She tapped the chart with a slender finger, and was talking with some intensity to a guard.

'Mama,' said Lu. 'We have to go back to the Castle now.'

The guard turned, and Kat saw that it was Jona. Marietta straightened.

'Is it that late already? Well, I suppose it is.' She opened her arms. 'Come and say goodbye properly.'

Lu gave a strange sort of gasp, almost a sob.

'I don't do it on purpose, Mama,' she said. 'It's not that I *want* us to fight.'

'I know,' said Marietta. 'Neither do I. It just happens.'

She hugged her daughter, and they held each other close for a moment, pale green and dark green, fair skin and dark.

They were almost the same height. And suddenly Kat could see the likeness very clearly.

'I've told Jona to see you back to the Castle tonight.'

'Oh, Mama . . .' said Lu, withdrawing from the hug. 'I can look after—'

'I know you can,' Marietta cut in. 'But these are unstable times. While Mustela is without maestra, anything can happen. I take my precautions when I can. I am responsible for Ceuta's security, and you are a part of Ceuta. You will take a guard, and like it.'

There was no mistaking the edge of command in that voice, and Kat half expected Lu to bridle at her mother's tone. But, strangely, Lu seemed almost pleased by it.

'Yes, Mama,' she said, and made no further protest.

'Katriona,' said Marietta, holding out her hand. Kat took it. 'I'm glad Lu has found a friend, and gladder still that it is someone with no part to play in the power games of the Seven. You are always welcome at Ceuta.' She kissed Kat briefly on the forehead. 'And now you had better get going, or you'll be locked out.'

THIRTEEN

It was a grey and windy day, a warning that late summer was about to turn into real autumn. Kat shivered in her linen shirt. She could have used a jacket, but so far she still only had the one that went with the dress greys, and she wasn't supposed to wear that on an ordinary day. She had been issued a winter cloak, but the heavy dark blue wool was nearly two fingers thick and much too hot and cumbersome for Master Bruna's classes. Glancing around, she saw that everyone else was wearing a jacket or a light cloak. She was the only one shivering in shirtsleeves.

Perhaps that was why Horsemaster Bruna called her into the Hippodrome first.

'Come here, Trivallia,' he said. 'And stand next to Moon.'

Moon was Bruna's hellhorse. She was of the rare blancacolouring – under the silver coat, her skin was as white as her mane and tail. She even showed a bit of pink around the muzzle and the eyes. This made the argent glow paler

259

than usual, and this, in turn, caused her eyes to seem darker, more coppery than the usual yellow-golden glare. Kat couldn't decide whether this made her look any less intimidating than the average hellhorse.

Moon was wearing neither bridle nor halter. She was entirely free. Free to run, free to stay, free to attack. Kat could not quite suppress a shiver of unease as she approached the hellhorse.

Moon snorted, and pawed the ground.

'Stand,' said Bruna, not to the hellhorse but to Kat. Kat stopped.

'Let go of your fear,' said Bruna.

'I'm not scared!' said Kat, outraged.

Moon squealed and half reared.

'Let it go,' said Bruna firmly. 'Purge your mind. Think of something calm and pleasant.'

The first thing that sprang to mind was her bed. She had had too little sleep, because she and Lu had been talking and giggling and drinking tea until the midnight bell. Perhaps that was why she was so easily chilled this morning. But at any rate, thoughts of soft, warm quilts and pillows were easy to concentrate on.

'Good,' said Bruna. 'Now approach.'

Kat took a step forward. Moon held still. Pillows, quilts, a lovely warm bed . . . she reached out and touched Moon's neck. Soft and warm, like the pillows she was picturing.

'Why are you in your shirtsleeves?' snapped Bruna suddenly, in a taunting tone.

What?

260

'Don't you know how to dress properly? Or perhaps you hadn't noticed that summer is over? And here I was, thinking that peasants were weather-wise, if nothing else.'

Suppressed giggles from the other prentices. Quilts and pillows evaporated, and she spun to face Bruna.

'It's not my fault that I haven't been issued a jacket yet.'

'Well, isn't that typical!' said Bruna implacably. 'If you need a jacket, why don't you buy one? Border brats coming here, wanting to become Silvers, yes, and expecting to have everything offered on a silver plate, too.'

She wanted to hit him. Kick him in the shins. Call him something extremely rude, at least. She didn't. She stood there, seething, but she restrained herself.

Moon showed no such restraint. She leaped forward, teeth bared, going for Bruna. Bruna stepped aside, and put one hand on her neck.

'Easy,' he murmured. 'Easy now.'

Moon stopped, looking confused, tossing her head in agitation.

'Purge your mind, Trivallia,' commanded Bruna, the scornful tone completely gone from his voice.

And only then did Kat understand why he had goaded her like that. It didn't make her any less angry; she felt cheated and betrayed. It was hard to force her thoughts back to calm and pleasant things. And it took several moments before Moon stopped jittering and snorting.

'Fear and anger,' said Bruna. 'Those are the two feelings that hellhorses respond to most strongly. If you want to

261

work with them, you must learn to control both. For what good is it, Trivallia, that *you* are too wise to hit your Master, if the hellhorse does it for you?' He patted Moon's neck. 'If Moon had been bonded to you, and not to me, I would have been in mortal danger just now.'

Kat felt her cheeks burning. It was true, she *had* felt like hitting him. And it was just as obvious that Moon had moved to the tune of that desire.

The shift from taunts and scorn to praise and soothing words, and back again, became a familiar pattern for the nine prentices in Bruna's class. One moment he gently and patiently helped Merian until she could approach Moon without fear. The next, he completely shattered Meiles's composure by tripping him so that he fell to the ground practically between the hellhorse's forefeet. Had Moon been an ordinary horse, the tasks he set them would have been simple: catch Moon, put a halter on her, lead her around, brush her, saddle her, and so forth. But one never knew when the next attack on one's composure would come. Unlike most Masters, Bruna sometimes allowed his students to tease and goad each other mercilessly. And whenever any strong emotion was aroused, Moon moved with it, like a wind chime in the wind, and gave you away. If you didn't already have a thick skin, Bruna saw to it that you got one.

*

'Trivallia's trying hard to rub elbows with the Ceutas, isn't she?' Rubio leaned across the barrier and spoke just loud enough for Kat to hear it. 'Guess she must be hoping for a few crumbs from the tables of the rich.'

'Well, I suppose if you haven't got it yourself, you can always sponge off somebody who has,' said DiCapra. 'You know, do a bit of brown-nosing. Hey, Trivallia, what's that on your face?'

Kat couldn't contain her fury. Moon reared to her full height and tried to batter down the wooden barrier that separated her from Rubio and DiCapra.

'Purge the mind, Trivallia!' yelled Bruna, and sprang forward to put his hand on Moon's neck. But Kat could not think away her rage, and Rubio's frightened cries did not make it any easier for Bruna to soothe the silver mare.

'Out!' he snapped. 'All three of you, out!'

Lu later told Kat that the mare had not settled even after they had left. She had been so agitated that Bruna would allow none of the prentices into the ring with him until the midmorning bell rang, and the class ended. Only then did Moon cease rearing and squealing.

Kat grew thoughtful when she heard that. Of course she had got into a fight with DiCapra and Rubio the minute they were out the door, and she had been so furious that she had not managed to calm down again – until the midmorning bell rang. Had Moon really been able to feel her fury all the way through gates and thick walls?

She might have taken Rubio on his own, and perhaps even DiCapra, though he was a better fighter. But not the two of them at once. They got her down on her belly and forced her hand up between her shoulders and told her to beg for mercy when she had had enough. There was nothing she hated more, and it took her so long to give in that her arm was swollen and painful for days. But the worst was having to watch DiCapra's triumphant grin. Oh, but she wanted to go for him again, to wipe that smile off his face. But there were, after all, certain rules even to illegal fights. Once you had asked for mercy, that was it. You had lost and they had won.

Losing stung. Worse than the arm, and worse than the bruises and the scrape on her cheek. And as if that wasn't enough, Bruna tore strips out of her once the others had left.

'One more lapse like that, and you are out of this class, Trivallia! I shudder to think what will happen if you ever bond a hellhorse of your own. Heaven help any poor bastard that gets in the way of that temper of yours. It's enough to give any Horsemaster evil dreams.'

'But they said—'

'I don't care *what* they said. It was probably moronic, offensive and injust. But a bredinari has to hear a thousand moronic, offensive remarks without letting his hellhorse kick the morons to bits. If you can't learn *that* lesson, you really have no business here!'

Later the same day, Master Haryn's keen eye immediately spotted the awkward way she moved her sword, and the abrasion on her cheek.

'Hold,' he said. 'There is no point in training if you are injured. Who was it this time – Meiles? Rubio? Essa?'

'Rubio,' she admitted sullenly. 'And DiCapra.'

'Come in here for a moment,' he said, and showed her into the small room at the back of the Armoury where he did his lists and kept his personal equipment. 'Let me have a look at that arm.'

The swelling wasn't gross, but just about any movement hurt both her elbow and her shoulder. Master Haryn shook his head at her.

'Next time, you might want to give in a little sooner,' he said. 'It will be a lot easier on your ligaments, and I doubt your pride will suffer any lasting damage.'

He pulled a box from under the bench and chose a slim, brown pottery flask among other pots and jars. When he pulled the cork, an eye-wateringly sharp smell rose from the small bottle.

'What's that?' asked Kat.

'Salamander oil. Though I doubt there are salamanders in it. Camphor, perhaps, and other essences. It will ease your muscles, if not your joints.'

He poured a bit of it on to her shoulder and rubbed her arm with it. It felt cool at first, but not for long. Soon, heat flushed through her arm, strong enough to make her gasp.

Master Haryn corked the bottle and returned it to the box.

'Listen, Kat,' he said, and the rare use of her first name sharpened her attention immediately. 'You are acquiring a certain reputation. A reputation for being a troublemaker and a fighter.' She opened her mouth to defend herself, but he held up a hand. 'I know – there is always a reason. An offensive remark, a push, a jabbing elbow. But why do you think they do it? They do it because they *know* it's so easy. Trivallia and her temper. Not hard to make you lose it, is it? And have you thought about what happens when you do? Who gets the bruises? You do. Who gets the blame? You do. Anyone who wants to pick a fight with you can basically go ahead and do it – because your Masters will assume you started it. And all those dimwits with their talk about how "border trash shouldn't be allowed into the Academy" – do you know what will happen if they get really lucky?'

Kat shook her head silently. Not that she didn't know what was coming. She just didn't want to say it herself.

'If they get really lucky, they'll prove their point. You will be expelled – and they will once more have proved that the Academy is no place for snotty brats from Three Valleys, or Ormark, or Joss, or Grana, or any other place that is not part of the actual heartlands. So please, Katriona. Next time it happens . . . don't. Don't fight.'

Discouraged, Kat picked at a splinter that was coming off the table leg. She knew he was right. She even knew that Horsemaster Bruna was right. But when so many people were picking fights with her, how could she avoid it?

'How . . . Master, how can I do that?'

Master Haryn gave a tiny snort of laughter. 'Aren't you being just a tiny bit dense, Katriona?'

'What . . . do you mean?'

'Has nothing I have said about posa ever made an impression on you?'

'Yes, but—'

266

'Yes, but you think it is something we use when we fight. Am I right?'

She nodded. Wasn't it?

'Has it never occurred to you that posa may just as easily be used to *not* fight?'

Only then did Kat realize that Bruna's classes and those of Master Haryn had the same basic aim: balance. A balance so perfect that nothing could upset it. But it was one thing to understand it, quite another to practise it.

'Purge the mind, purge the mind,' Lu groaned one day when she had been the target of Bruna's most gruelling form of teaching. 'If I purge myself any harder, I'll dry up and blow away like an empty peapod.'

'I know exactly how you feel,' said Kat. She was in a dark mood herself. Tomorrow was the first day of the Storm Season. Tomorrow was her birthday. And no one knew.

She could have told Lu. But that would sound as if she were begging for a present. And DiCapra's remarks had clung, long after the bruising on her arm had gone down. *I suppose if you haven't got it yourself, you can always sponge off somebody who has.* She wanted nobody to be able to say that she was sponging off Lu. And so she had told nobody at all.

Thirteen, she thought. I'm thirteen today. Let's hope that's not an unlucky number.

She opened the window and pushed back the shutters. It was such a foggy grey day that she could barely make out the hellhorses in the South Field. It had become a daily ritual of hers, this proprietory look. Next year, when the fillies down there were a year old, they would be taken from their mothers. And instead of that bond, another would arise: the bond to the Rider they would carry. Some would of course go to the grown Riders. But a few might be assigned to prentices. Perhaps even to a prentice called Trivallia – if she ever succeeded in learning the lessons Bruna and Haryn were trying to teach her.

They weren't on her schedule for today. This morning, she would first be put through the wringer by Wrestling Master Medes, and after that she would be sniped at by Archery Master Corthe. In the afternoon, after a brief stint with Master Osual, she had her weekly kitchen chores. Not that she minded. Sometimes it was pure relief to be doing something she thoroughly understood. And though she might be a bit behind the other prentices in most subjects, she was definitely the best potato peeler of the lot!

Besides, she liked Mistress Karolin, a small firm woman who had come to Breda as a 'drifter brat', and did nothing to hide the fact. Karolin worked herself hard and demanded as much from her helpers, but she knew that a breather and a joke or a cake that 'got dropped' made things run more smoothly in the long term. From Kat's earliest days at the Academy, the kitchens had been where she felt most at home.

In principle, all prentices owed the Academy one day's work a week, in the kitchens or in the stables, but most of the nobler families preferred paying a certain sum into the Academy accounts instead. Simon had not even mentioned that possibility to Tess, knowing how hard it would be for the inn to put that much ready cash on the table. But kitchen duties were sometimes given out as punishments too, even to the 'highborns'. And no amount of money would get them out of *that*. Every once in a while, Kat had the pleasure of seeing *them* struggle with tasks they had never done before. It would be a long time before she forgot the expression on Rubio's face when he had been told to pluck a chicken, and the headless fowl suddenly *moved*.

'Oh, there you are, Kat,' said Karolin. 'You can help Birch with the pots.'

That was another thing she liked – down here, she was not Trivallia. Here she was just Kat, and Karolin was just Karolin.

Karolin had laughed the first time Kat had tried to address her as 'Mistress'.

'When you're born in the back of a rover's cart, you're not that keen on titles. So you just call me Karolin.'

And that was the way it was.

Kat took an apron off the hook by the door and rolled up her white sleeves – the prentice uniform was not a marvel of practicality in a kitchen. Birch, one of the cook boys, was scrubbing the huge cast-iron pots that had been used for the noon meal. He smiled at her.

'Hello, Kitten,' he said. 'Good to see you. Be nice with a bit of help from a nifty pair of paws . . .'

'I'll give you paws,' said Kat, swiping at him with one hand, fingers curled into claws. Though he was only a few years older than Kat, Birch was already taller than some men, and strong with it. Hearing her name for the first time, he had smiled like an angel and told her she was lucky: he only knew one way to skin a cat, and he would never dream of trying that on her. And for some reason, he immediately became one of the few people Kat could never get mad at, no matter how many stupid cat jokes he came up with.

The afternoon passed quickly in the rush to clear one meal and prepare the next. Kat ate in the kitchen with the others and helped clear away the dishes afterwards, although her duties, strictly speaking, were now over.

'Well, that's that,' she said, rolling her shoulders and stretching her back. Muscles could get a bit tender, wrestling with the heavy pots. 'I'll be off, then.'

'Oh, no you won't,' said Karolin. 'Not quite yet. There is just one more thing . . .'

And Birch said, 'Hold still, Kitten,' and put his hands over her eyes. When he finally released her, the kitchen was suddenly full of people, and on the big table in the middle stood a huge cake.

'Happy birthday, Kitten,' said Birch, and gave her a hug, and so did Karolin, and Lu, and Merian, and Clerk Angia and at least a dozen other people.

'But how did you know?' stammered Kat.

'Jossa told us,' said Karolin. 'We have something for you from him. And then there was this other young man . . .'

The young man in question was wearing the black uniform of a Strigius caravan guard. It took her a moment to recognize him, because it was so unexpected, and because she hadn't seen him for more than two years. But it *was* Dan, her older brother.

'Hi there, Little-Kat,' he said, opening his arms.

'Dan!' Her voice soared and broke from sheer surprise, but it didn't take her long to throw her arms around his neck. He laughed and swung her around, then hugged her tightly. He had always been her favourite brother, and she had cried for days when he left home the first time.

'You've got so big,' she said, knowing even as she said it how childish that sounded. But he only laughed.

'At my age, it's called tall,' he said. 'You're the one who has become a big girl now.'

'What are you doing here? How have you been?' There were a million questions to ask, they buzzed in her head like a swarm of bees.

'I'm with a caravan now, and we came up from down south a couple of days ago. We passed the inn on the way, so I knew where to find you. I've got letters for you, and a couple of other things.'

'Show me, show me . . . How are they? Is everything all right at home?'

'Well enough. They've had a bit of bandit trouble again, it seems to have got worse lately. But it's been nothing Erold and Cornelius couldn't handle. Mattie has become quite the grown-up, now that she is the eldest. Rumours have it that she has even stood up to Tess once or twice . . .'

'Mattie? I don't believe it!' Kat took the letters and tried to make out the writing. This one had been written by Tess . . . and this one was from Tad. And this had to be from

271

Mattie. But no, she couldn't read them now. It needed peace and quiet, and better light. She pushed them inside her shirt.

'Come and cut the cake,' said Karolin. 'You have to have the first slice, or the luck won't work.'

Obediently, she carved a slice and ate it with all the others watching. Then they sang the Luck Song loudly and ringingly three times, and after that other people could get a taste too. Contented munching spread through the birthday crowd, and Dan opened his pack and got out the 'other things'. Tess had sent her money – not a lot, but enough so that she could buy something for herself and get Lu a Midwinter gift as well.

'Tad thought you might have finished Sari Moon-Daughter by now,' said Dan, 'so he sent you this.'

A new book – a small flat black one. 'Snow Rose and other Tales from Three Valleys', it was called. She knew the tale of Snow Rose, but she didn't know one could get it in a book. And then she looked more closely.

'Dan – he wrote this himself!'

Dan nodded. 'And look who he wrote it for.'

On the back of the title page it said: 'To Kat, so that she may always have something of Three Valleys with her.'

She had tears in her eyes.

'I miss him so,' she whispered. 'Him and all the others.'

'I think he misses you too, Little-Kat. But you'll be home again one day.'

She nodded. But it would be so long. All winter, probably, if the pass roads closed. Maybe even longer.

Someone was tuning a fiddle, and somebody else had produced a pair of pipes. Benches and tables were pushed back to make a dancing floor. Dan bowed gallantly.

'May I have this dance, Milady?'

Kat blinked away her tears. 'Well, all right then,' she said. 'Even though you're just an innkeeper's brat from the country.'

And after that there was no time for sad thoughts, because Birch wanted a dance, and Tarquin, one of the other prentices, and Master Haryn's journeyman Tobin, and finally, to her complete surprise, there was Master Haryn himself, demanding a dance with the birthday girl.

When she finally got back to her room that night she couldn't settle enough to go to bed. She read her letters over and over again, and sat looking at the gifts she had been given. Merian had given her a tiny folding knife that was good for sharpening quills. It was so small that it fitted into one of the secret compartments in Cornelius's old belt. Simon had given her one of his rugs, a small one, which lay now in front of her bed and glowed with colour, rose madder, gold and viridian. Lu had brought two Ceuta-made tea beakers with a small flower motif in richly coloured glass.

'It's supposed to be a glacier crowfoot, but our Glassmaster wasn't quite sure what they looked like,' she said shyly. 'But at least you can see it's a flower.'

'It looks just like a crowfoot,' said Kat. 'But Lu, you didn't have to—'

'It's because I intend to come round for tea quite often,' Lu said. 'In our wing we're not allowed that kind of thing in the rooms . . .'

That probably wasn't true, thought Kat. If Domnessa Ceuta was inclined to drink tea in her room, no Master was likely to forbid it. But it was just Lu's way of being Lu and *not* Domnessa Ceuta, and Kat appreciated it.

'Thirteen,' murmured Kat. It was as if she hadn't really discovered, before tonight, that she had actually made friends here. Apart from Lu, of course. Merian was nice, too. And Birch.

She smiled a bit. Maybe turning thirteen was not such a bad luck thing after all.

HELLHORSE MOUNTAIN

Moon would not step across the pole on the ground. Kat dug in her knees and tried to guide the hellhorse with her legs and her weight, but the mare calmly turned to walk around the pole instead of over it. For the third time. Kat sighed and thought intensely of her silver medallion. It was the best means she had of soothing her temper. But without saddle or bridle, how could Bruna expect you to make this *stupid* animal (Whoops! Moon lashed her tail and moved into an irritated trot . . . Easy now. Balance. Poise. Walk . . .) But well, just how *were* you expected to make the hellhorse do something she didn't want to do?

'Getting mad at her yet?' asked Bruna.

'I'm calm,' said Kat carefully.

'Good,' said Bruna. 'But try not to be.'

'What?'

'She knows what you want her to do, doesn't she?'

'Yes.'

'She just can't be bothered to.'

No – stupid beast.

'All right then,' said Bruna. 'Get mad at her.'

'Master. Do you want me to . . . ?'

'Yes. Let her feel your anger.'

Kat was so surprised that the tiny flicker of anger she was keeping so carefully under control guttered and died. Moon came to a complete standstill. Someone in the stands – probably DiCapra – laughed.

Kat looked at the pole carefully, and then, with as much intensity as she could muster, thought: Now *do* it, you dumb animal!

It was as if she had taken a whip to the silken silver hide. And suddenly the mare understood perfectly well the signals she gave it. Moon turned, headed for the pole, and leaped across it as if it were some mighty obstacle. Kat had to clutch the white mane with both hands to avoid being swept off.

'Whoa! . . . Easy. Halt!'

The mare stopped instantly.

'Well done,' was all Bruna said. 'Who's up next? Tarquin – you go.'

And as Kat got off and Tarquin got on, Bruna turned to the rest of the class.

'Hellhorses are not by nature obedient pets. You must teach them to respect you, even more so than with ordinary horses. And they cannot be tamed by violence. Hit a horse, and it will respond with fear. Hit a hellhorse, and it will attempt to take your head off. The only spur that will do any good is that of the Rider's will.'

Mario Essa was drumming his fingers impatiently on the wooden barrier separating the stands from the ring.

'How come we can't use saddle and bridle?' he asked. 'The Riders do.'

'Essa, if you cannot ride your hellhorse *without* a bridle, you haven't a hope of controlling it *with* one.'

Essa looked sceptical. He was a good horseman – perhaps the best rider in the class. Certainly he was the only one who had never fallen off Moon, no matter how suddenly she moved.

'But it would be so much easier to control—' he began.

'If you do not learn to do what Trivallia did today,' said Bruna, 'then a bridle will do you no earthly good. You *cannot* ride a hellhorse the way you would an ordinary horse. Moon is the quietest, most level-headed hellhorse in this place, which is the reason why she is the one who has to put up with all of you nine. Her bond with me is a very strong and solid one. But even Moon will not tolerate whips or spurs.' The Horsemaster looked thoughtfully at Essa. 'I think it is high time you get a better sense of what sort of animals we're dealing with here. The day after tomorrow we all go up on Hellhorse Mountain.'

The path was steep and slippery with rain. Kat was glad that she had put on her old clothes – the sheepskin jerkin and Dan's cast-off breeches and the hood Mattie had made from oilskin. And, of course, the mountain boots that were so much more comfortable for this kind of thing than the riding boots that went with the prentice greys. You had much better purchase too. And the hood covered her shoulders as well, so that the rain didn't trickle down the back of her neck. Rubio and DiCapra may laugh at my peasant clothes, she thought. But an hour from now, they will both be cold and wet, and they'll probably have slipped at least once. Then we'll see who's laughing!

The wind wasn't too bad here, as they were sheltered on both sides by tall stone walls. On one side lay the Black Stock territory, on the other that of Green Stock. Hawthorn and rosehip grew along the top of the wide walls and nettles aplenty. It was not possible to see across them, but at intervals there were steps set in the wall so that one could climb to the top and observe the territory. So far, however, Bruna had not permitted them to do that.

'Damn rain,' muttered Meiles in front of her. 'Why did it have to rain today? And why do we have to tramp about on the damn mountain, now that it *is* raining?'

Bruna heard. 'And if you were sent on a mission, Meiles, would you stay home in bed because it was raining?'

Meiles did not answer. There wasn't all that much he could say.

A little further up the mountain, DiCapra slipped, and he went down on his hands and knees. He cursed, and tried to wipe off the dirt with a tuft of wet grass. Kat bowed her head to hide a smile, but Merian, walking next to her, saw it.

'I think you're the only one of us properly dressed for this,' she said.

Kat cast a glance at Merian's heavy wool sweater and the old brown oilcloth cape she wore on top of it.

'You're not doing too badly yourself,' she said.

'The shoes are wrong,' said Merian. 'In Ormark, we are more used to water than mountains.'

Merian's shoes were of heavy canvas, with rope soles. Kat had seen the barge people at Idabrook wear them.

'You need a bit of support around the ankle,' said Kat, 'so you don't twist it.'

'Yes, I can feel that. But I thought that if they were good for climbing about in the rigging, one could climb a mountain in them as well.'

'It's probably not quite the same thing,' said Kat, looking down at her own metal-capped, hobnailed boots. They were a little bit too big for her – they had once been Dan's – but when she laced them tightly and wore an extra pair of thick socks, they fitted quite snugly.

Bruna signalled a halt and climbed on to the wall on the north side of the path.

'Can we look too?' asked Lu.

'There's nothing to see here,' said Bruna, and descended on to the path once more. 'We have to climb a bit further.'

Twice more he went scouting in this fashion, with the same lack of results. They trudged on, further and further up the mountain. Then the walls began to curve to the north, and for the first time the path dipped instead of rising. Shortly after that they came to a culvert, with a robust mountain brook that crossed the path and disappeared into Green Stock territory under a neat arch in the wall. They could have gone on – stepping stones made crossing the brook fairly easy – but Bruna gathered them on the near side instead.

'This is where we'll go in,' he said. 'And remember what I said. No straying from the group. No shouting, no noise. Single file. I'll be point, Ceuta will take the rear.'

Bruna had given them warnings aplenty, and the danger was underlined by the fact that he and Lu both had a crossbow slung across their backs. Hellhorse stallions were a great deal more savage than the mares, and the hellhorses whose territory they were about to enter were bonded to no man or woman.

So the risk was foremost in Kat's mind when she climbed to the top of the wall and then down on the other side by means of the rope ladder Bruna had brought. She felt as if they were entering hostile lands, in which they had to be careful not to be seen and discovered, so she was completely unprepared for the beauty of it.

They had come a fair way round the Mountain, and what they saw below was not the City but the wide river valley through which the Bredanavia flowed in slow, lazy sweeps. Some of it was marshland, lushly green, with little white clumps of sheep. Most of it, though, was brown and yellow fields, and orchards full of apple-laden trees, and houses bright with white and yellow walls and roofs of terracotta red, shiny wet with rain. And the rain itself – you could *see* it, like a glittering sail hung from the slate grey clouds. On the other side of the valley, the hills were aflame with autumn maples, and you could see the sun beyond the rain. She sniffed sharply. It was so like her own mountains, where you could sit on a hillside and watch the weather come and go.

In fact, it was so much like home that Kat could not feel frightened. For four months she had been between walls almost from dawn to dusk. Only now did she realize how much she had missed open fields and free skies and the smell of summer and of autumn. Why hadn't she used at least one of her Memory Days to discover all this? But no, she had crouched like a frightened mouse in the corner she knew, scared of getting lost if she moved beyond the familiar. But no longer. Next time she had some time to herself, it would be different, she swore.

They followed the brook up the mountain, but at a safe distance. Bruna explained that there was a good chance of coming across the hellhorses at their usual watering places. It would be unwise to trudge trustingly along the bank and suddenly find themselves in the middle of a herd.

The first hellhorse they came across was dead, and had been for some time. The curved ribs stuck out nakedly, and various scavengers had long since cleaned the skeleton of everything except a bit of hair and and a few remnants of dried-out hide. About half the ribs were broken, and the head, or rather, the skull, rested against a rock a short distance from the rest of the body. Several of the prentices grimaced in disgust, but it was not the first time Kat had come across a dead animal in the mountains. To her, there was nothing repellent about it, once the skeleton was more or less clean.

Bruna knelt by the bones.

'This was probably a colt,' he said. 'See how long the spine is? The males are much bigger than the females.'

'How did it die?' asked Merian.

'Probably the way most colts die. The lead stallion killed it.'

'In a fight?'

'Yes.'

'Do they always fight until death?' asked Kat. 'I mean – with ordinary horses, the fight usually only lasts until one of them backs off.'

Bruna ran a hand almost caressingly along one splintered rib. 'Hellhorses don't know how to back down. It's the curse of the breed. The instinct to fight is stronger than the will to survive.' He wiped his hand on the grass, and rose to his feet. 'In each territory there is only one stallion older than six or seven years, and that's the lead stallion. The colts survive for a time by staying away from the herd, but in the end the mares prove too great a draw.'

The prentices looked at the skeleton thoughtfully. When you looked more closely, the destruction was eerily thorough. Smashed ribs, broken spine – even the skull had been partially stoved in. The winner of this fight had kept at it long after the loser had died, had kept on kicking and trampling the body until hardly a bone was left undamaged.

'Come on,' said Bruna. 'We're quite close to the water

hole now. We need to draw back a bit, and find a good vantage point.

They settled on a ridge that gave them a good view of the watering place. Even on the hard and stony ground, many hoofprints were visible.

'We'll stay here,' said Bruna. 'There's a good chance some will show up. You may talk, if you keep your voices low, but don't get up. You'd be visible for miles.'

Kat had brought her old travelling blanket. She spread it on the ground and shared it with Lu and Merian. In return for the favour, Lu had carried Kat's flask as well as her own. They opened their lunch pouches and started eating. One could tell from Kat's that she had friends in the kitchen. There was eggs and sausage and cheese and new bread, and two small juicy apples from the new harvest.

'This is a great place,' said Kat, looking around her contentedly. 'Almost like home.'

Merian looked at her as though she were crazy.

'Well, I'm glad somebody's able to enjoy it,' she said. 'Personally I'm a bit too busy trying not to panic.'

'I hope you succeed,' said Kat with a grin. 'After all, we know how hellhorses respond to fear, don't we?'

'Thanks a lot,' said Merian. 'That was *just* what I needed to hear.'

Lu took no part in this. She was watching the cliffs above and below, with posa-distant eyes. The crossbow rested next to her on the blanket. She had cranked it so that all she had to do was set the bolt and shoot.

'Lu?' said Kat. 'Tarquin and Valente have the watch right now, not you.'

'Mmmh?' said Lu, without relaxing her watchfulness one bit.

'It's not your watch,' repeated Kat.

Lu became a bit less distant.

'Sorry,' she said. 'I know that. It's just that . . . well, Bruna gave that thing to me,' she nodded at the crossbow, 'so now I feel sort of responsible.'

'Confine your responsibilities to that sandwich,' said Kat. 'If you don't eat now, you'll be cold later. And it's hard to be a good lookout when you're tired and cold and hungry.'

Out in the open, the wind was much stronger. Thankfully, the rain had stopped, but not being able to stand up and move around made it hard to keep warm. Kat was very happy that she had her sheepskin coat. Rubio and DiCapra and a couple of the others were beginning to look a bit blue around the nose. They were more used to riding than walking, and their clothes were better suited to a quick canter round the fields than to a day on the Mountain. Virtuously, Kat didn't let her smugness show. Well, not much. Hardly at all.

Meiles and Essa took over from Tarquin and Valente at the top of the ridge. Still no hellhorse had been sighted. Merian had finally stopped looking so deliberately unscared. She rubbed a freckled cheek and blinked almost sleepily. Lu had finished her sandwich obediently, and had promptly returned her watchfulness to the surroundings.

'Merian?'

'Mmmh?'

'How come you're here? In Breda City, I mean. You're from Ormark, aren't you?'

'Yes,' said Merian, looking a bit more alert. 'And if you want to know, they don't regard Mark peasants any higher than Vale peasants, around here . . .' She grinned at Kat. 'I'm here because it's a place where I can learn something. But also because Mama needed to send me away from home, and this was the only respectable way of doing that.'

'Bit like me then,' said Kat. 'But why did you need to leave?'

Merian blushed. 'Well, you know that the Marklands do a fair bit of trade with Colmonte, don't you?'

Kat nodded. She doubted she would ever be able to forget about 'The Second Mark Conflict, its Cause and Effects', even if she wanted to.

'In the Eastlands people marry, like they do down South. And Matriarcha Sechuan, who is a very powerful merchant from Colmonte, thought it would be an excellent idea if I married her brother.'

'Married her . . . but . . . but how old are you?'

'Fourteen. Nearly fifteen. In Colmonte that's the perfect age for a girl's first marriage.'

'Couldn't you just say no?'

'That's not how things are done. It was up to my mother to accept or refuse. And my mother couldn't afford to offend the Matriarch. So she thanked her passionately for the honour and regretted deeply that it was impossible

285

for her daughter to accept the generous proposal, as she had already signed a prentice contract with the Academy in Breda a few weeks ago.'

'But – had you?'

'That's what it said on the contract. Even though the ink was still wet. It's very useful, knowing a bribable Clerk of Records.'

'Does that kind of thing happen often in Ormark?'

Merian shook her head. 'No. The Matriarch was showing our family a quite singular honour. Fortunately.'

Kat chewed the end of a very wet grass straw. She could hardly imagine what it would be like to be married . . . and to a man as old as the Matriarch's brother had to be.

'Do you like it here?' she asked cautiously.

Merian made a dubious face. 'Most of the time. I like learning things, and they have the most wonderful library in the world here. But to be honest, I'm not too keen on the hellhorses and all that. If I am ever to bond one, it would have to be a nice and quiet small one . . . and I don't think there are very many of those.'

Kat didn't think there were any. But telling Merian that would do no good.

Suddenly Meiles came scuttling down the ridge on all fours.

'They're coming!' he whispered.

Kat caught a white and blue glimpse of Merian's face. Anxious, wide blue eyes in a very pale face. Silently, she gave Merian's arm a small squeeze. Then she wormed her way up the ridge to get a look at the wild hellhorses.

286

This was not the herd, not the mares and the lead stallion. It was a group of colts, still young enough to stay together. Bruna had said that they became loners later on. As they matured, it became harder and harder for them to bear the scent of other stallions.

They came galloping down the slope, a bobbing wave of silver-white, silver-grey and silver-black backs and necks. Like a school of fish, shimmering brightly. There was even one among them that shone more brass than silver, the rare rossa colour. There were perhaps a score of them. And even though they were still very young, and even at this distance, one could tell that Bruna had told the truth: they were much bigger than the mares, taller and wider, with necks and chests and quarters that bunched and bulged with muscle.

'They're so beautiful,' whispered Merian next to Kat. 'Even more beautiful than the mares . . .'

The group turned and slowed before the last steep drop down to the watering place. By the brook, a skirmish of bites and squeals and kicks broke out. The foremost colt would not let the others get at the water until he had drunk his fill. He bared his teeth and reared, but the other hell-horses were thirsty too, and two of them drove him back into the clear water. Fiercely, he attacked one of them, and they began to do battle, there, in the middle of the brook, so that water rose in a bright spray around them.

'Oh no,' moaned Merian. 'Will they kill each other?'

'Not yet,' murmured Bruna. 'This is what you might call

a training match. It's only when they fight over the mares that it gets deadly.'

And so it proved. The fight tapered off into a more ordinary bickering of flattened ears and bared teeth, and finally the whole group was drinking almost peacefully.

Something screamed. Piercingly, like a bird of prey.

Every single prentice started at the sound, because it came from *behind*. There, on the slope just behind their vantage point, stood a hellhorse stallion. It was bigger, much bigger, than any hellhorse they had ever seen before, and nearly black under the silver sheen. It was so close that they could clearly see the yellow predator's eyes.

'Hold still,' said Bruna softly. 'Ceuta, only if it attacks.'

And Kat saw that Lu had the crossbow cocked and ready. That was somehow very reassuring.

'Let go of your fear,' said Bruna in the same low, calm voice. 'Purge your minds. Exactly like we do in class.'

Kat thought intensely of her medallion, of the way it felt to hold it in her hand, smooth and cool. Around her, the faces of other prentices grew absorbed and calm.

For a long, tense moment, the stallion stood, seemingly indecisive. Then it leaped forward, hurling itself down the slope with yet another of those skull-piercing screams. It ignored the humans on their ridge and swept on downwards towards the colts, screaming like a demon.

The colts startled and scattered. The rebellious one who had not wanted to let the others drink raised its head and answered the cry with a somewhat less forceful scream of its own. But the others had decided to run for it, and in their flight they swept the rebel with them. Soon, the group of colts had disappeared behind the next ridge.

The newcomer stopped at the brook. Head high, he stood with quivering nostrils, scenting the breeze. He shifted his weight and pounded the ground a couple of times with one forefoot. But at last he lowered his head to drink.

'A good time to leave,' said Bruna. 'Ceuta, you take the point, I'll bring up the rear this time.'

No one said anything until they had reached the stone wall. One by one they climbed the rope ladder and went down the steps on the other side. Only when Bruna reached the top of the wall and raised the ladder did the feeling of danger disappear, and the questions came tumbling, one on top of the other.

'Was that the lead stallion?'

'Would it have attacked us, Bruna? If the colts hadn't been there?'

'Hey, I was really nervous. Weren't you?'

'I'm covered in mud!'

'No, it wasn't the lead stallion,' said Bruna. 'He never lets the mares out of his sight. It must have been one of the oldest loners. Well done, Ceuta, that crossbow might have been needed. It was a good thing you were ready.' He glanced at the sky. 'And now, let's get going. Unless I'm much mistaken, those nice little rain clouds we had this morning went home to fetch their mother.'

All the way down Hellhorse Mountain, Kat kept seeing two things in her mind: the young colts bobbing down the slope, quick, strong and alive, and the splintered skeleton. The two pictures kept overlapping, the living and the dead, and it seemed to her almost unbearable that those young colts would end up like that, kicked and smashed and trampled, because they would one day be unable to back down, unable to turn and run.

'Master?'

'Yes, Trivallia?'

'Why don't we catch them? Why aren't they bonded and taken into service like the mares? More of them would survive.'

'It's been tried. Many times. It can't be done. Most of them won't bond at all, and with the few that do, the bond is never strong enough. Sooner or later, they go berserk. Too many people, Riders and others, have lost their lives in the past, and it's now forbidden.'

The downpour grew so heavy that they could barely see through the rain the last mile or so. Not even Kat's oilcloth and sheepskin were enough to save her from getting soaked. As soon as they were once more within the Castle walls, they headed straight for the baths.

'May I join you?' asked Ben Tarquin courteously. There were only five thermals in the boys' baths, and counting all the various arms prentices and stable boys, there were nearly three times as many boys as there were girls in the Academy part of the Castle. Among the Masters, it was even more disproportionate, but at least their baths were more spacious.

'Come on in,' said Merian. 'We'll be properly modest and keep our shifts on.'

Until she arrived at the Academy, Kat had never heard of anything so foolish – bathing with one's clothes on! But here it was not considered good manners to show your naked body to anyone, least of all to someone of the opposite sex. So in the tubs and thermals, one kept one's shift on, and there were tiny booths with slatted shutters behind which one could dry off and get dressed. Merian thought it was silly too, but to Lu and Valente, both raised in the City, it was entirely natural and right.

So there they were, all five of them – Lu, Kat, Tarquin, Valente and Merian – each soaking in a thermal, and letting the heat from the steaming water seep into their cold and stiffened muscles. At least this time, thought Kat, the shifts were so wet to begin with that the bathwater made little difference.

'What a day,' moaned Valente. 'I have blisters up to my knees!'

'Now, that's an exaggeration,' said Lu. 'How can anyone have blisters on their knees?'

'Well, I do!' said Valente. 'My breeches have rubbed my haunches raw.'

The others couldn't help laughing.

'That's not funny! It hurts like hell.'

'You should have worn some of your old breeches,' said Merian. 'New leather is too stiff.'

'I don't *have* any old breeches. I've outgrown them.'

'See,' said Lu. 'It's your own fault. You have to stop *growing* like that.'

'You'll end up like that girl in the song,' said Tarquin, and began to sing:

> 'My girlfriend is nearly twelve feet tall
> My girlfriend is nearly twelve feet tall
> When we're kissing, to get at her
> I must first go get a ladder
> Cos my girlfriend is nearly twelve feet tall!'

He had a nice deep voice, and he sang the song with exaggerated passion, as though it were some tragic tear-wringing ballad. Valente flung a sponge in his face. A very *wet* sponge.

'Really? How about this, then?' said Merian, and added a stanza:

> 'My boyfriend is uglier than sin
> My boyfried is uglier than sin
> So please give me for my wedding
> A sack to put his head in
> Cos my boyfriend is uglier than sin!'

'You made that up!' said Tarquin, pointing an accusing finger at her. 'It doesn't even rhyme properly!'

'So?' said Merian. 'There's a law against that?'

It turned into a contest after that. They took turns coming up with new verses, each one sillier than the other. The poor boy and girl in question gradually lost hair, teeth, an arm and a leg ('But don't think that I'm boo-hooing,/Cos we save a lot on shoeing,' sang Tarquin) and generally acquired one defect after another.

'Eeeeuuugh!' howled Lu. 'Will you stop it, the pair of you!'

Merian and Tarquin looked at each other with an air of injured feelings.

'Never mind, dear,' said Tarquin. 'Some people are just *insensitive* to true art. Whacked on the head with a sword once too often, I shouldn't wonder.'

This time, Lu threw the sponge. And set off a great splasher of a water fight, so that, for a while, they forgot all about blisters and tiredness.

Kat laughed until her stomach hurt. She thought no more of the dead hellhorse colt on the Mountain, or of polecat men and strange dreams full of owls and ermines. She felt at home. She had friends. And she had seen neither hide nor hair of any polecat for weeks now.

MUSTELA ERMINEA

'I am *not*!' said Kat, so loudly that heads turned all over the Refectory. Fortunately it was Waiting Day, the day before Memory Day, and many had already left to go home to their families. Bad enough, though. From across the hall, Master Haryn gave her a measured look, and she instantly regretted having raised her voice.

'Of course I'm not scared,' she said. 'Or I wouldn't have said anything, would I?'

'Oh, we all know you have a big mouth, Trivallia,' said DiCapra with a condescending smile. 'But talk is cheap. Which is good, or you wouldn't be able to afford it, would you? I'd like to see you prove it, that's all.'

Kat controlled herself with an effort.

'Think what you like,' she said. 'As it happens I'm not scared. If you act sensibly, it doesn't have to be dangerous. And at least I know what to wear on a mountain!'

DiCapra's lips tightened. The trip up the Mountain had ruined his almost new riding boots – to say nothing of what

295

it had done to his feet. Kat had been the only one with no blisters to show that day, and he didn't like being reminded of it. But his smile quickly returned, smugger and more superior than ever. To think she had ever thought it nice! Incredible.

'Get me back my knife, then, and I'll believe you. It's on that ridge we were watching the hellhorses from. For a mountain expert like you, finding it should be no trouble at all. Come on, Trivallia. Show us how clever you *really* are.'

A poppy seed had caught itself between Kat's front teeth. Still watching DiCapra, she tried to dislodge it with a fingernail.

'What are you up to?' she said suspiciously. 'Prentices aren't allowed on the Mountain.'

'Now, isn't *that* convenient?' He pitched his voice to mimic Kat's: 'It's not that I'm scared, but we're not *allowed* . . .'

'Think what you like,' she repeated, but she felt her cheeks heating. Putting it that way, her 'boast' did sound rather hollow.

DiCapra looked around quickly. No masters were within hearing.

'I'll make a bet with you,' he said. 'I'm betting three silver marks that you're too chicken to do it.'

'Do I look that stupid? You don't even have three silvers.'

'Don't I? Don't I?' He pulled out the purse he carried at his belt and shook three coins on to the table. Three beautiful silver coins, each the size of a belt buckle, with the royal kingfisher on one side and the number XII on the other, to show they had been minted in the reign of Cora Duodecima.

'Where did you get those?' said Kat suspiciously. It was more than half a year's wages for a fully trained bredinari.

'Not all of us come from a rag-arse family like yours,' said DiCapra scornfully. 'Well? Are we on? Three silvers to get me my knife back. Yes or no?'

She couldn't help seeing it: those three beautiful coins in her own hand. All the stuff she'd be able to buy with it. For a moment she actually considered it. Tomorrow was Memory Day and no one would miss her except Lu, and Lu would keep her mouth shut. And the satisfaction of slamming that knife down in front of DiCapra's superior nose and saying, all right then, pay up . . . that would be worth almost anything. But DiCapra being DiCapra, she didn't trust him. Where had he got the money? His family wasn't *that* rich. They weren't real Capras, just fosterlings and oathsmen who might or might not have fatherblood in their veins. And why would he risk such a sum? He wouldn't do it if he thought he could lose it, she was certain of that. Maybe there was no knife up there. Or maybe he'd rat on her, to get her expelled.

'No,' she said. 'I'm not doing it. I don't trust you.'

He sneered. 'You're scared,' he said. 'I knew it!'

That was by no means the last of it. DiCapra went on and on about the bet to any prentice who would listen.

'Three silvers to get me my knife back,' he would say, 'but she's too yellow to do it.'

'Get the damn thing yourself if it means so much to you,' she hissed one day, utterly sick of the whole thing.

'*I'm* not part mountain goat,' he said, and continued his taunts.

'If only I could be sure that the damn knife is really *there*,' she said to Lu that night. 'I'd get it, just to shut him up.'

'Don't even think about it,' said Lu. 'It might be there, or it might not, but he's up to *something*, that's for sure.'

'I could bring back something else if it isn't there,' Kat said, thinking out loud. 'Something that proved I had really been up there. A bone from that skeleton we saw, for instance. He wouldn't be able to call me yellow any more. And I'd be able to call *him* a liar.'

'Stop it, Kat. You're not that stupid.' And having thought about that for a while, Lu added: 'And if you do it anyway, don't you *dare* go without me!'

The library was on the ground floor of the Masters' Wing, nice and easy to find because you could get to it straight from the sunny flagstoned yard in which Karolin grew herbs for the kitchen, and plums, peaches and cherries. The trees had mostly shed their leaves now, but you could still close your eyes and catch a summer scent of rosemary and thyme if you nipped a few leaves from the plants and crushed them between your fingers. Now, though, it was empty and bare, and every once in a while, a cold wind gusted across the wall and made the oldest cherry trees creak and groan.

Kat stamped her feet on the flagstones so as not to drag in dirt and leaves. It was a gloomy afternoon, heavy and clouded, and through the glass doors she could see that someone had already lit the library lamps. That would be Bookmaster Hermes, the librarian. He practically lived in there, among shelves and scroll racks. He was a fat and gloomy man who hardly ever said a kind word to anybody – not someone in whose company Kat would ordinarily have chosen to spend several hours every afternoon. But the task she had set herself was an important one, and he had proved surprisingly helpful.

She had had a brilliant idea. Or rather, Tad had given her one. Because the perfect Midwinter gift for Merian was, of course, a book. And as she would never in a million years be able to afford to buy one, she would just have to make one. Master Osual had allowed her to spend his classes on this 'writing exercise' – she rather thought he didn't mind having a little free time himself. And when Bookmaster Hermes discovered that the book was for Merian, something as rare as a smile lit his gloomy features. He had helped her find the perfect book to copy. She was still much better at drawing than at writing, and the book the Master had picked off the shelves for her was full of lovely pictures, some in colour, some not. *Bestiarium Bredani*, it was called, and it was about all the animals that lived in Breda. The first few times Master Hermes had kept a keen, distrustful eye on her. She had felt as if he was constantly breathing down

299

her neck, presumably in terror that she'd deface his precious books. But by and by his confidence in her had grown, and he had even praised her drawings. Or rather:

'Adequate,' he had said, as he stood holding her drawing of *Bufo viridis* – *the green toad*. 'When you have finished Merian's book you may come here to do some copying for me. Half a copper penny for every acceptable line drawing, and a full penny for a coloured one.'

Kat had been open-mouthed with amazement. He wanted to pay *money* for her drawings. That was her kind of praise!

She pushed through the glass doors and called out a loud and clear 'Good afternoon!' so that the Master would know it was her. Had it been a 'stranger', he would have come trotting up like some officious guard dog, even though it always annoyed him to be interrupted in his work. As it was her, he merely yelled, 'Close the door!' before she had even had time to get through it. He fought a constant battle to be allotted enough fuel to keep the damp at bay.

She sat down at her usual spot by one of the windows facing the yard. It was a bit draughty there, but when the weather was clear she could usually avoid lighting the lamp. Today there was no help for it. She had to tolerate both the smell of burning oil, and the Master's complaints at the cost.

The animals in the book had been carefully sorted according to how they were related. She had just finished the dog family and had begun on the martens. Yesterday she had copied the pages on the stone marten and the pine marten and the badger. She knew what awaited her today, because she had taken a quick peek the day before. The polecat and the stoat, or ermine. She couldn't help giving a little shiver, but this was only lines on paper, letters and drawings, not people and masks and evil dreams. She folded a clean sheet of paper and placed the line sheet underneath it. The paper she wrote on was thin enough for her to see the heavy black lines through it, and in this way, she could print the letters neat and straight without actually lining the page she was writing on. The line sheet had a box, too, so that she could see how much room she had for her drawings. She unscrewed the lid on the ink bottle, dipped her pen, and started.

The library was such a quiet place. Just the low scratch of her own pen, and a rustle every time the Bookmaster turned a page. It was strange, but she had come to like sitting here, alone and unmoving, watching the drawings grow, line by line. And perhaps it was because she was so busy seeing everything, even the letters, as something that had to be drawn, a straight line here, here a curve, a fatter line here now, and there a thin one . . . perhaps it was because of this that it took her so long to see it.

The polecat. *Mustela putorius.*

The ermine. *Mustela erminea.*

Polecat and ermine – same family, same name. Mustela.

Her heart started pounding wildly, and she had to put down her pen. Polecat and ermine. Both Mustela.

She was back in the darkness of the old Resting Place in

Saratown's ghostly streets. She could almost feel Karel's grip on her arm, how much it had hurt. And she could hear that eerie voice, half-woman, half-man, unplaceable in the dark. *We must have her silence, Austerlin. One way or the other. Will you answer for her, on your life?*

And she remembered what Simon had said about Mustela's fugitive man-maestra: 'You must have seen them cut a colt.'

Ermine . . . she was almost certain. Ermine was Tedora Mustela, the most wanted man in Breda. And she couldn't tell a soul.

Suddenly it seemed to her that the book and the page she was working on screamed the secret for all to hear. *Mustela putorius. Mustela erminea.* It was so obvious. Feverishly, she folded the sheet, not caring that the wet ink smeared and blurred, and hid it inside her shirt. Her hands shook so badly that she had a hard time retying the laces. She closed the book, and then her eyes.

What was she going to do? There was no one she dared talk to. Not even Lu. Or maybe . . . maybe Lu? No. Because Lu also happened to be Domnessa Ceuta, and her family had its own part to play in the game of the Seven, the game to decide who would be Mustela's new maestra.

Mustela would have no new maestra until Tedora was dead. Until Ermine was dead.

One thought chased the other through her head, but she couldn't keep track of all the connections, all the tangled paths. Simon was right. She had no business in that game.

If only she could be sure that she wasn't already in it up to her neck and beyond.

'Are you leaving already?' said Bookmaster Hermes, and if she had been less shaken it might have amused her to hear the disappointment in his voice. Had he actually come to like her company?

'I'm not feeling too well,' she excused herself. 'I think I'll go and lie down a bit before supper.'

He raised his lamp to have a proper look at her.

'You do look pale,' he said. 'Go and rest, and come back tomorrow.'

The wind was wilder now, and tiny cold raindrops spattered her face and neck. She didn't want to draw attention by running, but she walked as fast as she could, through the long galleries and across the Weapons Yard, half expecting cruel polecat masks to come out of the gloom at every corner. But the only Lodge Brother she saw was a Salamander, and he had the mask pushed back on top of his head and was peacefully getting a drink of water from the well outside the Primanotte Chapel.

When she was finally safe in her own room, she pulled out the paper and looked at it again. The black ink had run and blurred a bit, but the letters were still clearly visible. *Mustela erminea.*

She felt an urge to hide the paper somewhere safe, as if it was evidence of something. But in itself, it proved nothing. Others might even have spotted the connection before her. When he asked about Ermine in the common room of the inn all those months ago, it might have been Tedora Mustela Simon had in mind, at least as a possibility.

The big difference lay in the fact that she had actually met Ermine. Not in broad daylight – she didn't think even Cornelius had had that honour. But she had heard that voice, neither male nor female. And she knew at least one of Ermine's bolt-holes.

She folded the paper again, looking around her. What should she do with it? In a room as small as hers, there weren't that many hiding places. Finally she raised the empty brazier and pushed the paper into the space between the flat metal pan and the brick socket it rested in. Then she locked the door behind her and went down to eat her supper.

For three days she tried to convince herself that nothing had changed. She had already decided, once and for all, that she could not tell anyone about Ermine, could not put Cornelius in such desperate danger. That she now felt certain that Ermine was Tedora Mustela did nothing to alter that. So, really, nothing had happened. Nothing important.

Her stomach told a different tale. Her stomach told her that hiding Ermine was bad enough. It was like having a small stone in your boot, rubbing away, a constant nuisance, but at least you could still walk. Hiding Ermine *and* Tedora, that was like having your boots full of rocks, so that you could barely move your feet.

304

She hadn't been to the library since. She just couldn't copy that page as if nothing had happened. And she couldn't just skip it either. Someone might notice it was missing. And what would she tell them if they asked her why?

Lu and Merian were suspicious enough already. They kept asking her what was wrong.

'Is it DiCapra and his lousy knife?' asked Lu. 'You're not about to do anything stupid, are you?'

Kat nearly laughed outright. DiCapra and his teasing was the last thing on her mind right now.

But perhaps it really didn't matter. What business was it of hers if they ever caught Tedora Mustela? It wasn't anything an ordinary Academy prentice needed to concern herself with. Simon had said as much. In a way, even Alcedina himself had said it: all that need concern her was becoming a good and dutiful bredinari. So she wore herself out working with Lu and Master Haryn, and she rode Moon with such decisiveness that she beat Essa's record on the small cross-country course they used now in Bruna's classes.

'Not bad, Trivallia,' said Bruna. 'Not bad. You might actually learn one day.'

Kat couldn't help smiling. That was high praise, coming from Bruna.

She was stiff and tender, returning to her room that night. It had been a day full of rain and mud and wear and tear, so it was lovely to open the door to a room already warm and snug. One of the fireboys must have been by to

SILVERHORSE

fill the brazier. The coals glowed red in the brazen pan, and the heat washed over her like sunshine on a summer's day. She draped her muddy coat across the chair and stood with her back to the brazier, letting the heat undo the worst of the knots in her shoulders.

She stood there, reliving Bruna's praise, for several minutes before the heat of the brazier finally unthawed her brain and made her think of something else. The paper! Was it burnt already?

She had to wrap a pair of her thickest socks around her hands before she could touch the hot pan without blistering her fingers. It's burnt, she thought, there's nothing left but ashes . . . But perhaps that's all for the best. Perhaps I should have set fire to it myself ages ago. Carefully, she tipped the brazier pan.

The paper hadn't been burnt. It was quite simply gone. Gone without a trace, no ashes, nothing. Someone must have taken it.

MASKS

It was Landing Day, the day that ushered in the Midwinter Festivals. The City was awash with festivity. Today, it was not just the Lodge Brothers who wore masks. Everyone who could afford it bought at least a small cheap paper mask, and people paraded about in bird beaks or badger stripes, drinking and eating too much, kissing perfect strangers in the streets, and generally behaving like happy idiots. Under the fine grey cat mask Birch had given her, Kat was gaping with wonder. There was a man with a torch, letting the flames lick at his naked chest as casually as though he was merely washing himself!

'Birch! Wait!' she called, but he just laughed and pulled her along through the bustle.

'Amateur!' he shouted. 'He's a butcher really, I know him. No, I want you to see Emilio Tigerroar; now *there's* a professional.'

They saw Emilio Tigerroar. They saw Rigo and Rosignola, who could walk a tightrope rigged between two houses, right above people's heads! They saw The Heart-Wrenching Tragedy of Remo and Julia, who weren't allowed to marry because Julia was to be the maestra of a Great House and could have no other spouse. Julia was a bit thick about the waist, but she had a voice like a blackbird's, soft and dark like velvet. She drank a poison to make her *look* dead, so that they would make her sister the maestra instead, but Remo thought her dead for real and stabbed himself in the chest. When Julia woke up and saw her dead lover, she took the same dagger and pushed it into her own heart, sang a song, and died. Kat cried buckets, making the grey felt mask rather damp.

'It's just a play,' said Birch, but even he had gone quiet and serious, or at least as serious as it was possible for someone like Birch to be.

Later, he paid a penny so that they could dance in a striped pavilion hung with lamps shaped like the moon and stars, and the fiddlers were from Joss where the dancing is lightning fast, and people swing and spin until they are dizzy. Birch pushed his otter's mask on to his forehead, sweating and laughing, and she told him that he had two noses now, so he had better not catch a cold.

'It's hot enough in here,' he said. 'And I'm thirsty now.'

He wouldn't let her drink beer. She wasn't old enough, he said.

'I was born at an inn,' she said, shaking her head at his silliness. 'They dipped the dummy in beer when they wanted me to sleep.'

But he would hear no arguments and bought her apple juice instead.

'Birch . . .' she said. 'The money. You mustn't spend so much.' She was embarrassed that she couldn't even afford to pay for her own apple juice.

'Oh, but I'm a rich man today,' he said, smiling so widely that the grin stretched his freckles. 'Half of the masks you see dancing here are of my making. And they fetch a pretty price, I can tell you.'

'Did you really . . . I mean . . .' She knew, of course that he was exaggerating, but it must mean that . . . 'You made this?' She touched her own cat mask.

'Sure did,' he said proudly. 'A cat for my Kitten.'

'But it's really pretty!' she burst out, realizing instantly, but too late, that her surprise was none too flattering.

'Of course it's pretty,' said Birch in injured tones. 'What do you think I am, some cheap bungler? My uncle makes most of the Lodge masks, and I've been helping him since l was seven.'

'But if you can do something like this, why do you work in the kitchens?'

He swallowed his beer and wiped the foam off his lips. 'Seasonal, isn't it? Twice a year, Landing Day and First of Spring, and that's that. Not a proper living. Anyway, I like the kitchens. Karolin is great. And she lets me have time off for this' – he pointed to her mask – 'when it's that time of year. Not all masters would do that.'

For a few moments, she considered his good-natured, freckled face which always looked like he was laughing or about to laugh. You had to watch his eyes to know what he was really feeling. Right now, they were serious enough.

'Birch,' she said firmly, 'I like you.'

His eyebrows rose, as if he didn't hear such declarations every day.

'Likewise,' he said. And then he leaned across the table and kissed her, gently, on the mouth. It was a somewhat beery kiss, but quite nice all the same. Still, it confused her a bit.

'I don't want babies,' she said. 'Just so you know.'

Something went down the wrong way, and he had to cough.

'Katriona,' he said, 'I just kissed you. You don't get babies from that.'

Her face flamed scarlet, and she was happy that the mask covered at least the top half of it.

'I know that,' she snapped. Just how stupid did he think she was? 'I just meant that . . . well, being kissed is nice, but that is all we'll do.'

Aren Journeyman, who had brought her from the inn to the Dyer's Yard, had warned her against accepting gifts from caravan people and other wayfarers. You never knew what they expected to get in return, he had said. Birch was no wayfarer, and she was no drifter girl, but all the same . . . You should speak plainly to men, Tess always said, so that they know where you stand. In trade, and in other matters.

'Kitten,' said Birch, scratching the back of his neck so that the otter mask jiggled, 'you are thirteen, and I'm sixteen. A kiss now and then is fine. And enough. Anything else can wait until you're a grown Kat.'

He emptied his tankard and made her finish her apple juice, and then they danced once more until they were flushed with sweat and out of breath. Squirrels and foxes and long red stork beaks whirled past them on the dance floor, so that Kat felt as if she had stumbled into a fairy-tale world where animals walked and talked and behaved like people, only with fur. Or feathers. One of the two storks had to be a fairly elderly one. At any rate, it was moulting so badly that white feathers scattered all over the floor when its fox partner spun it around in the dance.

'Enough,' she gasped to Birch. 'Let's take a breather.'

And so they stood for a while, leaning against the railing and watching others dance.

'Stay here,' he said, giving her hand a small squeeze. 'I need to find a place where a fellow can take a leak without hitting somebody.'

He ducked under the railing and leaped down on to the ground, and soon the crowd had swallowed him up.

She had been alone for only a moment when the squirrel next to her suddenly turned to her and spoke.

'Prentice Trivallia?' he said, with a cheerful smile. Or at least he looked cheerful. Chubby brown squirrel cheeks and two very large white front teeth lent him a very unfrightening appearance.

'Yes?' she said.

'A lady wants to see you,' he said. 'Follow me, please.'

'I'm waiting for a friend,' said Kat.

'This won't take long,' he said, taking her arm. 'Shall we go?'

'No,' objected Kat. 'I told you, I'm waiting for someone.'

Suddenly a badger had hold of her other arm.

'Come on,' it growled. 'The sooner we get there, the sooner we'll be back.'

'I am not going anywhere with you!' Kat tore her arm from his grasp.

'Listen . . .'

'I'll scream if you try to make me!' If only she had been Lu. Lu wouldn't have had to scream, she could just have taken care of them herself.

'I told you she was difficult,' muttered the badger, and suddenly she recognized him. It was Ola, the guard who had surprised her in the hospital gardens on her very first morning in the City.

'Ola,' she said. 'What is this? Why don't you just tell me what it is you want?'

The squirrel and the badger looked at each other. Finally the badger sighed, and pushed back its mask so that Ola's face appeared.

'Trivallia,' he said. 'How come you can never just do as you're told?'

Kat didn't say anything. How was she supposed to answer a question like that?

Ola wiped the sweat from his upper lip with the back of his hand.

'Listen,' he said. 'Felicia Capra-Mustela wants to see

you. Discreet, like. So if you'd just follow us – without screaming, please.'

Felicia Capra-Mustela. Kat's heart beat more rapidly. Stay away from those people, Simon had told her. Be polite, but stay away from them. Right now it seemed she couldn't do both.

'What about my friend? He'll worry if I'm not here when he gets back.'

'I'll stay here and tell him you'll be back in a minute,' said Ola.

'No,' said Kat. 'Mr Squirrel can stay. I'm not running about in the City with a man I don't know.'

Ola looked at Mr Squirrel. Mr Squirrel shrugged helplessly.

'If that is what it takes,' he said resignedly. 'Tell Felicia I'll be back as soon as I may.'

'Have you gone completely crazy?' snapped Ola, as soon as they were out of hearing. 'That was her own damn brother! You don't use the likes of him to run your errands like some messenger boy!'

'How was I to know? He didn't exactly introduce himself, did he? Besides, we're the ones doing the running. All he has to do is stay put.'

Ola gave her a look that said he wasn't quite sure whether to throttle her or laugh at her.

'Sweet Our Lady,' he muttered. 'One day you'll go too

far, I swear. Someone will take your head off, and that might not be just a phrase, do you hear?'

'But how was I to know he was her brother?' Kat repeated stubbornly. It was better to argue with Ola than to think about what Felicia Capra-Mustela might want. Other than to become Mustela's next maestra, of course.

Ola turned off the wide street into a narrower alley, and finally into a tiny, dark yard.

'Here we are,' he said, knocking some signal on a cracked and peeling door. 'Mind your head.'

The door was opened. It was so low that he had to bend almost in half to get through it, and even Kat, who was certainly no giant, had to duck her head. The doorman closed and locked the door behind them as soon as they were through. They were in a badly lit hallway, leading to a door no taller than the first.

'Why don't they have human-sized doors in this place?' she said in annoyance.

'This is safer,' said a woman's voice. 'Much easier to dispatch unwelcome visitors. But you, Katriona, are very welcome.'

Kat had recognized this careful, controlled way of speaking long before her eyes had adapted sufficiently to the weak light for her to make out Felicia Capra-Mustela's sharp features and tidy red-gold hair.

'Maestrina,' said Ola, bowing. Kat bowed too, but said nothing. Just that single word, she knew, was a way to choose sides.

The maestrina nodded briefly. When she realized that

no one else was coming through the low door, she asked sharply:

'Where is Antono?'

'He will be here as soon as he can,' said Ola, obviously ill at ease. 'He . . . er, he had to stay at the square to give Trivallia's friend a message.'

'I see,' said the maestrina. A short silence arose. Kat had a clear feeling that this meeting wasn't running quite according to schedule. 'Take off your mask, Katriona, and sit on the bench there, so we can talk. And thank you for your trouble, Guard. You may now leave. The man at the door will pay you your wages.'

Kat did not like to see Ola's familiar form disappear. But there was no help for it now. In this place, Felicia Capra-Mustela was giving the orders. Kat sat, pushing back her mask. It was not a large room, and it seemed an odd, rude setting for someone like the maestrina. An abandoned kitchen or perhaps a bakery. All of one wall was taken up by an oven and fireplace, but there were no food smells now, only a musty cellar-like smell, of dust and damp. The single window was shuttered closely, and the only light came from a branched candlestick, much too solidly silver to have belonged to the place originally. No doubt the maestrina's people had brought it with them, along with the slim folding chair in which Felicia sat enthroned. She was dressed in silk as red as flame, and at first she was the only person Kat really noticed. Only after a moment did her eyes move on to take in the presence of the three men standing behind the maestrina. Two of them wore polecat masks, causing

Kat's breath to catch. The third showed his face plainly and was dressed in a silken shirt almost as deeply red as Felicia's robes.

'I shall come straight to the point, Katriona, as I know you are anxious to return to your friend. It is in any case best that you do not stay too long. But I have acquired an item that I would like you to explain.'

Kat knew what it was long before the paper was spread before her, and she saw her own inky writing in the flickering light from the candles. *Mustela erminea. Mustela putorius.*

'Explain?' she said tentatively. What was she to say?

'Yes. Why did you set down those two names next to each other?'

'I'm making a book for a friend. *Bestiarium Bredani*. I smudged the ink on the page so I couldn't use it.' Why would her heart not stop pounding? She was afraid Felicia would be able to see her shirt tremble with the force of it.

The maestrina watched her for a while.

'I have to know whether you are telling the truth,' she said. 'Bernardo. The sphere . . .'

The man in the red shirt unwrapped an iron ball from a pouch he carried. A ball like the one Kat had been made to hold on her first day. A magus sphere.

'No,' said Kat. 'I won't let you do that. I hate that stuff!' She meant magic, sorcery, tricks played on the mind.

'It won't hurt,' said the man with the sphere. 'Not unless you're lying. And you're not, are you?'

'No,' said Kat. 'But I won't stand for that!'

Suddenly, the sphere was in her hand all the same. She

couldn't quite explain how it came to be there, but it wasn't really worth making such a fuss over. She wasn't going to lie, now, was she? So why make trouble, when it was so much easier just to listen to Bernardo's pleasant voice and answer his questions as best she could.

She blinked.

Ermine. Had she mentioned Ermine?

'Simon Jossa is looking for someone called Ermine,' she said, sweating. Had she said too much? Had she said more than that? 'A gang leader of some kind, that's all I know. It just struck me that polecats and ermines were related.'

'Did he say anything about where this Ermine might be found?' asked Felicia.

'No,' said Kat, grateful that the question had been posed like that. 'I don't think he knows more than that.'

'I see,' said Felicia once more, in her pointed way. But Kat had not lied, and the iron sphere was still dark and cool in her hand. And she felt, not quite knowing how, that Bernardo's grip on her will was slipping. Posa, she thought. Balance. My will is my own. I neither push nor yield.

'I was hoping for more,' said the maestrina, almost to herself. Then she suddenly grasped Kat's free hand. The physical contact was so unexpected that Kat started.

'This Ermine is a dangerous person,' she said. 'A criminal, a monster even, that has to be caught. Katriona, if you know anything else, tell me.'

'I can't help you,' said Kat tonelessly. And that was just as true as everything else she had said. She could not help

Felicia Capra-Mustela – not when it might cost Cornelius his life.

Twilight had come by the time she got out, but the city was not dark this evening. There were lights everywhere, lanterns and torches and oil lamps, and women with heavy shawls around their shoulders were roasting chestnuts and potatoes over large charcoal braziers. Elsewhere, one could buy tiny ships made from sugar or marchpane, or little animal figures. Landing Day was the day when the families on the seven Talisian ships had landed and begun the long trek that led them eventually to Breda.

Kat stood at the head of the narrow alley, looking bemusedly at the thronging main street. She was not at all sure whether to go left or right to get back to the striped pavilion. And there was something slightly intimidating about asking a rather drunken stag for directions. Finally she turned right, as that seemed to be the way most people were going.

She came to the square where she had seen Emilio Tigerroar perform, and then she was once more at a loss. There were six streets to choose from, and one looked just as good as the other to her. All were about equally busy. A hedgehog and a hare, with long, threadbare ears, had got into an argument and were pushing at each other, warming up to a proper fight. She caught a glimpse of white in the crowd and thought it looked like an ermine. This gave her a pang of unease, which was probably mostly guilt. Then a mob of Chamois Brothers came pouring out of a public house, all of them roaring drunk, and one of them put his arm around her waist and called her a 'shweet lissle pusshycat'. She pushed him away like she would have done with one of the guests back home who had had too much of Tess's good ale. He laughed good-humouredly and staggered onwards. But she couldn't help thinking that here there was no Cornelius to call for if she got into real trouble.

Finally she asked one of the chestnut roasters, who had pushed back a beaver mask so that one could see the reddened face underneath, glistening with the heat from the brazier.

'Pardon me, but how do I get to the dance pavilion?' Kat asked politely.

'Which one, dearie?'

Was there more than one? Kat became even more uncertain.

'I don't know,' she said. 'It's striped, red and white, and the musicians are from Joss.'

'Maybe you mean Mathilda's. You would have to go along Clerk Street over there, and then right along Our Lady's. The pavilion is in the square in front of the Motherhouse.'

Had there been a Motherhouse? Kat couldn't remember seeing one, but then, not all motherhouses were equally big and impressive, and there had been such a crowd . . . She thanked the chestnut woman and fought her way through the throng to Clerk Street, marked clearly with a sign bearing a quill and an inkwell. Why hadn't she paid more attention to the streets on her way to the meeting with Felicia Capra-Mustela? Because she had been too busy *thinking* about Felicia Capra-Mustela, of course. But if she had noticed just one or two signs, it would have been a help.

For a long time afterwards, that was all she remembered. That she had entered Clerk Street, beneath the handsomely enamelled inkwell sign, on her way to meet Birch at the pavilion.

She never got there.

THE MOONBEAM STALLION

She was lying with her feet in the water. Why was she lying with her feet in the water? It seemed a stupid thing to do. Her legs were getting wet. All very peculiar, but she was feeling too leaden to do anything about it. She could always move them tomorrow. Today was Landing Day, so tomorrow there was no school. Plenty of time then, to move heavy stuff like feet . . .

What was wrong with her?

What had happened?

She had kissed Birch. Well, all right, *he* had kissed *her*. Why was she thinking about that now? Because the kiss had tasted like beer. And this place stank of beer. Bad beer, at that, sour and much too yeasty. How had she come to drink such bad beer? He would only buy her apple juice.

It was really very uncomfortable here, with rocks and water all over the place. Her head hurt.

She was lying on her stomach, with her cheek crushed against something hard-edged and cutting. Gravel. Pebbles.

Rocks. She tried sitting up, but she was terribly dizzy. She rolled over on her side instead. Stars were out, she saw. It would be a cold night.

It *was* already night. It *was* cold.

What on earth had happened. Had she fallen?

The dizziness was less when she was lying still. But she had to find out what was going on. Legs. How did one make them move? She could barely remember. But she managed to draw up her knees, so that her feet were no longer in the water. They were so numb. She could hardly feel them at all. Finally she managed to prop herself against a boulder, so that she could take in her surroundings.

In front of her, the moon was mirrored in a waterhole between great boulders. Pretty. On both sides of the hole, the ground was pocked with hoofmarks. Other than that, the view was mostly blocked by a stand of frail birches, ghostly white in the moonlight.

She put a hand up to feel her head. The hair on one side was all matted and stiff, as if she had been bleeding. If so, it had stopped now. Then her fingers encountered a very tender spot. Ouch! There was a lump the size of a duck's egg, and it hurt. It hurt like hell, to be precise.

She must have fallen. On one side of the hole, the bank was quite steep. She could have slipped, tumbled down the slope, hit her head on a boulder. Perhaps even the nice one that propped her up right now. But where was this, and what was she doing here?

Her head nodded on to her chest. She raised it sharply, despite the jab of pain the movement sent through her skull.

She mustn't sleep. She had to get up. She could die, sitting here. Had to get up. Had to. But it was so very hard, and suddenly the moon had moved, and it was no longer just her feet that were numb. Time had slipped by, time that was simply gone, sucked down into the black hole the fall had made inside her head. And on the other side of the water, among the white birches, stood a hellhorse.

It was very young, barely more than a foal. The legs still looked spindly, with large lumpy knees. Maybe that was why she didn't get scared right away. It looked so timid itself, as if it hardly knew what to do with the world without its mother to guide it. And when she did get scared, so scared that the fear came crawling out of every dark nook and cranny inside her, it wasn't really the young colt she was terrified of. It was what its presence meant.

She was on Hellhorse Mountain.

Soft quilts, drifting clouds. Poise. Serenity.

'Hello, horse,' she said softly, when she felt calm enough. The young colt started. Maybe it hadn't seen her until now. It raised its head to get her scent, nostrils quivering. Then it spun, and trotted away among the trees.

There would be others. She sat by a pool that was frequently used, if the hoofmarks were anything to go by. And the next hellhorse visit might not be a single, timid youngling.

She clutched at the boulder and struggled to her feet. There was something wrong with one ankle. It didn't hurt, but that was probably because it was completely numb from the wet and the cold. It just felt shaky and strange, as if it didn't much want to support her.

First things first. She had to get away from the water hole. She limped from tree to tree, holding on to the trunks. Every once in a while she had to stop and wait for the dizziness to pass, but she found she could fight it if she could find her way to posa. Poise. Serenity. In the end, walking became an exercise like those Master Haryn had so often set her. She wasn't moving. It was the landscape that slipped slowly by. Trees and shrubs. Boulders. Grassy slopes. A brook.

A brook. What about it?

It wasn't *a* brook, she realized. It was *the* brook. If she followed it, she would reach the place where she could climb up the wall and into the safe passage between hellhorse territories. Safe from the hellhorses, at least, if not from the cold.

She staggered on. No more trees to support her. She fell. Everything spun and floated, and she wasn't sure she would ever be able to get up. She curled up on her side, with her knees against her chest and her hands clutched under her chin as if that might make them warmer. Her face was wet. Her neck was wet. It was only then she realized that she was crying.

There was a roll of thunder. Not from the sky, but from the ground, from the rocky ground she was lying on. She raised her head. And there they were. The hellhorses. This was no small group of exiled colts, not ten or a dozen. This was a herd. All of them. Like a river down the mountainside, a silver river in the moonlight, a stream of nodding heads and arched necks and shiny chests and flanks. The sound of drumming hooves rolled from one side of the valley to the other. Kat bit her lip and tasted salty tears, but just for a moment pain and cold and hopelessness were forgotten, because she knew that few, very few, people in the world had ever seen what she saw now.

They didn't halt, probably did not even notice a small human form crouched on the ground. But she was so close to them that she saw the dark skin of the nearest under-bellies and felt the spray from hooves splashing through the brook.

It was as if they drew her on, drew her to her feet when a moment ago she had not thought she would ever get up again.

One more step, she thought. I can always take one more step. And walking is warmer than lying still.

She was no longer afraid of the hellhorses. She had not forgotten how careful Bruna had been. She remembered Lu with the cocked crossbow, ready to shoot if the dark stallion had attacked them. But she no longer thought they would attack her. If she met a hellhorse now, they would pass each other quietly, she thought, like two strangers going each their own way.

Finally the stone wall appeared, a long line of shadow running down the mountain. When she reached it, she stood for a long time, breathing heavily, with her back against the stones. She didn't dare sit down, afraid that she might not be able to get up again. Now, where were the

325

stone steps? Where was that nice and easy way to the top of the wall?

And then she remembered. The steps were on the inside. On the passage side of the wall. When she and the others had climbed *this* side, they had had Bruna's rope ladder.

It was unbearable. So close to safety, and it did her no good at all. She couldn't climb the wall. Her hands and feet were numb, and if she fell . . . she didn't even want to think about that. One more knock would black her out completely.

There was only one thing to do. Follow the wall down the mountain. Somewhere down there was a gate, and even if it was locked, she could hammer at it until somebody heard her.

Crossing the brook was awful. She didn't dare try to leap it. She climbed laboriously down one bank and waded across the strong icy current, getting her feet completely soaked all over again. Fortunately, the bank on the other side was only waist high, so she could roll across it, crawl to the stone wall on her hands and knees, and haul her way back on to her feet with the support of the wall. Once there, she started walking again. One step at a time.

Tess had never been much of a singer. She had always maintained that she was tone deaf. But there was one song she used when she wanted Kat and her siblings to stop crying. It kept going round and round in Kat's head:

> Papa Barber he had gotten
> A leg of rotten mutton

Which he paid for, the old glutton,
With an old forgotten button.
Mama Farmer she was knittin'
A mitten for a kitten
Sittin' hidden in the midden –
Oh what a sight to see!

But the kitten's mitten didn't
Fit the kitten as was fittin'
And a-hissin' and a-spittin'
She went flittin' through the midden
And the rotten mutton gotten
With the old forgotten button
Made them dizzy of a sudden –
So now there's only me.

There were six more stanzas, every one as silly as the first.
She wasn't sure she could remember all of them.

'. . . So now there's only me,' she sang quietly, under her
breath. She wished that Tess was here to sing it to her. It
always worked. It was so completely silly that they could
never help laughing. There was one stanza about some
washerwomen wishing washing wasn't always wet and
sloshing, and one about three hairy hags who went sailing
in a leaky boat with a shoe for a paddle, 'Oh what a sight to
see,' and one of them tried to fix the leak with her dirty
shift, 'but the ship was soon a-driftin' and the shift was
shortly shiftin' . . . and now there's only me.' But Mama

327

Farmer and Papa Barber were the ones she remembered best, so she sang their verses once more.

And then one more time. And yet again. Out of the corner of her eye she could see a horse made from moonlight, white and silvery, and so silent she wasn't sure there was really anything there, other than some ghost that had come out of her own tired head. When she turned to get a proper look, it had gone. But there were so many shadows, so many shrubs and boulders and clouds drifting past the moon, it was hard to be certain of anything. And why would a moonshine horse follow her? Well, maybe it liked the song. She sang it again.

'. . . and now there's only me!'

A shower of pebbles rattled down the slope from somewhere above her. Kat paused. Carefully, she looked once more. And this time, she saw it quite clearly. It was as white-skinned as Moon, but other than that it looked nothing much like Bruna's patient mare. It towered above her, taller, broader, bigger in every way. A stallion. Its eyes were deeply orange, like embers. Its nostrils quivered.

How could she have been so stupid? To hobble down the Mountain, singing, like some dim-witted picnicker. Forgetting everything she had been taught. Thinking herself invulnerable. Thinking that the beautiful hellhorses would never hurt *her* . . .

The stallion snorted. It hadn't decided to attack yet. But it was obviously interested in her. She didn't dare turn her back on it. Better not to move at all. The stallion arched its neck and flung up its head in a gesture of impatience.

328

She stood stock still, hoping it would just lose interest and go away.

It didn't. Instead, it came closer, and she needed every last bit of her hard-earned serenity not to shrink from it. She could smell it now, the strong smell of horse that had been such a safe smell once, at home in the stables of Crowfoot Inn, a smell that went with warmth and summer-scented hay. For a few moments, the stallion stood, gauging her. Then it suddenly took one step closer and thrust its muzzle at her, pushing hard enough to send her stumbling back against the stone wall. It was not an attack. More the sort of forceful nudge it would use to direct a mare or a foal.

And she suddenly realized that it was lonely. No horse, not even a hellhorse, is meant to be alone. But the stallion was certainly old enough that it would no longer be able to bear the scent of other males. And apparently it was also still wise enough to stay away from the herd and the lead stallion. So right now, she was its herd, or the closest it could get to one. It did not mean to let her go.

Her back against the stone wall, she sweated in the chill of the night. The stallion took yet another step forward, crowding her.

'Go away, horse,' she said, without the proper determination. 'I'm no herd.'

Its ears flickered at the sound of a human voice, and it stopped. The moon slid free of its thin veil of clouds, making the ember eyes and the silver coat glow eerily. Kat let her hands wander over the wall behind her. Were there any handholds at all? Any place she could lodge a toe, so that she might climb over? The stones were hard-edged and uneven, and moss grew in the cracks. Perhaps she might be able to gain a foothold here . . . slowly she turned sideways from the stallion and tested the most promising crack with her toe.

'Just stay there, horsey,' she murmured, trying to turn it into an ordinary safe old nag in her mind, and not at all succeeding. She found an edge she could hang on to. Finally turning her back on the stallion completely, she clawed her way upwards. She had to be quick now. She flung up her left foot, her heel just catching the top of the wall. Now, just one last heave . . .

It was like being jabbed with a club. The hard ridge of the stallion's nose rammed her against the wall, and she lost her grip and tumbled to the ground. The black hole inside her head opened up again, and she knew she was very close to losing consciousness altogether.

'Mama Farmer she was knittin' a mitten for a kitten . . .'

She hardly knew what she was saying, knew only that she could not afford to faint now. Anything that held the black hole at bay could be used. Another nudge, softer this time. A get-on-your-feet nudge. And it was sound advice. Things lying on the ground looking half dead came much too close to looking like food. The hellhorses on the Mountain sometimes ate the flesh of both dead and living creatures, Bruna had said. With a huge effort, she climbed to her feet.

The stallion was watching her again, its ears flickering. It could probably only barely remember that it had once heard human voices, and felt human hands on its body. It had not been born up here, but the colts were only yearlings when they returned to the Mountain. What made it pause and listen like this could hardly be the memories.

Kat slowly turned to the wall again, but this time she kept talking.

'Papa Barber he had gotten a leg of rotten mutton . . .'

Foot wedged in the crack, right hand up, a quick scramble and then up with the left leg . . . Sweet Our Lady, *please* . . . The stallion was screaming madly, that shrill bird-like cry that should never come from something so horse-like . . . Heave, come *on*, now . . .

Teeth closed on her right calf, cutting through leather, skin and muscle, and the stallion tried to pull her off the wall. She clung to rock, to nettles, to hawthorn, to anything she could get a grip on, kicking fiercely with her trapped left leg, and managed to tear herself loose. She swung the left leg up too, and crouched there for a moment, and the silver-white hellhorse screamed yet again, rearing up as if to climb the wall to get at her. There was no herd instinct in the flaming eyes and bared teeth now, and she drew back, losing her balance and tumbling down the other side of the wall, on to the path.

It wasn't that hard a fall. It was more that she had spent every last bit of strength and will in that last scramble. She made one final heaving effort to get up. Then she collapsed into a sprawl, let her head sink on to her arm, and went out like a light.

*

331

She was alone on the mountain, and it was night. Her heart was hammering inside her chest, and she ran as best she could, but her feet were like lead. The moonbeam stallion galloped easily next to her; it slid across the rocks soundlessly, like snow on a windowpane. She knew it was there but did not dare to turn her head. If she slowed her pace for even a second, if she stumbled and fell, it would be over in seconds . . . it would tear her limb from limb with its sharp yellow fangs, and all they'd ever find of her would be a broken skeleton . . .

'*Kat!*'

The voice was much like Lu's, but Kat couldn't see her. Her eyes were blinded by feathers. The white owl swooped down silently, talons outstretched, eyes glowing like coals in the night . . . The Night Owl, *Strix aluco*, of the family Strigidae, and the order of Striges . . . lines on paper, talons in the darkness, whispering masks and iron spheres growing hot in her hand . . .

'Katriona – can you stand?'

That had to be Master Haryn.

'No,' she said. She wanted to stay where she was. Wasn't he the one who always told her there was no point in training when one was injured?

'We'll have to carry her. Lu, if you take her feet, Birch and I can—'

'*Ouch!*'

'Where does it hurt?'

'My foot . . . my leg . . .' She hardly knew which was worst, the jab in her ankle or the sharp tearing pain when the wound in her calf tore open once more and began to bleed.

'Sweet Our Lady . . .'

That was Birch. Birch, whom she'd kissed. Well, all right, who had kissed her.

'You'd only let me drink apple juice,' she said, affronted.

'Well, you seem to have made up for it since,' said Birch. 'The stench of bad beer is somewhat overpowering. Master, is that a hellhorse bite?'

'Yes. On your feet, Katriona. We'll help.'

And so they lifted her between them, with one of her arms draped around Master Haryn's neck and the other across Birch, to sit on their clasped hands.

'It's a good thing you're big for your age, Birch,' she muttered.

'Kat . . . Did you hit your head, or are you merely drunk?'

'Yes,' she said. 'Lump like a duck's egg.' She clenched her teeth. She was becoming dizzy again. 'And the rotten mutton gotten with the old forgotten button made them dizzy of a sudden . . .'

'Kat – will you *please* be quiet?'

'. . . and now there's only me!'

'How could you be so *stupid*?'

Kat didn't answer. She lay in her bed, picking bits of fuzz off her blanket, one minute grateful to be alive, the next consumed with a vast, burning desire to be dead. Or at least to be somewhere else. Anywhere else.

'You *promised* you would forget all about that stupid bet,' hissed Lu, eyes narrow with anger.

Kat didn't know what to say. She couldn't remember deciding to try to win the bet. But if not for the three silver marks, what on earth *had* she been doing on Hellhorse Mountain? In the middle of the night, too. She picked at the blanket.

Lu sighed, and hoisted one hip on to the bed.

'Stop that,' she said. 'Or you'll have no blanket left.' One brown hand came down on top of Kat's paler one, stilling it. 'Did you find it, then? The knife, I mean.'

'No,' said Kat. 'I can't even remember looking for it.'

Lu shook her head. 'How on earth did you get that drunk? It's not like you. I know it was Landing Day, but still . . .'

'I don't think I was drunk . . .' said Kat, considering it.

'Oh, please!' Lu snorted. 'You stank like a cheap alehouse.'

'That's precisely the point,' said Kat. 'I just can't see myself getting drunk on bad beer . . . my mother makes the stuff, for Lady's sake. I know good ale from bad. And how did I pay for it? I had no money.'

'None?'

Kat shook her head. 'Birch paid for everything. And he wouldn't buy me a beer. He said I was too young.'

'Well, how come you ended up smelling like that? I'm telling you, you absolute *stank* of it.'

'I know,' said Kat with a grimace. 'Maybe somebody spilled it on me. What do I know? I can't remember any of it.'

'You were dead lucky, you know,' said Lu. 'If it hadn't been for the mask we would never have thought of looking for you on the Mountain. We thought you'd got lost in town.'

'I did,' said Kat. 'At least, I think I did . . .' Then she realized what Lu had said. 'Mask? What mask?'

'Your cat mask. You'd hung it on the gatepost. Don't you remember that either?'

'No,' said Kat slowly. Masks. Something about masks . . . polecat masks. Owl masks. Oh, *why* couldn't she remember? She closed her eyes and lay back among the pillows.

'Kat?'

'Mmmh?'

'I'm sorry about Master Haryn.'

'What do you mean, sorry?'

'We didn't dare go up on the Mountain alone, Birch and me. And I thought Master Haryn might be willing to help us and keep quiet about it.'

'Yes.'

'Actually, I think he would have, only of course we had to run into Master Medes. And he couldn't stand there and lie to a fellow Master.'

'No. Of course not.'

'And you just wouldn't keep quiet. You kept singing that stupid song.'

'Mmmh.'

'What is it with that song, anyway?'

'It's one my mama taught me. She sings it to the little ones when she wants them to stop crying.'

'Oh.' Lu was quiet for a bit. 'I thought you were just being drunk.'

'I wasn't drunk.'

'No. I guess not.'

If Lu said anything after that, Kat didn't hear it. She fell asleep.

'Prentice Trivallia, were you aware that the Mountain was expressly forbidden to prentices?'

Kat ducked her head. 'Yes,' she muttered.

Alvar Alcedina stood leaning against his desk, arms crossed. Behind him, in armchairs, sat four members of his council. Kat recalled them from the day she had told them about Dorissa. The day she had been admitted to the corps.

'Please speak up, so that the councillors can hear you,' said Alcedina, his eyes positively glacial.

'Yes,' said Kat, very loud and clear. They've already made up their minds, she thought. Doesn't matter what I say now.

'Why, then, did you go there?'

Kat blinked. 'I don't know,' she said. It was the only true answer she could give them, yet she knew they would not believe it.

'You don't know?'

'No . . .'

'It would have nothing to do, then, with a certain bet? A bet you made with Prentice DiCapra?'

'I made no bet with DiCapra.' That, too, was perfectly true. She never had agreed to the bet.

'So you did not endanger yourself, and the lives of others, in order to win three silver marks?'

'No!' she said, very loudly. 'And what others? I was the only one who got hurt.'

'I'm thinking of your rescuers,' said Alcedina. 'It was pure luck that they did not actually have to enter hellhorse territory. And it is your claim that this had nothing to do with the three silver marks?'

'Yes.'

'Why, then, Prentice?'

Kat looked at her feet. 'I don't know,' she whispered. 'I don't remember very much about it . . .'

Alcedina straightened and brought his gloved hand down on his thigh with a whiplike snap.

'Because you were intoxicated?'

'I was not drunk!'

'Master Medes reports otherwise. I believe he used the words "yodelling and stinking like an alehouse".'

'I had hit my head!'

'Your account, Trivallia, is hardly thorough, nor consistent. In fact, the only consistent thing about you seems to be your insubordination. The fact is that you have been unable to abide by the rules that govern prentices in this place. The fact is that brawling, disobedience and irresponsible behaviour have marked your career here from your first day onwards. You have admittedly displayed a certain ability. Several of your Masters have spoken in your favour. But when talent is not coupled with discipline and responsibility, we have no use for it in the corps.'

I knew it, thought Kat. The decision was already made beforehand.

Alcedina seated himself behind his desk.

'Prentice DiCapra receives a warning. His behaviour has not been beyond reproach either. But as for you, Trivallia, I see only one solution. The prentice contract is hereby void.' He made a note on the paper in front of him. 'You will have three days to vacate your present quarters. I see you had a horse on your arrival. It will be released to you as soon as possible, and you will be paid an appropriate lease for the relevant category of animal. The uniforms you have been issued must be returned to Supplies.' He raised his eyes from the paper. 'Oh, and one more thing. I require Rider Granes's medallion.' He held out his hand.

That felt like a blow to her stomach. Unexpected. Unfair.

'She gave it to *me*!'

Alcedina's blue gaze trapped hers.

'You may have a suitable sum in coppers, as compensation. But I cannot let an ordinary citizen walk around wearing a bredinari medallion.'

His expression was adamant. If she did not give it up, he would have it taken from her, forcibly if need be. She could see the threat quite clearly in his face.

She brought out the small bag in which she kept her silverhorse medallion; clutched it for a moment, unwilling to let go; then let it drop into his palm. She would not cry. She would *not* cry.

'Thank you,' he said. 'You are dismissed.'

She turned and walked all the way out of that room without limping. Her ankle was still very sore and swollen, but she would rather die than hobble along like some lame pedlar's nag while they were watching.

RABBITS AND WEASELS

Kat stood there in her old, worn clothes waiting for the Quartermaster to finish noting and filing and checking and attesting that former Prentice Katriona Trivallia had not appropriated so much as a brass button that was rightfully the property of the corps. She had to remind herself not to resettle Cornelius's old belt all the time. It kept slipping down on to her hips, unusually heavy with everything she had packed into it – most notably the copper coins. She didn't want to draw attention to it. She wore it under her shift, against her bare skin, and had relegated the job of keeping her trousers up to a cheap string girdle.

She had never in all her life had so much money. Eighteen marks! Copper, of course, but even so. They had given her two silver marks for the services of her gelding for a little over four months, and three copper marks for the void prentice contract. Rane had earned more than she had . . . And then there was the compensation for Dorissa's

341

medallion. She had wanted to fling the money in their faces, she had wanted to shout at them that they could keep their filthy compensation. But she had finally hung on to just enough sense to know that she would need the money now. So she accepted, but asked to have everything paid in coppers instead. You could pay anywhere with coppers without calling attention to yourself.

Eighteen marks. It sounded like such a lot. But if she stayed in the capital, the money would drain away like bath water, even at the cheapest inn she could find. Prices were so steep. And what would she do here, anyway, now that she was not going to be a bredinari one day? She was no city girl. She was always losing her way.

Karolin had told her they could use her in the kitchens. But to be still here, day in, day out, watching the others, the ones not kicked out . . . watching as they became Silvers, while she still stood there with her hands in the dish-water . . . no, it didn't bear thinking about.

The Quartermaster's pen scratched its way down the list, marking each item that passed over the counter. Jerkin, shirts, the lovely warm cloak – she could have used that now . . .

Suddenly the scratching of the pen was stilled.

'These boots . . .' The Quartermaster had an ailment of the lungs and had to draw in a hissing breath every other word or so. 'These boots . . . they were issued . . . less than a month ago . . .'

'Yes,' said Kat, in affirmation. She had got them a few weeks before her birthday.

'How, then . . . may I ask . . . did they come . . . to be in this condition?'

The reproachful glare he gave her was certainly justified. The boots were more or less ruined. They had been a fine pair of dress boots in soft grey leather, but after that night on the Mountain, they looked like something the dogs had been fighting over. Now they were really in no better shape than DiCapra's. Worse, in fact.

'Manoeuvres, Master,' she said politely, hoping he would let it pass at that. If he told her she had to pay for them . . . she discovered she had put a hand on the belt, as if she meant to defend her meagre fortune with her fists.

And then a delayed light went on in her brain. Her boots looked exactly like DiCapra's had done after that tour of the Mountain Bruna had given them. And no matter how drunk she had got (and she had *not* been drunk, she was positive about that), no matter how moronic and confused she might have been, no matter how hard she had hit her head . . . she would never have gone walking on the Mountain in a pair of silly dress riding boots. Never. Not in a million years.

It followed that she had not gone walking on the Mountain – of her own free will.

Surprise made air hiss between her teeth, causing her to sound almost like the Quartermaster. He gave her a sharp look, as if suspecting her of insolence.

'Is there . . . a problem, Prentice?'

'No, Master,' she said, quickly. 'No problem.'

If she had decided to win DiCapra's stupid bet, she

would have worn sensible clothes, and at the very least, she would have used Dan's old mountain boots. And if she had, she probably wouldn't have taken that fall . . .

Once more, she was brought up short.

Fall . . . maybe she hadn't fallen. That lump on the back of her head – it might have been caused by something completely different. A blow with a bludgeon, for instance. Or something. And that big black gap in her memory . . . well, if she could not recall how she had got from Clerk Street to a waterhole on Hellhorse Mountain – it might be because she had been unconscious during the ride.

Oh, yes. It seemed glaringly obvious now. Someone had hit her on the head in Clerk Street, then brought her to the place where she had woken up and the beer – that same someone could have poured a pitcher of cheap ale over her head, just to convince everyone that she had been drunk. Drunk and irresponsible and untrustworthy.

'Very well,' hissed the Quartermaster. 'Here is your receipt. Do not lose it. The guard at the gate will require you to show it when you leave.'

'Thank you, Master,' she said automatically. Her thoughts were elsewhere. In a very dark and dangerous place.

Why? Why had they done it? *Who* had done it?

She pulled up her shirt and her shift and slid the receipt into one of the compartments in the belt. Belatedly, she remembered that she had meant to keep the belt a secret. She looked around quickly, but the Quartermaster was already deep in an argument with a young bredinari who

344

was of the – very loud – opinion that he could no longer *possibly* wear this rag of a shirt: the bredinari seemed to be losing the argument. The Quartermaster hissed one polite refusal after the other, and the regret in his voice did not sound particularly genuine.

They had to be crazy, she thought. Not the Quartermaster and his dissatisfied customer, but the mysterious someones who had dumped her on Hellhorse Mountain. They might have killed her!

A chill spread through her, starting in her backbone and working its way out. They might have killed her – and perhaps that had been more or less the intention. Perhaps they were even now regretting that the Moonbeam Stallion had only got hold of a leg.

Landing Day and its bobbing crowds of masks and people came back to her. Had there been a mask that bobbed up a little too often when she looked back? A polecat mask, perhaps? A polecat mask like those worn by Felicia Capra-Mustela's guards? But no. It made no sense. The maestrina did not want her silence, she wanted her to talk – and to reveal the whereabouts of Ermine. It suited Felicia not at all that Kat was now expelled from the Castle.

Mustela putorius. Mustela erminea.

Felicia wanted her to talk.

Ermine wanted her to be silent.

Ermine – *here*?

Unthinkingly, she looked around wildly, as if expecting the mysterious form to lurk behind the next corner. She hardly knew whether she was looking for a four-legged predator or a two-legged one. Ermine. The Nightmare beast with its red eyes and gaping jaws. The voice in the darkness, whispering words that meant silence or death. In her mind, they came together, and she hardly knew one from the other. From the black hole in her memory, something emerged – she was not sure whether real or dream. A glimpse of a mask among other masks, the mask of a beast of prey, with fur as cold and white as snow, and sharp white teeth in a red maw. *Had* she seen it, somewhere among friendly beavers and cheerful squirrels and weaving drunken stags? She became more and more certain. There had been an ermine. An ermine, following her.

For one long panicky moment she was deeply grateful that she was no longer apprenticed to the Academy. All she wanted to do was run. To get *away*. Away from this place and its terrible mazes. She walked as quickly as her sore ankle would let her; saddled Rane with shaking fingers; forced herself to fasten the packs properly, so that they would neither slip nor hurt nor hinder; showed the guard the Quartermaster's receipt.

And then she could finally ride through the gate and down the causeway. Free. And perhaps safe.

Three days out from Breda City, she became certain that someone was following her.

This late in the year, the caravan road saw few travellers. Those that did brave the weather usually took up with one another, for company and safety. She had heard hoofbeats behind her several times, but without getting any answer to her calls of greeting, and without being caught up or overtaken when she halted Rane for a rest.

On the fourth morning, she rose before the sun. She had chosen to sleep in the stable with Rane, as it was cheaper. If she didn't make it to the Vales before snow closed the passes, she and Rane might be in for a hungry winter, living off the meagre funds she kept stowed away in her belt. She saddled Rane and led him out the back way, past the middens, so as not to be spotted by her pursuer. With a big enough head start, perhaps she could lose him entirely.

Rane was grouchy and ill-mannered and had no desire to trot off into the darkness. Kat was in no mood to argue, however. She urged him forward firmly, and he grudgingly obliged. It was a cold and bitter morning, and the low hedge of hazel and willow did not break the force of the wind much. After less than a mile, her fingers were so numb and stiff they would hardly hold the reins. She had to stop and rummage in the pack for her mittens.

Suddenly Rane jerked up his head, and his nostrils quivered. She put a soothing hand on his neck and stood listening anxiously. Now that they weren't themselves making muddy clip-clop sounds, she heard it quite clearly: hoofbeats. And as she listened, they moved from a trot to a canter.

Quickly, she swung down off the gelding's back and gave his quarters a sharp slap. Rane started and leaped forward, trotting stiff-legged down the road. She dived behind the hedge, hoping the few puny leaves still clinging to it would be enough to hide her. Of course, the sun had chosen that moment to begin rising, so the leaves were no longer black but had acquired a trace of gold around the edges. She crouched, making herself as small as possible.

A large chestnut appeared, cantering along the road. Its rider was bent low over its neck, perhaps to make out Rane's trail. Kat held herself absolutely still, hardly daring to breathe. *Ride on*, she thought. There's no one here at all. Silence, silence . . . no one at all.

This careful silence was torn apart by an ear-splitting whinny. Oh, no! Rane had not liked his lonely freedom. Now he came trotting back, high-stepping and arching his neck almost like a hellhorse. The chestnut came to an abrupt halt. And the stranger on its back had no trouble spotting Rane's empty saddle.

'So that's the way of it . . .' The voice was low and menacing. The rider turned and looked straight into the hedge, directly at Kat. There was no face beneath the hood of the cloak. Just a mask. An ermine, glowing palely white in the morning gloom.

Kat turned to ice.

It was impossible to stir even a finger.

Rabbits sat like this, helpless in their cages, when the weasel slipped between the bars. Next morning, all that was left was the bodies. Too big to be dragged from the cage the way the heads had been. Kat had seen it several times, those headless bodies, bloody and dead. When she had been younger, she used to cry. Later she just cursed. Now, she neither cried nor cursed. She was a rabbit herself now, cowering, hugging the ground, and knowing it did no good.

'Come here . . .' whispered the voice. 'Come here, little one . . .'

Kat rose slowly. If she did *exactly* as he told her . . . if she was very, very obedient and good . . . maybe he would not . . . maybe she would not end up like those other rabbits. Headless. A small bloody mess at the bottom of the cage.

Rane extended his nose towards the chestnut, snorting. The chestnut squealed and pounded the ground with one hoof. Such a oddly ordinary sound. That was how it went whenever two strange horses met. One had to be careful they did not get into a fight.

Ermine did not care. He paid the horses no attention at all. He just reached for Kat with long, pale fingers and grasped both her shoulders, hard, close to her neck. He had strong hands. Hands like Master Haryn's, or Master Medes's. Soldier's hands.

And he had a beard.

'Little one . . . do you want to live?' That same voice, whispery and low.

Kat nodded dumbly. She was staring at the curly dark hairs on his chin and neck. A beard.

'You must learn then. Learn to keep your mouth shut.' His thumbs bored into the hollows beneath her collarbone, and Kat gasped in pain. Tears stung her eyes.

'Do you understand?'

Kat nodded once more. *But Tedora could not have a beard.* Was Ermine not Tedora, after all?

'And you must stay away from Breda. If you return, you'll die. Is that clear, little girl?'

'Yes,' whispered Kat.

'Run, then, little girl. Run while you can . . .'

Or was this not Ermine?

There was something in that thought that thawed her frozen limbs. If this was not Ermine, he was just a man in a mask. He let go of her shoulder with one hand, and she had just enough time to realize that he meant to hit her.

She spun to one side, out of his one-handed grasp, so that the blow hit nothing but the air next to her ear. Three paces brought her to Rane, and in a wild leap she made it almost on to his back. Almost; she hadn't been quite quick enough. She sensed him behind her and kicked both her legs backwards, straight and hard, not aiming for anything in particular.

Aimed or not, her kick was effective. The man stumbled back with a roar, both hands clutching his lower face. Blood welled between his fingers. With any luck, she had broken his nose. She got her leg across Rane and kicked him so hard he gave an offended grunt and took off at an unbalanced gallop.

Heedlessly, senselessly, she made him run, and Rane, catching her panic, stretched his short, strong legs with a will. The sun had cleared the horizon, but to Kat this only meant that she would be easier to see. Was there no farm-house, no village, nothing with people in it?

Finally some low, whitewashed buildings appeared; still she did not ease her pace, but sent Rane thundering into the yard, so that dogs and chickens scattered in all directions, barking and squawking. Safe. *Oh please, let this be safe.*

She had to lead Rane around the yard for a long time before he stopped blowing, and she knew any plans she had had of moving on that day were doomed. One couldn't ride a horse into a lather at dawn and then expect him to do a day's travel on top of it. She paid the farmwife two pennies for food and lodging for herself and Rane, and then spent some time rubbing down the gelding and grooming him, until he was happy and calm once more and her own nerves had settled a bit. And then she started thinking.

Perhaps she should have known right away that the ermine mask did not cover Ermine's own face. Surely he would not dare show himself so close to Breda City. But if not Ermine, who was he? Who would aid and abet an outlaw in that manner? And not just any outlaw – Tedora Mustela, the most notorious of them all, hunted from one end of the country to the other.

But perhaps that was it. She remembered what had happened at Saratown last year. Remembered how men had flocked to Ermine. Even Cornelius had been drawn to his side. Because . . . she fumbled for the words . . . because he had done the unthinkable. He had proved that a man *could* be a maestra, could even be maestra to a large and powerful clan, one of the Seven Families, no less. A man could hold land and not be struck down by lightning. The sun still rose every morning. The seasons still turned.

351

The Locus Spirit had shown not the slightest sign of offence. He had committed the worst sin a man could commit, and he had got away with it – at least for a while.

Once, Cornelius had shouted at Tess: *You think you know everything. But you don't. There is a place. And there are others like me. Why should a man not own a house, or a bit of land? Do we not work the land? Do we not defend it? Sweat for it and bleed for it, as much as you do? Why are we to be chased from place to place our whole life long, never to say, 'This is my place, here I stay'?*

There might be others dreaming the same dreams, thinking the same thoughts. Ermine might have his followers in places other than some distant hamlet in Three Valleys.

Do you want to live? You must learn then. Learn to keep your mouth shut.

If you return, you'll die.

They wanted her out of Breda City, that much was clear. Away from powerful people like Felicia Capra-Mustela and Alvar Alcedina who might even pay attention to what a lowly prentice was saying about ermines and polecats and other animals. They did not want her to tell tales. If they could shut her up without actually killing her, that was easier. But if not – well, she did not think they would shrink from killing. Only luck and accident had got her off Hellhorse Mountain alive.

She thought the rangy chestnut could easily have caught up with sturdy little Rane if the rider had wanted to. Perhaps she had kicked him harder than she thought. Or perhaps he had turned back because he had accomplished

352

what he had set out to do: scared her half to death and ensured that she would not return to Breda City.

Well, we shall see about that, she thought.

Although it was nearly noon, the barn had a twilight feel to it. Pale winter sunlight entered only sparsely through the cracks in the wooden walls, and most of the gloomy space was filled with hay and straw. There was a sweet and somehow warming smell of dried summer.

Kat stood in the empty space between the piles and stacks, barefoot and dressed only in her shirtsleeves. In one hand she grasped a stick somewhat longer than her arm. Slowly she raised it, and began First Wave, the first pattern she and Lu had ever practised together. She started it calmly, almost draggingly, then gradually increased her speed, still keeping her movements precise, exact, just as if she were faced with a real opponent, an opponent she was unable to see.

When the pattern came to an end, she was slick with sweat. Carefully, she put away her stick, even though it was just a length of hazelwood she had hastily cut for herself. A training weapon, Master Haryn would say, is still a weapon, and not to be treated with disrespect.

She put her woollen jerkin back on right away, so as not to chill herself, although heat went all the way through her right now, in every fibre of her body. She hadn't said goodbye to Master Haryn. She hadn't said goodbye to anyone, not even Lu. She had quite simply run away. Now she was ashamed to have been so easily panicked.

She had been afraid for such a long time; afraid, and confused, because it is hard to feel anger against someone you can't see. And her opponent had been invisible to her. Now that had changed.

The man in the ermine mask probably thought he had scared her out of her wits with his threats. That she would now be more scared than ever. But she wasn't. She was afraid, yes. Ordinarily afraid. Of ordinary things. Of people who could hurt her. But she was no longer scared of Nightmares and masks and whispering voices without faces, without bodies. Now she knew her enemy.

She thought of everything Ermine had taken away from her. Simon. She had not been able to be honest with Simon. Lu. Merian. Birch. All the friends she had found at the Castle. And the hellhorses. Ermine had taken her dream, her dream of becoming a bredinari, a bredinari of the right kind, who rode out to help people that *needed* help.

I won't stand for this, she thought, so fervently that she felt her silent words really should be echoing around the gloomy barn.

She still could not turn around and go back to Breda and put the whole matter into the hands of someone like Felicia Capra-Mustela or DomPrimus Alcedina. Not when Ermine held a knife at Cornelius's throat, in a manner of speaking. But Master Haryn had taught her that even such a knife could be dealt with. She just had to work out how.

*

354

She rode on the next day, shortly after dawn. She guessed the man in the ermine mask might still be watching her, so she took care to look like a thoroughly frightened country girl who wanted nothing more to do with the big city, or anyone in it. A small, terrified rabbit, fleeing for its life. In short – a coward on the run.

In reality, she wasn't running anywhere. She had decided to go and find Simon.

TROLL HEIGHTS

Snow fell heavily, but more calmly here, where the buildings broke the wind's main strength. Kat leaned forward and swung her leg over Rane's snow-covered quarters. She was glad she had decided to spend some of her eighteen marks on a blanket for him, but although she had chosen mostly to sleep in the stables with him instead of buying herself a bed, she now had only four marks left. It was a good thing her journey was over.

Standing on the ground felt strange. The last stretch had been a long one, because halting for a rest in this weather made little sense. What mattered was to reach warmth and shelter.

The Tora Vale Resting Place had once been large, well staffed and much used. It had four wings, but two of them now looked ill-kept and deserted. She wriggled her toes inside her boots, just to make sure they were still there. Then she waded through the snow to the main entrance, with Rane trudging wearily at her heels. He was tired and clearly thought he deserved a warm stable and a proper meal.

'You'll be taken good care of,' she told him, and reached for the rope of a large copper bell hanging in a frame next to the door. When she pulled it, it set up a satisfying clanging, like the sounds from a smithy.

The door opened.

'I thought I heard hooves . . . What crazy weather! Let's get your horse stabled right away, because I expect you want shelter, don't you? The stable is over there, but wait a moment, I just need to get my boots on . . .'

She had been expecting Simon. She had been imagining his surprise, and had armed herself with careful explanations. But this rapid stream of words came from a black-bearded young man she had never seen before. The rolling flow was a bit overwhelming, and she only managed a 'Yes' and a 'Please' and a 'Thank you', and then they were at the stable door. She loosened the straps of the pack with stiff fingers and shook the snow off Rane's blanket, so that it wouldn't melt into the wool in the sheltered warmth of the stable.

One half of the building was packed with straw and hay from floor to ceiling, so that the body heat of the few animals kept there would be enough to warm the room. There were only a couple of ponies, a goat with a half-grown kid, four sharp-hipped milch cows, and two hellhorses, Simon's Grizel and a mare Kat had not seen before. They looked ill-matched with the rest of the motley crew, like two royal ladies trying to mingle with the peasants.

'Oh good, at least Simon is here,' Kat said in relief. When he had not come to the door, she had been half afraid that he had vanished into the Southlands, like Dorissa.

'Simon?' said Blackbeard. 'You know him? No, I'm afraid he's not here, he's away on some business. But he'll be back in a few days, weather permitting.'

'But . . . without Grizel?'

'He thought that an ordinary mountain horse would be better able to make the trip.'

Kat felt a small, cold shiver of unease somewhere in the pit of her stomach. 'Where was he going, then?'

'South Vale, and the way the snow is coming down right now, there's always a risk the passes may close.'

Snow. And more snow. And no Simon. It was very nearly unbearable. The coldness in Kat's stomach turned into a permanent lump of ice – slippery and chilling and unwilling to settle for long. She tried to get Remus Varas, the black-bearded young bredinari, to say more about Simon's plans and whereabouts, but on this subject the talkative Remus had surprisingly little to say. He parried her questions with vague evasions – Oh, just some business of his. Don't worry about it. He'll be back any minute. Just something he had to do. Nothing special. Somewhere in South Vale. He'll be back. It's just the snow, delaying him.

It was driving her crazy. The snow kept coming down,

and she felt an increasingly strong desire to strangle young Varas, despite the liking she felt for him otherwise. Finally, she had had enough.

'I can't wait around any more,' she said firmly. 'I'm going home to my family.'

'Where do they live?' he asked suspiciously.

'Oh, somewhere in South Vale,' she said with barely hidden satisfaction.

He did not appreciate getting a taste of his own medicine.

'The pass is closed,' he said. 'You won't get through.'

'Don't worry about it,' she said cheerfully. 'I'll think of something.'

'Katriona! You mustn't! I won't permit it. Simon would be furious.'

'You can't forbid me anything,' she said. 'I'm nobody's prentice any more. Not yours, not Simon's, and not DomPrimus Alcedina's. I can do exactly as I please.'

And the next day, she did.

There is a way from Tora Vale to South Vale even when the pass is closed. There is a mountain path a little to the south. It is not for the caravans with their carts and heavy wagons, and most riders would probably hesitate and turn back. The track is narrow and in places dangerously steep, and a traveller has to be both stubborn and sure-footed. But for someone who had grown up in the Vales and had a mount that was steady and sensible and used to the mountains, it was possible even in this weather. Kat spent her last money at the Toratown Forge, having the smith hammer frostnails into Rane's shoes so that he would be better able to walk the slippery trails. And the smith, who knew her mother, lent her an old axe.

'It's a little rusty, but once I've sharpened it for you, it'll be almost good as new,' he said. 'Give Teresa my best wishes, will you?'

Kat listened to the way he said 'Teresa' instead of the usual everyday 'Tess'. Sweet Our Lady, she thought, is there any man in the Vales *not* in love with my mother? But the axe was a godsend: now she would be able to cut firewood along the way instead of having to drag it all with her. Rane would have quite enough to carry as it was.

Fortunately, the snow had stopped falling by the time she reached the first really steep rise. There were still some hours of daylight left, but she knew it would take her a full day to get across the mountain, and it was better to spend the night here, where the trees still provided shelter and protection. She cut enough pine-boughs to build a shelter big enough for both herself and Rane. On the outside, she packed the wall with snow, making the space inside snugger still. Then she chopped enough firewood to last the night. Luckily there was birch aplenty – and birchbark would burn, no matter how wet. She struck a spark with her tinder and fed the tiny flame carefully, first with needles and twigs and curls of bark, then with sturdier branches.

It was the first time she spent the night like this, alone in the snow. Cornelius had taught her how it was done – the fire, the shelter, and so on. Later he had taught Mattie and Tim the same lessons. It was something he insisted on before he would let you go on the mountain alone.

She stared into the flames. Cornelius had taught them a lot. So many clever tricks. So much about how to cope, how to survive. After she had left home, those lessons had gradually come to seem more important to her than the rows and the fights and the beltings. He did try to take care of them – of Tess, and of her children. And he had taught them how to take care of themselves.

She slept quite well for a few hours, probably because she was so tired. Then she woke up, because she was cold. She piled more fuel on the fire and snoozed on for a bit. Rane, too, slept, standing up but with floppy ears and one hind leg cocked and tucked under.

It was still dark when she finally gave up on sleep. Again, she put more wood on the fire and melted a bucketful of water for Rane, and then made some mint tea for herself. The gelding was awake now, too. His dark eyes glittered in the glow from the fire.

'Here you are,' she told him, making up his feedbag. 'Breakfast!'

She wasn't quite sure how long it would be until the sun rose. The sky was clouded and she couldn't see the moon. But dawn or not, they would have to move. This was too cold.

She ducked out of the shelter and gave her stiff muscles a good stretch. Then she got the hazel stick from her pack and practised First Wave as best she could wearing a sheepskin coat and mountain boots, on sloping, snow-slippery ground. It might even come in useful, she thought. Parry and evasion could become necessary at any time, and she might well need it wearing a sheepskin coat and mountain boots, and on sloping, snow-slippery ground.

When she had finished the pattern, the dark had grown less dark. The snow had begun to glow with a weak, rosy glow. She packed up and readied Rane for the trials of the day.

'Well, then,' she said, eyeing the trail that snaked up the slope towards the first ridge. 'Might as well get on with it, don't you think?'

There weren't many places she could actually ride. Mostly, she led him. The trail was marked here and there with white chalk smears on the dark tree trunks or on boulders along the path. This was a good thing, because she had come this way only twice before, and that was all a long time ago.

The trail rose steadily almost all the time, sometimes so steeply that she had to use the hazel stick as a 'third leg'. The stick was also handy in places where drifts made it hard to judge where the ground was.

Rane trudged along at her heels steadily and calmly, without twitching a hair on his muzzle. Not even once when she slipped and crashed into his forelegs. He just stood there stolidly, not shifting a hoof, until she had regained her balance and her footing.

'You may not shine like a fish in sunlight,' she told him,

patting his dull brown neck, 'but right now I wouldn't swap you for a herd of hellhorses!'

She hardly dared to rest. Heavy blue-black cloud hung just above the pinetops, and snow might start falling again any moment. If there was a blizzard like the one a few days ago, it would become very hard to continue. She had no desire to imagine what might happen if she lost her bearings in the snow.

The pines thinned and grew less tall. There was something cowed and creeping about them here, as if they were afraid of snapping if they stood properly upright. The path dropped. At first she thought it was just a small dip, but then she realized that she had made it across the first ridge, Pigeon Hill. At first the down-slope made a nice change. It was still a strain, but a different kind of strain, braking and holding back, so that the front of her thighs grew sore with it. There were hardly any trees now, only an even layer of snow and low bushes. Underneath the snow was grass, she remembered. In the summer, cows and goats were pastured here, but they had of course been brought down into the valley months ago.

The ground was even enough that she might actually ride for a while. She cast a gauging look at Rane, trying to measure his endurance. He didn't look particularly tired, but ahead of him waited the worst and steepest rise: Troll Heights. No, better not. She had tied two bundles of firewood to the pack as a safety measure, so he had enough to carry without her added weight.

In the open ground here, one could see much further.

The topmost ridge of Troll Heights poked up through the treeline, grey-white and bare, like an old man's bald crown. She would not need to go so high. The trail hugged the treeline most of the way, and she was going round Troll Heights more than over them, which was just as well. She would be going quite high enough as it was.

It was hard to tell what time of day it was. The sun was completely invisible behind the slate-grey cloud cover. She had a feeling it might be around noon. She dug into her food bag and fished out bread and sausage. She could gnaw the sausage as she walked. Rane begged most of the bread off her, as it had become a bit dry and boring.

Trees again now, mostly low fir and birch. Kat felt a new achey strain in her weary thighs and calves.

'Uphill again, horsey,' she said, and Rane snorted, blowing steam from his nostrils like some fairy-tale dragon. She glanced up at the Heights. There were many tales about how they had acquired their name, but Tad said it was just because some twisted stone pillars along the trail could be seen as trolls turned to stone, if one had a good enough imagination.

'Someone marked the trail that way once, and wind and weather did the rest,' she told Rane. That was what Tad had said, the one time she had come this way with him. But actually she thought that that 'someone' sounded a bit ominous in its own right. Who could casually tip huge boulders upright just because it suited them? Who, if not rock trolls?

She met the first of the 'trolls' just above the treeline, at

365

the highest and most dangerous stretch of the trail. She was grateful for Tad's explanations about weather and wind. When she stood at the foot of the pillar and looked up at its point, it was like looking up into a sad and furrowed face. Kat felt like putting a comforting hand on the troll's arm, or rather, on the mossy bulge along one side of the rock body. But in the end she refrained. Just to be on the safe side. She couldn't quite forget all the stories of curious shepherd boys and girls who had wakened something they should have left alone. *With a roar, the troll rose and bit off Little Olga's head in a single bite* . . . No, better not risk it.

Then it began to snow.

The timing couldn't have been worse.

On one side of the trail, a wall of rock rose steeply to such a height that she could barely make out the top of it. On the other, there was a drop almost as sharp. Not vertical, but if she stepped off the edge, it would take a very, very long time before she stopped tumbling. She might just possibly survive the fall, but she didn't feel like trying.

It was definitely *not* a place to camp.

There wasn't much she could do except go on, as cautiously as she could. And now the trolls were no longer sleeping monsters. Now they were something firm and secure, standing between her and the chasm. You could *see* them, even through the whirling fog of snow. Tall and dark they towered above her, and as long as she kept to the left of them, she was on firm ground.

Sometimes it felt almost like being back on Hellhorse Mountain. Step by careful step she walked, one foot in front of the other, keeping her balance almost as precariously as that night, though it was daylight now, and this time she was not dizzy from a knock on the head.

Finally, the trail levelled out, then dropped. At the foot of the first slope, the going became much more even, and ahead of her, she saw the first proper trees. And this time, these were woods she knew, woods that belonged to her own familiar Vale. In a few hours, she would be home at Crowfoot Inn, and then the snow might fall as it would!

It was nearly dark when a bone-weary Rane came to a dead halt in the yard behind the inn. He remembered the place, that much was clear. The last bit of the way he had been as eager as his tired legs allowed.

The snow probably muffled the sound of his hooves. At any rate, no one came to see what guest had arrived or to attend to the visitor's horse. Not that she minded. She knew her way around, of course, and after a day like today, she would trust no one else with Rane's care. Not after such a trip. She led the gelding into the stables. It was pretty full – more horses there than Cornelius normally kept during the winter. Had he become serious about horse-trading this year? But she did finally find an empty stall for her tired horse. She fed him well, groomed him carefully and made sure he had plenty of fresh water. Then she put out the lamp and let him rest and chomp away in peace.

She hardly had the energy to lug her packs across the yard to the inn. But in her head, she heard the combined voices of Cornelius and Simon: *Take care of your gear and your gear will take care of you.* So she gathered up the lot, pack, saddle and all, and stumbled across the snowy cobbles to the back door.

Mattie was in the kitchens. She was doing the dishes, and the light from the kitchen lamp fell on her fair hair and bent head, and threw long shadows on her face. When she saw Kat stumble stiff-leggedly across the threshold, she dropped the beer mug she was cleaning into the basin, so that soapy water splashed all over.

'Hello, Mattie,' said Kat.

'Kat? *Kat!*' Mattie's soft voice was hoarse with surprise. 'What are you doing here?'

'They kicked me out,' said Kat in what she hoped was a totally calm and matter-of-fact voice.

Mattie looked at her for a moment without saying anything. Then she threw the rag into the dishwater and flung herself into her older sister's arms, and started crying, in low, noiseless spasms.

'Don't cry like that,' said Kat in embarrassment. 'It's nothing to bawl about.' And then something tore loose inside her, and she too started sobbing, even louder than Mattie. They stood like that, on the kitchen threshold, holding each other tight and crying, each worse than the other.

Mattie was the first to pull away. She controlled herself with a visible effort, dabbing at her face with the hem of her apron.

'Sorry about that,' she said, with much greater composure. 'I didn't mean to go all weepy on you.'

Kat sniffed and blinked and watched her sister. She had grown. She would always be Kat's little sister, of course, but somehow she was no longer quite so little. She had become tougher, harder round the edges.

'What's wrong?' asked Kat quietly, because something clearly was.

'Nothing,' said the new, tough Mattie. 'I was just surprised to see you. I've missed you.'

'I've missed you too.' Kat picked up her pack and saddle from where she had dropped it and hung it on one of the pegs in the passageway. That would do for now, she felt. The rest – the cleaning and the oiling, and so on – would have to wait for tomorrow. Now that she was truly home, tiredness had set in with a vengeance. She was so tired it hurt.

'Where's Tad?' she asked, looking around the kitchens. It was not like Tad to leave Mattie to do all the hard work on her own.

Mattie had gone back to her dishwashing. Kat thought she kept her eyes a little too strictly on the basin.

'He isn't here right now,' she said. 'But Tess is in the common room.'

'Tess is right here,' said a quiet voice from the other doorway. 'How did you get into the Vale, Kat? I thought the pass was closed.'

'I took the Troll Heights trail,' said Kat, trying to sound as if that was the sort of thing she did all the time now. And then she stared.

Tess had grown old. Her hair was just as raven black,

369

and she had not suddenly acquired a faceful of wrinkles. That wasn't it. It was something inside. She seemed smaller, as if something inside her had broken.

Kat opened her mouth. Then closed it again. What's wrong? she wanted to say. Have you been ill? But you didn't ask Tess questions like that, not even now.

'Where is Tad?' she asked instead.

'Gone,' said Tess briefly. 'Mattie has taken over the kitchen now.'

Kat stood as stone still as the trolls up there along the trail. What did Tess mean? Tad, gone? Gone how? Where? He couldn't be! He had been here always. He was . . . he was nearly Kat's father, though she had never quite thought of it like that before. The one who was always there, always the same. The one you could trust.

'What do you mean, "gone"?' she whispered, terrified that it might somehow mean 'dead'.

'Left,' said Tess. 'With Cornelius. I don't know where they went.'

Men did leave. Men travelled, they came and they went. It was a common thing. But not Tad. Never Tad. And not even Cornelius.

'Is it your fault?' she asked her mother, shaking with sudden fury. 'Did you do this? *Did you chase them away?*'

'Watch your tongue!' snapped Tess with some of her old fire. But then the brief spark of temper died, and once more she looked as if she had already lived a hundred years too long. 'No,' she said tonelessly. 'It's not my fault. Why did you come home?'

'I . . . I wanted . . .' At first Kat could not remember a single one of her reasons for coming home. Then she seized on the easiest. 'I'm looking for Simon. In the Tora Vale Resting Place. They said he had come here.' All right, so Remus had just said 'somewhere in South Vale'. But Kat had always had the feeling that that 'somewhere' was here.

'We haven't seen him,' said Tess. 'You had better go back to the Resting Place and wait for him there.'

Kat was speechless. She had battled her way through the snows, she had fought her way across Troll Heights step by weary step, and now her mother just told her that 'you had better go back' – as if the whole hazardous trip had just been some summer picnic she had been on.

What was going on?

Tad was gone, Cornelius was gone, and Simon had never come here. Tess looked like a broken-spirited old woman. Mattie had become hard and almost a grown-up. And, she suddenly thought, adding one more piece to the puzzle, the stables were full of unfamiliar horses.

Something was very, very wrong here.

ERMINE TRACKS

In spite of her worries, she slept late the next morning. She was so exhausted that when she woke, the loft was empty. Mattie, Tim and Nicolas, and the three little ones, had all managed to get up and tiptoe downstairs without waking her.

Her legs felt as if they were made from wood. Big heavy logs that it would take six strong men to lift. But she did succeed in swinging them clear of the bed without such help. The air up here under the eaves had a chilly nip to it, and she pulled the quilt over her shoulders like a shawl while she sat in bed, wondering what to do.

Her sense that something was badly wrong at the inn had only increased. She had intended to interrogate Mattie once they were alone upstairs with the little ones asleep, but Mattie had stayed in the kitchen so long that Kat could barely keep her eyes open. And the few sleepy questions she had asked had been parried by Mattie in a style worthy of Remus Varas.

Tad and Cornelius had left. And that was all the information anyone would offer.

She clutched the quilt more firmly around her and settled herself in the attic window. It was close to the floor and with a wide sill, and in the old days it had been a sort of combined hideout and lookout post for her. No one spent much time in the loft during the daytime. In the summer it was too hot, and in the winter too cold. But with a quilt wrapped around you, you could sit like she did now, watching what went on in the yard through the yellowed windowpanes.

She saw Nicolas come out of the stables, carrying two buckets. He undid the well cover, hooked one bucket on to the rope and lowered it. He had to use all his strength to haul it back up again, she could see. He appeared to take care of the horses now, which was quite a job for a nine-year-old – no, a ten-year-old boy. And with so many horses to look after, too.

Nicolas suddenly froze in the middle of hauling up the second bucket. Someone had come into the yard. She couldn't see who, but she could hear a muffled voice. Then Nicolas replying. Then the voice again. It had to be a man. Nicolas let go of the winch. The handle spun round and round as the weight of the bucket pulled it back into the well.

'Oh, Nicolas, why did you do that?' she murmured. 'It was nearly all the way up! Now you have to do it all over again.'

The patron, or whatever he was, came further into the

yard. Kat could see him now, but recognizing people when you saw them from above was not easy, particularly not when they were wearing hats. He held the reins of a powerful grey horse. That was why Nicolas had had to let go of the winch, it seemed. The guest wanted him to take the horse, and at once. What would Nicolas do with it? Rane was now occupying the last free stall.

The guest stamped his boots to clear them of snow. Funny how some sounds echoed on a snowy day while others grew muffled. The stamping sounded like whip cracks. He unwound the wide woollen scarf wrapped around his neck and lower face, took off his hat and shook the snow from it. He looked a lot like . . .

He looked like Karel. At this distance, Kat couldn't be sure, but he certainly *looked* like him.

Karel, who had stayed with them for several weeks last year, and whom they later discovered was probably a highwayman and, certainly, one of Ermine's men.

Kat pressed her cheek against the glass, trying for a better view. Was it him? Same matted dark hair. Same big, heavy body, as far as she could see from up here. Not the same horse as the one he had been riding then, but people did change horses. The grey looked to be a better mount. Stronger and hardier. As if quite familiar, the man approached the back door, and was lost from sight.

She darted to the stairs and eased open the door. Sounds from the passage and the kitchens rose through the stairwell, and she could hear every word.

'Right then, Mattie my lass, go get your mother!'

Sweet Our Lady, it *was* him.

'People in the ale room,' said Mattie.

'Who?'

'Keri Herbwife. She's been to see Asa Farmer's old ma.'

'Has the old hag finally decided to die?' He sounded as if they were discussing the weather. Do you think it has decided to rain? It made Kat angry. Asa's ma was as old as the mountain and no longer in her right mind, but she was still a person!

'It looks like it.' Mattie wouldn't let on that she was bothered too, but Kat, knowing her so well, could hear the slight tremor in her voice.

'Is she staying long?'

'Till it's over. Unless someone else sends for her.'

'Damn.' A bench scraped across the flagstones. He had probably sat down. 'Give me some of that stuff. Why did you have to send for the herb witch? Surely the old woman could manage to die without her help.'

'Keri would think it funny if we didn't send.' A bowl rattled against the table top. 'And we were supposed to pretend everything was normal, right?'

'That would be the wise thing to do.' The threat in Karel's voice was unmistakable.

Silence for a while. Either he was thinking, or he had begun to eat. Eat, decided Kat, when she heard a slurping noise a little later.

'Pah!' he spat. 'This meat is not fit to eat!'

Kat grinned. Mattie had probably given him some of the stewing steak, which had to be boiled for hours before it was tender. Well, well. Little Mattie! Little Mattie who never disobeyed or answered back.

'I'm sorry,' said Mattie sweetly, 'but it was a very old cow. We didn't know you were coming.'

'Shut your mouth, girl, and get your mother. Tell her there's a man with . . . what sort of things do you buy at this time of year?'

'Hare,' said Mattie. 'Or grouse.'

'Hares, then. Tell her there's a man here with some hares to sell. And make sure she brings a mug of ale.'

The door to the ale room opened and closed. Karel slurped on. Apparently, he was hungry enough to eat, whether or not the meat was tender. Or perhaps he was just eating the soup and leaving the meat. Then the door opened once more, and she heard the clacking of her mother's heels.

'So?' said Tess.

'Ale first,' said Karel.

There was a brief pause. Kat could almost feel her mother's resistance. Then the mug was plonked down in front of him, and Kat heard him drink in great gulps. He made almost as much noise as a calf or a horse.

'Ahh,' he finally said, the satisfied sigh of a man after the first long draught. 'You're a troublesome bitch, Tess, but you make good ale.'

Kat listened carefully to the tone of his voice. But no, she didn't think Karel was in love with her mother. And by the sound of it, Tess hadn't fallen for him either, Lady be praised.

'The letter,' said Tess, as if she had not even heard Karel's remark.

'Easy now. Hold your horses.' He drank once more. 'Tell me, Tess, how does it feel not to be maestra in your own house?'

What?

'I am the maestra, as much as I've ever been. That piece of paper makes no difference. No Motherhouse in its right mind would ever acknowledge a *man* as maestra.'

'Well, you're probably right about that,' said Karel, unruffled. 'So we'll just have to do things a little differently, that's all. Entirely without Motherhouses, maybe . . .'

'You're all insane,' said Tess, but in a strangely tired way, as if she had said it a hundred times before and no longer believed it would make any difference. 'Now, give me the letter.'

'If you ask me nicely,' said Karel, in a mean voice. 'On your knees, like.'

On her knees? *Tess* on her knees? Not on your life.

'Or you know who will get hurt . . .' continued Karel silkily.

There was a pause. Then a rustle of skirts. 'Will you please give me my letter?' asked Tess, in a voice Kat had never in all her life heard her mother use.

Kat couldn't stand it any more. She pushed open the door and sneaked down the stairs, avoiding the steps that creaked. She got down flat on her belly on the landing and poked her head over the edge.

Tess was kneeling on the kitchen floor, the skirts of her

blue winter dress spreading around her like a pool of water. The only bit of Karel that Kat could see was one knee. Then he leaned forward and put his hand under Teresa's chin.

'A shame you're so high and mighty,' he said, and for the first time he sounded a little – just a little – like one of Teresa's many lovesick men.

Tess looked at him with a gaze that could have made flies drop dead in mid-flight. He released her, and finally brought out something from inside his shirt.

'Here.' He gave her a folded sheet of paper.

The door to the ale room opened.

'She's gone,' said Mattie. Then she came to an abrupt halt. 'Mama? Why—?' She looked from Tess to Karel and didn't finish her sentence.

'Go and get another mug of beer,' said Tess sharply. Mattie went away and came back soon after. By then, Tess was on her feet again, skirt neatly settled.

'Mama? Will you please read it out loud?'

'Yes,' said Tess, unfolding the letter. She began to read.

'The way it's snowing now, I can see why you've been thinking about icicles all week. Here, we are reasonably warm. Thank you for the raisin bread – it was delicious. Cornelius is better now, and his fever is down. Everyone else is doing fine. I am perfectly comfortable, and you have no need to worry about me. No one hurts a cook, you know. At least not as long as his cooking is good . . . This week I will be thinking of that raisin bread – so tasty. What will you be thinking? Kiss the children from me. Love from Tad.'

'Sniff, sniff,' sneered Karel. 'Isn't he brave? He's right,

though, about the cook bit. It's nice to have some decent grub for a change. Go on, then, write your bit. This one I'll keep – just in case, eh, ladies?' He snatched the letter from Tess's grasp. Mattie looked as if she would have liked to read it for herself, but she didn't say anything.

Tess went into the passage and through to the small enclosure she used for an office. Kat hastily snatched back her head. A while later, her mother came back, holding another folded sheet of paper.

'And what did you think of this time?' said Karel, taking the letter with a grin.

'Maggots,' answered Tess firmly, staring at him with a complete lack of expression.

The back of Karel's neck turned beetroot red, and he seized her roughly by the arm. 'If that's supposed to be an insult . . .'

'Insult?' said Tess tonelessly. 'What insult? It's a code word. That's the deal. We can think of whatever we like.'

Karel let go of her. 'As long as you remember the rest of the deal as well,' he said menacingly.

'Don't worry,' said Tess. 'We forget nothing. Not a single thing.'

'You never give up, do you? But this time the boot is on the other foot. Are the supplies ready?'

'It's all in the barn.'

'Get the boy to load it, then. Use two packhorses if you have to.'

'He's only ten,' Tess protested. 'He won't be able to lift the heavy sacks.'

'So? You'll just have to help him, then, won't you?' He stretched and yawned. 'I'll be upstairs, having a lie-down. Wake me when you're done.'

Kat snatched a breath. If he came up the kitchen stairs ... but he wasn't familiar enough with the layout of the house to think of that. He went into the ale room, and she heard him tramping up the stairs to the guest rooms. Quickly, she slipped down the few steps into the passage.

'Did you really write *maggots*?' whispered Mattie.

'No,' said Tess. 'I wrote that the cat had had a kitten, even though it was in the middle of winter, and I would be thinking of that. Maybe he'll guess that Kat has come home.' She sighed. 'Well, I had better give Nicolas a hand with the sacks.'

She came into the passage and stopped dead still when she caught sight of Kat.

'How much did you hear?' she asked, her voice low.

'All of it.'

Tess stood there for a moment, wiping her hands with her apron, though they didn't look particularly dirty to Kat.

'I told you you should have stayed in Tora Vale,' she finally said. 'Now we have to make sure he doesn't find out that you're here.'

They had no chance to talk properly while Karel was still around. And when he finally left, Keri Herbwife came back to rest for a while before tackling the night watch with Asa's old ma. Kat had to go and hide in the loft so that Keri wouldn't see her and start an endless trail of gossip about the sudden reappearance of 'that redhead at the Inn'. Tess took over the cooking, and Mattie took the little ones to play in the barn so that they wouldn't let the Kat out of the bag, so to speak, until Keri too had left. From her perch by the window, Kat looked on longingly as the twins screamed with laughter and threw snow at each other down there in the yard. She hadn't seen them for such a long time, and being stuck up here left her with far too much time to brood and think and get scared. It was impossible to talk properly until much later, when Keri had had her supper and had gone to sit with Asa's ma again, and the little ones had been put to bed.

'I suppose you've understood most of it,' said Tess, holding her mug under the ale tap at an angle, so that there wouldn't be too much of a head of foam.

'I think so,' said Kat and took a sip from her own mug. In the middle of everything Birch and his apple juice sprang to her mind. Well, there were things to be said for being home again.

'They've taken Tad and Cornelius and just about all the other men, too. Erold Smith, Aren Journeyman, Verle the Merchant and Asa's Gustav. There's no house in the village that hasn't lost someone. Minna Goats had no man in the house, so they took her youngest, and he's only nine! It might have been Nicolas or Tim – and it may still be, if we don't follow orders.' Tess took a long swallow. 'They took the men because that would be less noticeable to outsiders. If a daughter suddenly went missing, we would have some explaining to do. But I think they also thought there was a chance our men would buy into their damn nonsense.' She snorted. 'You heard him – they forced me to sign some piece of paper that says I'm giving over the maestra rights to someone else. Maestra Erminea, he calls himself. Ermine, I mean. A man! As if a man could ever be maestra of any-thing!' She drew a hand across her eyes. She looked tired, Kat thought. 'I don't know where this'll all end. Sooner or later someone is bound to spot that something is wrong here. But it's as if they don't even see the insanity of it. They have some wild, far-fetched plan to take over the whole Vale, I think. Karel's talking about making it "a Resting Place for men". A place where men have a right to the land. Apparently they can't see that the whole thing is so damned *unnatural*.'

'They've been living off our winter stores,' said Mattie. 'We might not have enough to last us till spring, now.'

'What was that about Cornelius's fever?' asked Kat.

'Wound fever,' said Tess, face carefully still. 'He just kept fighting them, that day. Kept coming at them. They had to almost—' she broke off. 'It was as if he *couldn't* surrender.'

Like the hellhorse stallions, thought Kat. Who fought to the death because they couldn't do anything else.

Tess pressed her palms flat against the table and stared down at her fingers. 'I was so afraid they'd kill him,' she said in a very small voice. 'It was then I signed their paper.' She raised her head slowly, painfully. Her eyes looked very dark, nearly black. 'I'm sorry, Kat.'

'Sorry? What for?'

'It is your inheritance. Yours and Mattie's. I should not have given up any part of it – for the sake of a man.'

'Nonsense,' said Kat firmly. 'You gave up nothing. And anyway – this was Cornelius. And *Tad*.' She had to bite her lip to keep from crying. 'Haven't you any . . . I mean, there must be something we can do.'

'If only we knew where they were,' said Tess. 'But we've been through the Vale with a fine-tooth comb, and we've found nothing. And yet . . . it can't be too far away, no more than a day or two on horseback, because Karel comes here at least once a week. Anna Weaver tried to follow him back once, but he caught on almost at once. He ambushed her and beat her to within an inch of her life. She still hasn't properly recovered. And he told her that if she tried that stunt again, Aren would get a beating to match hers. We haven't dared try it again. We sit here like mice in a trap, holding our breath for fear someone will find out what's going on. So far no one has become suspicious, but we're living on borrowed time.'

Kat thought for a while.

'If we knew where they keep the men . . . what would you do?' she finally asked.

'Try to free them,' said Tess promptly. 'We've nothing to lose. If we don't act, it's just a matter of time before things go wrong anyway.' She looked at her eldest daughter. 'But we don't know where they are – do we?'

'No,' said Kat. 'But I have an idea where to start looking.'

*

Karel's visits were not predictable, and at Anna Weaver's house and in the merchant's yard with Verle's wife there now lived men who were in Ermine's pay. Care was needed. So it was not yet dawn when Kat made her way up the hillside behind the inn. She was on foot – this was safer, although the way to Saratown was long and steep, and bitter at this time of year.

It took all morning to reach the ghost town. The day dawned bright and clear, and sunlight glittered on the snows. She had to take care not to go snow-blind from the glare. She had tied a strip of dark cloth across her face just below the eyes, the way Cornelius had taught her. She probably looked odd, Kat thought, like a highway robber who hadn't got his disguise quite right. But up here there was no one to see her. Or at least, she fervently hoped so. She had taken cover behind a stand of spruce trees on the ridge and now lay, belly down in the snow, watching the scattering of weather-bitten grey houses below her.

This was a barren, windswept place, and the only reason people had ever settled here was the old pass, now completely blocked by a rockslide. For a while, the Saratowners had held out, but it was hard to scratch a living from the bare, rocky slopes, now that no trading caravans came by to spend an occasional few coins. Most had given up and moved into the Vale. Only one old woman had stuck it out stubbornly until she had died in her bed, frozen stiff, probably because she had been too sick to get up and get firewood for her small stove. Many years had passed since. They said Mad Hanna haunted the hills, coming up to their fires at night to beg for firewood. Kat had heard one of them tell the story often enough, safely ensconced in Crowfoot Inn with a mug of Tess's good brew: how she had heard a voice moan, over and over again, 'I'm so cold . . .', right by her ear, though there was no one there but the goatherd herself and her goats and dogs.

'No way am *I* ever going up there again,' the goatherd said. 'Not if the Queen of Breda herself was to come and pay me pure gold to do it!'

'I don't suppose that's very likely,' Tess had replied drily, 'seeing that there hasn't been a queen in Breda for nigh on three hundred years.' Tess didn't hold with ghosts, or with people who believed in them.

Still, Kat was happy that it was bright daylight and that she had no fire that might lure Mad Hanna with its heat. Real life was quite scary enough, she thought. Down there was the Resting Place where Ermine's voice had once whispered its threats about silence or death. Now the settlement looked completely deserted. No smoke rose from the chimneys, and in this cold, surely no one would go without fire?

She crept closer, as carefully as she could. All the houses were empty. Doors and shutters swung lopsidedly, creaking in the wind, and several thresholds were buried knee-deep in snowdrifts. Dejected, she sat down on the porch in front of the Resting Place, letting the noonday sun warm her chilled body for a while. The sunbeams were warm enough to melt the top layers of snow on the roof, and a steady drip-drop splashed from the eaves on to the metal railing, coating it in a sheet of ice. Kat had not expected to find all the missing men here, and perhaps not even Ermine himself, but she had calculated that at least there would be some trace, some clue to his hidden bolt-hole. But the only tracks she had seen were her own, dark against the whiteness of the snow.

Tracks! If any of Ermine's men *were* to pass this way, it would be disastrous if they saw her trail. She leaped to her feet and started casting about for something with which to erase her tracks. Using the small penknife Merian had given her, she cut herself some birch twigs and used them for a broom. It still looked a bit conspicuous, but once a bit of snow had drifted across it, it might pass for the tracks of some animal, or just a natural unevenness in the snow. There were several other places where the snow was just as uneven.

Several other places . . . it took a little while before she caught on. Those lines in the snow, there . . . That had to be an old trail, now almost hidden by wind and snow. Almost – but not quite.

It was so faint there was no way she could determine what had made it – a rider with two packhorses, or just a couple of chamois. It was only because she had been standing here on the ridge, trying to gauge the effect of her own sweeping, that she had noticed the vague shadowy lines leading up to the old pass road. She was certain of nothing, and yet excitement stirred in her stomach, and she set off with the determination of a bird-dog scenting new game.

The trail – if it even was a trail – led towards the pass.

The road was no longer passable for someone with a cart or a wagon, since no one had bothered to clear it of shrubbery and fallen rocks. On foot it was quite feasible, and a rider who knew what he was doing might accomplish the climb. But why bother? The old cart road was nothing more than a dead end. Kat's conviction that it was Karel's trail she was following wavered and began to crumble. Here, between the steep slopes, the snow was much deeper, and wading through it took a lot of effort. Completely wasted effort, by the look of it. She really ought to turn back.

She kept going. Not because she believed this was the right trail, but simply because . . . if she turned back now, it would be over. And she had absolutely no idea where else to look for Cornelius and Tad and the others. It was this or nothing, and doing nothing was unbearable.

Then she ran out of road. Across the caravan road lay what looked like half a mountain. There was simply no longer a pass.

Feeling lost, Kat stared at the huge barrier of scree and rock in front of her. It had been there for so long that trees grew on it. There was nothing here except snow and rocks and trees. No Tad, no Cornelius, no Ermine. Not even Karel, it seemed. She wanted to sit down and cry.

Climbing the barrier was no use. She might just possibly succeed – but there was no way a rider with two pack-horses could have made it across. Which meant that Karel had not come this way. Which meant that she had been wrong. Which meant that all that was left for her to do was to trudge on back home to Tess to tell her that they were once again hopelessly cornered, with no leads and no plan. She could feel the tears, like a hot pressure, at the thought. She cast one last look at the blocked pass. Then she turned and began to make her way back to Saratown.

She had been walking for several minutes when she realized that there was something wrong with that picture. She turned and looked at it again. This time with greater care and keener suspicions. Snow and rock and trees. As before. But . . . why was there no snow on the branches of those two small pines?

She broke into a run and nearly stumbled and fell in the deep snow. The snowless pines were part of a group nestled below a narrow overhang. Now it was hard to understand why she hadn't spotted it right away. When she prodded one of the trees it sagged in a way no properly rooted tree would sag. And when she grasped the trunk and pulled, it came right out of the snow and collapsed next to her. The other tree was probably no more firmly rooted, but she left it in place, keen to inspect the hollow that was now revealed.

It was not the entrance to a cave, as she had half imagined. Someone had carved a tunnel through the rock, a narrow corridor just wide enough to admit a horse. She understood almost at once why it did not go through the rubble of the rock slide – it would be nearly impossible to make such a passage stable and safe. But a passage *around* the slide, through the mountainside itself – that was a different proposition. Feasible, yes, if one had the men, the time and the patience . . . as apparently Ermine had. It had to be him. It had to be the entrance to his lair.

She hesitated only for a moment on the threshold. Then she took the first step into the darkness.

She had to go slowly, with one hand firmly against the wall of the corridor. The daylight spilling through the entrance did not last long, and she had no lamp or torch to see by. And had she had one, she would hardly have dared to use it, for fear of discovery. Ermine might be quite close now – how close, she had no way of knowing.

They would have to use lanterns, though, when they brought the horses through. No horse would want to step into this deep black hole otherwise. She realized that she herself was walking in a sort of crouch, afraid to knock her head against the unseen ceiling, but at the thought of horses, she straightened up. If there was room enough for a horse, she would have no problem.

It felt very odd to walk like this, feeling her way through absolute darkness. It was nothing like being outside at night, when there was always some sort of light from the sky, however faint. After a while one's eyes got used to that and made use of what light there was. Here there was nothing. And still her eyes insisted on trying to see, filling the nothingness somehow. Maybe that was what happened when people started seeing ghosts. She remembered Mad Hanna, walking about in the darkness whispering, 'I'm so cold . . .' Kat shuddered, and wished she hadn't thought of ghosts at all.

When she finally did see a grey glow, it took a while before she dared to trust that it was daylight. She approached the opening with great care. Who knew what was on the other side? But at first glance there was nothing alarming to be seen. Just a grown-over, snow-covered cart-trail like the one on the other side of the pass. More tracks here, though, and clearer ones – someone had come to help Karel bring home the supplies.

She stood for a while, listening, but all she could hear was the wind and the soft whisper of drifting snow. The road looked completely deserted, so Ermine's hideaway was probably still some way off. She ate a bit of bread from the pouch at her belt – she was too tense to be really hungry, but once she stepped out of the tunnel, it was even less like-ly that she would feel like stopping for a picnic. She forced herself to eat the whole slice and a wedge of goat's cheese before she went on.

It happened almost at once. She had taken no more than a few dozen paces when there was a sharp crack and a whizzing sound as something came flying past her shoulder. She had only a brief glimpse of the slim black bolt before it buried itself in the snow ahead of her, but she recognized the sound at once.

A crossbow.

'Next one won't miss,' called a man somewhere behind her. 'Stand *absolutely* still.'

She stood absolutely still.

In a weird way, it reminded her of her first morning in Breda, but this was not the hospital gardens, and the man with the crossbow was definitely not easygoing Ola, who had laughed at her mistake. This was no mistake. This was deadly earnest.

How stupid. How utterly stupid of her to think that there would be no guard just because she couldn't see one. A sickening feeling of defeat spread through her body.

'Lie down,' ordered the voice. 'Flat on your belly, now!'

There was no point in refusing, and even less in trying to run. She lay down on her belly in the cold snow and stayed there while crunching footsteps came slowly closer.

'Hands behind your back.'

She put her hands behind her back. Practised fingers looped a rope around her wrists and tied knots that weren't the kind to come undone in a hurry.

'All right. Now get up and let's have a look at you.'

It was no easy task with her hands tied behind her back. She had to roll on to her back in order to get to her feet at all. In the middle of everything a strangely unaffected part of her noticed in irritation that she was now covered in snow on both her front and back.

The man who had tied her wrists looked at her without emotion. He was wearing a yellowish sheepskin cap and coat, and from beneath the cap poked a few greying wisps of hair. He was no longer young; might even be an old comrade from Cornelius's time in Marker's mercenary force, as Karel had once been. Somehow, he managed to look more like an old soldier than a highwayman. But Karel had taught her that a man could easily be both.

He was not alone. Well, he wouldn't be, not if Ermine had any sense. On the hillside, some feet above the opening, a small cabin had been built on a wooden platform. Two men stood on the porch, one of them armed with a cross-bow that rested against the railing, cranked and ready. From the cabin chimney, a thin column of smoke rose. Had she bothered to use her nose as well as her eyes and ears, she might have been able to catch the hint of wood-smoke. The wind was wrong, but still . . . she hadn't even thought of trying.

'Who is it?' called the one with the crossbow.

'No one we know,' said Greyhair. He reached for Kat's fur cap. As it came off, her stupid red hair came down, no doubt glowing like a bonfire against all the whiteness of the snow. 'But it looks like we've caught us a girl.'

One of the men on the platform shaded his eyes for a more careful look.

'I know her,' he said. 'That's Kat. The innkeeper's girl.'

Kat screwed up her eyes against the glare of the snow.

'Clipper?' she said hesitantly. 'Is that you?' Clipper had worked for Asa for several years. She couldn't remember his real name, but he got his nickname because he was the fastest sheep-shearer Kat had ever seen, and proud of that fact. Asa had had to tell him that she would prefer to have her sheep shorn more slowly and a little more gently. 'What are you doing here?'

'As little as possible,' said Greyhair grouchily. He

393

seemed to be in charge. 'Clipper, get down here and keep an
eye on the lass, seeing as you're such good friends. I need to
check the tunnel. Are you alone?'

'Yes,' said Kat quickly. 'I'm looking for Cornelius.'

'Cornelius?'

'Yes. Isn't he with you? Mama said he had left, but I was
so sure he had gone to join you again . . .' She pretended to
become uncertain. 'I mean . . . you are Ermine's people,
aren't you?'

Greyhair had not glanced away even for a second. Even
when he started talking to Clipper, who had come crunching up, his eyes remained on Kat with the steadfastness of a
beacon.

'Put her in the Nest. Don't talk to her. Don't untie her –
not even if she pleads cramp or wants to pee or something
like that. If I get into trouble, you use her for a hostage. *Stay
in the Nest; it's by far the best defensive position around.'
His grey-blue eyes remained on Kat still. 'And you,' he said,
poking her with a rough forefinger, 'no tricks. Girl or not,
they'll shoot you if they have to. Got that?'

Silently, Kat nodded. Perhaps it had not been such a
bright idea to mention Ermine. She had only meant to
reassure them, to make it seem like she was on their side,
but instead it seemed to have put Greyhair on full alert.

Slinging her over his shoulder like a sack of potatoes,
Clipper began to climb the rope ladder. The effort had him
puffing and red-faced before they were halfway there, and
Kat found no pleasure in the experience either. Dangling
head down, with his shoulder digging into her midriff, was

highly uncomfortable, but she didn't even dare to wriggle –
what if he dropped her?

'Take her into the shed,' said the crossbow man. 'I'll stay
out here.'

Clipper let her slide down and kept a hold of her arm
until she had recovered her balance. Then he opened the
door.

'Inside,' he said, jerking his head.

She went in.

The shed was a narrow, elongated room. A roughly
timbered bedstead took up most of one end. By the other
gable, firewood was piled floor to ceiling on both sides of a
fat little black stove. Apart from that, there was a table and
a bench, all made from rough boards and wood stumps.

'Sit,' he said, waving a hand. She sat cautiously on the
bench, which didn't look too solid. Clipper remained by
the open door, in a position that let him keep an eye both on
her and on the situation outside.

He wasn't that old, Kat thought, perhaps the same age as
her older brother Eskill. Early twenties. Wasn't he born
somewhere in Bryndale? She seemed to remember him talking about that. In the spring, he would travel from farm to
farm to help with the shearing – that was how he had come
to stay at Asa's farm. He hadn't been there all that long,
from the beginning of shearing season one year to the end
of it the following year. Still it was hard for her to believe –
someone from the Vales, someone she knew, here among
Ermine's men . . .

'Clipper? Why are you here?'

'Be quiet,' he muttered, sounding almost . . . shy? Could that be true?

'You might at least tell me what you're doing here,' she persisted.

'He said you were to be quiet,' said Clipper, more firmly this time. 'That means you keep your mouth shut.' He threw her a sidelong look. 'Do you even know where you are?'

'Some godforsaken bit of badland between South Vale and the Southlands.'

'No,' he said, smiling a peculiar, proud smile. 'You are in Val Erminea. Where men give the orders, because this is the land of men.' His smile widened. 'I guess that's what I'm doing here.'

She couldn't help herself – she just had to deflate his smugness a little.

'Among robbers and killers?'

His smile vanished.

'I told you to shut up!'

They waited in silence until Greyhair returned.

'Seems she really is alone,' he said. He glanced at the sky. The light was tawny now, edging towards twilight, and the shadows had grown long. Sunset was not far away. 'The two of you will have to split the night watch between you while I take her down to Erminegard. Don't fall asleep. Someone might come looking for her.'

'Even if they do,' said Crossbow, 'they'll never find the tunnel. Certainly not as long as it's dark.'

'Probably not. But keep your eyes open anyway. Clipper,

you carry her down for me. I'm getting too old for that kind of thing.'

'You could always untie me,' said Kat. 'Then no one would have to carry me.'

Greyhair looked sceptical. She tried to seem as small and harmless as possible.

'I won't try to run. What good would it do?'

'She has a point,' said Clipper. 'Three of us, and Pol with his crossbow . . . she wouldn't get very far, would she?'

'Oh, all right.' Greyhair undid his tough knots. 'I'll go down first. You wait until I tell you to start climbing.'

Kat rubbed her wrists and waited until he had completed the climb.

'Come on,' he finally said.

Kat took off her mittens and tucked them into her belt. Then she started down the ladder. Her fingers had already begun to cramp and stiffen, but it was still a fairly easy climb. The difficult part consisted of getting Merian's small penknife out of its belt compartment and into her hand without anybody seeing. As soon as her feet touched the ground, she put her mittens back on, completely hiding the knife.

She made no protest as Greyhair tied her up again and told her to start walking down the track. She merely hoped that Erminegard was still a long walk away and that the sun would set very soon.

They walked along the cart track, almost due west, with the sky ahead of them glowing gold and orange. The sun dropped slowly lower and lower and finally disappeared behind a mountain ridge. There was still some light in the sky, but now the track turned and Kat could see the valley Clipper had called Val Erminea. There was very little open land – hardly any fields or grazing, just dark pines and snowclad mountain slopes and a long narrow lake which had not yet frozen over. By the lake was a small cluster of buildings. Most of the windows were shuttered, but here and there slivers of light escaped to make long, slim golden stripes on the still, blue-black waters.

If she was going to do it, it had to be now, before they got too close to the small settlement down there. Resolutely, she put one foot down too close to the other, tripping herself up. She cried out sharply and tumbled down the hill. With her hands bound she was unable to break her fall. She ended up crashing into a tree trunk, and snow from the laden branches showered down on her in a small avalanche. For a moment, she just lay there, half stunned. But through it all, she hadn't let go of the knife.

He reached her quickly – so quickly, in fact, that the world still hadn't stopped spinning. He grabbed her by the arm and hauled her to her feet.

'What was that all about?' he asked suspiciously.

'I just fell.' Kat had no trouble looking dizzy and confused. 'It wasn't on purpose, if that's what you think!'

He gave a sort of growl. 'All right. Move along, then. We want to be home before nightfall.'

It might be home to you, Kat thought, but I've other plans. And at the first step, she yelped and quickly shifted her weight away from her right foot.

'Now what?'

'My ankle . . . I think I've broken my ankle!'

He snorted. 'Oh, sure.'

It was amazingly hard to cry on purpose, even though one would think she had enough to cry about. Kat thought with great intensity of Tad. Of Ermine, whom she feared so. Of Cornelius. But the memory that finally made the tears come was a more distant one: the day Tess had told her she would have to leave home.

'I can feel the bones move,' she said, and sobbed helplessly, tears pouring down her face.

'Oh, hell,' said Greyhair. 'Sit down. Let me have a look.'

Obediently, she sat, with one leg awkwardly stretched. Greyhair got down on one knee, took off his mittens and started to undo her bootlaces. She moaned and drew back her foot.

'It hurts!'

'Sit still,' he said in some annoyance and reached for the laces once more. And she kicked him as hard as she could, in the face.

He reeled back and collapsed in the snow, and she got to her feet, clumsily because of the bound hands, and started running. No time now to try to cut the rope. She had to get away fast, in among the pines, away from the road. At the moment that meant downhill, towards the houses, but right now that didn't matter. What mattered was keeping out of reach.

Now that she wanted to stop crying, she found she couldn't. Tears kept blurring her eyes as she ran, sniffing and gasping and getting more and more winded because she couldn't risk sobbing out loud. She dodged branches as best she could, but it wasn't easy, and a couple of times she fell for real. She changed directions more than once, hoping to put him off the track, hoping it would be too dark now for him to see her footprints in the snow. Finally she had to stop to ease the pain in her heaving chest. Her eyes still stung, but at least the tears had finally stopped.

For a while she stood among the pines, still as a mouse, listening. She couldn't hear him. Had she managed to kick him unconscious? Or was he standing still as she was, listening, waiting?

Jerk by laboured jerk, she tugged off one mitten and managed to unfold the knife. She was terrified of dropping it. In the deep snows, she might never find it again, and as long as her hands were bound, there was nothing she could do except stumble clumsily through the woods, waiting to be caught. Carefully, she pushed the blade through one loop of the rope and started cutting.

It took a long time. The small knife was sharp enough, but she could only reach a small section of the rope, and she had to go carefully, strand by strand. She tried not to imagine the mess it would make if the knife slipped, tried not to think of the many veins, of the blood pulsing just beneath the skin. Bleeding too much could kill you. Better, much better, to be careful. Sometimes she stopped for a few seconds to concentrate on listening, but the woods were still quiet, and night had fallen among the trees.

At last she felt the rope give. She forgot all about the

knife and pulled with all her strength, but the last few strands just wouldn't part. She had to go back to her careful filing again before she was finally free. Her hands shook. The knife had slipped twice, one superficial cut and one deeper one, but neither of them would cause her to bleed to death. She put her mouth against the bloodiest one and licked it. She had nothing that would make a bandage unless she tore strips off the clothes she was wearing. In the end she just put the mitten back on and walked on.

The most sensible plan would be to try and get back to South Vale and the inn. On her own, she had no chance of freeing Tad and the others, and once dawn came, her tracks would be only too easy to follow. But how would she get past Clipper and his crossbow friend? Maybe an idea would come to her as she walked. Standing still, at least, was no use at all.

She didn't dare return to the cart track, but she headed upslope and east, towards the rising moon. The skies were clear and the moon nearly full. Not entirely great, that. Easier to see – but also easier to be seen. Oh well, it couldn't be helped.

She had to try to climb *over* the wall of rubble that blocked the pass. It was the only way. She would never make it into the tunnel, let alone through it, without getting caught. Getting past Clipper and his mate with the crossbow would not be easy even so. She had to suppose their attention would be mainly on the tunnel, and that they would be on guard against someone trying to get in, not on a certain thirteen-year-old Vale girl trying to get out. They would not know that she had got away from Greyhair. Or so she hoped.

She slunk from tree to tree on the slope above the guard hut. She could see someone on the platform, but she couldn't tell whether it was Clipper or the other one. He was walking back and forth, stomping his feet and flapping his arms, trying to keep warm. Go in, then, thought Kat. Go into your nice warm hut with its nice warm stove . . . She caught hold of the next tree trunk with her mittened hands. The slope was now so steep that it was hard to stand without hanging on to something, but fortunately trees were plentiful. That would change a little further on. On the rockslide, she would not be entirely without cover, but a lot more exposed even so.

She stiffened in mid-movement. Hoofbeats? Were those hoofbeats? She peered into the darkness in the direction of the cart track, and there, sharply black against the white snows, was a rider on a galloping horse. Further away was something a lot bigger and more tangled, probably more riders, coming on at a less breakneck pace.

Damn. Just a little longer, and she would have been clear. But no. No such luck. She could hear Clipper shouting at the rider, and the rider shouting back. The little bitch had kicked Baldo in the face and done a runner, and would probably make for the pass. Reinforcements were on their way.

Her whole body had begun to shake. She was frightened, yes. Desperately afraid. But it was not just that. Her arms and legs could not hold on like this, she could not stay motionless much longer. Reinforcements or not, she had to move. The shouting continued. She could tell they thought she was still somewhere behind them. Maybe they supposed that her hands were still bound. It would be better to go now, while they were still busy with their own plans and traps and had not realized that she was in front of them and not behind.

She moved as soundlessly as she could, from tree to tree. A cloud – sweet friendly cloud – obscured the moon now, and she had to use the time as best she could. She was past the guard shed, at least. The going was more difficult here, the rough, knotted surface of the rock slide was full of cracks and stumps and other pitfalls, and she could break an ankle for real if she wasn't careful. Not much cover left now, either. A sapling here, a shrub, a craggy rock . . . but she was almost at the crest now, another ten yards and she would be –

Damn. And double damn. The friendly cloud drifted on, and pale blue moonlight lit up the mountainside. To Kat, it was as glaring as the noontime sun. She crouched behind her rock, shivery and ill. As soon as she stopped moving, the shakes came back. She had walked and trotted and climbed these stupid mountains since sunup, almost without rest. Her strength was nearly out. In all that time, she had fed her body nothing more than a slice of bread and a sodden bit of goat's cheese and a bit of Tess's ale from the flask. No wonder it rebelled.

Another cloud: thinner and hazier, but it would have to do. Once she was past the crest, they would not be able to see her, and she –

'Sweet Our Lady! There she is!'

The voice echoed through the pass. Kat jerked as if someone had hit her with a carter's whip, and poured every ounce of strength into reaching the crest, now, now, come on . . . the back of her neck crawled, any minute now there would be the crack of a crossbow, the pain of a bolt shearing through skin and flesh . . . If only she could pass the crest, they would have to climb very high on the slopes to get a decent shot again . . .

There was no sharp divide, no noticeable line to cross. Yet now she was moving downhill. She tumbled on with no thought for broken ankles now. They would have to be completely stupid not to send someone through the tunnel, to waylay her on the other side. Her only chance was to pass the slide before that happened. Still she stopped her headlong flight for a few seconds. She scratched letters in the snow, as large as her hurry permitted: WATCH OUT GUARD. She hung her goatskin flask on a branch where she hoped it would be nicely visible in the morning. Then she slid down the last sharp slope and pelted down the road towards Saratown.

She knew she would not have time to reach the ghost town. As soon as she was round the first bend, she dropped to her belly and wormed her way into cover beneath a large pine whose lower branches drooped almost to the ground with their load of snow.

Soon there were running footsteps. They passed by. She wasn't even sure how many. Two men? Three? Then snorts and hoofbeats. Shouting voices, answering calls. More and more distant. Were they searching the deserted houses in Saratown? She kept still, pressing herself against the cold ground, her shivers deep and permanent now.

Finally, when the silence had lasted a long time, she dared to poke her head out. She barely caught the gasp that would have warned him. There, no more than a few feet away, stood a man, leaning against a tree, quietly watching the pass. He hadn't seen her, didn't know she was there. She wasn't sure whether he was meant to be hiding behind the tree or merely resting against it. Then he turned his head, and his face became visible in the moonlight.

It was Simon!

Relief flooded through her. Finally. Finally a grown-up who could sort this mess out for her. Finally someone who would rescue her and save Tad and Cornelius and all the others. She got up carefully. She was close enough to touch him before he realized she was there.

'Oh, Simon!' she whispered and put both arms around his neck. 'I just knew you would come.'

He did not put his arms around her. That was the first hint that something was wrong.

'Sorry, Kat,' he said, very softly, with his lips so close to her ear that she could feel the warmth of his breath.

'Sorry? What for?'

He gently unhooked her arms from his neck but kept

hold of one wrist. Then he stepped out from under the tree, visible to everyone in the pass.

'Here!' he yelled. 'I've got her!'

For a moment she stood absolutely still, every muscle paralysed with shock. It was impossible. Inconceivable. Simon couldn't . . . Not Simon!

But men were heading their way from all around, Ermine's men, and there was no mistake, no possibility of doubt at all. Simon had betrayed her.

She flung herself at him with such violence that he lost his footing and crashed to the ground. There was no art to her attack, only fury: clawing and kicking like a wild animal, she managed to bite him thoroughly on the chin before rough hands dragged her away from him. He was bleeding. He was bleeding like a stuck pig, she thought with furious satisfaction. But although she made no sound, no sound at all, as they jerked her to her feet, twisted her arms behind her and tied her up again, she could not prevent the tears that flooded down her face.

Simon. Simon, whom she had trusted.

THE RIGHT PLACE

Ermine sat in a tall chair by the fireplace, gazing into the flames. At first he seemed not to have noticed that anyone had entered the room. Then he turned his head and looked directly at Kat.

'The innkeeper's daughter,' he said, and it was clearly no question. 'We've met before, haven't we?'

Kat nodded. She wasn't too sure of her voice.

It was the first time she'd ever seen Ermine clearly. He was thin. Uncannily so, as if someone had wrapped the absolute minimum of skin and muscle around a skeleton. His hair came to his shoulders, a coppery colour, not as dark as Kat's nor as curly. The hair and the sharp features made Kat think of Felicia Capra-Mustela. If she had ever doubted it, that doubt was gone. Ermine *was* Tedora Mustela.

Apart from a gold ring in one ear – and many men wore those, too – he had done nothing to look like a woman. He was dressed in perfectly ordinary clothes, dark leather

407

trousers and a white embroidered shirt. Yet when he spoke, he sounded more like a woman than like a man – and still not quite like either.

'Untie her,' he told Clipper, who was holding Kat's right arm in a firm grip.

'I'm not sure that's wise, maestra. She has a right temper. She kicked Baldo in the face, and the new man from Joss practically had his chin bitten off.'

'There will be no more of that,' said Ermine coldly. 'You know we have your stepfather here, don't you?'

Kat nodded again. 'He was the reason why I came,' she said cautiously. 'Mama said he had left, but I thought he must have come to join you.'

Ermine smiled – a thin, cold smile, no more than a tightening of the lips.

'Sadly, no. Austerlin's loyalty left much to be desired, as it happened. But I am still holding him responsible for your behaviour. Do you understand?'

Kat swallowed, and nodded once more.

'So no more escapades.'

'No.'

'Very well, then. Come closer. Tell me why you ran away from Baldo in such a . . . violent fashion.'

Kat took a few steps forward. She hung her head and tried to look guilt-ridden.

'I . . . I got angry about the crossbow. Shooting at people like that. And then he tied me up. I didn't like that. So I decided to run away.'

'Katriona . . . That is your name, isn't it?'

'Yes.'

'Katriona, come here. And look me in the eyes.'

Kat had not the slightest wish to do either. There was something about Ermine's yellow-brown eyes that made her think of iron spheres turning hot in one's hand. Something magus-like. As if Ermine had his own way of tearing the truth from people.

'I know you've been to Breda,' he said. 'I know you were a bredinari prentice. Don't try to play the peasant fool with me.'

'They threw me out,' said Kat. 'In their opinion I *am* an ignorant peasant fool.'

'I see. So you are no longer apprenticed to the corps?'

'I just said so, didn't I?'

'Katriona – do I really have to remind you what will happen if you don't mind your manners?' Ermine's cool and skinny fingers closed around her wrist, and she had to suppress an urgent wish to snatch back her hand.

'No, maestra,' she said, as obediently as she could.

'So. You've been to Breda. Do you know who I am?'

There was no escaping those eyes.

'I think so, maestra.'

'Who, then?'

'Tedora Mustela.' There. She had said it. It could not be kept hidden, not from those eyes and the hand that held her wrist so tightly that he could no doubt feel the hammering of her pulse, thump-thump-thump.

'I see . . .' It was a whisper, little more than a sigh. And the hardness, the prodding and the testing and the probing, seemed to leave him all at once. He smiled again, a different smile this time, without irony, and Kat suddenly understood how so many people had believed him to be a young girl for such a long time. She suddenly remembered that he was no older than Dan.

'Sit,' he said and pushed his footstool in her direction with one foot. Like the chair, the stool was upholstered in faded red wool and decorated with embroidery. A strange thing to find here, in the middle of nowhere, in a house where nearly everything else had been speedily put together from raw unpolished wood. Perhaps some rich merchant had kept it in his wagon. Kat sat down cautiously and rested her tired back against the side of the fireplace. It was hot enough to warm her stiff muscles even through her sheepskin jacket.

'Are you hungry? Would you like something to eat?'

Kat didn't understand. Why was Ermine suddenly treating her like some dear and long-expected guest instead of a captive who had been pushed into the room with her hands tied behind her? Was it a trap of some kind? But food was food, and she needed it.

'Yes, please,' she said. 'At least . . . if it pleases maestra to eat also?'

She added the last bit partly out of courtesy, partly because . . . well, one never knew what might find its way into one's food here.

'I rarely eat much,' said Ermine quietly.

Well, no, thought Kat, I don't suppose you do, or you wouldn't be so skinny.

410

And then, suddenly, she heard in her mind the words the Bredani used when a crime was too great to be forgiven: *You, Creature, my land will not suffer you. The earth you walk on shall burn beneath your feet. The food you eat shall turn to poison in your mouth. All gifts of the land shall be denied you – food, sleep and comfort – from this time till you die.*

The Bredani had made Tedora Mustela an outcast. Was this what was wrong with him? Did the Out-casting really *work*?

'What would you like? Brynna, get some – what do we have? Something hot? Soup? Meats?'

Brynna – that appeared to mean Clipper. He really was from Bryndale then.

'There's nothing hot now except mulled wine. But there's some cured lamb.'

She could hear Clipper's confusion in his voice. He too must be puzzled by this sudden show of hospitality.

'Two beakers of mulled wine, then, and bread and meat for the girl.' Ermine turned back to Kat and once more smiled that young-girl smile. 'Tell me the news from the City,' he said. 'What is happening there?'

'In Breda?'

'Yes. You've just come from there, haven't you? Tell me what goes on.'

Kat had no idea what to say. In the end, she dredged up her memories of the Landing Feast and told Tedora about that. The good part of it, anyway, before a squirrel and a badger came along to ruin the fun. She said nothing of her meeting with Felicia Capra-Mustela and, strangely

411

enough, Tedora had no questions about City politics. What interested him, it seemed, was everyday news about the weather, what people had been wearing, what performers had been there, and were there any new songs? Any new plays?

Kat kept looking for traps. But still there were no questions about the corps or the doings of the Seven. He didn't even ask about Mustela and the power struggle that was going on to find his replacement. And finally Kat realized: the gaunt young man in the chair was simply homesick. He wanted to hear about familiar things. Not about the problems and the plotting. Only about the good things. The parties. The clothes. The food. The music. All the things he no longer had.

In the end, Kat was barely coherent, and the room had begun to dim and sway like a curtain. She was utterly exhausted, and not used to the mulled wine either. Normally, she only tasted it once a year, at the Midwinter celebrations.

'Child, you are tired,' said Tedora, and smiled. 'We have to get you to bed.'

Kat made a huge effort to wake up just a little.

'Maestra . . .' she begged. 'Please, can I see my stepfather? And Tad – my mother's cook?'

Tedora's smile vanished instantly. But he nodded.

'Brynna!'

'Maestra?' Clipper sounded somewhat sleepy as well. Perhaps he had nodded off, over there in his spot by the door, leaning against the wall.

412

'Let her see Austerlin and the cook. But don't leave them alone.'

'Yes, maestra. And . . . after that?'

'A safe place. Not with the others. The stables, perhaps? At any rate, make sure she doesn't run off.' He sipped his wine and carefully dabbed his lips with a napkin. 'Once the innkeeper knows we have her daughter as well, I'm sure she will be more cooperative. And so, I think, will Austerlin.'

'Yes, maestra.' Clipper caught Kat's arm. 'Come on, Kat. Goodnight, maestra.'

'Goodnight.'

Kat stared. It was as if a completely different person had entered the room. The young girl was gone completely. Now he sat there, all sharp edges once more, as cold and forbidding and frightening as he had been when she first met him. It wasn't that one part of him was a man and the other a woman. Nothing that simple. His sharpness reminded Kat of Tess in a temper (though Tess was rarely cold). And Kat knew from the Eve of the Landing that Felicia Capra-Mustela could be just as ruthless and threatening when the outer shell of politeness fell away. No, if there were two Tedoras, then one had been given all the feelings – warmth, vulnerability, homesickness – while the other had the strength and the cunning, the ability to survive at impossible odds. Because Ermine had survived. He had survived by being cunning and cold, and by exploiting other people's feelings for each other. But he did not

413

know how to be strong *and* warm at the same time, the way Tess did.

Clipper pulled her along, and she came with him obediently. The last thing she saw before the door closed was Ermine, sitting thin and straight in his throne-like chair, eyes wide open and alert. Did he ever sleep? Or had that been taken away too, with the Out-casting?

The chill of the night woke her up a little, and she looked around with greater curiosity than she had been able to muster coming in, bound for her meeting with Ermine. The settlement consisted of perhaps half a score of houses, all of them built from logs. Most were old – once, this might have been a sort of Saratown. But some things had been built anew. Around the settlement, in a horseshoe shape with the lakeshore as the only opening, was a tall palisade fence, almost like a town wall. Unless one fancied a swim in the icy waters of the lake, the only way in or out was through the gate, and she did not think that was ever left unguarded. Ermine was not given to that kind of carelessness.

Clipper noticed her interest in the gate.

'Oh no you don't,' he said in a tone that was not actually too unfriendly, considering the trouble – and bruises – she'd caused him and his fellow guards. 'You've done enough running.'

'I still don't see what you're doing here,' she said.

'I told you. I'm here because it's a place where men can

live. I'm here to prove that the world doesn't come to an end because a man takes a piece of ground and calls it his own.'

Kat knew what Tess would have to say about talk like that, but she wasn't quite sure she agreed with Tess any more. Still, she had to argue.

'But Clipper . . . this way? By robbing and forcing and threatening people?'

'We do what we have to do,' said Clipper tightly. 'Do you think the maestras will give up their lands just for the asking?'

'You're not a . . . you're not like Karel.' Not a ruthless brute, she meant, and had stopped the words only just in time.

'Karel is good at what he does,' said Clipper, but seemed a bit less proud now. 'He makes people do what we want them to do.'

Kat halted, and Clipper, who was still folding her arm, had to stop too.'

'Seriously, Clipper. If you're with Karel, I'm no friend of yours!'

'No friend . . .' Clipper burst out laughing. 'Kat, you idiot, *nobody* expects you to be on our side.'

She gave him an irritated look, and walked on. He was still chuckling. But the strange thing was that in some weird way she really was on his side. Not that she in any way agreed with Ermine or Karel or their way of doing things. But once you had tried the odd homeless wandering that was what most men could expect from life, you could see their point. Men, like everyone else, had a need to settle. To live in a place where they had a *right* to be, and not just someone's grudging permission. A place where they could stay for as long as they wanted.

Only, not Ermine's way.

'Clipper,' she said cautiously, 'you said this was a place where men make the decisions . . . but aren't they mostly Ermine's decisions?'

'He is the maestra,' said Clipper. And that seemed to be all there was to say about that.

Clipper came to a halt by one of the longest cabins, but he didn't approach the door. Instead he unhooked a pair of heavy shutters and opened them. Behind them was nothing so fancy as window-panes, just iron bars.

'Austerlin,' he called, tapping the bars. 'Got a visitor.'

'Can't we go in?' asked Kat.

'No,' said Clipper. 'Not when I'm alone. Orders.'

Kat stood as tall as she could, and then on tiptoe. She still couldn't see through the window.

'Cornelius?' she called softly.

A bedstead creaked.

'Kat?' He was at the window now, but all she could see were his hands, grasping the bars. 'Kat – is that you?'

'Clipper,' she whispered, feeling tears on her face once more. 'I can't even *see* him.'

Clipper looked down on her and seemed to notice the difference in height for the first time.

416

'Oh damn,' he said. And then he got down on one knee. 'Here. Ride my shoulders.'

She did as he said. It was a strange feeling, like being a small child again. But at least she could see now.

Only his hands and face, though. The room behind him was black as night. But what she saw was enough to horrify her.

If Tess had begun to seem old, Cornelius looked as if he was teetering on the edge of his grave. His face, which had always had a rough and weathered look, was now deadly pale and furrowed, as if his skin was suddenly too big for his bones. His hair was matted and lifeless, and there was a smell about him, a sick and unclean smell so different from the mixture of horse and beer and sweat she was used to associating with him. Wound fever, Tess had said. Tad had written that he was better. If this was 'better', she was glad she hadn't been here to see him when he was 'bad'.

'Kat.' He caught her hands. 'What are you doing here? You were in Breda! You were safe!' He sounded as if he was scolding her. Like the times when he had yelled at her for forgetting to check a saddle girth, or raged because she had stayed out on the mountain too late. But he clutched her hands so hard it hurt, and his voice kept cracking, as if he had been shouting for days on end.

She couldn't say a word. She just sat there riding Clipper's shoulders and crying so hard she could barely see.

Clipper stirred uneasily.

'Right then. You've seen him. And you're not exactly light as a feather, you know.'

'At least let me talk to him,' she said, her voice shrill and croaking all at once. 'You can at least let me ask him how he is!'

'Ask away, then!'

But when she tried, she still couldn't say a word to Cornelius.

He let go of one hand and stroked her cheek rather clumsily. They were not used to such gentle gestures, he and she.

'Wipe your eyes, girl,' he muttered. 'We'll be all right.' But it was clear from his voice that he didn't believe in his own reassurances.

That finally loosened Kat's tongue.

'We *will* be all right,' she said, wishing she could tell him about the letters in the snow, about the goatskin flask and the plans she had made with Tess. There *is* hope, she tried to say, not with her words but with the way she said them.

'Right. Time to go,' said Clipper, and to do him justice she could feel his shoulders trembling with the strain.

'Sleep well,' she told Cornelius. 'I'll be back tomorrow.'

'That's for Ermine to decide,' said Clipper drily. 'Don't make promises you can't keep.'

Cornelius paid no attention to Clipper. He stroked Kat's cheek once more, his fingers rough and callused against her skin.

'Goodnight,' he said. And said nothing about tomorrow.

Clipper went down on one knee again and breathed a

sigh of relief when Kat's weight disappeared and he could get up again without a girl on his shoulders.

'Goodnight, Cornelius,' he said and began to close the shutters. Cornelius made no answer. Soon Kat heard the bedstead creak once more. She thought of him in the dark, alone and still dangerously ill. Had they even given him a proper mattress?

'He doesn't even have a stove in there,' she said, loudly and angrily. 'He'll be sick!'

'Oh, he won't freeze. There's a fireplace in the next room. If we gave him anything flammable, he'd only try to burn the place down. He's not exactly easy to deal with, I'll have you know.'

'And whose fault is that? Look at the way you treat him!'

'Oh, relax. Do you want to see Tad or not?'

'Of course I do!'

'Well, pipe down then. He's with some of the others.'

'So maybe you'll allow me into the room with him? Or is he "dangerous" too?'

'Relax, I said. I'll let you in.'

They went on to the next cabin. Clipper knocked.

'Who's there?' came a voice from behind the door.

'Clipper.'

The door opened. Kat took an involuntary step backwards, because the man opening it proved to be Greyhair, or Baldo as the others called him. His nose looked like a giant strawberry, and there were some ugly-looking scratches on one cheek. Her boots had studs on them, she recalled uncomfortably.

Baldo gave her a sour look. 'Brat,' he said. 'Come on in. *I* don't kick people. Or at least not people stupid enough to try and help me.'

'How are you feeling?' asked Clipper.

'Like I've been kicked by a mule. That's the last time I'll ever trust a girl just because she's bawling.'

He stepped aside and let them into a hallway which seemed to have been made into a sort of guard room. It was comfortably furnished with benches and a small stove and a cot on which Baldo promptly lay down. He put a kerchief full of what appeared to be half-melted snow on top of his nose and closed his eyes.

'Where's the cook?' asked Clipper.

'In there,' said Baldo and waved a hand in the direction of the most distant of three doors. 'Keep the noise down, I think the others are sleeping.'

Clipper unbarred the door.

'Go on, then,' he said. 'But only a few minutes. I want to get some shut-eye too.'

Kat moved hesitantly into the dim room. Here, too, there were shutters and bars, but apart from that it looked like a normal enough bedroom, with a large sleeping alcove and a washstand with pitcher and bowl. There was no lamp, but the light spilling through the door to the guardroom let her get her bearings.

'Tad?' she whispered. Two sleepers in the alcove, and she wasn't sure which one was him. 'Tad?'

The man closest to her sat up. She had been so afraid that he too would be changed in some awful way, like Tess and Cornelius. But he was exactly like himself. The same calm, the same warmth. Her Tad. He opened his arms to her, and she let herself be embraced. For a while they clung to each other, or rather, she clung to him. He held her the way he always did, lightly and openly. From way back when she was too small to remember anything much, she still remembered this: Tad never clutched, never hung on to you against your wish. You were always free to slip away, which was why you never wanted to.

'Katling. Why aren't you in Breda?'

'They threw me out,' she said, sniffing a little. And then she told him everything, the whole knotted story, in her lowest voice so that the guards wouldn't hear. And she told him about Tess and her plans and the letters and the flask.

'Do you think they'll be able to do it?' she asked. 'Now that I've warned them?'

'I can't answer that, Katling. But we'll be ready to do our bit. Most of us, anyway.'

'Enough of that whispering!' Clipper loomed in the doorway, and Kat couldn't suppress the start it gave her. Had he heard anything? 'Come on. Sleepy time.' Apparently not. Or if he had, he hid it very well.

Kat got to her feet. Tad gave her hand a last small squeeze.

'Sleep tight, Katling, and dream of Sari Moon-Daughter.'

Sari Moon-Daughter, who escaped from Breda Castle because she was wise and patient and brave. Yes, that would be a good dream to dream tonight. She smiled at Tad and wished him goodnight.

It turned out they were serious about the stables. Kat had slept in dozens, all the way from Breda to the Vales, so that in itself was not disturbing. But she had never been tied before.

'Sit.' Clipper pointed to one of the stalls.

'Why?' she said suspiciously.

'Just sit. Can't you do anything without arguing?'

She did as she was told.

'And no kicking,' he added. 'Remember what Ermine said about good behaviour.'

Sullenly, she nodded. But all obedient intentions fled when she saw what he had in mind.

'What on earth are you doing?'

'Making sure you don't run off.'

Under the crib was a chain of the sort that was familiar to her from the tie stalls at home. Some horses were perfectly capable of gnawing through a rope, and loose horses meant squeals and kicking and general uproar. But Clipper wrapped the chain speedily round her left ankle, dug out a padlock and pushed it through two links of the chain, and firmly locked it.

She looked at her chained leg in disbelief.

'I'm not a horse!'

'No,' said Clipper. 'Baldo seems to think you have more in common with a mule. And Ermine wants to be absolutely sure you aren't tempted into any little night-time adventures.' He looked around the empty stall – empty, that is, apart from Kat. 'I'll get you some sort of bedding and a bucket to pee in. It'll only be a night or two, then we'll find a better place for you. You should be warm enough, there are six horses altogether. Not counting you, that is.'

He moved too quickly, and her kick missed him. It had in any case been a half-hearted one. She kept thinking of Cornelius. What if he simply lay down and began to die, like Asa's old ma? He looked as if he had no strength left at all. No strength, and no hope.

Clipper came back, dragging a rough mattress stuffed with straw. Kat didn't care for the way it smelled. But at least he had also brought two blankets which were less damp and stale. She wrapped herself in them and tried not to feel the chain all the time, like a cold and bony hand around her foot.

'Kat?'

She woke up only slowly. Where was she? It was dark, and stable smells were all around. Then it all came back to her. The pass. The Vale. Ermine. Who had woken her? She sat up.

'Yes?'

There was a rasping sound as the bolt on the door to the stall was drawn back. The stall was not a bad prison even without the chain, she thought. High wooden walls and bars that reached all the way to the ceiling, so that the resident horse would not be able to fight with its neighbour.

'Are you all right?'

It was Simon.

'Go away.'

'I'm so sorry,' he said. 'But I swear, I had to do it.'

'Yes, well, everyone's very sorry it has to be this way, they just keep on doing it anyway,' she said bitterly. 'You and all your fine talk about men and land and justice for all!'

'No, I meant, I had to do it or I would have given myself away.'

'As what, exactly?'

He sighed.

'Think, my sweet. What do you *think* I'm doing here?'

'I *thought* you were my friend. I *thought* you were here to rescue me.'

But gradually a small light began to dawn. He had come here without Grizel. He was 'the new man from Joss', not 'the bredinari'.

'Don't they know you're with the corps?'

'If they did, do you think they would let me run around free? Of course they don't know. If you're that desperate to get even, all you have to do is tell them.' He squatted down next to her. 'Kat, I really am desperately sorry. I know how you must have felt. The look on your face . . . but I had to do it. They would have found you soon enough anyway. I thought . . . I thought perhaps it would be easier and safer if it was me.'

424

She knew he wanted to touch her, wanted to soothe her and stroke her hair or something, but he didn't want to risk it, wasn't sure she would allow it.'I don't understand anything any more,' she said tiredly. 'Can't you just leave me alone?'

'No,' he said. 'I have to know what plans you've made with Tess.'

Her heart beat faster. How did he know there was such a plan? Had he come here just to find out? And would he go directly to Ermine with the news, once she had opened her trusting little heart to him?

He must have felt her doubt.

'Dammit, Kat, do you think I could ever take orders from Dorissa's murderer?

No, she didn't think that.

'Did Ermine do it? Did he kill Dorissa?'

Simon shrugged helplessly. 'I have no proof. But I'm almost certain. She was here, Kat. At some point she was here. I've seen one of Ermine's men wearing her cloak and tunic.

Silence for a while. She could hear the horse in the next stall chomping its hay. Simon finally broke it.

'I talked to Tad earlier. I don't know what he meant, but he said you were to think of Robber Rodric's Tale.'

Rodric was a good man who had disguised himself as a robber in order to find their treasure. What Tad meant was that he thought Simon could be trusted.

'I've arranged with Mama that they were to come look-ing if I wasn't back before dark. So they'll begin the search tomorrow. They should be able to find the tunnel. I've marked it, and left a warning so they'll know about the guards. Keri Herbwife is with Asa right now. She'll have enough poppy juice to knock out the few men Ermine has left in the village. But if they are clever, they won't attack until full dark. Tomorrow night, perhaps.'

Now he dared to stroke her hair.

'Thank you, Kat. I'll see what I can do to make it easier for them to get through the gate. And I promise, we won't forget you, or Cornelius.'

'Can you get this off me?' She rattled the chain.

He cursed. 'There was no need for that!' His fingers found the padlock in the dark, and he tugged at it. 'No,' he said, 'I don't have a key for this. But I'll get one. And I will come to get you out of here as soon as I can.' He got to his feet. 'Try to sleep now. You must be exhausted. Goodnight.'

'Goodnight.'

He was almost at the door.

'Simon?'

'Yes?'

'I feel better now.'

'I'm glad.' He touched his chin. 'And I hope you'll *never* get that mad at me again . . .'

And then he was gone before she had time to apologize or get a closer look at the damage she had done. He bolted the door and disappeared as quietly as he had come.

*

Daylight came, but not much of it found its way into the dim recesses of the stables. A man Kat had never seen before came to feed the horses, but he paid absolutely no attention to her and simply ignored her efforts to lure him into undoing the chain. At least he left the top door open so that a little more light and fresh air entered. The horses chomped away at their feed. Somewhere she could hear someone hammering away at an anvil. It might even be Erold. She was thirsty. Time crept onwards, sluggish and slow.

She decided to try to free herself. Nothing could be done about the padlock, or the chain itself, but it had been fixed to the wall of the stall by means of a heavy clamp that had been driven into the wood. Naturally, she couldn't simply pull it out, or any self-respecting horse would have been able to get loose whenever it chose. But Kat got out her little knife and began to dig away at the wood, splinter by splinter. It was slow work, but at least it passed the time.

Around noon Clipper came along with a beaker of water and a bit of meat and bread. He then walked her to the latrines, but once that little adventure was done with, he tethered her as before. It made her feel more like an animal than a human being. If only she could *be* as calm and somnolent as the other inhabitants of the stable! But her stomach ached with nerves, and in her head a thousand questions teemed: What was happening at the inn, and at Saratown? Had they found the tunnel? Had they been able to deal with the men Ermine had left in the village? Would it be tonight? Or tomorrow night? And would Simon be

427

able to get the damn key so that she wouldn't have to sit here, no more use than the tethered horses, while all the fighting was going on?

Darkness fell. The sounds from the forge had stopped. She could hear men talking outside. One of them laughed loudly. Clearly, nothing had happened yet. Steps outside now, and the sound of someone stamping the snow from his feet. Clipper came in. He unlocked the padlock and tucked it into his belt.

'Come on,' he said.

'Where are we going?'

'Ermine wants to see you.'

That was the last place she wanted to be if the attack came tonight.

'Why? Can't it wait? I'm tired.'

Clipper didn't even bother to answer, he just hauled her to her feet and dragged her across the snow-covered yard to Ermine's cabin.

'Ah, there you are,' said Ermine as they came in. 'Sit down. Tell me more news of the City.'

It was unbearable. How could she sit here, telling him cosy little tales of city life, while her mother and the others might be heading for the settlement gate at this very moment? Kat could barely contain herself enough to sit on the stool by the fire. What on earth would she tell him?

'Is anything wrong?'

'No, maestra.'

'Well, then. Tell me about Ceuta. You say you've been to the house?'

'Yes, maestra.' And then she had to tell him about Lu and her family, about the many oathsmen and the ships on the Circle Sea, about the glass, the wonderful glass, that Ceuta made.

'Are you sure nothing is wrong, Katriona?'

'Yes, maestra. Nothing is wrong.'

At that moment there was sudden shouting and the sound of running feet, and then the sound of wood splintering. It had begun. Kat was on her feet, with no memory of standing up. Ermine, too, had risen.

'Lock the door, Brynna!'

'But . . .' Clipper had been about to open it instead, to see what was going on.

'Lock it, I said.'

Clipper obeyed.

'Get a lantern and light it. Katriona, come here.' There was a knife in Ermine's hand now, so quickly that it had to have been hidden up his sleeve. 'Come here, child.'

Instead, Kat backed away. She looked around wildly for some weapon to defend herself with. The poker! It was resting against the chimney, only a few feet away. She snatched at it, but Ermine had already moved to kick it away. Window? No. The shutters were closed. She danced sideways, backwards, sideways, keeping out of Ermine's reach. Wall of Air. Never be where harm can reach you . . . but it was a very small room, and two against one. From somewhere outside came the dry crack of a crossbow, and someone screamed. She grabbed the wine cup and threw it at Ermine. It hit him on the shoulder, and the red wine

429

soaked into the whiteness of his shirt, so that it looked like he was bleeding. The stool! Anything. Anything could be a weapon. She spun and swung it like a club, and Clipper had to leap aside and nearly fell over Ermine's chair. Someone was hammering at the door.

'Open up!' It sounded like Karel's voice.

'Go away,' shouted Ermine. 'I'll be there in a minute.'

The knife was a long one, almost a small sword. Kat held the stool in front of her like a shield. She danced backwards, backwards . . . until she could go back no further.

She stood with her back against the wall and couldn't sidestep without running into Clipper. She was cornered, and they all knew it. Ermine smiled his thinnest smile.

'Drop the stool. I won't hurt you.'

'Put up the knife, then.'

'Stubborn child. Brynna, take her.'

Clipper didn't look thrilled, but he did step forward. Kat swung the stool at him. He dodged, and before she had time for another swing, he leaped forward, knocking her into the wall.

That was more or less that. Clipper appeared to be well up on all the dirty tricks Cornelius had taught her, because he stepped on her foot before she had time to raise her knee, and then he grabbed at her hair with one hand and her left wrist with the other, spun her around and forced her hand up between her shoulder blades.

'Give in, Kat. I don't want to break your arm.'

Kat let go of the stool and kept still.

Ermine lit the lantern.

'Bring her here,' he said, unlocking the door. 'Hold the lantern high, so that they can see her.' Ermine's thin hand replaced Clipper's around her wrist, and the knife rested coldly against her throat. 'Now, open the door.'

Clipper opened the door and then leaped back, holding the lantern high. Ermine pushed Kat forward, on to the threshold.

Everything was in chaos. People were running from house to house, and she couldn't tell who was who. A panicky horse was running this way and that, wearing neither saddle nor bridle. A burning torch lay where someone had dropped it, on the porch in front of one of the cabins. An arrow suddenly bored into the wall, less than a foot from the door.

'No!' Tess came running out of the gatehouse. 'It's Kat!'

'Yes,' said Ermine in a voice that somehow cut through the shouting and the confusion. 'It's Kat. So please put down your bows. We don't want an accident, now, do we?' The pressure from the knife became just a fraction harder, but it was only when she felt the heat of the trickling blood that she knew the skin had been broken. It didn't hurt. Not yet, at any rate.

Most of the uproar and the movement died. Only the frightened horse still trotted back and forth, whinnying desperately.

'Come along, child. To the stables. Brynna, cover my back.'

Step by step through the snow. No one tried to stop them. No arrows came whizzing out of the dark.

431

They reached the stables. Ermine dragged Kat inside.

'Hang up the lantern, we want to be able to see what we're doing.' He pushed Kat into the stall where she had spent most of the day. 'Pass me the lock.'

Clipper did as he was told. With practised movements he wrapped the chain round Kat's ankle and clipped on the lock. Ermine released Kat and stepped back. Kat rubbed her arm and stretched it slowly. It felt numb and strange, like it had the time she had fought with Rubio and DiCapra.

'Saddle me a horse,' said Ermine. 'When I've left, you stay here with the girl until daybreak. If anyone tries to get into the stables or follow me on foot, you use the knife. Once dawn breaks, you can do as you like. Surrender, or try to get out with the girl as a hostage, it's up to you. Are we clear on that?'

'Yes, maestra,' said Clipper, who had wanted to be somewhere where men made the decisions. And then he went to saddle his maestra's horse.

The horses were restless and uneasy. They can probably smell the fear, thought Kat. And I don't think I'm the only one who's scared. Ermine was pacing the narrow space of the stall.

'Isn't that horse ready yet?' he called impatiently.

'Mmm, maestra,' came the mumbled answer – Clipper probably had the tip of one girth between his teeth. But finally the horse he was saddling emerged into the aisle.

No wonder it took so long, thought Kat. The man had no idea how to handle a horse, he was on the wrong side!

'Stop that fumbling,' snapped Ermine in annoyance and

took half a step forward, out of the stall. And suddenly
there was a bright glint of metal, and Ermine leaped back
with a cry of pain. Blood gleamed through a slash in one
white sleeve. But he still held the knife. The horse started
forward, and the man who had been hidden on its far side
was not Clipper but Simon, standing now on the threshold,
holding his sword. Standing still. Because he had seen that
his chance had been wasted.

'Yes, that's right, Jossa,' said Ermine in a chill voice. 'I
can get the girl before you get me.'

'Stand still, Kat,' said Simon. 'I'll take care of this.'

'Oh, I don't think so,' said Ermine. 'Back off, Jossa. Into
the aisle.' He feinted with the knife, not at Simon but at Kat.
Kat tried to leap aside, but was tripped up by the chain. The
knife made a brilliant arc above her shoulder and snicked a
lock of hair. Simon backed off.

'Very good. And now you may place the sword slowly
on the ground. Keep backing up. Into that stall there. Don't
worry, it's a very gentle animal.'

Simon let his sword slide to the floor. Then he let himself
into the stall next to Kat's. Ermine moved into the aisle and
bolted the door. He looked at it for a moment, then gave it
a couple of hard knocks with the hilt of Simon's sword. No
one would now be able to unbolt it in a hurry.

Ermine tested it. It didn't budge an inch.

'Do you think you'll be able to get out of that stall before
I can get to the girl?' asked Ermine in an oddly friendly
tone. 'Personally, I don't think so.'

Simon didn't answer.

Ermine put down the sword and disappeared into the stall where Clipper had been saddling the horse. As soon as he was out of sight, Kat started jerking and tugging at the chain, trying to wrest the weakened clamp free of the wood.

'Is Brynna dead?' asked Ermine.

'Hardly,' said Simon. 'But it might be a while before he wakes up.'

'Too bad. I shall have to take the girl with me, then.'

Simon changed his tone. 'Maestra, is it really worth it? Running all the time, always being hunted – what sort of a life is that?'

Ermine paused to look at Simon through the bars.

'The only one I have. And I'm not about to let you cart me off to Breda and let the Motherhouses kill me slowly with their poisons just so that everyone can see that the Out-casting really *works*.' He all but spat the last word, then caught the saddled horse and did a quick check of straps and buckles. 'Because you are from Breda, aren't you? A clever little spy owned by the Seven.'

'No. The corps.'

'Of course. I should have guessed. Because of that first one.'

'Yes,' said Simon through his teeth. 'Because of her. Dorissa Granes. What happened to her?'

'That's my little secret,' said Ermine with a show of distraction. 'We'll have to chat about that some other time.'

Simon kicked the door. It didn't budge.

'Temper, temper,' drawled Ermine. And then his voice lost any trace of jocularity. 'Where is the sword, Jossa?' He measured the space between the stall door and the floor with his eyes. 'That was stupid. Push it back out, nice and slow.'

Simon stood quite still. 'The sword?'

'Yes, the sword. Give it back.'

'But I don't have it.'

'Am I supposed to believe it took a walk on its own?'

'But . . . see for yourself.' Simon spread his arms wide. 'I really don't have it!'

'Don't be stupid. Who else could have taken it?'

'Me,' said Kat. 'Stand *quite* still.'

Ermine didn't. He turned.

'Well, well. Katriona. Now, be a good girl and give me that.'

'Stand still!' Kat wanted to sound firm and calm, but she herself could hear the trembles in her voice.

'Give me the sword . . .' Ermine reached for it, and Kat stumbled back a few steps. Simon tore furiously at the bolt, but to no avail.

'Stand, Kat!' he yelled. 'Don't let him drive you back!'

But Kat was moving back, because Ermine was moving forward, and she found she couldn't bring herself to swing the sword. The chain rattled along the floor every time she moved her left foot. Ermine once more made a grab for the sword, and she tottered backwards another few steps, nearly tripping herself.

'Stand!' shouted Simon. '*Use* that sword!' He had given up on the bolt and was trying to push his body through the narrow gap between the top of the door and the ceiling. Ermine spared a quick look at his progress.

'Reinforcements are on their way, sweetheart,' he told Kat. 'Do try to position that sword correctly. They must have taught you *something* at the Academy.'

He was no longer moving forward, and that might be what halted Kat's stumbling retreat. She brought up the sword into more or less the right position, with the point where she reckoned Ermine's heart must be.

'Ah, that's much better,' Tedora Mustela said. 'Your teacher would be proud. Now, hold it firmly so you won't drop it.'

With a grunt, Simon finally managed to squeeze himself through the gap and tumbled down into the aisle.

'Keep it in the right place,' said Tedora. 'Pointed at the heart.' He smiled at Kat, the warm open smile that made him look like a young girl. His fingers grasped the blade gently, as if he wanted to help her hold it right. Then he took a quick step forwards and leaned on the sword, so that it went through his chest.

Kat screamed. She held her hands to her mouth and kept screaming. The startled horse behind them leaped back and crashed into the wall. But Tedora merely smiled his young-girl smile and slid to the floor.

'Easy,' Simon said. 'Easy, girl.' He put his arms around her and cradled her like a child. 'Hush. He wanted it so. And it's all over now.'

*

That wasn't quite true. The night was full of noise and movement even after that. People searching and other people running. Once Ermine lay dead on the stable floor, most of his men ran off. The Vale folk shut the gates and barricaded themselves behind Ermine's own walls, waiting for the dawn. In the dark, it was so hard to tell who you could trust and who you couldn't.

Anna Weaver had caught a crossbow bolt through the chest, puncturing one lung. She died before dawn. The man who shot her was dead also. Erold had hit him with the leg of a chair, and the blow had split his skull.

When daylight finally did arrive, they left right away. No one wanted to linger in Val Erminea. The wounded got to ride. Cornelius objected, saying he was perfectly capable of walking on his own two feet, but Tess was having none of that.

'Take the damn horse,' she said. 'We're going home.'

Simon and a few of the others scouted ahead, but the Ermine men who had escaped no longer wanted to fight. The pass was clear.

CONTRACTS

Sunlight fell on Alvar Alcedina's desk, on inkwells, pens and yellowish sheets of paper. He held the red stick of sealing wax close to the candle so that the wax began to melt on to the paper he had been working on, finally imprinting it with the seal hidden in his ring. It left a clear silhouette of a kingfisher with the letters A–ALC–DomP–Bredinari in a circle round it.

'So,' he said. 'Welcome back to the corps, Prentice Trivallia.'

'Thank you.'

On the table, duly adorned with seal and signature, was her new prenticeship contract. DomPrimus Alcedina had not spared her a lecture on the rareness of this privilege – few students indeed had been given two chances at the Academy.

'But naturally, the circumstances are extraordinary.'

The circumstances are that you made a mistake, thought

439

Kat, but she didn't say it out loud. There had been enough talk of 'insubordinate Vale girls'.

'You may go. I expect you have quite a few people waiting for you.'

She did. Karolin had taken advantage of the fine spring day and had set up a table under the gate vault between the kitchens and the prentice baths. They would all be there, she thought, Lu and Merian and Birch and the others, possibly even Rubio and Meiles. She wouldn't mind, though, if those two stayed away. They would only be there for the food, she knew. But though she knew they were waiting, she went somewhere else first.

The cherry plums in the courtyard by the library had tiny new white flowers, and the library door, for once, was open. She stamped her feet to get rid of the dirt and went in.

'Good morning,' she called, so that Bookmaster Hermes would know it was her and wouldn't feel it necessary to break off his work. He did, anyway.

'Trivallia,' he said, coming to meet her. 'Are you finally going to finish that book of yours?'

'Not today,' she said. 'But I'll be back tomorrow. But there's something I need to find out.'

'And what might that be?'

'Do we have a law book?'

'Several dozen. Are you looking for anything in particular?'

Kat looked at this fat and serious man who had spent his life among books full of words and knowledge.

'How do you know if it's murder?' she asked.

'When someone intentionally and with full purpose causes the death of another human being, we deem it murder,' he said, and she could hear from his tone that he was quoting one of the several dozen law books.

'Intentionally – that means on purpose,' she said, just to be sure.

'Yes.'

'And if it's not on purpose?'

'We usually call it manslaughter. Involuntary manslaughter.'

'And if the other person . . . wants to die?'

'Then it is a mercy killing. Euthanasia.'

'Even if it's not on purpose?'

'No. I don't know what that is called. A sort of suicide, perhaps.'

'But not murder?'

'No. Murder takes intent.'

Kat nodded thoughtfully. 'Thank you,' she said. 'I'll be back tomorrow to work on the book.' She still had to do the drawing of *Mustela putorius* and *Mustela erminea*. This time, presumably, no one would steal it.

Lu came to meet her as she was passing through the Weapons Court.

'So,' she said. 'Did they put you back in their records?'

'Yes.'

'How was it? What was he like today?'

'Stiff. He doesn't like to admit a mistake, I think.'

Lu laughed. 'Who does? But there isn't a whole lot he can do about it. Are you happy now?'

441

'I suppose so.'

Lu stopped. 'You don't sound very happy.'

'Oh, I don't know . . . it's just that so much has happened. I can't just forget about it.'

'But isn't this what you want? To live here? To be a Silver one day?'

We thought of getting help, her mother had said. *But where would we have gone? Who would have come?*

I would have, Simon had answered rather gruffly. *The bredinari would have. It's what we are for, and things might never have gone so badly wrong if only you had asked for our help a little sooner.*

Because things had gone badly. Anna Weaver was dead, and Cornelius still looked more dead than alive, though Keri Herbwife said he would be all right eventually. A few of Ermine's men had been captured and sentenced to work in the mines in Oredale. More had escaped, and among them was Karel. This made Kat worry, particularly about Tess. And it could have been even worse. Much, much worse, in fact.

Lu was still waiting for her answer.

'Yes,' she said slowly. 'This is where I want to be. And I do want to be a Silver one day.'

Not so that she could gallop along on the back of a hell-horse, though that was part of it. But so that help might be a little closer the next time someone like her mother needed it.

Lu put her arm around Kat's neck and gave her a small shake. 'Well, let's not stand about then. The food is getting cold, and the others are waiting. And Tarquin has threatened to start singing if he is left hungry much longer.'

She let go of Kat and walked on. After a couple of steps she realized Kat still wasn't following.

'Katriona Trivallia!' she yelled, so loudly that the words echoed among the castle walls. 'Are you coming or not? We're all waiting for you!'

Kat looked up at the blue spring sky and at the pigeons circling the castle towers. And suddenly her heart felt lighter.

'Don't worry,' she said. 'Of course I'm coming.'

KATRIONA'S WORLD

BREDA

The history of Breda begins in a time of ice and darkness, in a twilight brought on by catastrophe. In Breda, children are taught that Man once made himself master of the earth, and of all creatures on it. He built houses so tall they scraped the skies. He bent the rivers to his will, rode the wind itself, and caused his words to echo everywhere, even among the stars. The very stuff of life was his to work with as he pleased, and he wrought from it new plants and animals such as had never been seen before. His might seemed limitless, and he himself believed that this was so.

But twilight came. The sea rose to destroy Man's cities, and the sun hid itself in endless fogs, and finally the ice came, to take what was left of the old lands. Only a few survived, to live desperate lives plagued by cold and starvation. It seemed to them that the earth itself had turned its back on them, and cared not whether they lived or died.

Then, in the midst of harshest winter, a wandering woman came upon a valley, lush and green when all else was covered in snow. Marvelling at the sight, she fell to her knees and closed her hand around a fistful of this soft, warm earth. She asked most fervently that she and her people might be allowed to stay in this valley, and wander no more. In return, she promised that they would never again abuse the land, would never again make themselves masters of it, nor trade with it as though it were a dead possession anyone could own.

The woman's name was Breda, and her people still live in the green valley. They have kept her promise: in her country, the land is not owned, nor can it be sold or bought. It falls to the women to care for it and treasure it. Men failed the earth once, it is said, and that must not be allowed to happen again. This is the reason why the Bredani is always a woman, and why Breda was ruled in the old days by queens, not kings. And this is the reason why men must wander still, having no place they can call their own.

TALIS

Two peoples share the country of Breda, though they have both been there for so long now that hardly anyone can tell them apart, nor do they care to. There are the Bredans, who were there first, and the Talisians, who came to Breda from a country called Talis. There, poisonous ice sickened both the land and the people, and survival became more and more difficult. Finally, most of the Talisians decided to take to their ships and sail south, in search of a new home.

They tried to land in the Norlands, north of Breda, but the Norlanders gave them cold welcome and would not let them settle, and they were a strong and war-hardened people against whom the newcomers could not fight and win. The Talisians faced a choice – they must either continue their voyage, or abandon their ships and strike inland in the hope of finding less hostile lands.

Most were afraid to leave the ships – they were a home, of sorts, and there were even those who had been born on board and had never known anything else. A land journey would mean abandoning most of their possessions too. But a woman called Kingfisher – Alcedina, in the Talisian tongue – had a strange dream. She saw Breda's green valley, and she saw seven animals find a home there: a kingfisher, a salamander, a pike, a raven, an owl, a polecat and a mountain goat. These seven happened to be the animals that seven of the Talisian Greatships were named for, and these seven ship-clans believed in Alcedina's vision and decided to embark on the land journey, along with all those who sailed in their daughter ships. To this day, the seven most powerful families in Breda are named for these animals: Alcedina, Salamandrida, Esocine, Corvinius, Strigius, Mustela and Capra.

SARI MOON-DAUGHTER

The Talisians came to Breda in the reign of Queen Mona Lunaria. At that time, the country had long been under threat from the West. Golia, or the Westland, as Bredans call it, had a different way of ordering their country. Here, men ruled. Hard times had given rise to a belief in the survival of the strongest. Weaklings died, and that was the way of things. In Golia, the warrior was king.

During the reign of the previous queen, the Goles had crossed the Lesser Ring Sea and had conquered Grana, the most westerly province of Breda. Now the Warrior King Imoges was standing by the Westwall, looking hungrily down at the rich heartlands.

'There is your wedding gift, Kana,' he told his youngest son. 'Make your way to the City of Breda and take the Princess Sari for a wife, and I shall make you King of all Breda.'

Kana did not need telling twice. With a small, hand-picked force, he climbed the steep cliffs of the Westwall and mounted a surprise attack on the City, ending in the capture of the Castle of Breda where Queen Mona and her daughter Sari had ensconced themselves. He set his sword at the throat of the Queen and told her daughter: 'I think you see now the cost of refusal. Will you then marry me – yes or no?'

But Sari did not say yes, and did not say no. She gave him no answer at all. And her Silence was such that all speech stopped, and all music died. Even the animals were still, and all over the realm open doors fell to and could not again be opened, no matter what the force. At this, Kana grew frightened. The sword fell from his hand, and the thought came to his mind that he had no wish to be

450

king of Breda after all – at least not if it meant having such a sorceress for a wife.

When Imoges heard of his son's indecision, he became furious. He gathered his army and headed for the City himself. But when he reached it, Sari Moon-Daughter had gone. She had managed to escape the Castle, and was nowhere to be found.

THE PEDLAR FROM JOSS

Long before Kana made his edged proposal, Sari had met someone else – a simple pedlar from Joss, with whom she had fallen in love. Having made good her escape, she sought her lover, only to find that he was not, in fact, a pedlar, nor, indeed, from Joss. He was Talisian, and he had come to Breda in disguise, as a spy. What Sari said when she learned of this we do not know, but her speech was probably not gentle; Sari was by no means a mild-tempered woman.

The fact remained, though, that the Bredans had far more in common with the Talisians than with the Goles. The Talisians, too, were ruled by women, and in Talis the land had been cared for by the women. For this reason, Sari proposed a treaty: the Talisians would be allowed to settle in Breda, if they would first help her oust Imoges and Kana and their forces from the land. The treaty was signed in the city of Luna, and became known as the Luna Covenant.

Sari and the Talisians were successful in their long struggle to drive the Goles from the heartland. But it took fifty more years before Grana, too, was liberated. The Talisians found a home, and Sari Moon-Daughter lived with her 'pedlar' for many eventful years.

BREDANI AND MAESTRA

Sari became the last queen to reign in Breda. The newcomers brought with them many new beliefs and customs. The language they spoke was very like the one Bredans called Latina. Before, only learned people in Breda knew Latina. Now many Talisian and Latina words became common among ordinary Bredans.

Locus, for instance. And *maestra*.

Locus means place, but to the Talisians it was much more than just a location. It was something personal, something living, something sacred: the *spirit* of the place. They, too, believed that land could not be bought or sold. Land rights could only be given to someone willing to wed themselves to the Locus Spirit, becoming the maestra, or mistress, of a house or a bit of land. The Talisians had priestesses who performed such wedding ceremonies and saw to it that the maestra and the people in her care remained firm in their duty and loyalty to the Locus Spirit. When Imoges had been able to conquer Breda, said the priestesses, it was because the bond between the queen and the spirit of the land was not strong enough. Had it been, the very earth would have refused to bear him, and the crops his soldiers picked would have turned to poison in their mouths.

The truth of this claim cannot, of course, be proved. But it is a fact that the Locus faith spread quickly throughout Breda, and that no foreign army has set foot in the heartland since Sari's daughter Cora was wedded to the spirit of the land and became Cora Prima, the first Bredani in the history of the realm.

What, then, is the difference between a queen and a Bredani? A queen is just a ruler. A Bredani is also a priestess and holds the highest office in the Locus faith. A sacred bond ties her not to one limited place, but to all places in the whole country. She is, in a manner of speaking, the maestra of all Breda. A queen might choose to have a man by her side and perhaps share her power with him. A Bredani can do no such thing – this would make her unfaithful to the Locus Spirit, and the Locus priestesses would reject her.

LOCUS AND CORA

Before the arrival of the Talisians, most Bredans believed mainly in Our Lady. Our Lady cares for us, they would say, the way a mother cares for her children. She gives us life when we are born, and she takes care of us when we die. Our Lady holds out the promise to all her children, male and female, that we will never be truly homeless.

Everyone is owed a resting place, in this life or beyond. There is a Breda other than the one human beings can chart with maps and rulers. It may sometimes be glimpsed in the morning mists rising over the fields, or seen as a reflection just below the surface of a mountain lake. It is in the sunset clouds, or in the shimmer of heat on the summer plains. This is the real Heartland, true home to us all. The Bredans believe that we go there when we die, and sometimes in our dreams too.

The Talisians call this Heartland Cora – which in Latina means heart, or core. And just as Bredans have adopted the belief in Locus and maestra, so the Talisians have taken Our Lady to their hearts. To men in particular, it is a gentler faith than the belief in a Locus Spirit that only a woman can have a true bond to. Our Lady cares for everyone, men and women alike.

Those who put their faith in the Heartland and Our Lady call themselves corans. Most people believe a little of both. All the twelve Bredani rulers of the realm have adopted the name Cora as a sign that the coran faith should be allowed to thrive side by side with the belief in Locus and maestra.

Breda's most famous historian, Darik Lunaria, writes in his *Historia Bredani*: 'Without Cora, men have no hope. Without Locus, the land has no law. On the day we no longer give room to both, peace will shatter, and strife and chaos will seize us. I beg I shall not live to see that day.'

THE BREDINARI

The Talisians brought more than just the Locus faith with them. Among them were also the magi, men who practised a form of sorcery called the Magus Arts. It was a Talisian magus who first discovered how to tame the feral Nightmares that were the terror of the highlands north of Joss and Luna.

The Nightmares were savage predators who were able to paralyse their prey merely by means of the fear they projected. Some say there is an ingredient in their smell that causes this panic. Others, that it is in the eyes – the golden predator's gaze that is so hard to escape. Pure-blooded Nightmares were almost impossible to ride, even for a magus. But crossbreeding with the small, fast plains horses of the Joss created the hellhorses, whose riders came to be known as the bredinari, or the Silvers.

In the beginning, the hellhorses and their riders served mainly as an effective weapon against Imoges and his forces. A single Silver could cause a wave of weakness and panic among scores of Goles. However, with the invention of the crossbow, their military usefulness was lessened. Armed with a crossbow, the Goles could pick off a Silver while still remaining out of panic-range. The bredinari tried various types of armouring, but the hellhorses were too slight-boned for massive plate armour.

The bredinari, then, were no longer mostly soldiers. Instead, they acquired other roles. A hellhorse is almost half as fast again as an ordinary horse, and has amazing stamina. The bredinari became messengers and border guards and rapid couriers. And eventually one of the first bredinari commanders, Nova Alcedina, founded the first Resting Place.

THE RESTING PLACES

Nova had thought about the resting place that Our Lady promises her children. She saw no reason why such a place should only exist after death. Every Resting Place she founded was meant to be a tiny plot of Heartland, a place where the tired, the frightened, the old and the sick could find 'shelter, rest and healing', as Resting signs all over Breda still proclaim. The Resting Places were for everyone, regardless of rank, gender, creed or past sins, and Nova even persuaded the Bredani to declare them sanctuaries under Bredan law.

There is a story of a man called Blackhand, a robber and a murderer, who once sought sanctuary at a Resting Place. The soldiers of the Bredani surrounded the place, but the Housemaster would not deliver the criminal into their hands as long as he observed the rules of the Place. For years, the soldiers waited for a chance to catch Blackhand if he set foot across the boundaries of the place, or if he gave the Housemaster cause to expel him. This never happened. Blackhand lived out his life in that Place, and the new ways he was forced to observe eventually

changed his mind and character to such a degree that he
even served as Housemaster for three years before he died.

In the present day, few Resting Places are kept
according to the old rules. This is a great pity, not least
because of the goodwill and respect they gave rise to
among people in the border provinces to whom the
distance to the Bredani and her City might otherwise seem
very great.

MORE BREDINARI TASKS

During the reign of Cora Septima, certain bredinari were
given the authority to act 'in loco Bredani', as the extended
hand of the Bredani. They were employed as envoys and
ambassadors, but as the Bredani is also the highest legal
authority in the land, they soon came to dispense justice to
some of the remoter places in the country, either because
there was no judge in the area, or because one of the
plaintiffs wanted to appeal to an impartial outsider.

A bredinari must, in other words, be prepared to face
many tasks: soldier, officer of the Law, messenger, healer,
diplomat and justice of the peace. Being able to control a
hellhorse is only the beginning. It takes many years of
training and education at the Akademia Bredinari before
one may call oneself a 'Silver'.

Dàrik writes in his *Historia Bredani*: 'The bredinari are
the threads that bind the border provinces to the
heartland. Without them, people in Grana, Joss, Ormark,

Ringmark, Sirimark, Fulmark and Three Valleys would hardly feel that they were part of Breda at all, and that the Laws and words of the Bredani pertained to them. As these threads begin to fray and wear thin the country falls apart, and each province looks only to its own profit, like islands no longer connected to any mainland. Each time a Resting Place is closed or degenerates into a common inn, another thread snaps. A child growing up without seeing a Silver, perhaps not even knowing what a bredinari is . . . such a child becomes an islander for whom Breda barely exists.'